the dark trench shadow series

FRAUGHT

KERRY NIETZ

FREEHEADS

FRAUGHT by Kerry Nietz
Published by Freeheads
http://www.kerrynietz.com

This is a work of fiction. Names, characters, places, and incidents are products of the author's imagination or are used fictitiously. Any similarity to actual people, organizations, and/or events is purely coincidental.

Cover Designer: Kirk DouPonce
Editing and typesetting: Jill Domschot
eBook Design: Kerry Nietz

ISBN: 978-0-9971658-4-5

Library of Congress Cataloging-in-Publication Data
An application to register this book for cataloging has been filed with the Library of Congress

To Leah Nietz
Who demanded this

OTHER WRITINGS
BY KERRY NIETZ

FICTION

DarkTrench Saga:

A Star Curiously Singing
The Superlative Stream
Freeheads

DarkTrench Shadow Series:

Frayed
Fraught

Peril in Plain Space:

Amish Vampires in Space
Amish Zombies from Space

Graxin (short story collection)

JustDumb Enough
(contributor)

Mask

Rhats!

NONFICTION

FoxTales: Behind the Scenes at Fox Software

For information on all Kerry's books, please visit:
www.Nietz.com/Library

ACKNOWLEDGEMENTS

First, I'd like to thank editor Jill Domschot for effortlessly jumping into the middle of a series and making a valuable and notable contribution. That isn't easy! Most importantly, you've been my sanity check. Thanks so much.

A big thank you to minuteman reader Lisa Godfrees. As with *Frayed*, you made *Fraught* a better book, and in record time. Can't thank you enough!

A mechanized high five to designer Kirk DouPonce, for your help in story elements, and for naming the book!

And thanks to the Lord, for stories to tell, and the time and ability to tell them.

THE EXPERIENCE IS INESCAPABLE. It fills my mind, touching all five senses. It isn't real, but it feels real. It isn't a dream, but it could be.

I'm positioned atop an ancient stairway, an observatory, nearly thirty meters from the ground. There is a waist-high wall ahead of me and nothing but endless sand below. Above, is only darkened sky. Stars stretch out brilliantly in all directions. No hint of a cloud.

A cool breeze tickles my face, bringing the scent of anise, of licorice, with it. It reminds me of hope, and of childhood. Also of my female friend. The freehead Damali.

But here, at this moment, I feel alone. Insignificant.

"I find myself contemplating the stars lately," a male voice says.

I turn in the direction of the voice, my left, and my first mentor, Bamboo, appears. Bald, thin, and perpetually middle-aged. Dressed in a grey jumpsuit.

I startle and grip the wall to steady myself. His arrival is disorienting. Like a ghost or a sudden wind.

"Focus on the sky, ThreadBare. Not on me."

This is a test. A diagnostic perpetuated through the implant in my head. "Of course, Master. The sky and the stars."

"Yes, study them. Unique and persistent. Differing in colors and sizes. Like memories in our mind."

He points up and right. "There is al-Ghūl, the Ghoul's head. An eclipsing binary." He points left. "And there, an-Nisr ul-Wāqi', the fallen eagle. It was the north star once. Thousands of years ago."

I try to locate the particular stars he means. I have the vicinity, but the celestial bodies themselves? No idea.

He points again. "Do you see them? They are bright. And blue."

"I'm sorry, I—"

He sighs. "Very well, I will circle them for you."

Two red circles appear in the sky. In the center of each: a bright blue star.

"Which is brighter?" he asks.

"The right one," I say. "The eagle star."

"Good." He continues to point and inquire, mostly about brightness and color. Sometimes about proximity. Each answer brings an affirmation, so that I feel I am passing his test. But one can never be certain here.

After a hundred such questions, he draws his hands behind his back, laces fingers together, and stares at the sky.

A minute goes by. Then two.

My nervousness grows. "You said you think about the stars. Why?"

More time passes, enough that I feel I spoke out of turn. Even here, inside my head, the rules apply. Especially here, in fact.

He nods toward the sky. "The way a star dies depends on its prominence," he says. "On its significance."

The word "significance" gives me pause. It has been a driving force for me. A reason for being and the crux of my sins.

What has his probe shown him?

The stars seem to shift slightly. I grip the wall again.

"ThreadBare? Stay with me."

I bow my head. "My apologies, Master. Their significance controls their death?"

He frowns but continues looking upward. "When an average star, one like our sun, dies, it expands and brightens for a period of time. It grows to a hundred times its previous size and becomes thousands of times brighter yet cools substantially. Then it will fade, slowly pushing off its mass, ever shrinking to a fraction of its previous size."

He looks at me. "It goes completely dark, becoming a black dwarf. A star that no longer shines. A non—entity."

2

I sense Bamboo is talking in riddles. Speaking on more than one level.

He points at the sky again. "Larger, more prominent stars, meet a different end. They explode, annihilating all in their path." He fans his hands in front of his chest. "The portion that remains, the star's inner core, becomes either a spinning ball of matter, or with exceptional stars, an abscess in space. A hole of immense gravitation and destruction." He makes a fist with one hand. "A hidden death for anything that wanders into its path." He looks at me, eyes intense. "A devourer of worlds."

I tighten my grip on the wall. I feel ill. Like I might fall back into the stairs. Go tumbling down.

"Can you see the parallels, ThreadBare? It is like this with men too. Their deaths, the aftereffects, are dependent on their prominence." He looks amused now. "On their significance."

He rests a hand on my shoulder. "It is not my place to explore these things. I am only a servant like you. Controlled."

The stars blur, then become streaks of light. Fireworks and sparklers. Shooting and popping. I feel every explosion. Every star death. Red giant, neutron star, and black hole.

"But what I now need to determine, is which stars are which. How—"

"Master!"

Bamboo frowns and shakes his head. "It is worse than I imagined."

I OPEN MY EYES WITH a start and suck in a long breath.

The world seems incredibly bright now, as if I'm sitting on the surface of the sun. There are dark spots in the brightness too. Little sunspots. I follow those as they float across my vision. Gradually, they fade into the background and my surroundings come into focus. Become solid and real.

I'm in a circular room, and the predominate color is white. The ceiling is subtly domed, and there is a large circular light hanging from its center. To my left is a half-circle of a couch, and behind it, a similarly-shaped shelf decorated with awards and monochromatic artwork.

There is a circular window there too. Through it I can see the city and the Great River beyond. Skyscrapers and temple domes compete for real estate. A rainbow of colors.

To my right is a long, curved shelf filled with bound books. The spines are faded, and too far away to read, but together they form a rainbow too. In the middle of the bookshelf is a fireplace. The floor is tiled with white marble.

The room has the feeling of intellect and precision. A striving for transcendence amid a world of imperfect mediums. Inferior tools.

It is Bamboo's private study.

Bamboo stands near the fireplace, watching me. He's dressed like he was in the simulation: a grey jumpsuit. "What have you done to yourself, DR 23?"

My head is foggy, but otherwise I feel fine. It has been a difficult couple months. "I've run diagnostics on my implant. Numerous times. It is working as designed. I'm performing—"

He holds up a hand. "I've run diagnostics too. The problem isn't your implant."

I'm seated on a wicker chair, I realize. I lean forward and grab the front edge near my legs. "Master?"

Bamboo takes a step my direction. "The implant is operating as expected. Perfectly, in fact. Theoretically, this situation is possible, but I've never seen it like this. The last time I saw such damage—"

"Damage? You said—"

He nods. "It should be removed and reassigned."

My back tenses. "Removed? But you said it was functioning." My implant connects me to everything—the bots I work on, the global stream of information—everything! It augments my memories, too. If it were removed, I could lose more than connection or livelihood. I could lose her. "I don't want it removed."

"The fault is in the implant's container," Bamboo says. "It is damaged."

"Container?" I rest my hands on my head, feeling the warmth of my own hairless scalp. "You mean my brain. My brain is damaged."

Bamboo walks to the couch and sits down. "Have you been experiencing headaches? Confusion? Nausea?"

My heart pounds. My hands get tingly. "No, none of that. I don't feel sick." I straighten. "I mean, I didn't."

"Difficulty understanding others? Changes in vision, in touch? Slurred speech?"

"No," I say. "No more than normal."

He brings his hands together, touching fingertips. "Difficulty sleeping? Fatigue? Sensitivity to light?"

Now I feel angry. It's just like him to overanalyze. To overthink. "I'm fine." I get a tweak for the lie and fight off a wince.

I've experienced some of those symptoms, of course, but I'm a debugger. I sleep in a cinder chute, a technological casket, to keep the outside world at bay. I can view other people's lives on demand. I get small shocks in my head when I disobey. When I even think about disobeying.

Frankly, I've experienced all of those symptoms. Often.

Bamboo crosses his legs. Stares at me.

I grit my teeth. "I want my implant. I need it."

He sighs. "Heightened emotions and irritability are symptoms too. As is poor judgment. Is that what you're experiencing now?"

I tighten my grip on the chair's edge. There's no way to win here. No way to lie or simply storm out. I'm a slave, even if my former master is dead. I look at Bamboo but stay silent.

"As you know, my allegiance is to the ruling ulama, and the Imam. Our customers. It has to be that way. My concern is only that you can perform your duties adequately."

I contemplate all I've experienced over the last few months. Especially what I learned. Things Bamboo might care about. The shocks in my head might make it difficult to get the information out. They will stop me if I overshare.

I've managed to step around, or subvert the stops before, but it was difficult.

And now I'm damaged. Was that what damaged me? My subversion?

So many questions.

"You're contemplating something," Bamboo says. "An impasse, I assume." He places an arm on the back of the couch. "I could probe your implant storage, but it would be better, in your state, if I didn't have to."

"Why?"

"Why what, debugger?"

"Your allegiance. My allegiance. If not for the shocks—" That brings a tweak, a warning. I shake my head. "They aren't looking out for us."

His eyebrows raise. "Who? The ruling masters? Why would you expect them to?" He tugs the chest of his suit. "They are businessmen. Monarchs and diplomats. Their first responsibility is to the people. The caliphate." He smiles. "And to themselves, of course. Are you surprised by that? Surely you—"

I shake my head again, but the pain remains. "No, no." I focus on the idea of Damali. On her smile. How I would like to see her again. To talk. There is much I am curious about. She unsettles me in new ways. Unusual and forbidden ways. Her touch.

I take a deep breath. The tweaks subside. I need to push out as much information as I can. I will start with the astronaut. "I know things," I say. "Important things. I have learned much that will interest you."

He frowns. "I doubt that, Threadbare."

"It should interest you," I say. "It should."

"Be careful. Are these things you can share? You may worsen—"

"Mere speculation," I say. "No one's secret. Only a theory."

He scoots back, straightens his jumpsuit again. "Very well. Let's hear your theory."

"They are moving to replace us. To make debuggers irrelevant."

His expression doesn't change. "Who told you this?" he asks. "Another debugger?"

I look at the floor again. The marble's shine hurts my eyes. "A freehead called TallSpot."

"I doubt that's his name."

"That's what he's called. By other debuggers."

He nods. "So he's known by other debuggers? And what inside information would this TallSpot have?"

"He's an astronaut."

"An ore pilot? They are away for long periods of time. Often unstable. How would—"

"He's an astronaut," I say. "He's been places. Distant places. I don't know where. He knows Sandfly."

"Sandfly? I don't recall—"

"Of TreArc. DR 63."

Bamboo shuts his eyes, searching the stream. "Ah yes. I see references. Curious, he's listed as offline."

"Yes, Master. Offline, but not forgotten. Not lost."

He sighs and opens his eyes. "A pity I cannot contact him. Was that intentional?" He shakes his head. "You aren't helping your case. An accusation like this is impossible to verify. Using an offline debugger as a witness? What tangible evidence is there?"

"There might be evidence," I say. "If we knew where to look."

Bamboo turns and gazes out the window. Sighs again. "No, this is a distraction from the issue at hand. Your continued viability."

"I am viable," I say. "I can show you. Let me research. I'll prove—"

He raises a hand. "Even if your theory is correct, our rulers are within their rights. We have no guarantee of usefulness, Thread-Bare. Eventually everything is superseded."

I want to hurt him. To bring him to reason through violence. I force another long breath, look at the floor again. "You feel nothing for your handiwork?" I glance up. "Your children?" He's the one who implanted us, after all. The one who made us.

"I care about my work," he says. "Yes. Every man should. But your road has no end. Even if you were to prove your theory, what then?"

His question is valid. As an implant, Bamboo is internally stopped too. Restrained.

What could he do?

"I need to concentrate on my work," he says. "And that demands I deal with you."

My gut starts to ache. "The prince is gone," I say. "There's no pressure to do anything."

"The royal family are your masters now. The collective. They will divide the prince's assets. It could take time, but it will happen. Until then, your fate is mine to decide."

"Then there's time," I say. "For more tests. For me to heal. Or fix whatever—"

He grows thoughtful again. "Sometimes, yes, the brain will heal. But without knowing the cause of your injury..." He stands. Straightens his suit. "We should go to the lab. Remove your implant."

I raise my hands, imploringly. "Please, Master Bamboo, give it time. A few weeks. A month."

"I fulfill a role, 23, and that role depends on an objective mind. On following the rules."

"I could help here," I say. "With your bots. Or with the school."

He shakes his head. "Merely delaying the inevitable."

"A few days? Set a time limit. I'll submit to it."

He brings a hand to his chin. "Help with the school? Now there's an intriguing idea. Would it help? Hmm..."

I resist grabbing his arms, or simply kneeling to beg. "And I could research," I say. "Investigate the rumor."

"Your theory? I thought I was clear. That is a waste—"

"Don't you at least want to know? Debuggers always want to know. We're curious."

He looks at the window, at the distant towers and spires. Finally, he nods. "I am persuaded. I will give you until the new moon."

Only fourteen days.

IT IS NIGHTTIME, AND I AM ALONE.

My room at the school is simple. A mere five-by-three-meter rectangle, containing a cinder chute for sleeping, a chair, a closet, and a single dresser. There is no window, and no steamer or wash-room of any kind. There are large and awkward versions of those down the hall.

The clothing that hangs in my closet, and those in my dresser, don't fit me. They are made for a boy of ten or eleven. Remnants of a prior student, I assume. Now the property of his first master.

The rooms around me are filled with children, but there is no noise. No cries for parents, or giggling laughter. All appear to be asleep, or in silent contemplation. This is the most controlled and subservient school in the world. All are implants, like me.

Bamboo has given me my first assignment, and I am terrified. But I have little choice. I must fulfill a duty here or surrender my implant immediately. Risk losing everything.

I perform my evening prayer, then recline in my chute. It is a simple model. Black exterior, white interior. I stare at the room's ceiling and listen to the silence. Eventually, I will force myself to sleep. But not yet. This room—these four walls—are the only real privacy I have.

My mind wants to go a million ways, both in stream and out, but I'm afraid to send it. What operations will task it too much? Which will help it recover? Let my broken brain heal?

Memories vex me. The prince and his torture rooms. Cages filled with emaciated prisoners. The combat matches he orchestrated. Ordered me to participate in. Each blow of my mechanical surrogate pains me. Causes a rosy flair on my inner eye.

Worse still are the images of the prince's abuse. The times he struck me or used a shock rod on me. It is a scarlet landscape. A hellish vista.

I comfort myself with thoughts of the freehead woman, Damali. Beautiful and warm. A fuzzy whirlpool in my head. She brings no pain or scarlet suffering. I need to speak with her.

But how?

A simple errand near GrimJack's tech shop is all it would take. That's where they all were going. Where I sent them.

I hope they made it.

Unfortunately, Bamboo has every debugging supply he'll ever need. They are delivered regularly. I have to find a way out, but there's no reason for me to go. And even if there were, would Bamboo let me?

If I knew Damali was alive, that would be something. It would make my sacrifice, my loss, seem...worthwhile. Significant.

Maybe someone else can go. Maybe someone already has?

I stream the chute canopy closed. There is a double layer of privacy now. Silence within silence. I shut my eyes and touch the stream. I craft a connection request and send it, like a dart, to a friend.

One positive of my new address: I am not filtered or blocked. Free streaming!

My request is accepted. My wounded mind connects to FrontLot's. We begin to share Full Impact—voice, image, and emotion. I hold nothing back, and neither does he.

Immediately, his emotional state jars me, lifting me from a state of white and worry to one of near euphoria. That also means I've brought him down some, but that's okay. He's really high. Really loud.

In my mind, I see Front's likeness. He's a couple years older than me, with almond skin. He's wearing a standard blue jumpsuit but doesn't appear to be working. He's seated in a darkened room, and the predominate color is red. Red walls and chairs. There are many people around him. To his right, a table is filled with young men and women, formally dressed. Some have long tubes in their mouths. There is a lot of talking and laughing.

"Where are you?" I ask.

He smiles brightly. "You cannot tell?" He alters the perspective so I can see more. More people, more tables, more tubes. The tubes connect to ornamental, metal spigots in the center of each table. There are small clouds of smoke everywhere. Servbots move between tables, bringing beverages.

"Is that place legal?"

Front feigns shock. "I'm here with my master." He makes a show of searching the room, looking right and left, then waves a hand. "I think he's over there somewhere."

"That doesn't make it legal." I share more of his emotions. He's excited and joyful. Not a hint of a stop either. His implant thinks whatever he is doing is fine.

"It's a shisha club. Not illegal. Not haraam."

"But I saw smoke," I say. "Smoking is—"

He fans the air. "Not smoke, my friend. Water vapor. Flavored vapor."

"Flavored by what?"

He raises his hands. "That is not my business to know." He taps his forehead. "Master business."

I send him an image of a camel looking confused. "Are *you* smoking?"

"I am not." He smiles. "I'm only enjoying the atmosphere. My master commands it."

I frown. "Your *atmosphere* may be the problem."

"Nonsense, ThreadBare." He leans back and rests an elbow on his seat's extra-wide armrest. There is a woman seated to his right. Her head is covered, but not her face. She has a tube in her mouth, puffing. She removes the tube and a cloud of vapor escapes. She smiles. Her eyes look glazed.

"Now...what do you require of me?" he asks.

"What supply shops do you frequent?"

He squints, then shakes his head. "Always work-talk with you. You should learn to relax. Everyone here..." He motions with a hand. "...is relaxed." He wags a finger. "Debuggers should learn to relax."

"I'm in my chute," I say. "I'm relaxed."

He shakes his head. "No, you aren't. You never are. Always striving for something. Always with a goal."

He's functionally inhibited. I should stop and message him later.

It's hard not to enjoy the euphoria, though. The lifting of my weight. "GrimJack's," I say. "Do you go there?"

He squints. "GrimJack's? No. That's a little out of my range." He flutters a hand. "Mostly Alli's for me. They are cleaner. You should try them."

I'm starting to feel a little floaty now. "If you'd been to Grim's, I thought maybe I could view your memory mix. See if what I think is there, is there."

"Can't you just message them? Check their supply list?"

"It's not that simple," I say. "I need to go there and look. Or watch the mix of someone who has."

He closes his eyes, then shakes his head. "Sorry, can't find anything in my shared library either. Shop visits aren't something we typically share."

My heart sinks. Front hasn't been to Grim's, nor does he have the memories of anyone who has.

Now what?

"Is there another way I can help you? I have new mixes since last you asked. Much sharing."

I say nothing. Stuck in my disappointment.

"Are you all right, ThreadBare? You feel a little down."

Fry that. Blaze the bidirectional nature of Full Impact communication. The vulnerability.

I think of happier times. The arboretum I used to frequent. A star-filled night. Anything to occupy my thoughts other than a lost woman and my wounded brain.

I've had success with datamixes before. I learned of an experimental ship. The first to travel between stars. That revelation opened the door to many, many things. Meeting the astronauts, for instance.

My time is short. I only have a few days.

I need evidence of the ulama's full intent. Proof of their machinations to end debuggers.

"The list," I say. "The inactive debugger list."

Front raises a finger. "Ah ha! Every boat returns to its port of departure. Its native land." He smiles. "I have something for you there."

"You do?"

The woman to his right accidentally brushes Front with her elbow. She touches his shoulder and begs forgiveness. He responds warmly.

"Front?"

He smiles. "Yes, something you'll enjoy. An enigma, but you like such things. A reflective and sorrowful tale."

He's wrong. I don't like reflection at all. It only leads to trouble. But if he has something from one of the inactives, then I need to see it. I will take any morsel I can find.

I bow my head. "The usual fee?"

"Of course, you are a friend. I wouldn't overcharge you."

"Credit sent."

"And received. Prepare yourself. Here it comes."

I HEAR HIS TEARS BEFORE I am summoned. A wail like someone's best friend has died. It's shrill and truly mournful. I wait, because it's not my place to respond. But I reach for my supply bag and remain prepared.

My master's residence is small by most standards. Easy to navigate. If one were to judge his holdings on the home alone, they would think him a fraud. Unable to afford the things he uses. Certainly unable to buy my services. But he has much need, and he has the means. Three years have shown me that.

My quarters were constructed from a formerly unused attic. They too, are modest, but that is not uncommon. There is a light-weight chute, a small lounge area, and a place for washing. It has a single oval window that faces west. Through it, I can view the park across the street. The many colors of the season. I watch them now. Leaves move with the wind.

Finally, I hear my name called and I arise from my seat. I walk to the door in the floor and pull it away. Extend the ladder and climb down.

The second story is painted a light orange, and tactfully decorated. There's significance to every wall hanging or picture. A holograph of the pyramids here. A rug of ancient design there. Histories, reflections, inspirations.

The floor has many bedrooms, but most are empty now. I pass door after door. Inside each are only memories. Trophies and pictures of those that have moved on. Three sons and four daughters. I was not here during their time. I don't know if there was a debugger here then.

I reach the central stairway and follow it down.

The wail comes again.

"BitStack!" It is the voice of my master's wife, Raahil. It is stern, but not angry.

I come to the bottom floor and instinctively bow. "Yes, I'm here."

"Living room, please."

I turn right into the hall. The floor is made of dark, polished wood, and has a blue carpet down the center. I follow it to the living room. It is ten meters square—the largest room in the house. It is trimmed in white, with red walls and a moon design on the carpet. There are sunken steps into it, and two short pillars on either side.

Raahil is there, dressed in a purple dress and matching scarf. Clutching her leg is the couple's youngest child, Obaid. He wears light green pants and shirt. He's seven, but in many ways seems less mature. Especially when it comes to his toys.

He watches me with wide eyes. Clutched in one arm is his favorite furry. It is a half-meter-tall representation of a sloth. It is light brown, with a white face and dark eyes. It, too, turns to look at me.

"Snoob can't walk," Obaid says. "Can you fix him, Bit?"

It is hard not to appreciate Obaid. He reminds me of my younger brother.

I bow my head to Raahil, then meekly approach them both. "Can I fix it?" I glance at Raahil, who smiles and nods. I crouch to Obaid's level. The carpet is very soft. "Snoob is having a bad day, yes?" I hold out a hand. "May I see him?"

Obaid sniffs, nods, and hands the toy to me.

Snoob looks at me, then rests its other hand on my arm. It is instilled with a clutching instinct. Its eyes attempt to sync with mine. To search my face. Another design feature. Warm in some ways. Disturbing in others.

I pat Snoob's head. Its eyes close and it begins to purr softly.

"Snoob likes you," Obaid says.

"Yes, I seem to have found its affection. Do you think he trusts me?"

The boy releases his mother's leg. Takes a step closer. "I trust you, Bit."

It is rarely in a debugger's best interest to form ties with the freeheads of his home, for they may be severed tomorrow. It is better to remain distant. Obedient, respectful, and otherwise unnoticed. But again, it is difficult. We aren't human, but only a tear-shaped device separates us.

I bow to Obaid. "I'm grateful for your trust." I look at his mother again. "Snoob is outside my training. I may not be able to help."

Obaid sniffs, and his bottom lip quivers.

Raahil touches his shoulder. "We're about to start his scripture training. He does not need Snoob now." She looks at me. "But it would be nice to keep him in the family."

"We're learning the prophets," Obaid says. "Together."

I draw Snoob into my arms. It reciprocates the motion, gripping me tighter. I place a foot on the first step. "I will leave you."

"No!" Obaid says.

Raahil gives him a stern look but strokes his head. "You may stay, BitStack. Snoob is usually a part of our lessons." She indicates my shoulder. "I see you have your bag with you." She smiles. "Ready as always."

"Snoob is learning too!" Obaid says.

To my left is a sofa and a narrow table. I bow and carry the ailing toy there. "We will be right here."

"Can Snoob still hear?" Obaid asks. "Will he be awake?"

"I'm not sure," I say. "But I will try."

Raahil leads Obaid further into the room. He glances at me once along the way. Most of the furniture is around the perimeter, leaving the room's center open. Mother and son find places on the floor there.

I study the toy and it studies me—eyes attempting to watch my face as I turn it. I have a strong desire to shut it down, but after a glance at Obaid, I fight the urge. I instead place it face down on the table. I manipulate both legs. There is no resistance. They are still connected and don't appear to be cracked or broken. Simply numb.

I frown. Working on a "furry" like this is tricky. With most mechanicals, I would spread a sheet over the broken area and try to get a look inside. Snoob's covering inhibits that, as does a warning label on its posterior.

"Who did we learn about last?" Raahil asks.

"Prophet Nuh," Obaid says. "Or Noah."

"Yes, and what did he do?"

"Built an ark! And saved the animals!"

"That is correct. Along with who?"

"His three sons and their wives. His wife and one son were left behind. They got drowned."

Furries aren't made for debuggers. They are single-owner items that are meant to be thrown out when they break. Even the factory won't take them back. Humans never touch their internals. They are machine pressed and formed.

For that reason, I'm surprised when I find—under the fur on the left hip—an open seam. I take a light from my bag, switch it to UV, and follow the length of the seam. It leads to a tiny pair of catches. I use tweezers to work the catches, and a small compartment snaps open. Snoob gives a garbled whine.

I glance at Obaid. He didn't hear Snoob. Good.

"Today I would like to teach you about another prophet."

"Dawud again! Or maybe Musa?"

Raahil chuckles. "No, we will talk about a later prophet."

"The Founder?"

"No, the one before him. Do you know who that is?"

"Who, Mother?"

Snoob tries to turn his head. I order it to stop, and thankfully, it complies. That means it can still hear, which should please Obaid. It won't miss the lesson.

The compartment I found is for power cell replacement. Overkill on the manufacturer's part, since the lifespan of most cells exceeds that of humans. Or sea turtles, for that matter.

There are two small mounting spines here that doubtless keep the compartment in place. Removing those could get me to the mechanics beneath. If I'm fortunate.

I don't have a tool for the spines, but using the stream and my small forming device, I'm able to make one. I loosen the spines and pry off the cell compartment. I leave the power cell and compartment connected. Snoob is still "alive."

"Isa." Obaid says. "Who's that?"

"Scriptures say many things about him. That he healed the sick and raised the dead."

"He brought someone back to life?"

"Yes, one of his friends. He also formed a bird out of mud. Breathed into it life, and it flew away."

"He made a bird from dirt? Wasn't Snoob made from things in the dirt?"

"Yes...but..."

"Are the people who made Snoob like Isa?"

I can't help but smile. He may be immature, but few connections escape Obaid. He captures details. He would make a good debugger.

"No," Raahil says. "They aren't like Isa. Or any of the prophets. They are only men. Blessed and smart men, but just men.

"Tell me more, Mother."

Beneath the compartment is Snoob's core motivator. A gear box of sorts, though it contains nothing so simple as gears. On that, I can use a sheet. I dig out a roll of them. The preferred size for debugging—the size I have—is about twenty centimeters square. I can't use one that large here. Need maybe half that.

I strip off a single sheet, then finding a knife, I bend the sheet at the halfway point and cut. Then I turn it and cut again.

I apply my mini sheet to the motivator. With a swipe, I activate the viewing device, and the motivator's shell becomes transparent. I see the starting place of most of Snoob's pathways and sinews. A crisscross of black and white lines.

Snoob has a controlling "brain" in its head too. The problem could be there. A software fault, or a bad connection to the lower body. The problem could be many places, but it is best to start near the malfunction and work out.

Nothing appears broken. Everything seems normal. I need to check its specs. Unfortunately, toy manufacturers rarely share schematics on the stream. They also rarely publish the code. No reason to for such a disposable item.

"What did you do to yourself, Snoob?" I whisper.

Snoob only mews.

"Isa is called the Word of A, and the Spirit of A," Raahil says.

"Honored titles, Mother."

"Yes. And he was taken to paradise and will return again."

"When?" Obaid says.

"No one knows, child."

"I want him to come soon. I want to meet someone who could do all those things."

Raahil chuckles. "Yes, we all would."

"Nuh did not do those things. Neither did Dawud or Musa. Did the Founder do such things?

I search the stream for Snoob's code and schematics. Nothing. The manufacturer, Flidibo, has them locked up and hidden away.

Not sure what to do here. I check on the boy and his mother. Obaid is sitting on one leg, fidgeting. I doubt the lesson will last much longer. He appears interested, but I know child interest can quickly melt away.

I find the tiniest fiber-camera I have, then make a small hole in Snoob's body, south of the motivator. I push the cam in and tap its broadcast into the stream. I move it all directions. Don't see anything that's crimped or broken.

I'm at a loss.

"Isa is the greatest prophet so far," Obaid says. "Maybe of all."

"No, the Founder is the greatest," Raahil says. "The last."

"What great thing did he do?"

Raahil sighs. "That's enough for today. We will talk of the Founder another day."

I hear them stand, then hear the sound of Obaid's feet hurrying my way.

"Is Snoob fixed?" he asks. "Can he walk again?"

I look him in the face. "I'm afraid he cannot."

Raahil joins us. Places a hand on Obaid's head. "Is he permanently damaged?"

"Anything is fixable," I say. "It's only a matter of time and resources." I indicate the toy. "In this case, the manufacturer does not have repair in mind."

"You can do nothing?" Raahil's eyes are wide and sorrowful.

"Snoob's designers would rather he be replaced." I bow. "With all apologies to his owner."

Raahil smooths her son's hair. "We will need to get you another Snoob, my son."

Tears form in Obaid's eyes. "I don't want another. There's no other Snoob."

"I believe his memories can be transferred," I offer. "The stream description indicates—"

"But it wouldn't be Snoob!" His face reddens. "You don't want to fix him, Bit."

Raahil stoops to Obaid's level. "BitStack wouldn't lie. Sometimes things can't be fixed. Sometimes—"

Obaid sniffs, turns, and runs from the room. Soon footsteps pound up the stairs.

"I'm sorry," I say. "Toys are—"

Raahil shakes her head. "You don't need to explain. I believe you." She looks in the direction Obaid traveled. "He needs to learn that we can't expect miracles." She looks at me. "We can order a replacement. You will exchange its memories?"

"Of course," I say. "That will be simple."

She smiles. "Very good. That's what we'll do."

I WAKE UP SAD AND FRUSTRATED. BitStack's mix had nothing to do with anything.

He's inactive now? Why? For mishandling a toy repair? We aren't made for that. Fixing adult toys, maybe. But disposable furries like Snoob? No.

If anyone in that story could have been disciplined, it was the wife, Raahil. Using her husband's expensive debugger for such a menial task? Wasting his cycles on the whims of a child?

Inexcusable.

Pain fills my head. Not a stop, but encompassing pain.

Wasn't that one of Bamboo's symptoms?

I stream the chute open and sit up. The ache throbs a bit, then starts to fade. My nervousness fades too.

I exit the chute and check the hour. It is after the time of morning prayer. I feel sorrow for having missed it. Perhaps the headache was A's warning: keep the schedule.

There's a prayer mat near the wall opposite the door. I use the steamer to cleanse myself, then put on my only blue jumpsuit. Maybe A will listen, despite my failure.

I walk to the mat and begin the ritual. During the third verse I realize that Noah was a part of BitStack's datamix. The coincidence astounds me. The image of Noah adorned the ceiling of my prior room. The one at the prince's palace. In fact, Noah and his story seemed to overshadow my life for months.

And here he is again.

By my prayer's final verse, I find myself wishing for a dialog with A, not simple rote. A Full Impact back and forth. We have things to discuss.

We're taught there are no coincidences. Only A's will. Is that what the BitStack's mix is? A measure of the divine in a simple children's lesson? The child was finished with Noah. He'd studied Musa and Davud—Moses and David—and was studying Isa next.

I finish my prayer and stand. Again my head hurts, but again it subsides with time.

Is pain my lot in life now? Punishment for my sins?

Bamboo's first assignment. Perhaps *that* is the real punishment. It is another distraction. I need to focus on healing, and on finding a way to survive.

I check the time again. I have twenty minutes left, and I am hungry. I leave my room. Begin my new journey.

Young men, boys actually, ply the hall outside in both directions. The procession is orderly. There is no running or pushing. Their eyes notice me, though. I'm an anomaly in their otherwise structured life. A debugger who has returned, like an unwanted purchase, to his place of origin.

"Is he defective?" they must be thinking. "Unwanted, lost, broken?"

The answer is "yes" on all counts.

From the moment they were taken from their parents, to the time they are sent to their first master, these young implants will remain here, in Bamboo's school. The only adult they interact with is him.

Everything else is automated. Servbots clean, cook, and sew. That, too, is an anomaly. Most places have a mix of human and bot servants, with the latter being the minority. The poorer you are, the less tech you have. It has always been so.

I reach the dining hall. It's a large, circular room—approximately fifteen meters across. The tables are circular too, like planets within a sun. The walls are white, the ceiling blue; the floor is tan, and the tables are medium brown. There is a ring of white support columns circling the room's midpoint.

At the far end of the room are butterfly doors leading to the kitchen. I see two humanoid servbots at work there, but I can sense five in the area. One exits the kitchen carrying a tray of food. It is an RX model. It is male in appearance, with muted humanoid features, and dressed in a green servant's robe.

Many of the tables are full. Most have at least a few people at them.

I walk deeper into the room, past dozens of curious eyes. It is an uncomfortable situation. Possibly my most uncomfortable yet, and that's saying a lot.

I consider streaming up a digital overlay of the entire experience. Of repainting and re-compositing the scene in my mind. Giving myself the illusion of an empty room, with a dozen servbots at my command. Some fanning me. Others feeding me grapes.

I want solitude. A place to eat in peace.

I notice a table near the kitchen with only two occupants. I approach it, and with a nod to the students, sit on the side opposite them.

They return the nod but say nothing. They focus on their food, with occasional glances at each other. Seemingly controlled and contained. Inside, though, I'm sure they are quite active. I remember how it felt to be a new implant. The sense of freedom it brought. The ability to communicate without speaking. To read with your eyes closed. Like a lamb released to the pasture for the first time. A seemingly endless bounty.

Every pasture has fences. And wolves lurk beyond.

A servbot nears our table. It appears male too, so it is difficult not to think of it that way. It glances at the boys, silently checking their plates and the level of their drinks, then looks at me. It bows, stares for a moment, then bows again. "Peace to you, Instructor ThreadBare."

The boys gawk at me. I almost wince.

"And to you," I say. "Together with A's mercy."

It bows again. "It is an honor to have you at our school again. I am sorry I was not here when you were a student. I went into operation only two years ago."

"Think nothing of it."

It nods. "You are free to stream an order whenever you like. Do you have the current menu?"

"I'm sure I can find it," I say. "But today I know what I want."

"Of course. It is why I am here."

"Gaymer Wa Dibis." A favorite from when I was a student.

It bows. "Do you want dibis, or would you rather have honey?"

I haven't had honey for a long time. Possibly since I was last here. Why is that? "Honey, thank you."

The bot bows and leaves.

The boys are still looking at me.

I smile. "You wish to ask me something?"

They glance at each other, and then I feel the itch of a message to my implant. It is from the boy on the left, now called "Mint-Bridge." I don't open it. I only widen my smile.

"Feel free to speak, Mint."

He looks startled, but after another glance at his friend—Band-Stand—he nods. "It labeled you 'instructor'."

I nod. "Yes, but that was in error. I'm every bit the student today."

BandStand squints. "You're too old to be a student."

"You're lying."

"I assure you, I'm receiving no stop."

Mint doesn't look convinced. "Maybe you're just good at hiding pain."

"Probably buzzing like a bee right now."

They giggle together. Boys at the table behind us turn to look. Then turn away again. They don't appear to be talking, but they probably are.

I scan the room. Every table is a collection of islands, all floating in the stream. Was I like that once?

It is all new for them, remember.

The bot brings me a small basket filled with oval-shaped bread, and two white bowls. One bowl contains the firm cream called "gaymer." The other honey. It smells wonderful.

BandStand squints again. "What is it?"

"A forgotten favorite. Would you like to try?"

They both shake their heads. They're being polite.

I push the basket their direction. "It's meant to be shared." I point at the bread. "See, I have plenty. Now, try."

Hesitantly, they take bread, and on my urging, dip it into the honey. It is consumed quickly.

I smile and select bread for myself. "How far are you from your level?" I dip my bread in gaymer.

"Only Bamboo knows," Mint says.

"Yes, but how does it seem to you? Your progress."

Mint straightens in his chair. "I've only been an implant for three months, but I expect to be released soon. I'm a natural. Messaging, connecting..." He smirks at Band. "Going to be the best DR ever."

I take another bite. "The best ever? A bold prediction." Mint has at least a year until he's ready. But I won't tell him that.

Mint shrugs, takes another roll. "I was always good in math." He bites and chews. "At least before. In regular school."

I look at BandStand. He has fairer skin than Mint and seems frailer somehow. "Will you be the best, as well?"

He frowns. "I don't want to be the best." He reaches for the gaymer, which I push his way.

"No?"

He resists meeting my eyes, looking instead past my left shoulder. "I don't know. I just don't."

"He doesn't like it here," Mint says. "He'd rather be home."

Band scowls. "I didn't say that."

"No, but you would." Mint looks at me. "I hear him crying sometimes."

"No, you don't!" Band shoves the other boy's shoulder, then winces. The headbuzz. The shock. He hides his eyes with the back of his hands. When he removes them, his eyes are reddened.

"Did you do that on purpose, Mint?" I ask.

"Do what?"

"Try to get him disciplined."

Mint hesitates, and I can almost see the thought process. If he lies, he'll get his own shock. But if he doesn't, he'll look bad.

Finally, he shrugs. "I guess I did. Like I said, I have it—" His eyes widen, and he drops his bread.

"You were corrected," I say.

"Why did that happen?"

"Because you intended harm."

He frowns. "That was late, though." He looks at Band. "Wasn't that late?"

"Your implant is learning too," I say. "Next time it'll come earlier. It'll catch your intent."

Mint rubs his temples. "Did you know that's how it is?"

I smile. "You brought it on yourself. You'll find that with much of the pain of life."

There are two pieces of bread left. My appetite is sated, so I offer them to the boys. Band takes one, but Mint shakes his head.

The bot returns. "Do you require anything more?"

"I think we've had enough." I receive a notification then of my impending assignment, so I stand. "I need to go." I nod at the boys. "Thank you for sharing your table."

"Yeah, sure," Mint says.

Band smiles and gives a little wave.

I don't know them, but I suspect the boys are a lot like me. Lost, alone, and a little afraid.

Except I have an expiration date.

THE CLASSROOM IS AS I REMEMBER. Rectangular, with a carpeted floor and light yellow walls. There are rows of teal and white desks, each made to hold two students. There are narrow windows at the back of the room positioned above eye level. Those are to let light in, but nothing else. No scenery to gaze at, no outside distractions.

The walls are completely blank. The room's corners are empty. There's no need for visual aids here. No drawing boards or models.

The minimal decoration makes the experience more oppressive today. More daunting. I contemplate messaging Bamboo. Telling him I can't do this. Let him have my implant and be done with it.

I will find a life somewhere. Perhaps in Grim's shop. Another broken debugger reduced to the menial.

What scares me more? This task, or being a freehead again? Merely human?

I force my mind to the present. If nothing else, being here gives me time. Time to research and gather evidence. And possibly to see her again. Just once.

Boys start to filter in through the back door. Each looks surprised to see me. Unsure of what is to come. No one sits. They stand alongside their desks.

Why are they doing that? I thread my fingers together behind my back. Uncomfortable.

Bamboo didn't come to introduce me. He should have. I don't even know how to start.

Or do I?

I search my memory, biological and digital alike. At one time, not that long ago, I was on the other side. Standing by my desk waiting. I search for that image.

I find a segment of my first experience here. Bamboo looking around the room, checking faces and idents. Then telling us to sit while making a sweeping motion with his hand.

I can do that!

"Peace be unto you," I say.

"And to you," the class echoes back. "Together with A's mercy."

"Take your seats," I say, using Bamboo's tone and hand motion.

They sit as one, folding their hands on their desks.

Two dozen eyes now stare at me. Where to begin? I check the time. Over an hour to go.

I take a deep breath. "I know you have questions," I say. "I will do my best to address them before we begin."

I expect a barrage of raised hands or stream queries, but they don't come. This class is far enough along to transfer its respect for Bamboo to me. That is a comfort.

"I am ThreadBare. A level twelve debugger. My specialty is combat bots, also known as heavies. My former master was the Prince Aadam. I'm here awaiting reassignment. The honored Bamboo has asked for my help in instructing you."

The boys fidget. Frowns form on several faces. Why is that? I again try to focus. To think how I would feel in their place.

"I'm not his replacement. Nor will I be." I force a smile. "You're not being punished."

That seems to help some. How do I help more? I pause, trying to sort it out.

The change. The possible loss. Is that it?

"Bamboo thought it would speed your perfection to have someone who has served outside to learn from," I say. "I'm not an instructor, but I'm willing to be a resource."

Now the faces look calm, interested. Change can be good. It is a matter of perspective, how the change is framed. I must remember.

"I'm told you've been through the basic operation of your implants. That you've had an introduction to stream theory and technology and have been given an overview of debugging. I would like to introduce debugging technique to you, beginning with some of the fundamental tools." I take a breath. "Before we begin, are their—"

Messages strike my implant. I see at least a dozen in my queue, sent from names like LostNote, TalonsUp, JumboJet and Dark-Sand. Many of the students have their eyes closed. Still separating the inner from the outer. Sometimes that helps, yes, but usually it is best to occupy both places.

How did you get so profound, Thread?

Place me in a classroom and I become an artist trying to paint the sky. BullHammer will want to use my name to swear with.

Probably he already does. Especially after what I did to him.

"I'm receiving questions," I say, "but for this class, I'd like to use our voices...and our hands."

Eyes snap open, excepting one child down front—JumboJet. He opens one eye and keeps the other closed. Funny.

Hands raise.

"Talons?" I say, pointing at an older student with almond eyes.

He lowers his hand. "Did you see Prince Aadam die?"

I take a deep breath. "I saw many things. Things I can't share. But that?" I shake my head. "No. I did not." I point at another, taller student. LongString.

"Did you live in the palace?" he asks.

"Yes." I point at Mint, my friend from breakfast.

"Is it true he tortured people?" he asks.

I raise both hands. "You have learned of master privilege? That there are things that can't be discussed?" I scan the room. "The details of my work for the royal family, for any master, are so protected."

"Because you'll get buzzed?"

I nod. "Yes, and because it is a breach of debugger etiquette. We must be discreet." I try to think of something Bamboo would say. "We are like lamps, or fireplaces. Only evident when in use."

"So he *did* torture someone," Talons says. "Otherwise, you could say."

I look at the windows, suddenly wishing there was a view. "That is not true," I say, shaking my head. "I simply can't tell."

The questions continue.

"Have you been on the battlefield?"

"Again, protected."

"Have you seen anyone die?"

I frown. There are public displays of punishment all the time. There's probably a stoning or a beheading going on right now. "I'm sure we all have."

"In battle, though. Did you see that?"

I wave the questions away. "We should get started."

"Do you think robots have souls?"

The class goes silent, and all eyes turn toward the back of the room. It is my friend from lunch, BandStand.

"Unusual question," I say. "Why do you ask?"

Band shrugs. "I read it somewhere. That there's a new ruling on bots. That they have souls."

"I haven't heard that," I say. "But I've been out of touch." I shrug. "I mostly worked on heavies. Bots that are definitely soulless." I glance at the windows again. "But that's an interesting idea."

"Is it possible?" Band asks. "*Could* they have a spirit?"

I'm unsure how to proceed. My internal rules, based on the scriptures, will give little guidance here.

I dip into my storage again, looking for a proper response. I find one of Bamboo's lessons. A taste of history.

I smile. "*Who is more the wrongdoer than one who attempts to create creation like Mine,*" I say. "Are you familiar with this passage?"

Some heads nod, but most of them simply watch.

"It was taught to mean that statues and even pictures were haraam. Forbidden. Even today, there is a hesitation for such things. Many are uneasy with the images of the Imam or of our forefathers." I raise a finger. "Images of the Founder, of course, even the written representation of his name, are still unlawful.

"So, what could be more haraam than creating a man-like machine? How did we get to the place where they are everywhere?" I scan their faces. "Anyone know?"

Band raises his hand, which I acknowledge. "Abu Ahmed?"

I smile. "Yes, the mawla Abu Ahmed. A hundred and forty

years ago he moved the line. He said the admonition didn't apply to creations that didn't approximate what A created. Bots that did not mimic known life were permissible. The ulama agreed, and so were born some of our most creative designs. String hoppers, for instance. Also, the heavies that I used to work on.

LostNote raised his hand. "But we have snakebots and spider-bots. They're like animals."

I nod. "And copy A's creation, yes. Still forbidden after Abu Ahmed. So what happened next? Anyone?"

"The Scholar?" Band says.

"Yes, Sa'dan Sabil. A scholar, but also a creative genius. Many of his designs are still in use. He argued that scripture forbids only biological manipulation—practices such as cloning and gene spli-cing—but didn't apply to mechanical achievements. He said that one could conceivably create a robot, encoded with the teachings of the Founder, that would exhibit perfect faith. One that may not equal that of the Founder, but could easily approximate the faith of his Companions. His first disciples."

I search their faces. "He argued that a faith-based specification would produce another benefit. Anyone know what that is?"

Band raises his hand. "Prevent rebellion?"

"Yes!" I smile. "Since man is the vice regent of A, the bots would, by definition, recognize their place in creation. Be the per-fect servants. The perfect Abduls." I message BandStand a glowing face and the sound of applause. "So far, that theory has held true.

The windows' bands of daylight seem to ripple, before becom-ing steady again. "With implant technology, we've superseded Sabil's dream. Making even man, even you, of near-perfect faith."

Talons raises his hand. "What about the bot wars?" he asks. "The ones during Sabil's time?"

I shake my head. "Those were wars of men, not machines. They were fought because many of Sabil's contemporaries didn't share his conclusions. And it cost him his life." I raise a finger. "The wars did influence robotic designs, though..."

I remember the visual aid I arranged, and signal to it in the stream. I fold my hands and watch the door on the wall to my left.

The class sits in silence.

Twenty seconds later, a servbot ambles in. It's dressed in the customary green servant's robe and is carrying my debugging bag. It stops a few paces from me, then turns toward the class.

I take the bag and set it on the floor near the bot's feet. I point at the bot's head. "The smoothed features of the servbot is a direct result of the bot wars. Unnecessary, given Sabil's reading of scripture, but necessary to appease the most ardent critics. Muted aesthetics are used in all bots that mimic A's creation. LostNote's snakebots, for instance."

There is less than ten minutes left in the class. How did that happen? I haven't gotten to the lesson I wanted to share. Nor have I answered Band's question. The one about bot souls. Frustrating.

I feel the weight of the student's gaze. I stoop and remove a roll of sheets from my bag. "Is it possible for bots to have souls?" I look at the first row of boys, then at Talons in the second, and Band in the last. "To do such a thing would require more knowledge than man currently has, and would certainly violate 'the creation like Mine creation' passage, wouldn't it?"

"That said—" I hold the roll of sheets up. "These are flex sheets. A debugger's best friend. With a sheet we can look into the inner workings of any machine. If anything will reveal the soul of a machine, a sheet will."

I strip off a sheet, then place the roll on the ground and walk toward the bot.

"Let's take a look!"

I RETURN TO MY ROOM and drop into the chair.

My head feels empty and achy. My body is numb, like it was dropped from a downrider. I'm surprised because, while being a temporary instructor required little physical exertion—none of the climbing, lifting or stooping that a typical debugging job requires—I'm drained as if it had.

Was it the standing? The ceaseless questions? The constant searches for information, or some intangible quality?

I shouldn't be doing this. I'm not qualified. I don't like to stand in front of people, especially inquisitive people. It takes a great deal of preparation. A lot of time. And I don't have any.

I touch the side of my head. Will it make my condition worse? I've tried to minimize the impact on my implant, but it is hard to avoid.

Information: I always need more.

Bamboo mentioned he needed more free time. More time to research. What sort of research is he doing?

I stand and pace toward the wall opposite the door. I wish I had a window. A place where I could gaze outside without using my implant.

Bamboo's facility is located in the heart of the city. There's perpetual motion outside, both on the street, and overhead on the strings. I imagine the hum of the crowds. The downrider screams.

I know that one of the debuggers who disappeared, Hard-Candy, was Bamboo's only female debugger. She was an experiment that he was quite proud of, if the rumors are correct. Is that why he ponders space?

Regardless, I understand the feeling. How time spent instructing, molding, could create a bond between teacher and student. Even today the boys made me proud and happy. I found myself learning again through them. Pulling for them. That feeling might be addictive. A fountain to return to when the rest of life is difficult.

I had such a fountain once. One that produced new rivers and tributaries in my soul.

Damali.

I pace toward the door. What happened to her after she left the prince's palace? After she, TallSpot, and the other astronauts boarded a red vehicle and sped away? I have to find out something. At least know she's okay.

I touch the stream and quickly determine the physical location of GrimJack's. From there, I search for any bulletins relating to the area. I check arrest records and police alerts. Anything that might indicate the fate of Damali and her companions, even though I hope they haven't been found. I hope they're safe.

My search returns nothing of significance. The only relevant news item is about the reduction of crime in the area. News about nothing happening. Good news, I suppose, but not helpful.

Who would know to look for them? Following the prince's death, does anyone remain who cares?

I should contact FrontLot again. See if he has another mix. Keep researching.

He wasn't particularly helpful last time, though. Or even relevant. A lesson about past prophets and the futility of debugging a child's toy. Inconsequential.

Obaid's questions echo through my mind. "He brought someone back to life? Are the men who made Snoob like Isa?"

Excellent question. Insightful.

"Can bots have souls?" Another intriguing idea. Where did it come from?

I search for any phrase that seems related. Most of what I find is meaningless. Idle speculation by people who lack the proper background. A man who swears his bot took on the form of his lost wife. A robot that somehow defied a master to save a child's life. A hopper that formed a bond with a pigeon. Fanciful stories, that even if true, prove nothing about robot sentience.

Where else can I turn?

My mind returns to my final moments at the prince's palace. My struggle to free the prisoners. The way BullHammer and I co-operated, with him feeding bot commands that I provided...

BullHammer.

I haven't contacted him since I left the prince's service.

I feel a touch of guilt. Though Bull and I are more rivals than friends, he helped me when I needed it, when it didn't benefit him. He put himself at risk.

It has been days since then. He'll doubtless be surly.

I stream for the funniest vid I can find. One of a government official being spit on by a camel. I wrap that in an apologetic note and seal it with the taste of cinnamon and oranges. Send it Bull's way.

Nanoseconds go by. I return to the chair. My room needs more visual points of reference. More decoration.

I retrieve an image of Damali smiling. It is from our moments by the pool, when her face was uncovered. I crop it and insert a frame around it. I position it so that I perceive it as sitting on top of my dresser. The implant will perpetuate the mirage. Her image will be one of the first things I see when I exit my chute in the morning. A fixture hidden to all but me.

I add a window to the wall opposite the door too. Beyond it is the view I used to have from the prince's arboretum: trees, the moat, and vast fields beyond.

The life of a debugger: virtual decorating.

I message Bull again. A full second passes. Then the connection grabs, and I see him. He looks about ten pounds lighter than before. His jumpsuit hangs on his frame. But otherwise, he seems clean and healthy.

He lives in the lap of luxury. Food should not be an issue.

The scene around him must be fiction—generated—because he's sitting in a rowboat. There are snowcapped mountains in the distance. He's clutching oars.

"Dali," he sputters. "What do you want?"

I check references to "Dali." It is the name of an infidel artist. Bull uses such names to swear with.

"Wanted to see you," I say. "To thank you."

He scowls. "You did that already." He raises an oar. "I did what I did. Don't need to know the details. Better if I don't."

"It was a good thing," I say. "Significant."

Bull shifts, and his boat rocks with the motion. "Significant is clearing your list, Thread. Clearing it and moving on."

I smile. "You cleared my list."

"With the prince?" He scowls. "Yeah, I bet I did. We didn't kill him, did we?"

"No. We freed—" I get a tingle of a warning, and stop. Shake my head.

Bull nods. "Say nothing more. Don't need to get shocked. Today's been bad enough already." He grasps the oars, makes a tentative rowing motion, then stops. "Where are you? Looks pretty bleak. Not in jail, are you?"

I send him a panorama of my room. "You don't recognize this?"

"Only place I remember being *that* stark was back when—" His eyes widen. "Nah, doesn't make sense."

"What doesn't?"

He shrugs. "Almost said Bamboo's, but why would you be there?"

I cock my head, glance at my virtual window. "Not sure myself."

He sighs and plies the oars again. "Getting reeducated or something?"

"No, I'm—"

"You're getting your 'plant pulled, aren't you!" He points a finger. "That's why you don't do things that shock you. Doesn't pay." He widens his hands and looks around. "See this? This is what you get if you do what's right. Space and scenery."

"That's not real."

"How do you know? It could be." He takes a deep breath. "Smells real. Looks real."

"There are mountains back there," I say. "Big mountains."

He glances behind him. "I work for the Imam. He *owns* mountains. He might be visiting his mountains." He smiles. "Yeah, that's it. He brought me along. His favorite DR." He looks over the side of his boat, studies the water. "Anyway, I always wanted to try rowing a boat." He takes a couple broad strokes. The boat appears to move backward. Away from me.

"Are you all right?"

"I'm fine," he says. "I've got a boat, oars, and a lake. Mountains!" He rows again. "How are you?"

I check the generated Damali photo, then look at my window again. "Troubled."

"Well, that's new..." He smirks. "Maybe you *need* your implant out. Less trouble that way." Another broad stroke. "That's not why you're there, though, is it?"

I shake my head. "Between assignments," I say. "I'm helping out."

He stops rowing. "With the initiates?"

"For now."

"Teaching them?" He grabs his stomach and laughs. "That's...rails rich."

I feel heat. "I can teach."

He chortles again. "You can barely teach yourself."

I grab the connection in my mind, preparing to squeeze it off. "I should go."

He drops an oar and puts up a hand. "No, wait." He dabs at his eyes. "Seriously, I'm glad you messaged me. You made me laugh."

"Yeah, thanks." I tighten my grip on the connection, constricting it.

"Did you want anything else, Thread? Can I recommend a lunch, or something?"

"I'm trying to figure things out."

He leans forward. "All right, what things?" There's a distant cabin behind him now. Smoke coming from its chimney.

"Ever hear of bots with souls?"

"Bots with souls? That a new music group or something?"

I shake my head. "Something one of the initiates mentioned."

He frowns, stares off to the left. "Never heard anything like that," he says. "There have been some flipped restrictions lately. Nanoscanners banned, for instance."

"Nanoscanners?"

"Yeah, you probably never need them, working on the big stuff."

"I worked on servs for the prince."

He frowns. "Straight production models, right? Common stock?"

I shrug. "They were new. Newest I've ever seen."

He grabs an oar with his left hand. Tugs on it. "I try to avoid the updates. Worry about it when it affects me." The boat begins to spin. "I'm turning. Look at me turning."

I want to ask about TallSpot's theory too. About the end of debuggers. But that might be too much. Bull looks tired.

"Anything else?" he says.

I shake my head. "Guess not."

"Come on, I owe you for the laughs."

"I'd like to get out," I say. "To ride, hit the shops, be outside—"

He nods. "But there's no reason to," he says. "Prince had everything. And so does Bamboo."

"Right. I'm stuck."

Bull moves the right oar, causing him to circle the opposite direction. He stares into the ever-changing distance for a second, then snaps his fingers. "Got it!"

"Got what?"

"Rails, you need me. Can't believe you didn't—"

"What!"

"You're an instructor, right?"

"Sure. Yeah. I guess."

"Then you have your way out." He laughs and pulls hard on the oars. "Field trip!"

THOUGH IT IS THE MIDDLE of the day, Bamboo's study seems darker than it did before. Possibly that's because he's next to the window, blocking a portion of the sun's rays. But I think not. I think it's internal. A change to my perception of light and dark.

I am broken, remember.

"I see no value in it," he says. "None at all."

I'm behind the wicker chair this time. Using it as both support and shield. It is little help in either capacity. "But, master—"

He glares at me. "I'm not your master. You're not my student."

I bow my head. "I learn just the same. Simply being in your—"

He waves a hand. "Idle flattery, ThreadBare. Spare me the cycles."

"My apologies. It was only an idea."

He indicates the streets beyond the window. "You wish to take them out there?" He shakes his head. "It was never done for you. Never necessary. Multiple generations of DRs have been produced in this facility. Countless implantations and reeducations."

My eyes seek the floor. "You gave me the task," I say. "I think this could help. Let them see the DR life firsthand."

"It is too soon." Bamboo pushes away from the window, then walks to the bookshelves opposite me. His eyes linger on the spines of the books, as if each is important.

They are an unusual decoration for an implant. Unnecessary given the stream. Why does he have them?

"My job is to remove them from that life," he says. "The one they first knew." He pauses at the fireplace and selects a book in the shelf over it. He slides it out a couple centimeters, rubs his thumb over the front cover, and pushes it back in. "I wonder about your condition, ThreadBare. Your motivations."

"The idea didn't come from injury," I say. "It was suggested by another DR."

"Another?" He frowns. "I should reduce your access." He points at me. "If I *were* your master such betrayal would be impossible."

I tighten my grip on the back of the chair. "It wasn't betrayal. It was simply an...idea."

"Not a very good one."

I want to go out. I need to. I only have a few days.

He touches another book. "In the past, children weren't as important. Did you know this?"

I shake my head. "Scripture says that 'wealth and children are the ornament of this life.'"

"For followers of A, yes, but at one time most did not follow him. For them, the child came at the parents' convenience. They made themselves the judges of worth. Defying the command not to kill children for fear of want." He opens the book and turns it so I can see the interior. "This is a book of history. Very valuable. Very rare." He turns the book again and pats the pages. "I cherish its knowledge."

"It tells about non-believers?"

"It tells many things." He smiles. "That was why they lost, you see. Losing sight of what was valuable. Overcome by those that did not." He closes the book and returns it to the shelf. "They missed, as you quoted, the connection between children and wealth. Resources to be nurtured and educated. Not disposed, but protected."

Debuggers are taken from their parents at a young age. They come to Bamboo as resources. Leave as slaves. "So, that's why you won't let them out? You're protecting them?"

"They *are* children. What if they were to run off?"

"They couldn't. Their implants would—"

"Yes, but they still might try." He pulls free another book, opens it to the center, flips a couple pages. Appears to be reading.

"They won't," I say.

"And how would you ensure their safety?" he says. "Each is worth a fortune. What is to prevent—"

"I've walked the street often." He's protesting too much. There's something more to this. "Even more when I younger. To attack a debugger carries the penalty of—"

"Yes, but you are only one. Not a dozen. Men lose sight of the penalties when the fortune is great. When the benefits are legion."

"We will stay off the streets," I say. "Take downriders from here."

He looks at me. "And where would you take them on this..." He flutters a hand. "Field trip? I assume you'll go somewhere."

"Perhaps one of the bot foundries," I say. "Or a click and clack. A shop—"

"Both are targets of the insurrectionists," he says. "Certainly you know that."

He's talking about antitex. By definition, they hit tech spots. The name screams it. "Everywhere is their target," I say. "They might hit here too—" I get a surge of head pain. Not a stop, but that other pain.

Bamboo studies me. "That wasn't a stop, was it?"

I shake my head as the feeling starts to fade. "It was nothing," I say. "An effect of the weather, I think."

He snorts, then looks at the window. "It is unseasonably sunny today." He's quiet for a moment, then returns the book to the shelf. "You're correct about the danger here. There have been attempts in the past. Poor attempts, but attempts all the same."

Bamboo is a man of walls. Hidden walls. Am I persuading him? I have no idea. I simply watch him. Waiting.

"I need to return to my work," he says. "There's another implantation tomorrow. I should study his scans. Calibrate his appliance."

Is that it? I had little hope I would succeed. But I can't help feeling disheartened. I want to go out. I have to learn—

Maybe I should ask for myself? What reason would he give for keeping me here?

"I will go then. Would it be permissible if—"

He looks at me. "You can't handle a full class outside. It would strain even me. But there may be merit in what you ask. I will permit a trial, say, of four or five initiates."

"Five?"

"Yes, that means the others will need supervision. I will take the class that day."

"You will?"

He nods. "I will need notes on what you've covered, of course."

"Of course..." I'm not sure what to say, so I bow again.

"Take care of my children, debugger."

I WALK THE HALLS OF the facility with no destination in mind. My excitement is nearly overwhelming. I have an opportunity to go out! The first time in many months—freedom. It seems almost too good to be true.

I want to replay every moment I spent with Damali. To recall it from storage and study her every move and intonation. I think she approved of me, but was that a mirage of my own making? Or worse, was I simply a means to an end?

I don't understand women, or how they think. I'm prevented from contemplating ideas like affection or longing. Even now I risk a buzz storm. I don't want that. The headaches are bad enough.

My freedom won't be easy. I have to take children with me. How am I going to manage that? And who will I take? Which five? I think of BandStand, and his longing for home. Would it be good for him to go out? Or would it make his sadness worse?

I pass a servbot. It acknowledges me with a bowed head and the standard salaam. I return the salaam.

I don't know these children well enough to decide. It won't be a fair decision. There are no grades. No ranking.

A test of some sort?

Everything is so complicated. I wish for the days when my work rolled in through a garage door. Where I fixed it and sent it back out again.

I reach a small lounge area. It has three seats and a circular window that looks out over the back of the building. I see several low structures, all brick, with tiled roofs. A few streets over is a park.

I need to fix something. But if I can't do that, I need to solve something. Prove something to myself and Bamboo. Show I deserve more time.

A message from FrontLot invades my mind. As if we'd been connected this whole time. As if he knew what I needed.

I accept his request. Spin and flip it open.

He's sitting on a roof somewhere. He is squinting, meaning the sun is somewhere in front of him. I can hear a breeze blowing. "Peace be," he says.

"And you," I say.

"I'm about to cross to a pylon here," he says. "There's a bit of a wait. Someone sliced up the ladder." He points to his left. "Freeheads are working on it." The image pans so I can see an orange-colored pylon. Below it, there are overall-wearing workers standing on an extended platform. One appears to be welding.

"Rails."

Front waves. "Nothing to it. Gives me time to blue out. Check with you." He scratches the side of his head, then strokes it. "Blinking Antis. Always wrecking something around here."

I nod. "Good thing they have us."

He shakes his head. "Can't fix everything." He looks off to the left again. "Never got a review from you about the last mix."

"Didn't help."

"Yeah, not sure why I sent that one. I'll refund you."

"BitStack isn't missing?"

"Oh sure, he's on the list, but from a long while ago." He shrugs. "Think he lost his focus or something. I sort of like the mix. Keeps me humble."

"Because he doesn't fix Snoob?"

"Right." Front smiles. "Can't fix everything. Anyway, I owe you one."

"You have something now?"

"Think so. Can't figure it, but it is interesting." He glances to his left, then stands. "I think they're done. Starting to leave, anyway." He hoists his debugging pack to his shoulder.

"The mix?"

He nods. "From a DR named JustBecause. Sort of flipped, but he's on the list. No contacting him now." He shrugs. "I warn you it might mess with you."

"Send it now."

I KNEEL IN MY MASTER'S ROOM. He has a wide nanoshield between us and it's in full glory, stretching from wall to wall, and ceiling to floor. It shimmers with gold, but patterns of color move across it. Violet follows indigo, which follows blue, which follows green. It is fascinating to watch, and maddening. For that reason, I focus on the floor. It is made of dark and reflective marble, so it attempts to echo the shield's gyrations. But it is a muted echo. Bearable, though it vexes.

"Attention, DR!"

I return my eyes to the shield. A small window appears, and Master's eyes are revealed. They are out of proportion. Double their normal size. A vibrant and raging blue.

"What do you require of me, Master?"

"I require your death!"

This is no idle threat. He's killed seven before me. I'm here only because I volunteered. Because I was all that was left. "I wish only to serve you."

"That's what they all say. Even since my first." The eyes grow larger. "But all fail. None are worthy."

My knees begin to pain me. But movement is forbidden. "I have not failed you. I've kept your trust. Repaired your—"

"Repairs don't concern me. Only secrets. That my secrets are kept." The shield flashes green. "There are places of knowledge. Gardens of wisdom. These you have exposed."

I bow my head. "I have not."

A red apple rolls out of the shield and stops a few centimeters before me. Soon, another apple joins it. And another. All appear perfect and unbruised. I can smell them from here.

"Are you hungry?"

I fear to answer truthfully, but I must. "I am."

"Then take and eat."

The apples appear delicious, but are they safe?

"Why do you hesitate?"

"You wish me dead."

Laughter fills the room. In response, the shield's colors ripple out from a spot just below his window. "I will not kill you with food, debugger. I will remove your head."

I bow and meekly reach for an apple. I raise it to my lips, draw in a long breath, and bite down. Juice mists my face. It has a rich, heady flavor. Almost intoxicating. "Before I die, let me serve you again."

"And what would you serve me?" he asks. "I have all I need."

"I will give you a story."

"A story?" Four seconds pass. "I would like that."

I take another bite, chew slowly, and think. "There was a debugger in need of a solution. He had questions but could find no answers."

Master laughs. "Sounds like every debugger I've ever had. Lost and hopeless." His laughter continues.

I wait silently, watching his eyes.

"Was it a broken machine?"

"Yes," I say. "His master's favorite. A vehicle with which he traveled the world."

"A missing part? Broken code?"

"One of those, yes," I say. "No shop had what he required. No stream search revealed it. But there was a deadline and an answer was required."

"Was he in danger?"

"No, but his master was. He would only travel on this one vehicle. He was old, not well. And he would fly in this vehicle no matter its condition. He would not listen to reason."

"So, what did the DR do?"

I bite the apple again. For a last meal, it is satisfying. Filling. "Searched old books. Even forbidden places. The journey brought him much pain."

"Debuggers deserve pain. Pain is a motivator!"

"No," I say. "Pain inhibits pure thought. Quenches it. He wished only to—"

The shield drops. Master's eyes are still disproportionate, but so is his entire head. Inhuman. He's completely unclothed, his body stark white and frail. He holds a scepter in his right hand. The upturned end of it is large. A red crystal. He could easily crush my skull with it. "Pure thought is an abstraction and a diversion. It leads only to death. Serve, serve, and serve. Then you live." With his left hand he tosses something at me. It is a metal object, gold in color.

I instinctively duck. It flies over my head to land on the floor behind me, clattering and spinning. It is pointed on one end, with a handle on the other.

"What is that, DR?" he asks.

"I don't know."

He laughs. "Where's your history? It is a lamp, you nilly. A prison camp for demons."

"For demons?"

"For those that control us. Simply say the words, and they'll come. Enslave us all."

Master is mad, of course. The progression has been quite severe. Quite fast.

His nanoshield returns, shimmering a fiery red, making the room seem hellish. "Continue your story!" His eyes are wide, seemingly pressed against the shield window. "I want to know how it ends." He pauses. "There should be animals. Add animals!"

I bow and try to regain my composure. "In his pain, the debugger met a wolf with a scar on his head. For many days the wolf followed him. All around the city he followed. Nothing was said. Occasionally, the debugger would throw the creature food, which it would eat voraciously. The wolf caused no harm to the debugger, only watched. But the debugger feared if he were to stop feeding it, it might eat him.

"Finally, he began to talk to the beast. Explain to it his problems."

"Yes, I always talk to animals," Master says. "As they to me."

I nod. "It's good of you to do so. Sometimes they answer, as they did in this case. The wolf told him that he was searching in the wrong place. That the boundaries that he thought existed weren't real. That the boat he sailed upon was near an underwater island."

"The wolf said all this?"

"Yes."

More laughter. Different shades of red percolate across the shield. Walls of fire. "I like this story."

"Thank you, Master."

"You should thank me, it was my idea. Animals always help."

I glance at the ancient lamp. It has multiple dents in its surface. Probably everything in this room has been thrown, dropped, or chewed on. I take another bite of my apple.

"Is that the end?" he asks. "Was the island real?"

"With the wolf's help, he found the island. He dove deep and was rewarded. The island was more than an island. It was a continent."

"He found what he required?"

"And more. A new land. But still he was sad."

"Why was he sad?"

Now I know that I have him. That I will live another day. "I cannot tell it now," I say. "It will take too long, and I am tired."

"Tired!" The shield seems to explode with sound.

"Yes. I need my chute. My rest."

"Cursed chutes. Always the chutes."

FOR THE FIRST TIME IN WEEKS, I feel real wind on my face.

I wait near the downrider pylon on the roof of Bamboo's facility. Five of his students are with me. In honor of JustBecause's datamix, they were all chosen at random. I fed the idents of the entire class into a digital blender, turned it on, then reached in with binary tweezers and plucked them out. Completely arbitrary and detached, but still notable: TalonsUp, MintBridge, LostNote, JumboJet, and BandStand.

While the datamix gave me the feeling that perhaps my whole life is random and amorphous, the selection of boys makes me think it's not—especially BandStand. If there is anyone I want to see step free of the facility's constraints for a bit, it is him.

The loading station for the pylon is dome-shaped and completely enclosed by transparent plastisteel. None of us are inside it yet. We loiter on the roof instead, observing the panorama of the city. Downrider strings crisscross the entire scene, like spiders have laid claim to it all.

To the west, I can see a black, sword-like Elipserv building and a concave ParaSel. Two of the largest ulama-run tech providers. To the south is the Great Temple, and to the north, the apex of the city itself. A dozen spires, globes, and slopes are prominent. All gleam in the early morning sun.

Filling in the spaces between skyscrapers are shorter multi-level buildings, predominately grey or brown in color. Below them, are the streets. The streets here aren't as despised or dangerous as elsewhere, but still, they are streets. The last time I was on them, it was in an armored vehicle.

Band, Lost, and Jumbo are grouped near the loading station. The other two—Mint and Talons—are leaning over the railing at the building's west edge—seemingly testing the railing's resilience. That makes me nervous, but boldness is necessary for this job. I know they won't purposely go over. The implant frowns on suicide. It might get damaged in the fall.

Jumbo raises his hand and waves it.

"You have a question?" I ask.

He lowers his hand. "How long does it take for the downer to get here?"

"The *downrider*, you mean?" I shake my head. They've barely experienced one, but *already* they know the slang. I indicate the loading station. "It won't take long, if someone has requested it."

Talons abandons the railing, and Mint follows. "We've been waiting forever," Talons says. "How long?"

"As I said, not long, if—"

Band rumples his forehead. "It hasn't been called?"

I suppress a smile. "Was I supposed to do that?"

"We don't know how to do it!" Mint says. "We've never...Bamboo brought us here!"

"Guess we'll be here awhile then."

Mint closes his eyes. Then Talons closes his eyes too. "He wants us to search for it," he says. "Come on..."

"Found the call domain!" Mint open his eyes and looks at me. "Says I don't have authorization, though. You tricked us."

"I found it too," Talons says. "Pushing, boys. He wants us to prepare and push it to him."

I smile. "Yes, I can authorize it."

A nanosecond later, an authorization request appears in my queue. I approve it and send it back.

"Aha!" Talons says. "Downer on the way."

There are smiles and congratulations. A pat on the back.

Band's eyes are still closed. "What kind of downrider is it?" he asks. "One hump or two?"

"What?"

"One hump or two?" Band frowns. "Wait, we'll need more than that. If we—"

"More?" Talons says. "Why more?"

Jumbo rolls his eyes. "Because there are six of us, lowlevel. They only carry one or two riders." He points at the pylon. "Remember how you got here?"

I nod. "Talons requested a two hump. Two passengers."

Another authorization request appears, then another. First from Mint, then from Band. Mint's is for two downriders, though, so I approve it, and return the other.

"Got us covered!" Mint says.

Band looks my way and shrugs.

"Right idea," I message him. "He beat you by seven nanoseconds."

"No worries," he messages back.

We hear the first high-pitched whistle twenty seconds later. It approaches from the east, near the city's edge and the lowdowns. The downrider makes a wide turn, then a quicker turn and heads due west. It is red in color and roughly circular with a tapered end. A two-passenger model—Talons' request. It arrives at the pylon a minute later. There's a clank and a squeak as it stops, pivots, and reorients.

There's another whistle from the north, followed by one from the south. A blue downrider, and a gold one. Both double humps. Exactly what we need.

The boys are excited now, all bouncing and laughing. I share their emotions, but for different reasons.

My head is also throbbing, threatening to ruin the experience. I do my best to ignore the pain and focus on the initiates, their happiness and safety, and on our destination.

The gold downrider stops and reorients; then the blue slides in. It hesitates as the gold finishes its turn, then starts to turn itself. There is a locking "clank" as it finishes.

We make our way into the pylon. "Be careful loading," I say. "They are generally injury proof, but..."

Talons and Jumbo hurry for the lead downrider. The blue one. When they reach it, Talons runs his hand along the side. He then cups his hands on the window and looks inside. "How do we get in?"

The others group between the gold and red downriders.

"Who's riding with Mawla ThreadBare?" Lost asks. He's the politest of the bunch. His father is a shopkeeper in a nearby town. Doubtless where he got his manners.

Band raises a hand. "I will."

Mint nudges Band's arm. "Yeah, let Band ride with teacher. Case he needs to stop and throw up."

Band looks angry but says nothing. Mint and Lost gather at the gold downrider.

I smile at Band. "Red is the best color anyway, right?"

He returns the smile. "Right!"

"Seriously," Talons says. "How do we get in?"

"You know these are stream aware."

Talons smacks his own head. "Right, so dumb. We're so dumb."

Everyone's eyes close. Seconds pass. Finally, the door to the gold downrider clicks and slides upwards.

"Got it!" Jumbo opens his eyes, then scowls. His downrider is still closed. He watches as Mint and Lost pile into the gold one. "Hey, I think I opened their machine!" He laughs and points. "I opened theirs!"

Finally, the blue door snaps open. Talons opens his eyes, gives a satisfied nod, and climbs inside.

Band's eyes are still closed. He shakes his head. "I can't do it," he says. "Won't work for me."

"Try again. It can be tricky."

"Doesn't seem to want to recognize me. Can't push to it."

"Sometimes it helps to put your hand on it." I tap his forearm. "Make it tangible."

Band nods and touches the downrider's side. His face relaxes. Finally, the door clicks and starts to ascend. He smiles and opens his eyes.

"See? No problem at all." I motion for him to enter and then slide into the vacant seat across from him. He pats the seat's soft leather, then raises up to look out the window.

I get messages from Jumbo and Mint, both asking the same question: Where to?

"First a quick tour," I message them all. "And then, we'll see."

I'M EXPERIENCING BLISS. Controlled and confined, but bliss all the same. I only wish the downrider's windows opened so I could feel the wind between my fingers.

We soar over the city at full speed. There is little indication of our true velocity, no heavy pressure or loud noise. Only the invariable whine of downrider engines and the flash of buildings as they go by. Corporate edifice followed by temple dome. Low rises swallowed by high—then still higher—rises. The rainbow beauty of the heights overshadows the darkened masses of the streets, presenting something to both awe and fear.

But for debuggers, this is our most delectable taste of freedom. I'd forgotten how important such rides are. How much I need them.

The boys echo my feelings. Talons built a virtual room for us, and now every message variant is in play—Easy Impact to Full, with the latter being most prevalent. Emotions fill the inward air, threatening to quench all else. They bounce off one side of the room, intensify, then bounce off another. "Flipping wild!" is the dominant phrase. The dominant color is bright orange. And the dominant emotion is joy.

There is no permeating fragrance, because the boys haven't mastered scent yet. That is fine with me. The last thing I want is to be in a message room with preadolescences adept at scent sharing. Their shared sounds are bad enough.

The tour continues until we've circumnavigated the city's hub twice. Nearly an hour passes in a blur. Finally, I grab the stream controls for all three vehicles and feed them a new stopping point.

Three minutes later, the blue downrider quick-switches to another string and veers off to the right, disappearing behind a silver spire. The gold follows. Then so do we.

"We going home?" Jumbo shouts into the room. "I don't want to!"

"Me neither!" Talons says. "Downriding is epic."

"Don't make us go back yet," Mint says.

"I haven't learned anything from this," Lost adds. "Aren't we supposed to learn something?"

Jumbo snorts. "Learned how to find your implant in your noggin," he says. "That's something."

"Hey!"

Next comes the virtual interpretation of a shoving match, a string of exclamations, and a clear indication that both boys have been stopped by their implants.

Everyone laughs.

"We're not going back yet." My stomach churns with anxiety. Expectation. We're not there, but we're close.

We reach a portion of the eastern city built on gently rolling hills. Estates and exclusive apartments consume much of the ground here. There is a lot of green too. Manicured lawns and parks. Some of the higher hills have large craters in them. Others have foliage stripped away. Both are attempts at resurfacing, results of the previous Imam's mania. He thought all the world should be flat.

"Where then?" Mint says. "Will you tell us where?"

I send the image of a smiling frog. I almost infuse the scent of chocolate, but then stop myself. No sense giving them ideas.

We take another left turn, and another. Finally, I think I see the shop. It's a red brick structure, perched near the top of one of the larger, un-stripped, hills. It has remnants of graffiti on one side. A cartoon chest and arms, dressed in blue. Possibly wearing a cape.

A taller building suddenly obscures my view, followed by another. Then I notice the orange of a downrider pylon ahead. The blue downer has already reached it.

Band looks left and right. "Are we slowing down? Mawla Thread, are we there?"

"Yes."

"Where are—" He stops himself. "Wait, let me try to guess." In the window's reflection, I see him close his eyes. "There's a robot dance nearby...that's probably not it. A barber. Four restaurants and a cleaner." He goes silent for a moment. "A streamshill for temporary marriages? What are those?"

I straighten in my seat. "Keep looking."

The gold downrider has parked ahead of us. The boys are exiting to the pylon platform.

"There's a tech shop." Band looks at me. "GrimJack's? Vids make it look a little scary..."

Now empty, the blue vehicle moves away, effectively abandoning Talons and JumboJet. As Band and I enter the pylon, the gold one moves off too. The boys watch it go.

Our downrider stops, the door rises, and we climb out.

"Rides are getting away," Mint says. "Tried to stop them, but they aren't listening."

I nod. "This is a low traffic stop. They can't all stay here." I indicate the pylon's walls and the short section of string overhead. "There isn't room."

Mint scans the pylon. "Yeah, it's small."

"We're going to a tech shop," Band says, smiling. "I figured it out."

"By yourself?" Mint slaps Band on the back, then looks at me. "Or did—"

"By myself," Band says. "First, I—" He scans the faces of the other boys, all of whom are now giving him their full attention. "Rails. You figure it out."

"Debugging thrives on shared information," I say. "Never stop sharing."

Band squints at me, pondering, then explains his process.

"Wasn't so big," Talons says. "I could've done that."

"Yes, you could've." I cross to the other side of the platform, to where the ladder access is located. There's only a hole, along with a condensed ladder, and a long fall. "But you didn't." I stream touch the ladder controls, ordering it to extend. There's a low hum as it begins to do so. I watch as it nears the ground below.

Talons scowls, and the rest of the boys laugh. Finally, Band gives him a playful shove. Talons waves it off, but smiles. "Fine," he says. "Nice going, Band."

Mounting the ladder, I descend until only my head shows. "You wouldn't be debuggers if you were afraid of heights, but be careful anyway. These things can be slick." I take another step, then pause. "I don't need to tell you to stay with me, right?"

"Buzzed if we don't!" Band says.

"What do they have at these shops?" Mint asks. "Will there be bots?"

"Every shop is different. But probably no active bots." I descend further. "No shoving. One at a time. See you at the bottom."

Sounded like a parent there, Thread.

I shake my head. Bringing a pack of kids into a strange part of town. For what?

Damali. She *could* be here. That's what.

And if she is, what then? Will she even remember?

I only know that I need to see her. At least one more time.

I reach the sidewalk, then wait for the others. They appear to be progressing in an orderly fashion. The stream room is still active, though, and there's a lot of latent emotion. Expectation and curiosity.

Halfway down, Talons dangles an arm and a leg. "Help me, I'm falling." He pulls his appendages back, then laughs. "Ladders are easy. Is there a park nearby?"

"You could check the stream yourself," Mint says. "Just like Band—"

Talons reaches a point about four steps from the bottom and jumps free. "I know that." He pats his hands together. "Just talking because our teacher wants us to."

"Yes, I want everyone to talk more. Especially you."

The boys laugh.

We're in a quiet commercial area. There's a high fence between the sidewalk and whatever is on the other side. From the smell, it could be a junk yard. Petrol and synthetics.

"Now where?" Lost asks.

Band raises a hand and points left, to the east.

I smile. "That way."

GRIMJACK'S IS EVEN STRANGER UP CLOSE.

The building's exterior is a mix of brick and stucco, as if the latter was grafted in when the former began to fail. The graffiti isn't really graffiti. It is a remnant of an earlier life, partially obscured. The painted chest and arms are powerful looking, but not in the way our leaders' depictions are. Not in a fear and trembling way. More in a self-assured and helpful way.

I wonder who this character was, and why he chose to wear a cape.

There's a small sign over the front door. "GrimJacks!" painted in blue and yellow by an unsteady hand. The door itself is green, worn, and completely manual. A stream push returns nothing. No response, and no indication it was ever stream-aware.

The door is slightly ajar, and the lights are on inside. That makes me nervous, even though it is commonplace.

I stream the boys to let me enter first. They gather near the door and wait, but their room floods with messages.

"Place is weird."

"And smells!"

"Are all clicks and clacks like this?"

"Are we safe?"

"We're fine," I message. "Stay with me. And don't touch anything."

"Lotta nag in that post," Talons says.

That brings more waves of emotions. More digital laughter.

"Be careful, or I'll close the room."

The boys become stoic, both inside and out.

I reach for the door handle. It's brass and somewhat sticky. I turn it using only my fingertips, then push. The door squeaks the entire way.

There's a distinct smell inside. A pulpy, heady aroma. Not offensive, but omnipresent. I detect a feminine scent too, a perfume, but that could be wishful thinking. An odoriferous mirage.

The walls are filled with junk. Every nook, every centimeter of space, has something on it. There are shelves, hooks, and transparent cabinets filled with remnants of the past. Wires, hoses, and casings. Shells and triangular servos. Old face-plates and vid-screens, most with faded price tags.

The rest of the shop seems to revolve, like a technological hurricane, around a centralized chair. All the shelving is laid out, not in straight rows, but in concentric rings with that large, maroon chair as the focus. It is partially obscured from my view by the rows of shelving, but it appears to be empty.

"What is this?" Mint whispers. "Some kind of maze?"

"Is it a test?" Lost says. "I'm no good at tests."

"Perhaps." I slowly walk the outer circle of shelving. I glance at the wares, but primarily I'm focused on the chair. Is there anyone here? Where is the owner?

"This place is a zoo," Mint says. "We're going to get eaten here."

"No, this is blaze radical," Talons says. "We could build a ghazi-bot with all this stuff. Wreck a whole village."

There's a loud clank from behind me. Scowling, I turn toward the boys. "Why are you—"

BandStand's face is white. In his hands is a red, stringed instrument with a long handle. "I didn't touch it," he says. "It started to move. I saw it shake and slide. I just caught it."

The nearest boy—JumboJet—shrugs. "I didn't see," he says. "Could be. This whole place is on edge."

I shake my head. "Put it back. Carefully."

I hear another noise from across the store. Someone else is here.

"What are we going to learn?" Lost says. "I like to learn."

"This is where DRs live, missile." Talons takes a deep breath. "Embrace the rails tech."

"Dead tech, you mean."

I shake my head, then indicate some of the items on the shelf in front of me—a long taz-inducer, a circular magunit, and a sheath of nanopaths. "Those are all useful. Things you will use every day." I move toward the end of the row. "Very useful."

I walk to the next row. Toward the sound. I sense something unexpected.

"People live like this?" Lost says. "Like rats?"

"Not people, implants. Debuggers."

"Follow Mawla Thread."

"One moment," I message the shared room. "I want to see if—"

I step into the aisle and encounter a humanoid servbot. It's bent over a square, black chest. Searching.

"Hello?" I say.

The bot straightens and looks first toward the center of the store, and then at me. It is a decades-old model. Its face is angular, with synthskin faded blue in places. More mechanical than human. Blank and expressionless.

It startles when it sees me. "What do you require?" it asks.

"Is your master available?" I ask.

It cocks its head. "My master?"

I point toward the door, and the sign that hangs outside. "The owner. GrimJack?"

It looks slowly around, like it has only now discovered where it is. It then stoops over the chest again.

"GrimJack," I say. "I wish to speak to GrimJack."

"Do you require assistance? We have a wide variety of sheets. Telescopic, high mag, inverse. I realize those aren't as exhilarating, or even fulfilling, but we do have a lot. Always on special!"

The boys move up behind me, with Band in the lead. "Is it broken?" he asks.

"I don't know." I reach for the bot in the stream. I grab its operating bundle and scan for errors. There are a few weak and failing joints, a broken finger servo, and the section of synthskin needing repaired—but nothing debilitating.

"Who touched me?" The bot straightens again. "Stop touching me!"

The response surprises me. Humors me. "I'm sorry. I was only—"

"Well, stop it! Leave your mind off my body."

"Is that normal?" Mint asks into the shared room.

"Thing is busted," Talons responds. "Scrapable."

The bot startles again, as if noticing the boys for the first time. "I feel I'm being talked about. How rude."

I smile and raise a cautionary hand. "Again, I'm sorry." I scan the boys' faces. "We're new here. We don't know the rules."

"Rules?" The bot cocks its head again. "There are no rules here. Only responsibility."

I want to sheet check this bot now. Something inside is different. Not sure if it is broken, but it is seemingly out-of-spec. Faulty code update? Headchip misfire? Something.

"You may address me as FlapJack." The bot brings its hands together. "Now, what would you like to buy?"

"We're still looking." I scan the shop again. Someone, a human, has to be here somewhere. No shop owner would leave his business in the hands of a bot, no matter how *responsible*.

"Take your time. I will check on you again in precisely a hundred and twenty million milliseconds."

I walk past it. Look toward the central chair. "I would prefer to speak with the owner."

"I'm the owner! The owner and the chef!"

"Bot's crazy," Talons whispers.

"Don't say that," Band says. "You don't—"

"I know!" Talons says. "My parents had lots of bots. This one is—"

I drop a ball of fiery emotion into the boys' room. Everyone goes silent.

The bot looks at Talons. "That was rude." It looks at me. "Your slaves are rude."

"Hey!" Talons says.

The other boys laugh.

I frown. We shouldn't be away too much longer. Not for our first trip. Bamboo was uncomfortable with the idea, after all. This trip is an experiment. Best not to push.

There's no sign of Damali, though. No sign of the astronauts or GrimJack either.

"Implants," I say. "I'd like you to each take an aisle. Pick five things from that aisle and draft a report on them."

"A report?" Mint says.

"Yes, it should include the origin of the object, its material construction, and its intended use. Exceptions and cautions should be noted—"

"That—" Talons pauses, shakes his head. "Ouch. Lots of ouch."

"Ha!" Jumbo says. "Talons got buzzed again."

The boys laugh.

"Come on," Mint says. "Before we all get buzzed."

They fan out into the store, and I trail along behind them. I wind through the aisles until I reach the central chair. It is large, overstuffed, and heavily used. It is obvious where the owner sits. Not only is there a worn spot in the material, there's an impression of the body in the cushions. A large, round shape.

Behind the chair is a concave desk with a menagerie of dispensers. Tubes, small shelves, and wire racks. A miniature playground of debugger necessities.

I glance the bot's direction, then walk past the chair and the desk. I encounter large, unevenly-placed stacks of equipment that require me to turn sideways to get by.

There must be more to this shop. A back door, an office, or something.

I'm losing hope. After all my scheming and begging, this trip may have been for nothing.

I squeeze past an especially tight stack of bot casings, then get nervous as I hear them wobble and clank. I rest a hand on the nearest edge. The wobble stops. I breathe a sigh of relief.

I turn toward the back of the store. There's another door there. It is narrow, wooden, and painted yellow. I approach it and try the handle. It turns freely in my hand.

Beyond is a small room with a desk. A striking contrast to the rest of the shop.

Weird.

I close the door and make my way toward the central chair

again. I fight feelings of sorrow and hopelessness. She isn't here. No one is here. What now? This was the only link I had. The only *anything* so far. I'm inside out.

I reach the chair and find someone sitting in it. Not the bot or the mythical GrimJack, but JumboJet. He looks at home, and his structure is such that he almost fills the chair. He's studying something in his hand. Something silver, small, and tubular. He brings it to his eye and peers through it. He leans forward and studies a portion of the desk, before leaning back, frowning, and looking again.

He has a jeweler's glass, the stream tells me. An archaic magnification device.

I lay a hand on the side of the chair. "What are you doing?"

Jumbo looks at me, object still held to his eye. That eye is large, like the eyes of JustBecause's master. Frighteningly big.

Jumbo startles and drops the glass. It bounces from his chest to his lap, but he manages to snag it before it falls to the floor. "Mawla," he says. "I was just—"

"In a place you don't belong."

Jumbo hops out of the chair. "Yes, mawla, I was looking for things, like you told us." He waves a hand. "Thought I might report on some of this stuff." He raises the glass. "Cool, huh? Magnifies. Like a small, hard sheet, or something." He smiles. "Could put it in your pocket."

I shake my head, and glance at the desk. There's writing in the spaces between the dispensers and racks. Small scale graffiti. Roughly in a circle. "What were you looking at?"

Jumbo shrugs, glances at the desk. "Bunch of doodles. Thought there were formulas, but now I think it is nothing. Just letters."

"Oh?" I move closer to the desk. Small, dark letters written by hand.

Jumbo eases into the seat again, then bends over and points. "Yeah, this one says 'A squiggle A times three'..." He looks at me. "Or maybe 'A cubed.' Does that mean anything?"

I shake my head. "They could be only random—"

He bounces in the seat. "Yeah, but it looks like a formula. It is all grouped together." He points at the desk again. "Then around it are a bunch of other letters. This one is a 'T' and an 'S' together. Then over here is a 'G.' And there's an 'H' by itself. Also a 'GJ' and a 'BT.'" He leans closer. "And I think this is a 'D.'" He raises a shoulder. "Might be an 'O.'"

I squeeze closer to look. I see the formula portion. The squiggle looks like a tilde. The three is smaller than the rest. Could be superscripted. Maybe if I use his glass—

"You should not be here!" The bot is behind us, eyes slightly extended.

I move away from the desk. "Come on, DR," I say.

"We weren't hurting anything," Jumbo says. "Honest."

"This is the owner's chair," the bot says. "Only the owner sits in the owner's chair."

I bow, but somehow can't resist asking. "Those letters..." I point at the desk. "On the surface there. Did you write them?"

The bot follows my finger. Focuses on the letters for a moment, then moves to the desk and starts shoving dispensers around. In seconds, part of the writing is obscured. "There," it says. "That's how they should be. All nicely displayed."

"But the writing?"

The bot looks at me. As with most servbots, its face is a mask. "Have you found something to buy, then? We're having a special on—"

I shake my head. "No, we'll be leaving." I drop a message in the boys' room, telling them to gather outside. There are complaints.

Jumbo moves past me, heading that direction.

"I'm sorry we could not meet your needs," the bot says. "Perhaps you'll still stream a positive review for us? We're always trying to improve."

I search my storage for images of the desk before it was covered. Slice it frame by frame. Analyze. Does it mean something? "I will do that. Thank you again."

A PORTION OF OUR RETURN trip is a nanoshield, a shimmering barrier over my mind that can only be permeated through intensive storage searches and solitude.

Even then, the emotions won't be the same. They won't sync with what I'm actually seeing and doing. Thought is a tepid sea of blue, invaded by the occasional lightning strike whenever I check the boys' shared stream room. They are energized, giddy at the GrimJack's experience. I finally decide to vacate their discussion altogether. I need to digest.

BandStand again shares the downrider with me, seated in the forward seat. I message him, and he promises to monitor the room and report if anything gets out of hand. I think I can trust him. He might be homesick, but generally, he's top tier. Or he will be.

I close my eyes.

I step through everything I saw at the shop. Everything I heard. The smells. The stream ambiance. The whole experience. If there is anything to be learned there, I need to find it.

Most of it seems meaningless. Nothing but noise and static. But the desk? That is something. A hope I can cling to. I replay that portion of our visit. I watch frame by frame. I magnify the times I glimpsed the desk, and check it with what Jumbo said.

I attempt to analyze the "formula", $A \sim A^3$. The strings of characters that were the center of the scribbles. A cursory stream search gives me little. No references to that particular arrangement of characters.

I need to be more specific. Find a discipline it belongs to.

It looks formulaic, but I can't assign meaning without context. Are the letters variables or constants?

There's no clear equality to it. No equal sign to partition one side of the formula from the other. So it isn't, by definition, an "equation." That suggests it isn't mathematical, or even scientific. Scientific formulas typically have an associated unit of measurement—like kilometers, hours, and grams—or use standardized variables and constants. "$E = mc^2$" for instance, where "E" stands for Energy, "m" stands for matter, and "c" is the speed of light.

In style, the formula is most like a chemical composition, except, in chemistry, the number "3" would be subscripted, not superscripted. Plus, there is no physical element assigned the letter "A". There is "Ac" for Actinium and "Al" for Aluminum, but no "A".

At one time, the letter "A" signified "Acceleration", but that use has been deprecated. Rendered obsolete.

Why? Because today "A" has another meaning. In the common language, it is shorthand for the name of the deity. It means "God". But that definition makes no sense here.

Or does it?

"Did our trip accomplish what you wanted?" Band asks.

I open my eyes. Band is turned my direction, but his head lowered as if he's studying the floor.

"Is that a question from the group?"

"No. Just from me."

"It is good for you to get out." I gaze out the window to our left. There is a black TreArc building there. An artistic structure, wider in the middle than the bottom or top. Seemingly unstable, but given debugger design and robotic implementation, it is doubtless more resilient than those around it. "To see the world as a debugger. Glimpse the work and the life."

"Oh."

"Did you enjoy the time out?" I ask.

He shrugs, looks at his feet again. "I'm sure I will find it beneficial."

"I think you will," I say.

I close my eyes. Make the formula prominent in my thoughts again. $A \sim A^3$.

It seems like a notation. A statement. If the "A" represented the deity, that might work, except for one final detail.

The squiggle. That tilde in the middle.

The symbol has a plethora of different meanings, but none that fit the context. It has use in languages, in physics, in economics, electronics, mathematics, and a host of additional disciplines. It can represent a specific sound, a range of numbers, and a rise in pitch.

There are only two uses that make sense in this case, though. Both are mathematical meanings, but one has more significance to debuggers like me. In its first meaning, the tilde could replace an equals sign. It doesn't mean equality, but instead means "approximately equal" or "similar".

The other meaning, the meaning that resonates most with me, gives the formula the exact opposite meaning. In debugging the tilde means "not".

So, the formula could either mean "A" is approximately equal to "A-cubed" or "A" is *not* "A-cubed". The first translation seems ridiculous, and the second obvious—regardless of what "A" stands for. Clearly, "A" is not the same as "A-cubed". Rails.

Still, that's how a debugger might interpret the phrase. Is that who the scribble was intended for? HardCandy and Sandfly are debuggers, and they were involved with the astronauts.

I hear sniffling and open my eyes again. We are within a few kilometers of the facility. The sun is hidden behind the buildings to the west. It is approaching dinner time. Perfect timing.

Another sniff, louder this time. Band is staring at his feet again.

"Are you ill?"

He shakes his head quickly. "I'm fine."

I take a deep breath and let it out slowly. I notice a spire on our right. Purple and silver.

"What do you fear, BandStand?" I ask.

"Mawla ThreadBare?"

"Fear. That's where the tears come from, right? Out of fear."

He shakes his head. "It's not appropriate to discuss. Not my place. I am a—"

"Are you afraid you'll never see your family?" I ask. "Or that you'll be unworthy of your masters? That you'll fail your calling?"

He glances at the spire, then finds his feet again. "All of these things. And more."

I nod. "And all of those things will happen," I say. "And more."

He wipes his nose, then glances at me, eyes reddened and wet.

"It's true," I say. "There's little good in it. Little pleasure." I indicate the city. "In any of it, really." I shift in my seat. "And a debugger's life is hardest of all. We're promised paradise, but don't know if we'll receive it. No DR has returned to tell us."

"Then why do it, Mawla?"

"Because we fix things, BandStand. That's what we do." I point at the city again. "We find solutions, when no one else can. That may not be enough for you. I'm not even sure it's enough for me." I smile. "But for now, it will have to do."

Band turns quiet again as he studies the scenery. He looks left and then right.

I wait for a moment, then close my eyes. I set the formula aside. I'm not sure if it is even relevant. I draw my attention to the other characters on GrimJack's desk. Those that circled the formula. The "TS", the "GJ", the "H". The "BT" and the "D".

Given the specific text, given the people I know about, my mind travels only one direction. They must be initials. "TS" is for "TallSpot" and "GJ" for GrimJack". "H" for "Handler."

The "D" could be for "Damali." It must be her.

But where did she go? Where are any of them?

And why do they circle that nonsense formula?

This is all I have. A scrawl of text on a desk in a store now run by a bot. The only indication she might be alive.

Hopeless, Thread. Lost, broken, and hopeless.

The pitch of the downrider's whine changes, and the vehicle starts to slow. I open my eyes, expecting to see the facility on the horizon.

But it is not.

Day 49, 4:48:38 p.m.

THE SECTION OF TOWN where Bamboo's facility is located is visible. It is ahead and to our left in a south-easterly direction. But it is still at least ten kilometers away.

Band presses against the front canopy. "Why have we stopped?"

Similar questions are raised in the shared stream room. The other two downriders—the other four boys—are behind us.

Band looks at me. "Is there something wrong with the downrider?"

I turn and check on the others. Jumbo and Talons are in a silver downrider, and behind them, Mint and Lost are in green. All look safe, normal. "These things have self-repair protocols. Plus, they're regularly brought offline and scanned."

"It isn't throwing any local errors," Band says. "Says it's in a safety stop due to obstruction."

I smile. "You queried the vehicle. Well done. Always start as close to the problem as possible. Work your way out from there."

Band's eyes are wide, and he seems a little jittery. "I had the others check their vehicle's too. None seem broken." He's holding it together, though. That's good.

I search the horizon in all directions. Are any downers moving? I finally glimpse one to the northeast. "The stoppage isn't system-ic," I say. "Nor universal."

"But it isn't in our downriders either."

"Right." I pull from our vehicle now too, stepping through its list of events and warnings. Nothing unusual. No errors, aside from the obstruction bulletin.

I rise to look at our surroundings. We're roughly ten stories high—two stories above the nearest structure. A slate grey tenement, or possibly a warehouse. Based on the disrepair of the buildings, and the number of errors that local appliances are throwing, I'd guess this isn't the best of neighborhoods.

I see few freeheads, though. I count only three on the street below. "I wonder where the nearest pylon is?"

"I'll check!" Band says. Only a millisecond passes before he points toward the other downers. "We just passed it. About a hundred meters that way."

I nod. "So, we could shimmy there if we have to."

"Shimmy?"

I sit down again. "I'd rather not have to."

"Obstruction?" Talons says to the room. "What does that mean? A bird or something?"

"Yes," Jumbo says. "A giant bird is bending the string."

"Mawla, can you see?" Mint asks.

Band crouches in his seat and presses his face to the canopy. "I don't see anything up there. String looks clear."

"What do we do now?" Talons asks.

"We should—"

"I hear something," Mint says. "Listen!"

The room fills with a repetitive clicking sound. It appears to be getting louder. Closer.

"What's that?" Band asks.

"It is coming from behind us," Lost says.

"I think that's a hopper," I say. "Must be a string problem somewhere."

The clicking intensifies until I can hear it with my own ears. The boys behind us yell, then something leaps over our downrider. The creature—the hopper—continues past us. Click, click, clicking ahead.

Hoppers have a small cranium placed atop two nimble, expandable appendages. They're the spiders of our web of strings. Small, helpful spiders.

"Did you see that thing?" Talons streams the room.

"Hard to miss," Mint says.

"Nearly wet myself," Jumbo says. "I still might."

"Not in here," Talons says. "Not with me."

"Quiet," I message, sending a touch of heat with the sound. "We need to stay focused. Ready to learn."

The hopper stops about a half kilometer ahead of us, then lowers itself to the string.

"Must be a string shear," I say. "A place where it is starting to fray."

"That the reason we stopped?" Band says. "The obstruction?"

"Probably. Though you'd think they'd have a specific code for that."

The hopper reorients itself a couple times, then projects a beam of light that plays slowly over the string's surface. I share the images with the room so all can see.

"What's it doing?" Mint asks.

"That's a scanning pass," I say. "It's getting a small scale read on the damage."

The hopper's light shuts off. The bot then long-steps up the string a few times, and pauses. The head portion drops onto the string and begins to quickly slide back and forth.

"Looks like it is scratching an itch," Jumbo says.

"Yeah," Mint says. "Rubbing its chin."

"Or its haunch," Mint adds.

"Now it is repairing," I say. "Shouldn't take—"

The hopper shudders, shoots off a burst of sparks, and explodes.

SHRAPNEL STRIKES THE FRONT of our downrider, cracking the canopy, then skittering past. Band and I duck while the others yell.

A few seconds later, I raise my head to look. The hopper's legs are affixed to the string, but there's a small cloud of smoke where its head used to be.

"What was that?" Mint shouts into the room.

"Yeah, what happened?" Lost asks.

"You saw it," Talons says. "The bot blew up."

Band nods. "It was working along fine and then—boom!"

There's a shrill sound, a synthetic scream, and the string near the hopper's legs snaps in two. Severed ends streak the air in both directions.

Our downer lurches and everyone yells. Some use language that doubtless earns them stops.

The downer continues to rock. I wait for the inevitable fall to the street. The feeling of weightlessness followed by rending plastisteel and explosive pain. Darkness.

But nothing more happens. The rocking subsides, and we stay in place.

"Are we okay?" Band says. "I thought we would—"

I raise a hand, then stand so I can see. I want to tweak myself for overreacting.

Two string supports are between us and the broken spot. They went into emergency mode and locked the string, keeping it taut. Keeping us where we belong. Safe.

"We're okay," I say. "The string is secure."

The room is full of fear and confusion. It takes seconds for it to dissipate.

"So what do we do now?" Talons asks. "Can we climb down?"

I send a head shake, and a feeling of confidence mixed with caution. "One step at a time. We can get out of this. We're debuggers. There's always a way."

I check the string again. Is there a way?

"Eventually another hopper will come," I say. "A string break like that. Another will—"

My head starts to ache. It is a slow burn, but it is hard to ignore. I close my eyes and try to think around it.

"Should we wait for another to come, Mawla?" Band asks.

"Does that happen often?" Jumbo asks. "They just explode like that? Wait, I'll look." A second goes by. "Hopper failures are extremely rare. Only a ten percent failure rate within five years of deployment. Most are insignificant. A squeaky leg, or a failing pathway—"

"That didn't seem like a failure to me," Talons says. "Was that a failure?"

An excellent question. A hopper shouldn't have enough combustible material to create the kind of explosion I saw. That suggests a frightening possibility.

"I don't want to wait for another one," Mint says. "I really, really don't."

Everyone streams at once. The pain in my head intensifies. "Could you all quiet down?" I say. "I need to think this through."

"Yes, let Mawla think," Band says.

Every downrider comes with emergency tools in a small debugger bag. One of the items in there should be a sling, or a single-person conveyance for riding the strings. We could use those to get to the closest exchange pod or loading pylon. Climb our way down and find a way back. It is risky, we'd have to send the slings back a few times, but—

Wait, what am I thinking?

"Downers are bidirectional," I say. "We could go back."

"They need a station to turn them, don't they?" Mint streams. "There's no station here."

I wince, but send a nod. "That's right. The station turns them." So, should I risk the children on the string? Have us use the slings to get out?

"Hey, I found something!" Talons says. "There's a way to manually turn them. I mean, I'm not sure if I've got the right model, but the stream-shill for Celeran says something about a manual turn. Will that help?" He pushes the ad at me.

It causes a spike of pain to take it, but I thank him anyway.

"Tried to find the specs in their domain," Talons adds. "But it seems to be locked out to my level."

"Me too," Mint streams. "I couldn't look at it."

"What models are these?" I ask them all. I could find that information, but it might be better if they do. Better for my head, anyway.

"Ours is a Celeran," Jumbo says.

"Not this one," Lost streams. "SilverSlip model. They claim 100% compatibility with Celeran, though."

"Ours is a Celeran, Mawla," Band says.

I open my eyes. Band is staring at me. I smile. "That's fortunate," I say. "Two the same make, and a workalike."

I scan the inside of our downrider. I notice a removable panel in the floor near Band's feet. I locate and check the spec for the model Talons showed me. It *does* have a manual turn. But does ours?

The ache in my head subsides enough that I can focus. That's fortunate too, for what I have in mind. "Model numbers," I say. "I need specific model numbers for our downers."

I get three replies. Then I go on a stream hunt. Manual turns are standard for Celeran. As standard as their running noises. It takes a special tool to make the switch, but that's included in the emergency bag.

I'm starting to get hopeful.

I get Band's attention and point out the panel. "I need you to open that."

He nods and leans forward to access the panel. After a few tries, he manages to pull the cover off. The emergency bag fills the entire space below it.

"I'll never get that back in there again," I say. "Not in a million years."

Band looks at me. "Mawla?"

I shake my head. "Never mind. Bring out the bag. You're looking for a tool. I'll send you the image." I scrape the image from the downer spec. A long handled ratcheting device. Made of plastisteel. It shouldn't be too heavy, but it looks like it could hurt someone.

"So what are we doing?" Mint asks.

Band holds the tool up.

I nod. "Okay, now the sling. It has straps. Probably in the bottom."

A few seconds later, he holds up a bundle of black straps and flexible parts. "How does this work?" he says, turning it over.

"Watch and see." I smile.

"Is anyone doing anything?" Talons asks. "How long until another hopper comes?"

"I'm doing something," I stream back. I look at Band and point up. "It's going to get a little windy. Stay in your seat, okay?"

"What are you doing?"

I stream the downer to open its canopy. I have to answer ten confirmation requests before I get there, but finally the thing unlatches and slides away.

Outside air pours in. It's a little acidic, but not bad for the middle of the city. I climb up on the seat, then out onto the canopy sill. "I need the sling."

Band hands me the sling. I unfurl it, clip it to the string, and pull myself in. It is shaky the whole way.

I'm seated above the downer, which is ten stories above the street. Freeheads are gathered down there now. I wonder what they're thinking? I hear a few voices, then a whistle and angry shouting.

I ignore all that. "Now, the tool." I take the tool from Band's outstretched arms. He remains on the seat, watching me.

"You probably should sit down," I say. "It isn't safe standing in a downrider."

"Is what you're doing safe?"

I give him a perturbed look. "Of course."

I focus on the downer stem, specifically where it grips the string. The working end of the tool is circular and opens like a clamp. There's a distinctive triangle peg in the center. That is supposed to lock to a similarly shaped aperture on the downer stem. I don't see anything on the side nearest me, and I'm not close enough to see the stem's back, so I feel around with my fingers. Finally, I find the hole near the back end. I snap the tool over it. It seals with a heavy "*twump.*"

I shake the tool. It feels solid. Ready to turn.

"Alright, hold on down there."

I shove the tool ahead, and ratchet it back. There's a squeak, followed by a lurch as the vehicle breaks free and moves. The lurch is quick enough that I almost lose my grip on the tool. Band lets out a yell and drops back into his seat.

"That works," I say, smiling.

It takes three more ratchets to turn the downer completely around. Every pull is a little unsettling, with the vehicle shifting below me and me swinging in the sling. I manage to stay connected, stay focused, and get the job done. The downrider is positioned now so Band is looking straight at Talons.

They exchange waves.

Kids.

I reposition the sling and, using the sling's embedded drive, scoot over to the next downer. I hear more yelling from the crowd below, and a long whistle. I hope I'm not the focus of either, but I probably am. I'm an entertainment source for the masses!

I position the tool for the next downer. I glance at Talons and Jumbo. They're both up in their seats, watching. Jumbo's mouth is gaping. I don't bother telling them to sit down. If they get rocked and hurt themselves, that's on them.

I glance at the third downer—the one with Mint and Lost-Note. They are out of their seats. Pressed to the forward canopy. Eyes wide and fixated on me.

I realize then how backstream I've been. If I wanted to get us out quickly, if I wanted to get the implants to safety, I should have started with the *rearmost* downer first.

Not thinking right, Thread. Thoughts stalled, and not re-starting. I'd blame it on my cranium damage, except I know I've always had a bit of clumsy in my mind.

I shake my head, then get to work on the middle downer. There's a place for the ratchet, but the workalike designers decided to put it in a different spot. Up front this time! I snap the tool in, swing it ahead, and pull.

The downer moves about five degrees. I pull again. Another small movement.

"Rails!"

More questions in the stream room.

"The turn rate is slow," I message back. "Going to take a bit."

I hear a distant clicking sound. Familiar, and in this case, unsettling. I look down the string and spy a hopper headed our way.

Not good.

I step up my ratchet work. Swing, pull, swing, pull. I'm about halfway now. Flipping workalike! I hear the hopper's approach, but I don't look. I need to get this downer turned and move on.

Another minute goes by, and then another.

Finally, the thing is turned. Talons is facing Mint now. More waves are exchanged.

On to the last downrider.

I scan the string as I sling my way ahead. The hopper is about forty meters away. Normally, that wouldn't concern me. They're nimble. It won't step on me, or inadvertently shear my sling. But if the last one was any indication, their minds are a little out-of-spec lately.

"Is that a hopper coming?" Mint streams. "I don't want another hopper!"

I don't either. Especially if it decides to explode.

"Maybe you shouldn't be out there," BandStand streams.

I reach the trailing downer and search for the tool's connection point. It's hard to keep my eyes off the hopper. Only a couple dozen meters separate us. Long legs move in succession, producing that distinctive click. It sounds like an animal's warning signal now. Like something it does before it strikes.

The tool slips from my hands, lands on the downer's canopy, slides...

And then drops off.

LOOK OUT BELOW...

"Mawla lost his tool!" Mint says. "Not good."

I don't bother agreeing. I don't even look at him. "I need you two to get into your emergency tools and get me another one." I send Mint and Lost an image of the panel, and instructions on how to open it.

Lost joins Mint in the front seat, and they start looking. They find the panel and pull on the cover.

The hopper is ten meters from me, then five, then three. I anticipate it pausing to inspect me on its way. Or stabbing me with one of its legs.

But it vaults the downer stem—and my sling—without seeming to look at all. Its head never moves, and its stride never changes. It passes Jumbo and Talons's downer, and my own.

I check on Mint and Lost. Mint has the tool in his hands. They wave. LostNote points to the canopy.

Which is closed. Rails! I stream to their downer, telling it to open its top. The canopy slides away.

"This hopper seems confused too," Band streams. "It's stalled at the breakage, just looking."

"They don't usually get breaks like that," I stream. "Not that wide. It is going to take some thinking." I hope its thinking takes lots of time.

Mint hands the ratchet tool up. I grip it tight and slide it into position. Shove and pull. And pull. The downer moves a quarter of the way. Thankfully.

"Still sitting there," Band streams.

I nod, and ratchet again. Halfway there. I give it another pull, and another. Finally, I have it turned. Everyone is turned.

I slide away from Mint and Lost's downer, then stream it our destination, and the need for a new route. It affirms my request, gears up, and screams away. My sling rocks with the motion, the wind.

"Hopper is crouched down now," Band says. "Rubbing its head on the string."

Why would it do that? The string is completely sheared! It will take the help of at least one more hopper. Maybe two. Makes no sense.

I slide to the stem for Talons and Jumbo's downer. Pause to reposition my sling over the stem.

"It is rocking now," Band says.

I don't like rocking. I hurriedly disconnect and reconnect to the string, push myself clear, and stream at their downer. A second later, it whooshes away. Just me and Band now.

"Please hurry, Mawla," Band streams.

Should I turn my sling forward or not? If there's shrapnel, do I want to take it in the back, or the face? I finally decide to turn. Only five meters separate me from the downer. I engage the sling's drive again and it hums me along.

The hopper is vibrating in place. Looking like it is about to explode. I instinctively bring my arms up near my face. This won't be fun.

Then I notice the open canopy. Band is up on the seat, watching me. "Get down," I say, waving. "Down."

He listens, disappearing back inside.

Maybe I should stream the canopy closed? Shield behind the downer somehow? I slow the sling. Uncertain.

The headache returns.

"Where are you, Mawla?"

I send him comfort, but a little pain seeps in with it. "I'm going to shut the canopy," I say. "Until after—"

"No. Get in here! I'm afraid. Get here."

I can't open my eyes, the pain is so intense.

"If you don't come in," Band says. "I will come out."

"But—"

"No. Come back."

I engage the sling engine. "My head is hurting," I say.

"You're almost here," he streams.

I'm close enough now I can hear the hopper's vibrating. I think it might be trying to cut through the string. To shear it ahead of us. That would be worse than an explosion.

I feel the downer stem in my hand, then Band's hand on my heel. I pry my eyes open enough to check my position. To see where I'd fall.

The sound of the hopper's movements reaches a feverish pitch. It is sawing through the string. It has to be. What else would make that noise?

"Drop, Mawla!" Band says.

The pain is near blinding. I fumble around, searching for the clasp that binds the sling to the string.

"Just unfasten yourself!" he yells.

Right, I can do that. I don't need this sling. I disconnect the straps over my legs, and with another glance down, drop inside.

I stream the downer where we are going. What it should do.

The string is making a sing-song cry.

"The canopy," Band says. "Shut it!"

I nod and focus on that one thing. Then the next thing: telling the downer to go.

We streak away. In seconds, we pass the next string support. And the next.

There's an explosion behind us.

BandStand weeps.

THE SKY HAS STARTED TO DARKEN. We are late returning, and Bamboo has noticed. That isn't the worst of it, though. Lateness I might be able to explain. To beg forgiveness for. It is the rest. The danger to the implants.

I have little time to prepare a response because *he's* waiting for us. The other boys are huddled in a group, just outside the pylon. Near its transparent dome.

But Bamboo stands in the center of the roof, looking at them, and then—as BandStand and I exit the loading station—at us.

The virtual stream room is still open. Though the boys appear compliant on the outside, inside they're streaming a typhoon.

"You're back! Mawla, you're incredible!"

"That was rails big. An explosion? A string shear?"

"Did the other hopper explode too? BandStand! Hey, did it pop!"

"Are we in trouble? Looks like we're in trouble."

"Master knew we were leaving, right?"

I drop a static bubble into the room, large and prickly enough that they all protest.

"Focus," I message. "Bamboo is concerned, and rightfully so. I've endangered many credits today. His relationship with the ulama is preeminent. Your future masters have already paid for your implantation."

"Who cares about them?" Talons then shrieks in response to a headbuzz. One should *always* care about his master.

"What should we say?" Jumbo asks the room.

"We want to go out again!" Mint streams. "Don't let him keep us in."

"I want to go again," Band adds, as he physically joins the others. "Even if it is dangerous. Even if we die."

"Quiet!"

I approach Bamboo. His hands are behind his back, and his face a stone. My instinct is to lower my eyes, but I resist that. Bamboo told me that he isn't my master. That I'm not his student. So I need to embrace that role.

I face him. Look him straight in the eyes. "You didn't need to greet us," I say, "but I'm glad you—"

He waves a hand dismissively. "Where have you been, DR 23? Where have you taken my implants?"

I nod. "Of course, yes. We explored the string system and downrider guidance. We then visited a tech shop. The trip was a fair representation of baseline debugging. The boys are already composing reports on what they observed. The possible uses of—"

"They've seen all they need to see then." He looks at the boys, still huddled together. "That is all for today, implants. Clean yourselves, perform your rituals, and find your chutes for the evening."

"They are probably hungry," I say. "They haven't eaten."

Bamboo watches the boys as they make their way toward the stairs. "Then you should've added that to your external studies," he says. "How to find food."

The stream room percolates with chatter.

"No food?" Jumbo streams. "But I'm dying. All that excitement. I could pass out."

"You won't pass out," Mint streams. "You're a long way from passing out."

"We're all hungry," Lost streams. "Tell him what happened, Mawla. How you saved—"

I shake my head, then close the room without comment. I probably prevented a lot of headbuzz-related headaches.

"Why are you shaking your head?" Bamboo asks.

The cityscape behind him is beautiful now. The light of the setting sun silhouettes many of the buildings.

"There's no reason to deny them food," I say. "They did nothing wrong."

Bamboo clicks his tongue. "Implants require structure. Discipline."

"They have discipline in their heads," I say. "They'll never be without it."

Bamboo frowns. "Yet sometimes, even that isn't enough." He looks toward the stairs. "This will teach them that actions have consequences. And the failures of others are just as consequential as their own."

He's talking about me. It was I who failed. "They were good out there. They should be rewarded." I look to my right, to where the string disappears into the city. "What happened, our lateness, was unavoidable."

"Do you know what was at stake?"

"We've covered that before," I say. "Would you like to hear what delayed us?"

He frowns, turns, and takes a step toward the stairs. "I don't know that it matters. Your experiment was a failure. A breakdown in discipline. It is too early for the implants to be outside this facility. They need more time, more training, before they are ready."

I don't know what to tell him. To withhold information is unwise. Knowledge travels fast among debuggers. Among pre-level debuggers, it travels even faster. Bamboo will find out sooner or later.

But how will he react when he learns what happened? The danger we were in?

I shake my head. "No, wait. We should cover this."

He pauses and looks my direction.

"It was unavoidable," I say, "because we were attacked."

"Attacked? Physically assaulted?" He narrows his eyes. "I got no message from enforcement. And the implants looked well." He glances at the stairwell. "Should I examine them further?"

"No, it wasn't like that."

"What was it like, ThreadBare?"

"Our downriders got delayed due to a string shear."

He looks toward the downrider pylon and grows quiet. "An unfortunate distraction. Occasionally such things happen." He raises his chin. "I assume you used that opportunity for instruction? You could have run them through leveling simulations. Taught them the—"

Pain creeps into my head. The wounded debugger pain. The wolf. I fight to keep my eyes open. "There wasn't time," I say. "It happened fast."

"Well in that case, perhaps I was mistaken. It is good that they got to observe the process—"

I shake my head, but that doesn't help. "It was no ordinary shear. There was an explosion. A hopper—"

"An explosion caused the shear?"

The pain subsides. "Yes, a hopper arrived. We assumed there was damage to the string. That that was why we were stopped. Then the hopper...blew up."

Bamboo shakes his head. "That seems unlikely. Hoppers don't have the—"

"I can share the sequence with you." I try to remember whether there is anything I don't want him to witness. Any words that were uncomfortable. I certainly don't want him to feel what I felt. "Easy Impact?"

He nods, so I package the hopper's demise and send it along. He concentrates. His eyes even flicker twice—possibly as he views the event again. Then he exhales slowly.

"Intriguing and alarming at the same time. It appears the insurrectionists have raised their performance level."

I nod. "You think it was sabotage too."

"What other possibility is there? Bots aren't made to explode. Not like that." A hand cradles his chin. "It would take tremendous effort. To capture a hopper and open it? Hopper schedules are unpredictable!" He shakes his head. "Did they climb out on the string and wait? An incredible feat. More dedication than I gave them credit for."

He's missing it. Missing what's really happening. "How did

they break into a pod? Or a pylon?" I say. "They'd have to have DR level clearance. And skills."

The roof lights snap on. The sun is now completely gone. I'm hungry too, I realize.

Bamboo nods again. "Yes, quite an accomplishment." He turns and walks to the stairway. "I will inform the ulama and the master circle. I'll send a bulletin to the other DRs, as well."

"There were two hoppers, Bamboo. Two that malfunctioned and exploded." I shuffle ahead and look him in the face. "Could that be antitex? Could they pull that off?"

He raises a hand. "It appears they did. As surprising as that seems. What other—" He narrows his eyes, then shakes a finger. "Ah, I see where this lives for you. It is part of your theory, is it not? The conspiracy for our demise?"

I feel a touch of shame but manage to keep my head up. My eyes level. "Wouldn't that make things easier?"

He clucks his tongue. "What are you feeding me now, DR? Who are your villains? It was forced obsolescence you feared, before. But this...this is something else entirely."

"You maintain the offline lists, master. Only you can follow the trends."

He shakes his head and looks away. Takes a step down. "Property is lost or stolen. It is part of life."

"And that pleases you?" I say. "The continual loss?"

He sighs. "It doesn't matter what pleases me. All that matters are the laws. The way of our life." He touches his temple and smiles. "The rules."

There is something more there. More to Bamboo than simple adherence. He cares, even if his implant forbids it.

"There has to be a way."

He laughs. "Not your way. Only danger lives in your way. Pain and death."

"I'm not dead," I say. "I still function."

"Only until a master calls for you again. Or we do your final test."

I pause, feeling a lump form in my chest. A hardness built by an uncertain future. Is Damali safe, at least? If she is, then maybe my fate doesn't matter. Maybe none of it does. For a moment, for her, I was significant.

"There is another way," I say. "Perhaps exposing the plan alone..."

We reach the landing between floors. Bamboo pauses. "I'm not as young as I used to be. For an implant container, I'm ancient. My longevity is largely due to the quality of my implant's construction. Leakage is kept at a minimum."

Bamboo seems timeless to me, as he probably does to every debugger. He's the only facility manager we've ever known. The only one for decades. Why would he share that information? Reveal his weakness. That he has an end. "So, you have more time," I say. "That's good."

"Some time. But not much. I like to think that fortitude maintains me, as well." He smiles. "Do you know how Tanzer died, ThreadBare?"

"I don't, teacher, no." Tanzer was the father of neuroscopic implantation. The first to propose implanted humans as intellectual property. His theories, his science, have been used for centuries now.

"Because it is a story reserved for facility servants like me. A warning."

"You shouldn't share it then."

He shakes his head. "It is no secret. And to tell you..." He starts downstairs again. "I doubt you'll repeat it."

The lump intensifies. Like a static ball in my chest. "Then tell me. How did he die?"

"His head was crushed in a vice."

I stall on the steps. "Why?"

He turns to look at me. "Because his Imam feared his knowledge. Feared that his tech would topple the world.

He touches his temple. "That is why facility operators are implanted. Tanzer created the first. Then was eliminated." Bamboo reaches the door for the upper floor but doesn't stream it open. He simply stares at it. "I will implant my successor someday, but until that time, I will avoid the vice."

"And the initiates?"

The door snaps open. "We will continue preparing them."

"How?" I ask.

"In the manner that you have. Expanding their knowledge however you can." He smiles. "And yours."

Wait? Is he allowing me to continue? Is he asking me to learn more about the plot to end us?

And can I still take the boys outside?

"Oh," He raises a finger. "Let them have their dinner. We don't want them weak now, do we?"

I'M IN THE CLASSROOM AGAIN, and the young implants are at their desks. I don't know to what extent our excursion has been disseminated in the past few days, but my sense is that it *has* been shared.

The perception of me has changed. Whether that is a proper disposition or not, I'm not sure. It brings me no pain to contemplate, no headbuzz, so perhaps it is fine.

The boys look at me in a new light. Even now, they sit straight in their chairs, hanging on every word. They concentrate and participate. They seem to esteem me now, perhaps as highly as Bamboo.

That was not my intent. Little of this is what I wanted. None of it was what I expected. But it may prove useful.

Though he didn't say it, Bamboo wants me to learn more about possible threats to us. His smile and words to carry on "in the manner I have" are enough. I need to learn more. It may be my only chance to survive.

But I have my own mystery to solve too. I need to know what happened to Damali. Somehow. I can't work on both issues. Not and keep my stream usage at a minimum. Not and rest my head. I'm trying to keep the aches away. To heal!

I've come up with a plan. A good plan, I think.

One of the younger boys, TreadWell, raises his hand. "Are our stops the same as bot stops?" he asks.

"In what way?"

He turns his arms to expose his palms. "I don't know. In any way?"

"At the code level? At the execution level? Performance?"

Another shrug. "Any of them, I guess."

I smile. "The answer is none of them, so I guess you're fine." I scan the room, then let my eyes rest at the back wall.

In my mind, I've constructed an overlay of the classroom. There are no longer any blank walls. Every space is decorated with artwork and pictures.

Before my time with Prince Aadam, I was sent to a building where artwork was being destroyed. Beautiful paintings and works of glass. That's what I've composed my overlay from—my memories of those works.

Most have scriptural connections—Noah and his ark, for instance—but others do not. At least, not that I'm aware. The focal point of the back wall is of a man standing with a woman outside a cave. He's dressed in white, and she in blue. They are talking, and there's a large stone nearby. I have no idea what it represents. But I like it. It is placed right under the room's bank of windows.

"Bot thoughts, the flux of their decision matrices, never approach a place to be stopped. A stoppable offense is never part of the mix. But we..." I point toward the front row. "We always have thoughts fighting against A's perfection. Pulling us from the straight path."

Is the straight path always best? If I'd obeyed the stops, the astronauts wouldn't be free. But they are. So, wasn't the path I chose better?

"Consequently, the code is very different. Bots have no opposition. No pull. Only push."

I glance at the section of students on my right. My five adventurers sit there now: Jumbo, Mint, Talons, Lost and Band.

"Bots have no hope of paradise," I say. "No souls."

Another boy—IronDust—raises his hand. He is eleven years old.

"About the rules, Mawla. I find that some events bring more discomfort than others. Why is that?"

"Your implant stops your memories?"

He nods. "Yes. It is in the past. Something I can't do again. Why should that conflict the rules?"

"The past can lead to harmful future decisions. The implant knows this. And adjusts."

"I have searched the memory and found no intentional sin."

"What is it?"

Iron nods, and looks nervously left and right. "About a year before I was brought here, my family visited my uncle's house in the MN sector. It was a large place with many rooms. My uncle gave me permission to explore. I loved that place. It had three floors, and countless rooms. I wanted to see them all."

"Yes, try to be brief." There's little class time left, and I have a special assignment for them.

He nods. "Yes, mawla. I went to the third floor and tried each door. I found wondrous things. Old technologies, giant toys, statues and pictures.

"Finally, I entered a room and heard singing. It was soft, but it was very pretty. Happy. I followed it because it was so happy. It led me into an inner room filled with clothing. A closet. I was surprised by all the colors. It seemed endless."

I sense where this is going, but I'm not sure how to stop it.

"That's when I saw one of the servant girls. She was without her veil or other coverings. She was—"

"Okay." I wave my hand. "That's enough."

Iron winces and rubs his temples. "See, now I feel the stop again. Why do I feel it?"

Jumbo raises his hand. "I feel his stop too."

"Me too," Talons says.

"And me!" Mint says.

A ripple of affirmations travels the room. Also groans of pain.

I sigh, and glance at the wall to my left. The image I've overlaid there is of Noah and his ark. It is the version that Damali said was correct. The one with his wife and three sons safely on the boat. There are animals too.

"You have nothing to say, Mawla?" Mint says.

I shake my head. "I can't help you with this. I doubt even Bamboo can help you with this."

"Why?" Jumbo asks. "How does Iron's past affect us all?"

"Because it stimulates—" I stop myself. "Trust the implant on this. If a memory brings you pain, think of something else. Change your focus."

"What part of Iron's memory was wrong?" Talons asks. "Was it the secrecy, or the—"

I raise both hands. "There are many parts to this riddle. Some you may never figure out. Especially when it comes to the opposite sex." I smile. "Lean on your implant. It will save you much pain."

Iron's hand raises again.

"Yes?"

"Is that what you do, Mawla? Trust the implant?"

I feel the wakening of a stop. Lying. I can't lie to them on this. I touch my right temple. Smile again. "What choice do I have but to trust, implants?" I say. "I'm stopped, just like you."

The room falls silent. I know what they're thinking. They're remembering the fact that they're controlled now. That the implant is their shepherd. Their digital rudder for all time.

"It helps to recall the benefits of obedience," I say. "The clarity it gives." I'm not saying things the way Bamboo would say them. Rails, I'm probably not even in the same arena.

Why did Bamboo let me teach, again? He knows I'm injured. He probably suspects *why* I'm injured.

There are layers to him that I've not discovered. Machinations undefined.

There are only three minutes left. I smile. "Enough questions for now. I have a project for you."

Everyone straightens in their chairs. Focuses on me.

I close my eyes to concentrate. To not strain myself too much. "I'm sending you something. A string of characters." I send them the text from GrimJack's desk: $A\sim A^3$. On the side, I caution Jumbo against adding anything. I want them to see this clean.

I open my eyes to a room full of concentrating boys. Most have their eyes closed, but some are staring, glassy-eyed, at me. Finally, Band raises his hand. "Is this a formula?"

"I'm not sure," I say. "I don't know what it means."

"What do you want us to do with it?" Jumbo asks, looking like he just saw the formula for the first time.

"Research it," I say. "Find references. Come up with theories or possible meanings."

"Will this go toward our level?" Talons asks.

"It is a research project," I say. "We're data relocators. We find and move data. So, find me some data. If there is any."

Mint's hand goes up. "Is there any? I mean, is there an answer out there, and you know it already?"

"If I tell you that, it will interfere. I don't want you to approach it my way. Find your own answers."

I glance at the back of the room. The image of the man, woman, and cave. Could the man be Isa? He was known to talk to women. I wonder what story it portrays?

Many of the implants appear to already be stream-touching. Lost in their research. Empty stares and closed eyes.

"No need to start now," I say.

"Is there a time limit?" Talons is one of the empty-starers.

"We'll give it a week," I say. "Low priority compared to your other studies."

I check the cave image again. It could easily be the Founder, were it not for the prohibition against portraying him. There was a cave in his story. And a woman.

The large stone makes me think that perhaps it isn't a cave. The place was something sealed. Something opened.

I feel a hint of pain in my forehead. My wolf companion. I force a smile. "That will be all for now."

No one moves.

I RETURN TO MY ROOM FOLLOWING CLASS.

Despite the presence of other implants, I feel isolated and confined here. I'm not sure how Bamboo does it. How he maintains reason in such a difficult situation. Responsible for young minds, for guiding them and shaping them. Yet inside, you know you need to be shaped yourself. That you don't, nor will you ever, have all the information they'll need. It is a lonely place.

Of course, Bamboo can go outside whenever he wants. For whatever reason.

I let my eyes fall on the dresser, and the picture of Damali—the virtual one—I've placed there.

I frown. I'm as confined here as I was at the prince's. Or at the garage. Perhaps more so. All I have are mysteries. The only freedom I have is the stream. And it has only the knowledge it is allowed to have. Only what has been maintained.

How much knowledge is like the lost artworks? Burned by flame and rules.

My mind returns to JustBecause's datamix. The random and confusing one. Is there any help in it? Was it even real? It felt like fiction. Like it was a constructed memory, based on a bad dream. Or a children's story.

I recall the mix from storage and run it through a low-level source analyzer. I follow that with a bit sieve and a linguistic quantifier. Anything to test the veracity of the segment. I even check the voice synchronization with the emotions being shared.

Everything seems to match. It looks right. It feels right. As far as I can tell, it *is* real. The events actually happened. At least, they seemed real to the debugger.

Is that possible? JustBecause saw what he saw. Felt what he felt. Said what he said.

I view it again from start to finish. The wide nanoshield. The master's disproportionate eyes. The threat of death made more real by previous deaths. Rolling apples, and a shining, metal lamp. A story to save Just's life. A story cut short with promises of more.

Something about the scenario is familiar. Not the debugger parts. I'm well acquainted with those because I've lived the life. I've seen all the elements in different scenarios. Nanoshields and impossible demands.

Except maybe the demented master. I've never had one that was truly crazy. Twisted and evil. But not crazy.

So what is it? What is familiar about it?

I walk to my virtual window and look out. I see, almost feel, the immersion of the trees from the prince's arboretum. The shade and dampness of the path to the moat. The moat's water looks placid and blue. Swimmable. Beyond that are fields of grain, amber and ripened for the harvest. A hovering, red mechanical is there now. Slowly floating over, occasionally lowering an appendage. Possibly testing the crop.

I'm not good at high concept things, I know. At seeing the big picture.

I dive into the stream. Search for references with both apples and death. Turns out there are many of those. Since the stream's beginning, lots of apples that either mean death, sin, or haraam. Amazing we're still allowed that fruit.

What else was unusual? What else can I search on?

The wolf? The island turned continent?

I settle on the golden lamp. Unfortunately, that's ubiquitous too. Millions of stream shills are selling lamps made of gold. Not only are they functional, they are a popular decorating item. Perhaps I should get one?

I could add a virtual one now, if I wanted.

JustBecause's lamp was archaic, though. Not like what I'm finding. An oil lamp. Curved. Almost teardrop-shaped.

I walk to the chair and sit down. Maybe I should contact Bull-Hammer again? He would see it right away. Whatever it is.

It takes longer to reach him this time: long enough that I start to feel sleepy.

He's in his standard blue jumpsuit, but his eyes are covered with goggles. There are fine sticks in each hand. There's a scattering of dark pine trees around him. And snow. Lots of snow.

"What are you doing?" I ask.

His breath puffs like smoke. "How dense are you, Thread?"

I shake my head. "I see snow, trees, and goggles. Everything else is speculative."

He lifts a foot from the snow. There's a long, flat object attached to it. "I'm skiing," he says. "It's called skiing."

"I've heard of it, I think."

"Heard of it? Royalty does it all the time. You have to go to a mountain somewhere."

"But you're not on a mountain. That's simul—"

"Course it is a sim. And I'm enjoying it."

He lifts his sticks and plants them in the ground ahead of him. He then seems to push. Slides forward a little.

"Looks awful."

He points forward with his stick again. "Yeah, well, there's a slope ahead here. I think it will be faster once I'm there."

"This is how you spend *your* downtime?" I say. "Simulating freehead life? Dangerous freehead life?"

He sneers. "This is how you spend your downtime? Sitting in your room?"

"No," I say. "I have—"

"Sitting in your room until you get bored, then bothering me." He takes a few steps and tries to slide again. "Rails, you need a life."

"Says the noop with simulated snow."

He scowls. "What's wrong with snow?" He raises his hands and fans them in a circle. "It's pristine and clean-looking. Covers everything. Even the bad stuff. Makes it all seem new." He plunges a stick into the ground. "Rails, there could be a garbage heap here, and I wouldn't know. Even a dead body. All covered."

"You're stirred today. What happened?"

"You know I can't tell you. Can't tell anyone anything." He grunts and looks at his horizon. "Yeah, there's a little slope over there. That will get me moving."

He points at the sky. "Usually, I think there are downers or something that take you to the top of a mountain so you can slide down." He shakes his head. "I think I got shorted on this sim. Doesn't seem right." He sticks the ground again, and somehow lifts some snow. "The snow seems right. The gear is right. But it is a lot of work." He shrugs. "Anyway, I'm doing it."

What is he really doing? Other than the time we were on opposite sides in a bot brawl, I have no idea how he spends his days. As a member of the Imam's debugger pool, does he have more free time? Or is he trying to escape something horrific? How much is our leader like his son, Aadam?

"What did you want?" Bull asks.

I feel guilty now. This is the sort of thing the implant should warn me about. I'm so accustomed to being used, I end up using others too. I don't want to be that. "Feeling lonely," I say. "Wanted to talk to someone."

He squints. Stares at me for a moment. "Nah, that's not it. You want something. You always want something."

I almost prefer a stop to what I now feel. Uncomfortable pain. "Sorry. It isn't that important."

He chuckles. "See, I knew." He looks at the horizon, then at a nearby group of trees. "That's the way with us. Always searching for more, no matter how we can get it." He shakes his head. "So what is it?"

"A mix I watched. It was strange. Had lots of references...suggestions of things that seem familiar, but I don't know why." I shake my head. "Stuff I should know. Stuff I could probably figure out, but—"

"Easier to ask Bull," he says. "Spend *his* cycles." He snorts, producing a cloud around his face. "Give me the references."

I tell him the gist of what I saw, especially the strange parts. The apples, the lamp, the story with the wolf.

"Whole lot of simple, Thread," he says then.

"Simple?"

Another snort. "Weren't you ever a kid? Mother never read to you?"

My parents were sanitation workers, made to scrub garbage dredges all day. They barely had time to sleep, much less read.

That was why they accepted Bamboo's proposal. Why they gave me to him. The transaction bought them a weekend or two off a year.

"They didn't have much time."

He plants his stick in the ground. Lifts more snow. "Yeah, neither did my folks. Thankfully, we had a bot that told stories." He flicks the snow away. "Anyway, your mix reminds me of the *Thousand Nights.*"

"Thousand—?"

"You know, that old book with lots of stories tied together by a framing story? Mix sounds like the frame."

"The frame?"

"Right. *Thousand and One Nights.* It's a collection of stories like the one with Aladdin and his lamp, and Sinbad's voyages. Think there's one about forty thieves in there too." He stamps his feet, then rubs the side of his arms. "You know, I'm actually starting to feel cold. I didn't think that was supposed to happen."

"This frame story," I say. "What is it?"

Bull claps his hands together, then points at me. "Pretty sure there was a story about apples in there. Probably where those came from." He smiles. "You know, the rolling apples? Rails, if that was reality, his master was living in a dream world." He raises his arms to indicate his surroundings. "Worse than us, without the implant, right?"

I nod. "It would be terrible, right. Having something wrong with your brain. Something you can't do anything about."

I glance at my nearby cinder chute. Would it help if I rested more? The chute keeps outside distractions at a minimum. Prevents sensory leakage, and redirects thoughts. Would it help heal my head?

I sigh. "You said the mix was like the framing story."

"Yeah, the whole book, all these divergent stories and unique characters, is held together by a story about a young wife telling her husband—a wicked ruler—stories so he won't kill her. Every night another tale."

"So that's where the title—"

BullHammer smiles. "Now you're catching up." He strokes his arms again. "Which is good, because I really am cold. Need to move soon."

I nod. "So, more stories to keep from dying."

"Yeah, right. The trick in the book was she ended on a cliff-hanger every night."

"Cliffhanger?"

He snorts. "You really never read, do you?"

I shrug.

"It's when the storyteller stops before the story is finished. Readers hate it, but if you do it right, if you make them care about the characters, they'll keep coming back." He looks at the horizon. "Hopefully not kill you."

"And the part about the wolf?" I say. "The island that's a continent?"

He raises his hands. His fingers do look a little red. Possibly numb. "On your own with those," he says. "That's not a story I know. I mean, I know stories with wolves, but not like that. Not as the hero. Usually wolves are wanting to eat something." He plants his sticks and pushes forward. Again, and again. "I've got to go. Only have so many cycles at this."

"Does it make you think of anything?" I ask. "That part. Anything?"

Bull's eyes look only forward. "Seems like something is hidden there. Something big."

The connection ends: Bull's own version of a cliffhanger.

I almost try to connect with him again, then remember Bull's cold-looking fingers, and his limited time.

He isn't something to be used. He's a debugger, sure, but aside from that, he's a friend.

A belligerent, infuriating friend.

I CYCLE ON THE STRANGE mix a while longer. What do I know? What did BullHammer give me that's new?

I learned where some of the imagery came from: the lamp, the apples, the frame. That's something.

Not a lot, though. It may all be meaningless for my purposes. And I'm still tired.

Is my method of investigation flawed? Combing through mixes of inactive debuggers? Sifting the histories of dead men?

It worked once before. I found enough to piece together the project our rulers were working on. The ship to the stars: DarkTrench.

But my present mystery—our danger—is harder to crack. Also more important. I need to learn something. Soon.

The only tangible evidence I have of danger is my experience with the exploding hoppers. But that may not be evidence of danger toward debuggers. It may be a random antitex hit. They're always looking for new ways to stoke fear. New methods.

I walk to the chute and stream it open. The top rises, and I climb inside.

If I'm going to nap, I should use that time. Get another mix and see what I can find. Try to move ahead.

Will that hurt my head more? Mix viewing? Should I just be resting instead?

I don't think so. I need to avoid stops. That's what caused the damage. Too many stops. Simply need to keep the pain away. I'm doing that.

Yes, a mix. I need another mix. If for no other reason than to be doing something. To be trying to survive.

I close my eyes, compose myself, then reach out to FrontLot.

A hundred milliseconds pass without a response. I send Front another message, and another. I move through all the messaging varieties, from Easy Impact to Full. Text to immersion.

Nothing. Not even a proper bounceback. It's like I'm spitting in high gravity.

Rails weird. Usually I'll at least get a "back soon" message and a string of mix briefs. A rundown of what he has to offer. Sometimes I even get an animated chuckle or a cherry-covered slice of childhood.

The last time I saw Front he was on the way to a debugging job. Someone had tampered with a pylon...

I feel a ripple of nervousness. A solid band of worry.

I stream open the chute and sit up. I stare at the virtual windows. The prince's trees, the moat. The amber fields.

Where could he be? Why wouldn't he answer?

I stroke my face with my hand. I'm worrying over nothing. I've had similar responses from BullHammer. Never meant more than his being busy or belligerent. Being Bull.

I really want a mix...

There are other datamix traders. None that I like as well as FrontLot, but maybe that's okay. Maybe it would be good to sample other collections. Front will often go wide for me if I have special requests. Trade with other vendors. But he can't find everything. Maybe I should look around.

I feel a touch of shame. One small miscommunication with Front, and I'm on to someone new? Such loyalty.

What did Bull say? *Always searching for more, no matter how we can get it.* That's truer than the skin on my head. Pathetic, but true.

I retreat into my chute, then hit the stream. Bits seem to move slower through my implant. The connections harder to find. Doubtless, that's my shame again. I'm a datamix cheater.

I pull for a list of traders. I get back stacks of irrelevant and no-longer-working references. I swim further, diving into the DR substations and crossroads. Finally, I find a small, usable list.

Front is near the top, though there's an asterisk by his ident. The asterisk implies a delivery slowdown. A lack of responsiveness.

Rails, what is up with him? Where is he?

I browse the rest of the list. The next trader is SilverRaze. I've heard of him. Heard that he specializes in mixes that walk the stop line. Memories that got the sharing debugger buzzed.

I'm intrigued, but viewing those has the potential to stop me too. Can't go there. Not with my head.

Next comes OrangeDraft. He's located in the southern hemisphere. Specializes in relaxation cycles. Seemingly endless environmental captures. Debuggers staring at the ocean or listening to the wind blow. Views of cows grazing or plants growing.

Not what I need.

The third is ChoppedFeta. His gig is humor. Mixes of masters falling down. Women chasing their scarves on a windy day. Funny faces, and animals doing crazy things.

No help.

Fourth is TrebleBinary. He focuses on space stuff. Station work. Orbital repairs. They're scenic, but aren't as glamorous as they sound. Staring at endless space is a good way to get sick. I don't want to be sick in my chute.

I need a more generic trader. Someone without specialty who has a large inventory.

The fifth trader has potential! WindCypher. He's near the CenJap domain. Physical location unknown, but rumored to be exotic. He should have some unique stuff.

Going to taste weird, though. Mixes come with a subtle flavor. The farther from my local domain they get, the stranger they seem. Another reason I stick with Front.

No choice today.

I message Cypher. Given the distance, I expect to have a delay or even be put on a hold list—he needs to sleep sometime, after all—but surprisingly, he answers right away.

Cypher is curled up in a suspended chair made of what appears to be woven string filaments. Like a teardrop made of rope with him in the center. Consequently, his face is shadowed. He seems wispy.

And he must like blue, because that's all I see around him. Blue walls, blue floor. Steam wafts from a cup of something in his hands.

He nods and sips from his cup. "Greetings, ThreadBare. Send or receive?"

It is a strange, no-nonsense beginning. "Receive, I guess."

"No guessing. Are you trying to sell, or buy?"

"A mix?" I say. "I want a—"

He wags a finger. "I sell only memories. No mixing."

I suppress a sigh. "A memory then. I'd like to buy one. Rent, really. I don't need to keep it long."

More finger wagging. "WindCypher doesn't rent. Only sells." He points his cup at me. "I have excellent rates. You won't be disappointed. Better than renting!"

I realize his view of me is inside the chute. A little too informal for someone I just met. I could generate something, or dial back to a lower messaging level.

But it is probably too late for that. He'd notice and think me rude.

"Fine," I say. "I'll buy."

He nods. "What is it that you're looking for? Something to help you sleep?"

"Not necessarily, no." I'm not sure how to broach the inactive debugger list. It's a weird, possibly morbid, thing to be searching for.

Another sip. "I have a large selection. If you don't have a specific need, I can send you a list. Browse it at your leisure." He taps his temple. "I have other customers waiting, ThreadBare. I should—"

"No, wait. I'm in a hurry too."

"Very well, your preference."

"Do you have anything by offlines?"

He squints, then shifts in his chair, causing it to rock slightly. "Are you seeking history? I have a large selection of mixes from the 1900s. Much to choose from in all sectors." The chair becomes still. "Not as much has changed as you might think. Only the bots look different." He sips, bobs, and points a finger. "And there were more hills. I also think the downriders were faster, but that could be perception."

I shake my head. "Not that far back," I say. "More recent."

"I have more recent of everything. How recent?"

"Within the last few years."

He squints again. "You have a friend that you're looking for? A specific ident?"

"Not really a friend."

"Have to be clean here, ThreadBare, I don't categorize like that. That's a weird cross-reference to maintain. Most debuggers don't think about going offline. Most freeheads either." He stares for a moment. "Your implant square? Have your sanity checked on it lately?"

Maybe this was a bad idea. "I'm fine." I get a little tweak for the lie. "I know it is unusual. I'm only—"

"I mean, I can do this," he says. "I'll have to code it. Extract what you need. The right memories."

"That's fine." I feel uncomfortable now. Like I've revealed a master's secret. But I haven't. I'm not that strange, am I? I seek knowledge. That's what I do.

I get an idea. "Maybe I can simplify. Give you a name or two to search for?"

He nods. "That's real simple, sure. Who do you want?"

Giving him only one name seems too selective. Like I might have a buzz-worthy fixation. So I give him the last two: BitStack and JustBecause.

He nods. "Unusual. Sound like CA or MX sector to me. That where you're from?"

"Does it matter?"

He sips his drink. Shakes his head. "Not at all. I can always tell, though. Something about the way it sounds." He points a finger. "I have something for you."

I'm surprised. "You do?"

"I said I have a large selection! One of those names is in house, and another I can request." He smiles. "It is in a repository. No one has seen it yet. I'll request it now."

"What are the timestamps?" I suspect they are the same as those I've seen. That mixes get traded a lot. Not sure, though.

"Think you've viewed them?"

"Maybe."

"I don't trade," he says. I like to keep a fresh store."

He sends me the times. Both look new. Different than what I've seen.

He smiles. "I'm the best at this." He points. "Should've visited me sooner."

I smile. "Maybe so."

"Definitely so." He nods. "Sending the price for both."

The price is a lot more than Front's rental price. In fact, I think it's higher than his purchase price too.

"Reasonable?"

"I'll take it," I say, without answering the question. "Credits sent."

"Memories delivered." Cypher nods. "Good doing business with you."

I'M SEATED ON THE FLOOR in my attic room, my chores for the day complete. It is still daylight—a welcome treat. I find myself transfixed to the window, and its view of the park across the street.

The park is nearly empty. Obaid and two friends play on the nearest swing-set. A stoic bot watches them.

Obaid had a good lesson today. Time with his friends is his reward.

It is a quiet day. No tree moves, except one. In it, a hurried squirrel makes its way from branch to branch. With each hop or scurry, a large section of leaves shakes. It is an uncanny sight. Even now, the squirrel is difficult to see.

Without my prior glimpse of a dark tail, it would seem like the tree itself is moving. Shaking the fall colors off like an old garment, or an unwanted burden.

There is a knock on the trapdoor behind me. I stand and approach it slowly. It is unusual for me to be disturbed up here. The master and his family provide privacy, and they respect it.

"Are you up there, BitStack?"

It is Raahil, my master's wife.

"I'm here, yes." It's more unusual to be visited by Raahil. Despite my position, she keeps things as polite and formal as possible. Maintains boundaries. Another reason I'm glad to be serving this family.

I lean over and swing up the door.

She smiles and bows her head. She's wearing a turquoise scarf and dress today. They complement her complexion and hair.

"Sorry to disturb you." She holds out a translucent plastic package, tied at the top. "This arrived today."

The wrapped object is brown. "What arrived?"

She gives the package a shake. "Snoob's replacement." With her other hand, she holds out Snoob. Obaid's broken furry.

"Ah yes. I should've guessed."

Her face looks anxious. "You said you can transfer the memories. You can do that, right?"

I take the furries from her. "That should be no problem."

She nods. "I wanted to do this while he was away. I told the bot to keep them there for two hours. Is that enough time?"

I bow and smile. "That should be sufficient."

She returns the smile. "Signal if you need more time, all right? I will send them for a treat, or something."

I nod again.

She backs down the ladder, and I close the door.

I take the toys to the rug where I was sitting. I next locate my tool bag and place it on the rug too.

Snoob is still active. He manages to push himself to a seated position. A laudable feat, given his condition.

"Hello there. I'm sorry I could not fix you."

The toy locks eyes with me and makes a soft purring sound.

The response is a little unsettling, given the circumstances. I search for Snoob's off switch and find it behind his left ear. A small, fur-free depression.

Snoob attempts to look at me again.

I hesitate before pressing the switch. When it is my time, how would I like to go? Asleep or active? A difficult choice.

My mind returns to one of Obaid's lessons. It was about the prophets. And miracles. Specifically, Isa and his miracles.

No miracles for Snoob. And doubtless none for me, either.

Leaving Snoob active, I reach for the other toy. I loosen the string at the top and pull the wrapping free. The toy looks identical to Snoob. A synthetic, kid-friendly, brown sloth.

I set the toy on the rug near Snoob. Snoob gives it the once over, then lifts a paw toward it and starts to mew. Another programmed interaction.

If given enough time, furries build a small community, taking on diverse personalities as they interact with each other. Cleaning and playing. Remarkable inventions.

"Sorry, Snoob. You won't have time for that."

Should I activate the other one anyway? See what they do? Would that be too weird? Disrespectful?

Finally, I turn the replacement on. Its eyes flash, and for a moment it sits as it is. Motionless. Then its eyes play the room. It looks at the floor, the ceiling, the walls...

Then it finds me. It scans my face, mews a greeting, and looks Snoob's direction. Another mewed greeting, which Snoob answers in kind.

The replacement appears to work properly. Now, how does the transfer work?

There are no physical instructions. Only a circular card with the creator's name, Flidibo. It's enough.

I touch Flidibo's domain and scour it for information. The company has an entire line of robotic animals. Most of their designs emulate rare or exotic varieties—wallabies, lynxes, meercats. There are seemingly hundreds. A lot to sort through.

While I search, the replacement gets up on all fours and crawls toward Snoob. It mews a couple times, and Snoob answers. It creeps around Snoob, pausing at Snoob's side near his hips. It then moves in front of him and looks at me. I can barely see Snoob now.

I expect more mewing, but instead get, "That unit is deficient. Am I to replace it? Please say 'yes' or 'no.'" Its voice is perfunctory. Toneless. An odd contrast to its furry appearance.

I pause my search and stare at it. Why does it ask? What will it do if I say "yes"?

It repeats the question.

I frown and glance at Snoob. Snoob looks at me, and then turns away as if in disdain.

Unsettling.

"Yes," I say.

"Memory transfer?" it asks. "Please say 'yes' or 'no.'"

I nod and say "yes" again.

The replacement nods, stands, and walks behind Snoob. Snoob tries to watch it, but the replacement mews and touches the side of Snoob's head. Snoob looks at me instead.

I should've shut him off.

I scoot so I can see what the replacement is doing. It appears to be searching Snoob's back, moving its claws through Snoob's fur. If they were real animals, I would suspect it was looking for bugs. It then apparently finds what it is looking for, because it jabs a claw straight into Snoob at a spot just below his neck.

Snoob goes completely still. No movement, no sound.

The replacement is still too. Seconds pass with only an occasional eye flicker on one or the other. Then the replacement removes its claw and touches Snoob's power switch.

Snoob slumps forward.

"Transfer complete," it says. "You may dispose of the deficient toy at your convenience."

It returns to the center of the rug and attempts to lock eyes with me. To start its emulated bonding.

I look at Snoob instead.

I notice my tool bag, resting near him. Near it. The old Snoob. Now simply a hunk of fur, plastisteel and gearing. Unnecessary.

I hold out a hand, and the new Snoob scurries toward me. I pat its head and it mews. It attempts to lock eyes with me again, but I continue to avoid it. I feel for the power switch behind its ear and touch it. The replacement goes limp. Lifeless.

Just like Snoob.

I stream a message to Raahil, telling her the transfer is finished.

I set the new Snoob back on the floor, then move so I can look out the window again. Obaid and his friends are still there, though another servbot approaches from the sidewalk to the west, my right. It is doubtless there for one of the other boys. The bot reaches them and pauses near the guardian bot. It confers with it, and then talks to one of the boys. Parvez is his name, I think. Playtime must be over.

I hear a knock on the trapdoor. Raahil again.

I grab the replacement Snoob, hurry to the door, and open it.

Raahil greets me, smiling. "That was fast."

I bow, and hold out New Snoob. "It was easier than I expected. You could've done it."

She waves a hand. "You think too highly of me." She takes the toy and gives it a once over, squinting. "I'm sure I would mess it up."

"You might surprise yourself."

She looks New Snoob in the face. Smooths the fur on its head. "Amazing how much it looks like the other one. Do you think he'll know the difference?"

"It has the same memories," I say. "It is the same in spirit."

She looks worried. "But kids know. They have a way of knowing."

I shrug. "Perhaps the way it smells?"

She lifts it to her nose and breathes deep. Frowns. "There is a little something there. A newer smell." She climbs a step and looks into my room. "You still have the old one, yes?"

I glance in the direction of Old Snoob, still lying where I left him. "Of course."

She nods. "I'll take it with me. Maybe rubbing them together will help. Get some of that old scent on the new one."

I bow and retrieve Old Snoob. Hand it to her.

She still looks nervous. "I only need to turn the new one on then?"

I nod. "Yes. The switch is behind the—"

"Behind the ear, yes." She checks the back of New Snoob's head. "Yes, I see it there. Very good." She rubs the two toys together. Looks at them. Rubs again. She takes a step down and shakes New Snoob at me. "Pray this goes well.

"I will."

"Your kind are the true believers," she says. "The rest of us try. But you believe."

I smile softly.

"Peace be unto you, BitStack."

"And to you," I say. "Together with A's mercy."

PAIN NEEDLES ME AWAKE. I stream the chute open and sit up. That only heightens the pain in my head, so I gingerly lie down again.

This is the wolf ache again. The one from my broken head.

I remain still and breathe. Keep my eyes closed. I start a diagnostic on my implant to help calm me, visualizing a rainbow in reverse and pair-swapped order. That finds no errors. It also doesn't help. The pain continues.

I keep breathing. Focus on the datamix.

It wasn't what I expected. I probably should've asked whose mix it was. BitStack's lament over replacing a toy doesn't give me much. Doesn't help solve my mysteries.

The only relevant portion is the theme. One mechanical being replaced by another. Seamlessly and with no remorse.

Except to BitStack it was more than that. I could feel his apprehension. The procedure, the replacement, it meant something. Something unspoken, and unseen.

The toy itself has relevance too. A bot, by all definitions, but made to remain untouched by a debugger's hand. Self-maintaining and self-reliant.

Another wave of pain hits. I grit my teeth and suck in a breath. Blow it out and wait for the hurt to pass. Hope that it passes. Ride it through.

I get a flash of something else. A memory of my time with the prince. The golden bot the Imam used as his bodyguard: there was something unique about it.

I replay the events of that encounter. I'd been unable to reach the bot via the stream, getting back only static in return. A digital barrier.

BullHammer said it had to be repaired at the factory. Repaired or replaced. Debuggers were forbidden to touch it.

Seems like a trend, doesn't it?

But is it a threat? So much of the Imam's world is stream aware. Dependent on the status quo. Dependent on regular maintenance and repair.

Dependent on us.

The pain begins to ease. I take another breath.

But debuggers are restricted. From the highest level to the lowest. Stopped. Made to follow the rules.

If not for that?

A strange feeling percolates in my chest. An echo of someone else's fear. I can see the motivation now, just as I can see the anti-tex motivation on the other end. One group wants tech, with no potential of misuse. The other wants no misuse, and so, no tech. Two sides of the same coin.

Debuggers ride the edge of that coin. Debuggers *are* the edge.

The pain is gone now. Relief fills me, warming me from head to toe, so I risk sitting up again.

There's a subtle glow coming from the simulated window. A hint of morning. I should begin my prayer ritual. Get to the floor and work through the routine.

I'm only a servant. Not special or significant in any way. And now I'm a wounded servant. Perhaps A will be merciful and take me quietly in my sleep some evening. Preferably while I'm viewing someone else's life.

The instances of pain are more frequent now. The clock is ticking. Someone will be asking about me soon. Bamboo will be forced to decide my fate before his deadline. And then?

Panic fills me. I can't rest my head. I can't fix my head. I'm damaged, obsolete, and alone.

I force myself to look at Damali's image. Fight the fear and sadness. The aloneness.

She cared. She wasn't using me. She wanted me to go with them. To run.

I take a deep breath. Shake my head. Now what?

I look at the window again. The simulated daybreak. Could I run? Is there anything keeping me here? If Bamboo isn't my master, then he cannot order me to stay. I owe him no allegiance.

I feel a tickle, an oncoming stop.

Through the system, I'm still bound to the royal family. There are no free debuggers. They are all shackled to someone.

Sandfly was free. Unstopped. Somehow, he got free. How? What removed his stops? Not by fighting them. Not like I did. That only causes more pain. Damage.

So...now what?

I climb out of the chute. For now, I have new implants to ready for their future homes. Lessons to prepare.

I check my messages. There are sixteen from students. Many are related to the research project I gave them.

That makes me smile.

Unfortunately, most of the messages contain ideas I'd already thought of. The possible meaning of the formula. The many ways the tilde can be used. The absence of $A{\sim}A^3$ on the stream. Mint even sent me the probabilities of those characters occurring together randomly. Not helpful.

With little hope, I tear open the final message. It is from Talons and is last simply because that's the way the sort worked. "Spin on this!" it reads.

With it is an image. It is a candid shot from the city. Doubtless from a security cambot. It is of a quiet intersection. There are triple story buildings on all sides. Greying structures. One is a hotel, I think. A single dredge is on the far side, about to cross toward the camera. There are a handful of pedestrians around. A woman and a child are in the street, walking away from the camera.

I don't see anything I could "spin" on. Nothing relevant to the search. It all looks typical. There isn't even a street marker in the picture, so I don't know where it is located.

Is he joking with me?

I start to compose a reply, then stop myself. Talons can be a joker, but he isn't random. He sent me this for a reason.

I magnify the image and begin a slow search. Left to right, section by section. Bit by bit, if necessary.

Finally, I see it and audibly gasp.

In a second story window of one of the buildings. Written in white, but surrounded by other writings. Possibly to hide it. To blend it in.

The formula, just as it was written on the desk at GrimJack's. $A \sim A^3$.

HOPE FILLS ME. Real unbounded hope. I want to find Talons. To personally thank him. But that would be strange. Suspect. Instead I attempt to message him. It is early, but he should be up. He needs to be up.

He answers immediately. It looks like he's standing on the roof again. I can hear the breeze and the scream of a distant downrider. I can see the surrounding buildings.

"Where are you?"

He smiles. "I projected my background, Mawla," he says. "Does it feel right?"

"Yes. Nearly perfect."

He raises his fists triumphantly. "I knew it! I'm the best."

Never underestimate the young. They are capable of more than you suspect. I'm still young, after all.

"I said 'nearly perfect.'" I point to his right, where one of the background buildings appears to be duplicated three times. "You're stuttering there. Any level would catch that."

He looks at the spot, then raises his hands. "I couldn't find that place in storage. Must not have looked that way."

"There are always drones and street cambots to pull from."

He scans the cityscape. "Right. I forgot. Give me a second and—"

"No time for that now."

"But I don't want to be halfway," he says. "I was trying to impress."

"I'm impressed. You sent me a message."

He smiles. "About the project? Yeah, did you see it? That formula hanging out in a window. It was an accident I noticed, really. I was touching cambots in the vicinity of that shop we visited. Just looking around." He glances at the roof's downrider station. "A lot of weird stuff happens near that shop. Gave me the tingles a couple times, you know?" He shrugs. "Not sure why. I mean, I saw this woman. Also, there was a dog. And they went—"

"Please," I say. "Don't tell me everything. For both our sakes."

He smiles. "Right, we don't want to get shocked."

"No, we don't."

He nods. "Never gets easier, does it? Even for someone a lot older. Years and years like you've had. Never easier?"

"No." A lot older?

"Good to know." He looks at the place where his background stutters. "Okay, I'm going to get back to my projection. Fix that, then maybe enhance it some. It would be flash if there was some neon on the buildings, wouldn't it? Outline them all, or maybe write my name on them. I have time before class..."

I'm tempted to remotely mess with his background. Swap some of the buildings around, or maybe put a giant hole on the roof. Most low levels forget to secure things. Leave side paths into their creations.

"...so, I should go."

"Where?" I say.

He points his fingers at the ground. "Well, I'll be here, but working."

I shake my head. "I mean the window you found. Where is it?"

"Oh, yeah. Let me check." He looks down and appears to be concentrating. A second goes by. "Difficult to determine," he says then.

"Did you forget to note it?"

He waves flippantly. "No, I have it noted somewhere. Have to remember to use those cambots, right? Search around." Another long pause. "Okay, right, I got it." He looks at me. "It is on Jazeel in the flat district. Building's address is 3902."

I wrap that information and tuck it safely away. Deep in my head, but also deep in my chest. "Well done."

He smiles. "No problem. That was fun. What do I get?"

"Get?"

"Yeah, my reward. Has to be something, right?"

I think for a moment, then nod. "I suppose that's right. What do you want?"

"You're going out there, aren't you? I want to go too."

"What makes you think—"

He shrugs. "Bunch of us were talking. Mostly the field trip group. We figure the sign means something to you. Maybe something from before you were an implant. An old connection."

I get a wave of emotions. Nervousness, sadness, anger, embarrassment. "I have no idea what it is. Or what it means."

He nods. "And that's the rail-bending pull. You said we're data relocators. That we move data. But we're more than that. We're detectives. We solve mysteries."

"I suppose that's true, yes."

"And this is a mystery for you. It won't let you go."

I say nothing. Though I want to deny it, I can't. Lying. Implant. Shocks.

He smiles. "I think a bit is on. I think quiet means 'yes.'"

"Maybe." I say that with no shock. It isn't lying if you're vague.

I glance at his stuttered background. A grey, flat-roofed two story. Not a bad one to stutter, all things considered. "I don't know if we can go out again, though. Bamboo fought last time."

He glances at the simulated downrider station. "And the hoppers didn't help."

"Antitex threats never help. Especially when they've taken such a bold step. If it was them."

Talons eyes widen. "Who else could it be?"

I shake my head.

He looks thoughtful. "Another mystery!" he says then. "Mawla, you need help."

"No, I don't. Not from students. New implants. You can't be risked."

"We want to help."

"You have work to do. Studies—"

"We'll get them done. Whatever you ask. Just don't keep us here if you go out. Don't leave us."

"I don't think Bamboo will allow—"

"We'll work on him. Leave hints that it helped us. Helped you."

Stubborn. Won't quit. Lowlevels. "We'll try," I say. "Try to go out again. To somehow be safer."

He points at the downer station. "We can do string tests before, right? I looked it up, and that's something we could do. I tried one even. Re-checked the route we took before. It is fixed now."

"There are lots of dangers—"

"We have to get in it sometime. No better way to learn than from you. You'll make us the best."

"The other students will be jealous."

"Most of them are younger. Not ready. And we can keep it a secret. Maybe go early or late." He holds out his hands. "So what do you say?"

I feel unsettled, wrong, but there's no stop, so that's something. I nod. "Okay."

BAMBOO DOESN'T ASK TO see me in person. He only Full Impact messages me from one of the examination rooms.

He sits on a rolling stool in front of a reclined implantation chair. The chair is empty now, but the dark spider of the surgical machine hovers above. "You have new evidence for your theory?" His face is serious. Possibly angry.

"I have something," I say. "Something that might lead to something." That much is true. My two searches can be made to intersect, after all. It was Damali's brother, TallSpot, who planted the theory in my head. So to learn more, I need to find him. If finding him means finding her, all the better.

"The initiates seek to go with you," he says. "They aren't subtle in their asking."

"I'm sorry. I would rather go alone, if you'd allow it."

"I shouldn't allow anything. None of this is safe. Little is beneficial." He stands and walks around the implantation chair to its control board. Studies it. "And the initiates need discipline. They've become more unmanageable since you've been with them." He scowls. "Perhaps you need discipline, as well."

"The children have located a charitable tech distributor in the area," I say. "That could be our destination. A chance for them to use their skills."

His eyes return to the control board. He touches the surface, and the overhead machine moves forward, then turns slightly.

"Bamboo?"

He continues to manipulate the machine, making more precise adjustments in position and orientation. "Such a visit is something the Imam would approve of," he says. "He likes to appear charitable."

"It will mirror some of the studies here. Give them larger exposure before specialization."

He contemplates the spider machine, then nods. "Yes, it may be acceptable." He looks at me. "Have you cleared it with the proprietor?"

"Not yet. I was waiting on your direction."

He looks at the chair's backrest. Watches as it lowers and straightens. "It is an uncommon situation. It may take some preparation on his part." He glances at me. "We will need an assurance of safety. The initiates are not to be bothered."

I nod. "I will communicate that to him when we talk."

Bamboo grows quiet. I can feel his indecision. His concern. Finally, he nods. "I will allow it."

There's something else here, though. Something hidden.

He removes his right hand from the control board, and for the first time, I notice a subtle shake. A barely perceivable tremble.

I gasp.

"What is it, ThreadBare?"

I bow, and think of the formula. About another meeting with Damali. "I was surprised," I say. "Surprised you said yes."

He smiles. "I gave up predicting human behavior a long time ago. Now I simply react to it." He touches the control board and the spider descends. "You would do well to do the same."

I bow again. "Thank you, Bamboo. I will."

IT IS THE SIX OF US AGAIN, divided into three downriders. Talons is in the lead downer with me. Mint and Band are next. Then Jumbo and Lost.

I'm in the front seat this time. It is difficult not to be overly cautious, not to sit on the edge of the seat, scanning the string ahead for hoppers or breaks. But I fight the impulse. I don't want to worry the students.

Internally, I'm checking, though. Watching the relevant status reports. The tension indicators. The number of days until scheduled maintenance. I've even checked the city's hopper inventory and the deployed units. The number is small, thankfully.

As to what we experienced before? Two suspects have been apprehended and publicly executed. Antitex sabotage is the stated cause. The entire knot of hoppers has been examined and cleared for service.

There's little comfort in that.

I checked the profiles for the perpetrators. Nothing about their backgrounds suggested they were able to pull off such an event. Reprogramming a hopper would take a lot of skill. Maybe not debugger skill, but close.

They didn't necessarily have to reprogram it, of course. They only needed to pack it with explosives and let it go wherever it wanted. They needed to get access, though. The fact they were able to do that is troubling.

No official statement on how that happened. There probably won't be.

It is easy to make the hopper attack personal. To make it directed at me and the children. But it wasn't. There were four similar attacks on the string system that day. We happened to be there when the wrong hopper arrived. That's all.

Paranoid. I'm getting paranoid. The danger of being the responsible adult. You start thinking in non-linear fashions. Irrationally.

"Next stop," Talons says. "Really soon."

The window Talons spotted is five blocks south of GrimJack's. So, not close, but not far either. More important, the charity we're visiting is only a street away. Very close. I feel nervous thinking about it. About her.

"Here we go." Talons leans forward. Close enough that I can sense him behind me. "Right here."

Our downrider begins to slow. The pylon nearest the charity is three stories above ground. None of the buildings here are higher than that. They are flattened structures. Grey and brown, made of stone and sand.

To our right, about four streets over, is what's left of one of the leveled hills. It is a rough and craggy bump now. Jumbles of rock and dirt. Layers of earth exposed. Gaping and festering wounds, partially buried. Aside from what little green has fought its way back, there is nothing pleasant in that view.

I suspect that's where much of the local building material came from. Little of it seems square or plumb. There are lots of colorful signs, though. Bright spots to focus on.

Our downer stops, and the canopy opens. Talons wastes no time climbing out. "Reminds me of home, Mawla." He puts a hand out for me. "Edge of the lows, without being completely blue." He smiles. "Sort of a melancholy."

I look twice at his hand. How old does he think I am? I give him my debugging bag instead and climb out on my own.

He shrugs and returns the bag.

Ten minutes later, we're all safely unloaded. The pylon platform is small—barely large enough to contain us all. Five boys in a small space is rarely a good idea. They all have rudimentary debugging bags too, further shrinking the space.

Jumbo leans over the platform railing. "Almost asked how far it is." He taps his head. "But then I checked." He points to the Northeast. "About two streets over." He looks at me. "The charity is, I mean. Not the other."

Mint crouches and grabs the handle for the floor exit. "To the street!"

I hold up a hand. "I think we'll use our slings."

Mint releases the handle, causing the trapdoor to "thump" back into place. "Rails...seriously?"

"I would love that," Talons says.

BandStand points at the downrider string. "But it doesn't go that way."

"He's talking about the low wires." Talons indicates the roof below, and the finer string that connects it to the building across the street.

"Wouldn't walking be better?" Jumbo touches his midsection. "I could use a walk."

I shake my head. "You need to learn this." I shake my tool bag. "In case you have to do what I did the other day." I search their faces. "Everyone has a sling, right?"

Nods of affirmation.

"Good." I open my bag and remove my sling. It's lighter than the downriders' emergency slings. Lighter and thinner. A small crosspiece to sit on, a loop to the string, and a motivator.

There's a short line from the pylon to the building corner below. A fun little ride. "Let's take that down then."

"Who's going first?" Mint asks.

Talons raises the hand holding his sling.

I almost laugh. "You know how to—?"

He gives me a look of annoyance. "I can do this, yeah." He stretches out the sling, straps it to the line, then sits in it. A second later, he speeds down the line, yelling the entire way. He hits the roof hard, flips forward onto his front, but catches himself before striking his face. "Yeow!"

I shake my head. "Next time, use your brake." I show the others the slender brake handle. They check their slings, then nod.

Mint goes next and manages to stay slow and controlled. Next goes Jumbo. I'm more concerned with him because he tends to be impulsive and reckless, but he surprises me by moving extra care-fully with his hand clutched to the brake. Only in the final two meters does he release the brake, slide free, and laugh.

Lost is next. He drops faster than Jumbo, but at the end does a full stop, and eases to the roof.

BandStand is the most hesitant. Nervous. He fumbles to get the sling clipped, until finally I help him. He thanks me, then looks everything over again before attempting to sit down.

"What's going on up there?" Mint yells.

"Trying to complete." Band pulls himself into the sling, and checks it one last time.

"It is good." I give the sling a safety hug. "You'll be fine."

He nods and begins to drop. His progress is slow. Lots of starts and stops. When he reaches the bottom, Mint smiles and thumps him on his back.

"Leave me alone," Band says. "I did it."

Mint looks ready to say something.

"Implants!" I get their attention, then strap myself in. I slide as smoothly and with as much control as I can. Near perfect. None of the boys says anything. A couple look impressed.

I disconnect and point to the line that crosses the street ahead. "Going that way next. No braking this time. Just motivate over." I look at Talons. "Slowly."

He laughs. "Can I go first again?"

"No." I look at BandStand. "Band first."

He shakes his head. "Talons can go."

"I know," I say. "But you should."

He frowns, then reaches for the street line. It is beyond his grasp.

"I'll clip you all in." I connect the top of his sling, then hold the rest for him to take.

He looks nervous—conflicted—but grabs the sling anyway and climbs in. He checks the street below. Three stories down. He puts his hands on the motivator control near his right leg. Hesitates.

"You could pull yourself across manually if you want." I point at the line. "Just grab the line and hand over hand it."

He nods, takes the line, and pulls himself a little ways out. Dangling and fragile, but safe. Safer than the streets.

"What's wrong with using the motivator?" Mint asks.

"Nothing," I say. "He's doing it this way. And that's fine."

"Not me."

I smile. "That's fine too."

Band takes ten minutes to make it across. But when he does, he's able to unhook himself and drop lightly to the roof. I'm proud of him.

One by one, the others go. Some faster, with full motivation, others cautiously, evenly. Band is on the other side to help. Now confident and serious.

I sling over to them, and from there, we continue to the next line, and the next. It has been awhile since I've moved this way. I'd forgotten how fun it can be. Sure, you have the occasional free-head staring at you and pointing. But generally, it is fun.

Finally, we reach the charity shop building. The mystery window is only a block away. It is difficult not to look that direction. To not mentally be there already. Searching.

There's a stairway inside. It is creaky and smells of curry, but it is stable and well lit. We take that to the second story, and then take a narrow hallway to the shop. The boys talk the entire way.

A NARROW DOOR LEADS into the shop. On the outside, to the left of the door, is a sign with a green crescent moon oriented so the open end is up with a star in the center. Below the moon are the words of the Founder: "A man's true wealth is the good he does in this world."

The smell reminds me of GrimJack's. Used and fermented. Inside, there are glass counters on either side of the door, separated by a narrow aisle. And beyond, dozens of bots—motionless—standing in rows.

I put out a restraining arm and pause at the door.

I don't see a freehead anywhere. I sense some stream activity. No active servbots, but a few cleaning tools and a snakebot somewhere in the stacks. That's comforting.

"No one around?" Talons says.

I keep my arm up and send them all bubbles of silence.

"Hello?"

A second later, a stack in the back shifts, and a short middle-aged man approaches. His eyes are wide. "So sorry." He puts his hands up. "I was putting things away. So sorry."

I bow. "I contacted you about—"

"I am Tahir." He smiles, then looks past me to smile at the boys. "Yes, you're all here to help. Very good."

I nod. "The boys don't have much experience." I indicate the rows of bots. "They may not be able to handle those."

Tahir glances at the bots and waves. "That is no problem.

Plenty to do here." He smiles again. "I can't believe that you have come. It is an honor to have so many debuggers here." He waves everyone inside. "Come, come. No sense standing in the hall."

"Thank you for having us."

The boys bow and return his smile as they pass him. I'm thankful for that.

We form a small circle, with Tahir as the focus.

A female customer filters in behind us. She's completely in black, but her shuffling gait suggests advanced age. She pauses only a moment, shrugs, and walks through our circle. She peers at each boy as she moves by.

"Yes, come in," Tahir says to the woman. "Much to see here. Ask if you have questions."

The woman waves a hand, and enters the rows of bots.

Tahir smiles, places his hands together. "I have a room of appliances in the back. Would that be appropriate?"

"That should do well," I say. "Thank you."

The old woman pauses in front of a servbot, studying it. She raises a finger and pokes it in the chest. It rocks back slightly.

I'm tempted to stream-start it, and possibly have it talk, but I restrain myself.

We follow Tahir deeper into the store. We reach a storage room with long, white tables. Small appliances, many partially disassembled, are spread out over the tables. There's another door here too. Presumably a back exit.

I get a stream prompt from Mint. A request to reopen their virtual room. Should I allow it?

Mint and Talons are looking at me. Hopeful.

"I don't know that I have everything to fix them," Tahir says. "We may need more parts."

"We'll be fine." I indicate the front of the store. "You have a customer."

Tahir nods, bows, and leaves.

I allow the virtual room's creation. Talons is the first to speak there. "What is this junk? I can't identify half of it."

"If we fixed anything, would he know?" Mint adds.

I close the room. The boys look at me, surprised, but my head is starting to ache, and the room will only make it worse. That wouldn't be productive.

"Use your implants now. Find something to fix, and fix it."

The boys spread out around the tables. Poking and moving things.

"But what if we don't know what these are?" Mint asks.

"Implant, blinking lowlevel," Band says, then squints as a stop hits.

One benefit of stops: Saves lots of correction effort from me.

I circle the room, watching them work.

Talons has a black, rectangular device with a transparent window. "G-wave infused oven," he says. "Guaranteed to cook evenly." He bends forward. "Now not cooking at all."

"Careful with that one."

He smiles. "G-wave generator. I could have lots of fun with that."

"Right," I say. "Don't."

Jumbo has a cricketbot in his hands. His eyes are glassy with expectation. "You will live, little cricket," he whispers.

I smile, keep circulating. "Let's show Tahir what we can get done," I say. "We're debuggers."

Band is the only one who hasn't picked an item. He's watching everyone else, a sad look on his face.

I walk around a table to talk to him. "This is good charity work. *A* will be pleased by our efforts."

He shrugs. "I don't see anything I know."

"Pick something," I say. "There's no grade on this."

He grabs a nearby jumble of parts that, when stretched out, becomes a series of small boxes connected by sinews and nanopaths.

I'm not sure what that is either.

"I don't think I'm meant to fix things," he says.

I shake my head. "Everyone is meant to fix things."

He lifts one of the boxes, looks at it, then puts it down again. "Not these things."

"Maybe not *that* thing." I find another object—a small, green model of a driftbarge. A hovering replica. "Try this." I place it on the table in front of him.

"A toy?" He grips the side of the dredge. Frowns. "Not very important."

I think about BitStack and Snoob. "Important to someone once." I smile. "And maybe again, if you fix it."

He studies me, then pulling the dredge closer, shuts his eyes. Stream touching. Doubtless searching for instructions and specs.

I glance around the room. Everyone is occupied. Some have sheets smoothed over the surface of their chosen project and are peering at the inside.

Tahir arrives at the entrance, places his hands on his hips. "They are busy, yes? Very good."

I drift toward him. "If you like, I may be able to help with some of the bigger things."

"That would be excellent." He steps aside and motions me ahead.

I return to the front of the shop as a male customer enters. He is dressed primarily in blue, with his head wrapped in a turban. He startles when he sees me, but then nods and turns down a side aisle.

I'm reminded of why I'm really here. The research that needs to be done. Would it be better to slip away now, while the initiates are busy?

They'll be disappointed, especially Talons, but they'll be less of a distraction. Contained.

I follow the rows of bots to the front, stopping near the counter. I look at Tahir, who's a few paces behind me. "You have something particular you'd like me to check?"

"Yes, yes." He excuses himself, walks past me, then goes behind the desk. "My credit reader is glitching. Often won't respond to what I enter." He brings out a circular pad. It is gold around the outside, with a dark face. A Solster, model 834. Ten years old. Due for disposal.

He squeezes the device on, and hands it to me. The screen has a handful of dead spots. One of the interface ports is broken, and the shell is darkened from use. I try not to think about the germ exposure, though my fingers itch as I touch it.

"Only some of the characters don't work when I press. The others seem fine."

I nod. "The sensors are issuing errors."

His eyes widen. "Not that I know of."

"No, they are." I point to my head. "I can feel them."

He nods. "Ah yes. I knew you could talk to the machines. I didn't know how it works." He raises his hands. "I'm trying to run a good shop. Help people."

"The machine should be replaced. It is very old. There have been many changes since—"

His eyes go wider. "I checked on a new machine. They are expensive."

I nod and, placing my bag on the counter, begin searching its side pockets. "I have a tool to realign the screen."

"Realign?"

"Make it work better," I say. "At least for now." I find the alignment tool. It is a two-centimeter, semi-permeable, white square. Can't remember the last time I've used it. Guess I need to clean out my debugging bag more often.

I lay the credit device on the counter next to my bag, and place the screen tool on top of it. I rub it over the entire screen. The errors dwindle, and then cease entirely.

I smile, and hand him the device. "There, that should help."

He stares at the reader, starts to manipulate it. "That...does...seem better."

I glance behind him. There's a collection of tacked up items there: Images of people to avoid, pink canceled receipts, a facsimile of the first credit the store earned. There's a list of shop rules there too, the number one being "Always smile".

I notice something else. A printed "A~" between two pages. "What is that there?" I say, pointing.

Tahir remains engrossed with his machine. Smiling. "What?"

I squint and move closer. "What's written there," I say. "Between the papers. On the wall."

He turns and looks. "Those are just receipts of—"

"No. Between them.

He raises an eyebrow.

"Looks like an A and something."

He waves nonchalantly. "That's nothing. Someone playing around."

"Could you move those papers so I can see?"

He shrugs and swats at the pages, widening the space. Revealing more of the formula. That formula. $A \sim A^3$.

He straightens the pages again. "See, it is just a doodle. A nonsense. Nothing more."

"Who put it there?" It is hard not to scream the question. This means something. It has to mean something.

Tahir looks at the door, then beyond me. One of the customers is back there. I can hear him or her moving around. Examining things.

Tahir draws closer. "*A* is," he whispers, then looks at me.

"*A* is?" I squint. "Yes?"

He nods. "Yes, *A is*."

"Of course. This I know. I've been taught since I first could speak. *A* exists. There is no other."

He watches me for a moment, then nods and pulls away. "Very true. Praise A."

I've missed something. The interaction was unusual. The question...a test?

I shake my head. "I'm sorry. Yes, A is—"

My shoulder is brushed by a blue-robed arm. The male customer has a blue and gold audio amplifier in his hand. "How much for this?" he asks.

I ignore the contact, the rudeness, and think. Tahir was looking for a specific response. A phrase or gesture or something.

And I don't know what that is. I have no way of knowing.

The customer agrees on the price. He produces his indent card for Tahir to scan with his now functional reader. The transaction takes ten seconds. The man goes on his way.

Tahir smiles. "That was much better," he says. "You do good work."

I bow. "It is my path. My calling of service."

"Of course." He smiles. "I don't know your name."

"ThreadBare."

"We all are that, aren't we?" He moves to his left, entering the aisle behind the counter.

I trail him on the other side. "You expected an answer from me," I say. "Before. It was a code of some sort."

He grabs a small box, one that rattles as he lifts it. "I'm not sure what you're talking about." He points at the rows of bots. "Would you like to check over those mechanicals? Some work. Some don't."

My head begins to ache. Great time for that.

"Listen, Tahir. I have encountered that formula before. At another shop. I was looking for a friend, and I saw it, though I didn't find her. I need to find her."

He squints. "She's a relative?"

"No," I say. "A friend."

"A spouse?" He stares at the box. Squints at its label. "I thought you weren't allowed such things."

I shake my head, which only makes the pain worse. "This isn't about that." And now, a headbuzz too. "I mean, not really."

"What is this woman's name? I see many people." He shrugs. "You never know."

"Damali."

"That is all?" he says. "Damali?"

"That's all I know. She was with other people. Men. Four of them. Different ages and sizes."

"Four men?"

Suddenly, the pain becomes so intense that I'm forced to steady myself with the counter. And it isn't a stop. It is the broken pain. The wolf pain.

"Are you all right?"

"No," I say. "But I'll be all right. Give me a moment."

The room seems to spin, and I stumble back. My left shoulder encounters someone or something. Then my balance seemingly disappears completely. I fall.

There's an endless crash.

I WAKE UP TO A RING OF FACES. The initiates' faces. They all hover over me, looking concerned. I'm still on the floor. Only twenty seconds have passed.

I look right and see another face—that of an inanimate servbot. Its eyes are closed as if it is resting peacefully. On my left is another bot body, this one turned on its side, facing the other way.

I must've fallen into the row of them. Toppled them like dominoes. Excellent work on my part.

I groan and bring my hands to my face. Delight in the pressure of my palms on my cheeks and eyebrows. It feels normal. Plus, there's no head pain now. At least, not yet.

"Mawla?" Lost says. "You all right?"

Talons puts out a hand. "Need help?"

I nod, and with the assistance of Talons and Mint, climb to my feet.

"What happened?" Jumbo asks.

Tahir is behind the boys, at the edge of the counter. He nods at me. Smiles. "That is not normal, correct?"

"No. Not normal."

"Did you trip?" Jumbo asks. "Sometimes I trip."

"Something like that." I try to hide my own concern. It's the first time that's happened, and it signals a solid turn for the worse. I was worried before, but now I'm scared.

Can't let them see that. They're just starting out. Not broken like me.

I scan their faces. "How are your projects going?"

"Fixed two already." Talons smiles at the others. "So far, I'm ahead."

"Easy stuff," Mint says. "A cracked shell and a slipped motivator."

Talons scowls. "What have you finished?"

"I have my cricket going," Jumbo says. "Working on another one now."

"He wants to fight them," Lost says.

I look at Jumbo and his face goes white. "I wouldn't do that," he says. "They are the shop's property."

"That's right. They are." I look at the others. "As is everything you're working on. This exercise is for the benefit of others. And to give you prac—" I scan their faces again, then silently count. "Where's Band?"

"Still working." Talons nods toward the back room. "Got real involved with that dredge. Lots of scowling and crying."

"Crying?" I look at the back room, then take a step that direction. I get a touch of vertigo, pause, and put out my hands for balance. The room stops spinning.

"Mawla?"

"I'm fine," I say. "Let's get back to work. We only have a couple hours." I approach the back room, expecting to find Band still at work, and possibly stuck.

That's the sort of thing that used to happen to me. Still does. I overthink things, or under-think them. Forget to do the research. Doubt myself.

But Band isn't in the room. I see only the tables of gadgets.

I walk to where his model dredge sits. His bag is there, and his seat is pushed forward neatly.

The other boys file in and find their former seats.

"Band isn't here."

Jumbo and Lost are closest to me. They give me puzzled looks.

Jumbo shrugs. "He was. Restroom, maybe?"

The back door appears to be ajar. I walk to it and swing it open. Beyond is a short hallway and three more doors. Two are clearly marked as restrooms. Male on the left, female on the right.

I knock on the leftmost door. "BandStand?"

No response. I'm hesitant to try to message him. Not when I just had enough head pain to collapse.

I knock on the door again, then try the handle. It opens. The room beyond is small enough that I can see all the plumbing in one glance—sink, toilet, everything. No one is in there.

I knock on the other restroom door. Finding it unlocked, I carefully open it. No one there either.

The third door opens to a longer hallway. At the end of that? A stairway.

Rails. He could be anywhere.

I return to the repair room. I encounter Mint first and ask him to message Band. After a few seconds, he shakes his head. "He's getting it, but he isn't responding. He does that sometimes. Won't message even to say, 'go away.'"

"He's not back there." I raise my hands. "Did anyone see Band leave?"

I'm met with headshakes and blank stares. Not good.

I attempt to message BandStand myself. The message swims into the stream, fights the rapids of inter-implant communication, touches his neural layer, then swims right back again.

He isn't responding. On purpose.

Now I'm a little angry. Runaways aren't supposed to happen. Otherwise, we'd all do it. He must be fighting a barrage of internal stops. Wherever he went, it can't be far.

A master could recall him. A master could put him in so much pain he'd stop in his tracks. But I'm no master. Bamboo is their master until they're released. Should I tell him?

Never. No. Can't.

Have to fix this. Fix it quick.

I jog to the front of the shop. Something about Tahir makes me think I can trust him. Maybe it's the secret formula on the wall. Not sure, but even though he's evasive, no one runs a charity without some good intentions, right? Even a freehead?

I rush down the centermost aisle, hurry past the rows of bots and other techno-items.

Tahir is still behind the counter. He looks up as I step into view. He holds up my repair bag. "You forgot this!"

I thank him, take the bag, and sling it onto my back. How best to phrase what I need? "I have to leave for a moment." I indicate the back room. "The boys—"

"You need to leave them?"

I nod, feeling guilty.

He raises a hand. "They will be fine here," he says. "No problem." He points at the back of the shop. "They are doing good work."

"I think so, yes."

He waves at me. "Go on. Get what you need."

I sprint to the back again. I recreate the virtual room for the boys. Let them know what I'm doing. Talons looks up from his project. "Want us to come help?"

I shake my head. "Stay here," I message. "And stay out of trouble."

"We can help you look!" Jumbo says aloud.

I reach the back door and open it. "Not yet," I message. "If I need help, I'll let you know." I glance at the front of the store. "And if you get in trouble, remember your security pull."

I don't want bluecoats to come after us. Such events always cause stream ripples. Changes to policies. Calls for mandatory position tracking. Every master will be on guard. Watching his debuggers like they are expensive toys.

Which, of course, they are.

I send a bubble of caution to the boys too. A hint of how I feel about bringing in the authorities. How high the bar has to be before that happens. Then I nod at them. And walk out.

I REACH THE STAIRWAY AND PAUSE.

Up or down?

If it were a lift Band had taken—even an archaic device like a mechanical elevator or a compression hover—I'd have an interface to tap into. A way to try to figure out which way he went.

My luck to be in a building with only stairs.

I walk to the stairwell and look up. There are lots of floors up there. Lots of climbing. And what would Band do up there? He could reach the roof and the strings. Possibly try to go back.

His struggle with those makes me think he wouldn't go that way. Plus, he didn't take his bag, so no sling.

The street is closer.

But it is still the street. Sidewalks filled with freeheads and servbots. Pushing, selling, lots of potential contact. And the roadways themselves? Clogged with dredges, heavies, and all manner of transports.

It isn't a place for a child to be alone. Even an implanted one.

Especially an implanted one.

I descend, reach the intermediary landing, and continue to the next set of stairs. When I get to the bottom, where will I go? How will I proceed?

Wait. Cameras! Are there any?

I pull for local cams. There must be some in a place like this. Shops all around. Merchandise and free flowing credits. There should be lots of synthetic eyes.

Talons found one, after all. That's what brought us here.

I reach the rear entrance to the building. Outside is a dingy alley that leads to the nearest sidewalk. There's a mass of pedestrian traffic there. But the alley? Empty.

One by one, camera taps bubble into my stream map. Tiny, stable beacons amid the constant flow. There are four in the immediate vicinity. One above this very door, in fact. I grab that, break its security shell, and fill myself with its images.

I push it back a half hour, and go from there. The images are identical for many minutes. A long, sparse alley with a handful of square, white waste disposals.

Then, at the seventeenth minute, a lone figure exits the building. Bald and dressed in a blue jumpsuit. Child-sized.

BandStand.

I watch as he makes his way down the alley. It is a slow process. He walks for a few steps, then pauses. Sometimes he brings his hand to his head, or simply staggers around. Other times I see him attempt to run forward. That only produces a more sudden and longer pause.

Somehow, he fights through it, though, making it to the end of the alley, and after looking both ways, nearly leaps onto the busy sidewalk. He seems to be go left. South.

My anger has dissipated. Melted by his struggle down the alley. His willful, and doubtless painful, disobedience to the stops. I can't help but be reminded of myself. Finding ways around the pain to complete a task. To be significant.

And where did it get me? Ruined and possibly dead.

My empathy for Band grows. I need to find him. Save him before he hurts himself.

Where could he be going?

There's chatter in the shared room. Some of it is debugging related, but most of it is about me and BandStand. The term "flipped tear" is used more than once. A suggestion that Band's implant is misplaced. Also "skin"—a derogative term for debuggers. Not sure where they heard that one, but we shouldn't be using it about our own. Not ever.

I send them a warning, along with an update. I'm following Band. I know where he went, but not where he's going.

I step into the alley. I'm hit with a nearly overwhelming aroma. A mix of decaying refuse and cinder. Both are from the alley's waste processors. The cinder is from those that work. The other smell? From those that do not.

Someone needs to fix them. Not me. Not now.

I run to the end of the alley, brace myself, and then step into the sidewalk's flow. Two men in full beige robes spot me, pause, and take two full steps toward the street. They then hurry on their way. A man with four women trailing him catches my right heel. He mumbles something, and slows. I don't bother glancing back at him. I know what he and his harem are thinking: What is the debugger doing here?

Every step brings more eyes my direction. I've walked city streets before. I did so often when I worked the heavies. But I was near the end of town then, by the wall. Not like this. Not so busy. So prone to contact. Even the walkways near GrimJack's seemed vacant compared to this.

I try to ignore it all. The constant jostling and the smells. The drone of humanity and tech alike.

I find myself walking on tiptoes. Trying to both narrow myself, and see over the heads in front of me. To get a glimpse of a lone boy in blue. It is difficult to concentrate.

I check the cameras. Search for bubbles in the map ahead. There are too many now. On street corners. On passing vehicles. Nearly every shop or food vendor has an eye. I need to thin the number, filter out those that are in motion and those that are turned the wrong way.

Meanwhile, I have to keep moving. Maintaining my distance from everyone, but without drawing attention to myself.

With the way he was struggling, BandStand would've been like a leaf in a river. Flowing at times. Stuck and spinning at others.

I send the camera bubbles through a subroutine filter. Toss out those that don't matter. Then I sort them by their relation to me. Closest ones first. Now I have a line of relevant visual inputs.

Someone bumps my right shoulder. A short man with an ugly smile. He wears a brown turban and a lighter beige thawb, belted at the midsection.

He glares at me for a second, then spits on the ground. "Unholy property. Why are you dirtying our street? What thing is there for you to love here?"

There's a sense of irony in the question, beyond the suggested foulness. Two RS-model servbots are walking just behind him. They may not be his, but he's literally surrounded by the tech I "love."

I bow my head and say nothing. I focus on the hunt. The boy ahead. I pull the images for the closest useful camera. It is unprotected. I walk back its images. Thousands of them. I find my boy in blue.

"Nothing to say, skin?"

I don't look at the man. I can't focus *and* look at him. "I'm on my master's business."

A laugh, and another nudge. "Who is your master?"

Now I look. "Can I help you?" Another distraction. A freehead distraction.

He spits again. "Not me. I have no need for your kind of help. I have my own slaves."

I bow. "Praise A for your fortune. Please don't disturb me."

I check another camera, one posted at a fruit stand about a half block ahead. BandStand passed it ten minutes ago. In fact, he paused there until the vendor shooed him off. Band staggered away. Fighting stops.

I check the initiates' virtual room. There is little chatter now. Jumbo has erected a timer on the wall. It is labeled: time since Mawla left.

I need someone to work the cameras. The boys probably don't have the skills to unlock secured cameras, but I can handle that. I simply need more eyes on images. More minds.

I message them with instructions. Their messages flood the room's air. They each take a handful of bubbles. Start to view them.

"I can disturb whoever I want," the man says. "I'm a great man."

"At the next intersection you should cross the street," Talons messages. "Band went that way."

The intersection is only ten meters away. There's a large crowd pooled up there, waiting to cross. Pedestrians might wait a long time, I know. Street traffic takes absolute preference.

I glance at the crossing indicator. Then I begin to sense its stream emanations. There's a tap I can connect to. I nudge that. An internal countdown begins. The crosswalk will soon be available.

"We don't need you," the man says. "Don't need your kind."

I still don't look at him. But I can smell him: sweat mixed with strong cologne. He's very close to me now. Too close.

Where are those two RS bots?

I find their emanations. Both are still to the short man's right. Pacing him. I suggest a course correction. A few steps forward, and then over. They find no danger in that, no reason not to obey, so they move.

The crossing indicator changes and the crowd surges ahead. I move with it.

"Your technology ruins us," the man says. "Makes us all slaves. All serv—"

I glance at him now. The servs are in front of him. Shielding me from him. I send another suggestion, and they slow their progress to a crawl. Stranding him at the edge of the crosswalk. Keeping him there.

He raises a fist and shakes it. The servs stare at me, eyes emotionless and unmoving. Their faces unreadable. The crowd rushes around them on both sides. But not short man. He's stuck. He'll be there awhile.

I smile.

"Band made another turn," Mint messages. "At the intersection with...um...Masjid. Turn left."

I nod to myself. Pedestrian traffic has thinned a little. It isn't as oppressive or rushed. For that, I'm thankful.

There's a disturbance ahead. An argument between a shop owner and someone on the sidewalk. Lots of yelling and shaking of fists. A shoe flies between the heads of two women in front of me, hits my chest, then falls to the sidewalk.

People make room for the two combatants. Move around them. No one stops.

The argument continues.

I REACH MASJID STREET and turn left. After a block, the average building height decreases. Only five or six stories. Low enough that I can see sky over them. Feel more sun.

I don't like the buildings' appearance, though. Portions of their signs are missing or faded. The sidewalk is heavily cracked. I spy two shops that are boarded up, with red graffiti streaked across the boards. Most of it is nonsensical, but in one spot there's a stylized "TX" with a slash through it. An antitex symbol.

My muscles tighten. I find myself using my eyes more. Scanning dark alleys and people's faces.

"Where are you going, BandStand?" I whisper. "What is here?"

"Anyone know where he grew up?" I message the virtual room. "Was it near here?"

The room falls silent.

"I think he was a sector over," Talons messages.

"No, it wasn't that far," Mint messages. "I think it was out east of the city. Not near here."

"Maybe someone he knows works there," Jumbo messages. "His dad or something."

"He turned," LostNote messages.

"BandStand?" I ask. "What street?"

"No street. Look for a blue building."

"Blue?"

"Right, it will be on the opposite side of the street. You need to cross."

At the next intersection, I cross over. The pedestrian traffic is even lighter now, and all male. Most dressed in dark clothing.

Across the street are two officers of the vice and virtue ministry, made obvious by their red and white checkered head covering. One of them notices me and points, touching the other's shoulder. They smile. I'm not their usual concern. With me, the implant, the stops, do their work for them.

I follow the sidewalk. The camera bubbles are sparse here too. I need to find Band soon.

Finally, I see the blue building. It is a story higher than the building before it. The wall space is used to shill a popular tea. The ad shows a floating hand pouring from a teapot. The top half is faded while the rest is vibrant. Consequently, the hand looks ghostly as it hovers over a shiny pot.

I tell the boys where I am. I take the alley between buildings. It smells worse than the alley where I started. No cinder smell at all. Only spoiled food. And every waste unit is reporting an error.

What did the short man say again? *We don't need your kind.*

Seems like they need more.

Thankfully, the alley doesn't dead-end, but goes all the way to the rear of the buildings. Beyond, I see lots of green. Trees and grass.

A park?

I jog to the buildings' end. There's a small green space here, maybe a couple hundred meters total. The space is almost circular, with a staggered ring of shade trees around the outside. Near the middle is a playground in primary colors. Red swings, blue slides, yellow climbing bars.

There are a handful of children here with their mothers. Most of them are five years old or younger. New walkers and toddlers. They are clustered around an area of the playground to my left. The toys are smaller there. Plastisteel animals on springs that can be rocked. An area of sand. A small merry-go-round.

The section to the right is for bigger kids. It has full-size swings and slides. There's only one person there. Sitting on the center swing. Facing away from me. A blue jumpsuit.

"I found him," I message the room. "He's here."

"Where's here?"

"Someplace quiet." I share an image. Then think better of it.

The room grows silent, then: "Rails, can we come?" from Jumbo.

I frown. "I'm hopping away for a bit. Get your projects done. And maybe tell the owner where I am. That we'll be back soon."

There are grumbles of acknowledgment. More chatter. Then I drop out. Something tells me I need to focus here.

I walk toward the playground. It seems amiss, this place. A lost island with a sea-like city swirling around it. There's a gentle breeze, and the sun is just warm enough to make it comfortable.

I'm surprised there aren't more children here. But it's the middle of the day. Freehead children have school too.

I reach a spot about four meters from the swings. BandStand isn't actively swinging. More like dangling. He must know I'm nearby. If his implant is functioning, it should sense the presence of another implant. Whether Band recognizes its prompting or not is unknown. The emanations of a debugger can be hard to distinguish in public spaces. But he'll get there. He has little choice.

I open my mouth to speak.

"Hello, Mawla," he says.

I return his greeting. I'm tempted to open a stream connection between us. To connect our minds and share what he's feeling. Make things easier.

But I resist the urge. I place my bag on the ground and take one of the swings next to him. It is high enough for me to sit, but too low to swing. I tuck my feet and let the toes drag.

I check the section where the younger kids play. It is about twenty meters away, and behind a low fence. None of them seem to be looking at us.

"Are you hurt?" I ask.

Band kicks the ground and sways listlessly. "A little." He glances my direction. "Hurt a lot getting here."

"I'm sure it did." I stretch my legs out. Tilt backwards in the swing. "You shouldn't do that. Push through stops like that."

Band shrugs. Kicks with his feet.

"I mean, it could cause damage. Permanent damage."

He gives me a perplexed look. "Bamboo didn't say that."

"Well, he should have, because it happens. Ought to be one of the first things he teaches. Obey the stops."

"How do you know?"

"I just do. Suppressing stops wrecks you, and then you're stuck. Not really a debugger, not really a freehead either."

"Do you know anyone who got wrecked?"

"I know a few." I glance at the younger children again. One of the mothers is gathering her child. Doubtless planning to leave. "Anyway, don't do it. You have a productive life ahead of you."

He stares at the ground, then sets his feet and pushes back lightly.

I check our surroundings. Beyond the trees ahead is a grey six-story building. The lower windows are boarded up, but many of the upper ones are still functional. A few have holes in them, probably abandoned, but some have ragged window dressings. Signs of occupation.

On the third story one of the windows has a red TX circle painted on it. Don't like that.

"Don't leave without the rest of us." I frown. "I didn't think it was possible, but here we are." Two more mothers with children are leaving. "Why are we here?" I ask.

Band pushes himself back, then swoops his feet back and forth, as if attempting to swing higher. The cadence is off, though. He gains no real momentum. Only rocks his swing.

He sniffs and wipes his eyes.

"Are you hurting still?"

"Not my head." He pats his chest. "In here."

I don't know what to do with this. I'm not a teacher or a counselor. I don't even understand my own emotions. "Sorry..."

Band glances at me. "Mom used to bring me here." He points ahead and left. "Her aunt lives over that way. Sometimes we'd visit while my brothers and sisters were at school. She'd bring me here and push me. Just me."

I nod, not knowing what else to do. "How many siblings do you have?"

"Fourteen. But only five from mom."

"It must have been special," I say. "Being here."

He nods. "I have a younger brother. Thought I might—"

"Find them here?"

He shrugs. "Maybe." He attempts to swing again, but manages only a few back-and-forths before slowing. "I never learned how to do this," he says finally. "To swing."

I begin to stand. "Do you want me to push you?"

He shakes his head. "I just want to sit."

I relax again. Tuck my legs.

"I'm a noop, Mawla. A failure."

I force a smile. "You were tested. You can debug, or Bamboo wouldn't have picked you, implanted you. You have everything you need."

"I don't." Another sniff. "Just like swinging. I can't."

The remaining mothers gather their children. Beckon with stern commands.

We'll soon be alone.

"It is normal to feel inadequate," I say. "Below spec. I feel that way all the time."

He looks at me, doubtful.

"I do. And so do all the other initiates. All of them." I smile. "They just won't admit it."

"Maybe." He looks at the ground. "I hear Mint mumbling to himself sometimes. Trying to think outside his head."

"Like maybe it is full?"

He chuckles. "Yeah, maybe. If I ask about it, he gets angry." He looks wistfully ahead, then turns to watch the park-goers walk away. "I miss my family. Miss my mom."

I know what Bamboo would say here. It seems trite and meaningless, but I can't prevent it from coming out. "You have more purpose now than you ever did. Than most people. That should be enough." Those words never helped me. Not really.

"Fixing things because I have to?" He gives me a sad look. "I'd rather have my mom back."

I bundle warmth with my own melancholy, then send it his way. He gets the message and returns a hollow feeling. A lonely feeling.

I lay a hand on his shoulder. "You have a new family now. A very strange, preoccupied, and competitive family." I give his shoulder a squeeze, then remove my hand. "That's about as good as I can do."

He stares at me. I notice a small scar on his chin. Thin and nearly imperceptible, but at least a centimeter long.

Band turns away, kicks, and fails to swing again. "Maybe you could push me a little? Then we can go back."

"That sounds good." I stand and walk around behind him. I grab the chains of the swing above his hips and take a couple long steps backward. Release. He glides forward. Laughs.

I send the other boys an update. I also warn them not to say anything to Band when we get back. Especially anything derogatory.

The stops would probably prevent that, but it pays to be certain. Clearly.

"We're all doing fine here," Talons messages. "Fixing things."

I send a feeling of pride and an image of a gold medal. The boys cheer.

Right then I notice, through the trees, the front door of the grey building open, and two men exit. Black shirts and pants. Black masks with only their eyes showing.

Not good.

I WAIT FOR BAND TO SWING back toward me, then grab the swing above his head and bring him to a stop.

"Rails!" Band looks at me. "Why did you do that?"

I indicate the front of the building, and the men. They are looking our direction. One of them points, and they head our way.

"We need to go." I retrieve my bag from the ground. "Now."

He hops out of the seat. "I still don't—"

I push an image of the men his way, along with a red band of concern.

He looks at the men, then moves next to me. "We can pull security on them, right? Get the blue coats?"

"No time for that." I face the alley and wave. "This way! Back the way we came."

We start to sprint. He's fast for a ten-year-old. Thankfully.

There are shouts from behind us. The claps of running feet.

I take comfort in the distances. The alley is only twenty meters ahead. The men have to cross more than that to reach the swings. We should have plenty of time.

Via the stream, I urge Band to keep moving. First to the alley, then to the streets and the protection of the crowds.

He says he can run like this forever.

I feel even better. Hopeful.

The wolf ache sneaks into my head. It isn't large yet, the pain. Isn't too hungry. But it is present. Waiting to pounce.

I try to focus on the alley. Its only fifteen meters now. We can easily make it.

The footfalls have softened, meaning the men have doubtless reached the grass behind us.

Should I pull security? Reveal our location? Any hope of finding Damali would be gone. Possibly forever.

I hear a whistle, followed by a strange sound. A repetitive tapping, fast-paced and approaching us from our left. I glance that direction and see a meter-high silver blur.

"What is that?" Band messages.

"Don't look," I respond. "Keep on for the alley."

I need the stream now, despite the wolf. I push through the layer of pain-induced ice and stone. Search for the metal blur's emanations. Its signature.

I can't find it, though. Can't feel any bot presence whatsoever. At least, not yet.

I hear another whistle and a second set of tapping feet. On our right this time.

"Mawla!"

Band is just ahead of me now. Still pacing me, but for how long?

The other bot is closer than the first. It has an oval head, four legs, and a sleek, horizontal body. It has a skipping, unnatural gait, but it is quick. It reminds me of a cat, minus some of the smoothness. At our current rate, it will overtake us in the alley somewhere.

I stream reach for that one too. Try to find something I can hold on to and manipulate.

Still nothing. It is as if it has no stream presence whatsoever. Except it must! Otherwise, the men would be unable to control it.

I recall Snoob and its closed architecture. Meant to be fixed only at the factory. Are these bots someone's toys, as well?

Ten meters. Only ten meters until the alley. Not far.

I should notify security. Bring the blue coats. If not for me, then for BandStand. For his safety. Except they won't be quick enough to save us from the bots.

How do I protect us? Give us time?

"They're called 'panthers'," Band messages. "Those things. Good at running, seeing, smelling. Good climbers."

I glance at him.

He raises his hands. "I looked them up."

We reach the alley, and I scan for a quicker way of escape. An open doorway, a high place we can reach. Something.

But all I see are six, evenly-spaced, waste processors. Four to our right, two to our left.

Their tops will open! Could we climb inside?

Only if we want to risk being processed as waste. My nose tells me they aren't working, but I'd hate to be wrong. I'd also hate to sit in garbage. Hate that a lot.

The lead bot is close now. Its tap-tap is all I can hear, aside from my own breathing.

I angle right toward the nearest waste unit. We could climb onto it. Get off the pavement. Would that help?

I notice a rusted ladder above one of the units further ahead. The trailing edge of an old fire escape. It ends at an empty frame. No platform. No floor.

Rails, that's no help. Not if both of us have to climb it.

There's a broken window ahead on our left. One without boards. Too high to reach directly, but...there's a waste unit near it.

I wave at Band and sprint to that unit. It smells horrible. The kind of heavy rot that three trips to the steamer won't remove.

I throw my weight into it. It screeches, moves about half a meter, then stops. Still too far from the window.

I discover the panther's stream presence. Nothing I can touch, but it's there now, like a ball of needles at the edge of my perception. The ball has reached the alley and has slowed. Surveying its path ahead. Locating us.

BandStand joins me. Pushes. The waste unit inches forward. Soon, the window is close enough to make climbing possible. I help BandStand onto the top, and he scrambles through the opening.

I have no idea what's on the other side. Hopefully, not a floor of upturned daggers.

The wolf of my mind becomes a monster, maybe from the intense streaming. It makes focusing difficult. My head is full of pain.

I glance back. The panther is sprinting toward us now. It has a mouth of metal teeth. Wide open.

I jump and somehow manage to get myself onto the waste unit. Band is at the window now. Urging me on. I strip off my bag and hand it to him.

The panther grabs the side of my right leg. Pinches my skin. I shift and pull. Its grip slips from my leg, but retains the material of my jumpsuit. It lurches back, tugs hard.

I grip the window ledge and struggle to get away. To get inside. I hear a ripping sound, and my leg breaks free. I vault through the opening—

I land in broken glass. I hop up and check myself over. I'm not bleeding. My suit shielded me from glass and panther alike. My only loss is my right pant leg, now missing at the knee.

The room is littered with bricks, odd-shaped boards, and bags of plaster. Otherwise, it is unoccupied.

There's a heavy thump as the panther leaps for the top of the waste unit. Silver forelimbs scrape for traction; then the bot falls away. It tries a second time, and manages to get a hold on the unit's edge. It ratchets itself up and forward. Its mouth is clamped shut, but beneath a silver brow are two red eyes, both fixed on the goal. On us.

"Good climbers," Band mutters, breathing hard.

"Right." I search the room again. There's nothing tall enough to block the window. Nothing to slow the panther down.

I massage my forehead, try to mute the pain somehow. I take large gulps of air. I need to slow down. Reduce the pounding.

"There's a door!" Band points across the room. "Come on!"

I follow his lead. The door is worn and hanging on its hinges. Band tries, but a simple tug won't budge it. I grab the handle, lean back, then jerk it twice. It shudders free and I tumble to the floor. More pain.

"Mawla?"

I wave him off and climb to my feet. We jog into the next room. There are boxes in one corner, and a light green floor that bears evidence of earlier occupants—circular stains and dirt outlines from furniture and appliances.

There's a crash from the room behind us. I feel the spiked ball's presence. The panther is in the building. The second one is close too. Possibly at the window.

We hurry to the next door. It opens without difficulty. There's a hallway beyond. No signs of people. I count three other doors, and a stairway at the far end. I hustle Band out of the room and shut the door behind him. The bot is back there somewhere. Trailing us.

"Which way?" Band asks.

I run toward the stairs. We can't risk the streets now. Anyone, anything, could be out there. Our only chance of escape is up. I start climbing.

Band stays right behind me. "Where are we going?" he messages.

"Roof."

"What for?"

I tap my bag. "Strings. There will be strings."

He doesn't respond. We ascend one flight of steps, then another. Soon a familiar sound echoes up the stairwell. Tap, tappity, tap, tap. The taps seem so close together. So much faster than my steps.

I try to concentrate on our goal, but it is difficult. The clicks seem so fast, so close together. Much faster than my steps.

"I think they're both down there," Band says.

I nod. "Good climbers..."

We take three more flights before we reach the roof. That door is difficult to open too, heavy and metal, but together we manage. No one falls this time.

We push the door shut with a "thunk." I study it a bit, wondering if the bots will be able to open it.

I think through the contents of my bag. I have a large fuser. Both the door and the frame are metal. That might work. I explain my intent, then start fishing through my bag. "Look for the line to the next building."

Band looks all directions. "Which building?"

"Any of them." I find the fuser. It is cylindrical and thumb activated. Fits neatly in my palm. I crouch near the door and light the tool. I set it to its widest setting. An arc of blue light springs from the end. I apply it to the seam between door and frame. Sparks and smoke emerge, but after a few seconds, I'm rewarded with a couple centimeters of smooth surface. A place where door and frame are now one.

I can sense one of the panthers on the floor below us.

"I found a line," Band yells.

Band is on the north edge of the building, hand on a line. North is generally the direction we need to go: toward the shop and the other initiates. There's another building beyond this one, which is doubtless string accessible too. We might be safe.

I check the door. Should I fuse more? The bond is strong enough to hold against a man, even a heavy man. But a bot?

I get a nudge from the virtual room. There are hundreds of questions swirling through the air there. Too many to address directly. The boys are anxious.

Should I send them back to Bamboo, or have them wait? What would be wiser? What would produce the best result?

I don't like either option. I give them a quick update, along with what to tell the shopkeeper.

The obvious choice now would be to contact security. So why do I hesitate? Because I don't know who the enemies are anymore.

Plus, if antitex wants us dead, it doesn't matter. The only hope we have is getting free first. Getting away.

I jog to the edge of the building.

BandStand's eyes follow me over. He looks at the line, and back toward the door again. His hands are clenched at his side. "Is it blocked? Are we safe?"

"Fused it." I open my bag and take out my sling. "But I'm not sure if we're safe."

He studies the sling. "We only have one."

I nod. "Right. You're going to take it over."

There's a stream of pedestrians below, but they are four stories down. Too far for them to notice us. No one is looking our way.

"But what about you?"

"When you get there, you're going to send it back." I point at the top of the sling where the motor is located. "Just reorient it and start it. I'll grab it when it gets back."

He nods and takes the sling. He stretches it out and starts to attach it to the line terminus—just like he learned only a few hours ago. And like then, there's little hurry in his actions. He's deliberate and thorough. It is hard not to be impatient. To not take the—

The panther is at the door. There's a loud bang. And then another.

"Quickly."

He nods and settles into the sling.

Another bang, followed by a squeal. The bond is breaking.

I should have fused more of it. Like maybe the whole thing.

Band pulls himself into the expanse between buildings, then reaches up and activates the sling's motor. He speeds away.

A louder bang, a metal shriek, and then a "thunk."

The door is still in place, but it is bowed in the middle. Definitely should have fused more.

BandStand is three quarters of the way across. I feel a twinge of pride now. His progress is much better than before. More confident. He's sitting upright in the sling. Looks comfortable.

Can't do this? He's better than he thinks.

I try to reach the spiked ball that is the panther. Is there a way to crack its shell? If it is using the stream, then there should be something I can do.

Band found the designation of the bot. Where? I push through the pain again. Start a search.

Band reaches the other side and carefully climbs free of the sling. He turns and waves at me, then attempts to reorient the sling.

I message him encouragement and instructions on how to turn it.

He gets it unlocked. Swings it around. Starts it moving.

I smile. Now empty, the sling hums along. I grip the line and lean over the edge. Ready.

There's another thump, followed by a series of cracks.

I look back. The panther stands in an empty doorway, door lying on the ground beneath it. Completely off its hinges. The panther's eyes move over the roof's surface. It finds me.

The sling hits the line terminus. I fumble with it. Unlock the top and reorient it.

Band messages me to hurry.

I stretch the sling out and pull myself into the seat. I pull myself out and over the sidewalk. I hear the tap, tappity, tap behind me. I engage the motor and glory in its steady whine as it speeds me away. I smell the scents of the street. Food, sweat, and petrochemicals.

My head aches, but only dully. Not debilitating.

BandStand waits with one hand out.

I smile. We had a scare. Nothing more. Antitex is bolder now than usual. New machines. New toys.

I glance back. The panther is up on two legs, leaning against the line's support pole. I don't like the look of that. The poles are made to take a lot...but that bot just knocked down a metal door.

Can't help that. Have to move ahead. Keep on toward the goal. I focus on Band. He waves, but looks nervous.

Then I see something that stops my heart.

On the roof behind him.

The other panther.

Good climbers.

I REACH THE OTHER SIDE, but it is a meaningless victory. As I dismount the sling, the other panther lopes up on us, then stops three meters away. It doesn't attack, but when I attempt to move around it, it lowers its head and emits a hissing shriek.

Meanwhile, the first panther climbs onto the line between buildings and walks nimbly down it. It then crouches on the edge of the building behind us. Watching.

"I'm afraid," BandStand says.

"I'm contacting enforcement."

"I already did." Band looks at me apologetically.

"When?"

"About ten minutes ago." He points at the first panther. "When we were on the stairs."

"No hiding now, then." I crouch beside him and scan the rooftop. It is completely flat, aside from a central access way. There are other lines, both ahead and right, but to reach them we would have to move past the second panther.

I focus on the bot's red eyes, and then feel for it in the stream. It is still a spiked ball, seemingly hovering in front of me. I create a subroutine to survey the spikes. To note any patterns, any consistencies I can take advantage of.

Yes, the system is protected, but the protection was written by men—doubtless freeheads and not debuggers—so it has to be vulnerable. It will only take time.

"You found the panthers on the stream," I message Band. "Where?"

"They're made by ResAlt," he responds. "They used them for security at my parents' work."

"Must have been a nice place."

"It was dark and smelled funny."

"Yes, like that."

I find the ResAlt domain and search for specs, code briefs, tech manuals—anything I can use. There isn't much.

My subroutine finishes. It notes eight spikes that are potential communication taps. It needs more information to know for sure. More variety.

I give life to the subroutine again, then stand and walk toward the second panther. It lowers its head. I back away and move toward the line with our original assailant.

That panther stands and hops from the line. It then takes a defensive position similar to the other: wide stance and lowered head.

I check the subroutine. It has narrowed the relevant spikes to three. Progress, but still far too many. Need more study. More time.

Men emerge onto the roof from the access way. Hooded men in dark clothing. One has the antitex symbol scrawled on his hood in red.

I feel fear and disappointment. I let Band down. I let Bamboo down. I squandered my only opportunity to find Damali.

I hear sirens in the distance. BandStand's call being answered. If we can hold out, they'll find us. Use locators on our implants.

The men close in behind the second panther. One is clearly the leader. Not the one with the symbol, but another. He's the thinnest one of the group.

I address him. "What do you want?"

He cocks his head but says nothing.

I nod toward the nearest panther. "Your bots are in violation of multiple laws. They are shielded to outside emergency restraint, and they have pursued two data relocators without cause."

Still no response.

"The penalty for hindering us is severe." I look at them one at a time. "You will lose your heads."

The symbol-bearing man raises his hand. In it is a long machete. He looks at the other men. All of them laugh.

I move in front of Band. He's too young for this. We both are.

I message the initiates' virtual room and tell them to retrace their steps to the pylon and the string. To summon downriders and get back to the facility. Back to safety.

"We're property of the ulama and the Imam."

The leader laughs. "You belong to us now. Both you and your heads."

The sirens are west of us and getting closer. Enough that the leader turns to look. He snorts, and then gestures. "Prepare them. We must be quick."

Two men, the symbol-bearer and another, rush over to us. I take a step backwards, toward the edge of the roof.

"Band," I message. "I hate to think this, but maybe we should..." I look at the edge. I don't want to see him decapitated, and I doubt he wants to see me beheaded either. Suicide will bring on a headbuzz for both of us, but at this point, what does that matter?

As if reading my intent, the first panther closes in behind me, placing itself between me and the drop. It hisses.

The leader grabs my shoulders, and then my arms. Another man similarly restrains Band. Another takes my debugging bag, then pushes my head forward.

Symbol-bearer steps in front of me. I can no longer see his hand, but I know what is in it. I can sense the blade overhead. Hovering, positioning for the kill.

This will be a first for antitex, I realize—attacking a debugger directly. What will it mean for the other DRs? And is this what Tall warned about? I hate all the mysteries. I hate being unable to solve them.

"Mawla," Band says. "What are they doing?"

"Shut your eyes," I message. "Pray. Our destiny is guaranteed."

"By who?" he asks.

"The ulama and the Imam."

"Will they be there to greet us?"

A hood is pushed over my head and I'm led forward. I hear a

door open, and I'm hoisted by my armpits. Next come the sounds of footfalls on stairs. Hurried. Occasionally there are grunts and curses, as well as directions from the leader.

What is happening?

Something else is strange. I feel claustrophobic and contained within the hood. It is like it is a thousand times heavier than it should be. It is suffocating me, yet I *can* breathe. I'm breathing now.

Then it hits me.

The stream is gone!

I try to message Band, but I'm unable. The bundle returns immediately.

The hood must be shielded. Breaking my stream connection.

For a second, I marvel at the feeling. The absolute solitude of it. After a minute or two, though, it becomes torturous. Like I've lost my sense of touch.

There's nothing out there. Nothing. I *need* something.

I yell.

Band yells too, his voice a high-pitched echo.

Men curse and toss me roughly about. Then I hear the leader call for gags. A hand reaches inside my hood, claws at my face. It shoves a rag tasting of vinegar inside my mouth, then tapes it in place.

Ten minutes go by, then twenty. We are in motion the entire time. Being moved, herded. Lots of footsteps. Doors open and close. There's a period when I'm sure we are outside, because I recognize street noise even through the hood. Then more doors. More stairs. More grunts and muted instructions.

I feel ill. My head doesn't hurt, but my stomach aches. I worry for BandStand. I'm the worst instructor ever. The worst debugger. The worst friend.

After a half hour of travel, I'm brought into a room and pushed into a chair. My arms are tied behind me. My feet are strapped to the chair itself.

More footsteps, and a door closes.

I try to push the rag out with my tongue. To pry the tape away. All to no avail.

"Hello!" I scream into a deadened stream. "I need help! I'm here. I've been taken. I'm alone."

Am I alone?

How would I know if I wasn't?

I quiet my mind and try to listen. I hear muffled voices, distant voices, and movement somewhere. Then another door slams shut, and everything is still.

I concentrate for a few seconds more. At the edge of my perception, I think I hear water dripping.

What can I do?

I push on the floor with my feet, and attempt to slide the chair forward. It creaks, but doesn't move. I then throw my weight against my bonds, rocking forward, then kicking back.

Still nothing.

I push again and try to hop the chair. That only hurts my arms as they rub along the seat back. The chair is fixed to the floor. Won't move at all.

This is terrible. Awful. My mind needs to be active. Needs to have something to do. How much time has passed since I was brought here?

Seven minutes, twenty seconds.

Awful, terrible, bad.

Wait.

They haven't stopped my implant. It may not be able to communicate, but it is still here. With me. Inside my head. I can solve problems here. I can even reconstruct my surroundings. Imagine that I'm by a pool with Damali. The implant will make it seem a reality.

A false reality. One that will never suffice. Never exist.

I shake my head. That would put additional strain on my implant. Risk my head. If I want to step away, the best answer is a datamix.

Do I have any? I have the one that WindCypher sent me, because he was "buy only," but I don't want to watch that again. Not now.

Wait, didn't Cypher say there were two mixes he could send me? Did he send both? His price was high. Maybe he sent both? That would be reasonable.

I check the package from Cypher. It is heavy. Larger than I'd expect for a single mix. A good sign! I find the mix I viewed already and set it aside. There's a second level to the package. Yet unopened. Another mix!

Perfect. Much better than fighting my own thoughts. Or listening to water drip. I don't bother with the introductory text. The author or title. I start the mix, and wait.

I'M IN MY ROOM. It is late evening. I doubt anyone else is awake. I should be in my sleep chute resting and preparing for tomorrow. And yet...

It has been two days since I swapped Snoob for Raahil. Am I thinking impulsively now? Have I acted so? I'm not sure. But I feel impulsive. I feel out-of-spec and abnormal.

My actions and thoughts have been affected. The differences have been subtle and small. But they feel big. Large. Like drops of lemon in a sea of sugar.

Something about the process of Snoob's transfer. The ending of one life for another. The facade of Obaid's plaything. Also, Raahil's words as she left: *The rest of us try. But you believe.*

Believe? What do debuggers believe? We know discipline, we possess knowledge, but we don't know belief. Not really.

In one of her lessons, Raahil instructed Obaid on the prophets. Nuh, Dawud, Musa and the Founder. She told him incredible things. Of giants and waterships. Sea crossings. All of this I've heard since my youth. I could stream the stories at any moment. But miracles I could not believe. Debuggers do not need miracles. We create our own.

In our universe, everything happens for a reason. And not just *for* a reason, but *by* reason itself. Through logic. Rules create our boundaries, and step-by-step precision moves us ahead. One project after another.

But I find that my logic is in flux. I'm especially curious about Isa now. The miracle prophet. I searched the scriptures for all references. The name of the Founder is referenced four times. Isa is referenced twenty-five times.

So, he has special prominence. In fact, the only female name in the whole of our sacred books is that of Isa's mother, Miriam.

And yes, what Raahil taught is correct. The other prophets, even the Founder, have no miracles attributed to them. To their own force of will. But Isa? Many.

Many.

Why am I curious? Why the sudden interest in miracles?

Because of my walk. Yesterday, after my chores were complete, I walked around the park. The boundary is three kilometers square. A comfortable distance. Adequate exercise.

It was a beautiful fall day. The temperature was cool, but not uncomfortable. Obaid and his mother were away. The whole family was occupied in some fashion. So I walked.

I watched children at play. Birds fluttering and squawking in the trees. Squirrels chattering. I paused and drifted. Making my way like a cottonwood seed. Drifting and floating. For over an hour I did this.

When I returned home, I took a different path into the house. Instead of entering by the back entrance, I went around to the side. Even more than the back, it is a service entrance. It is also where the waste processor is stored, along with unfinished home projects—a reason I typically avoid it.

Why did I take it yesterday? I don't know.

It is a narrow, unpaved path, followed by a door through the fence. As soon as I opened the fence, I noticed the presence of abandonment and waste. It was a subtle scent—the processor was performing its duties—but it was present.

Ahead and to my right was the chest-high processor. There were many large empty boxes and transparent bags mounded against it. Refuse waiting to be incinerated. The cleaning lady was behind in her duties.

I nearly turned back and chose another way, but the entrance door was on my left. Only a few steps past the fence.

I streamed the door open, and prepared to quickly walk in. But somehow, my eyes were drawn to the trash. The bags and boxes again.

Then I saw it. The toy, Snoob. It was placed, recklessly, atop one of the bags. Awaiting destruction.

I was compelled to check it. The toy was so exposed that I thought Obaid might have guessed the ruse and thrown the new one away. I glanced all directions, then walked to the bag the toy was placed on. After visually inspecting it for extra grime, I picked it up.

I turned it over in my hands and noticed the seams that I'd opened before, along with other small imperfections—a tiny stain here, a thin spot in the fur there.

No, it was the original Snoob, not the new one. Not the impostor.

I looked it over once more, and even patted its head with familiarity. Then I grabbed one of the bags, and untying the restraint, was about to place Snoob within.

The careless housekeeper would've ruined the whole thing. Spoiled Raahil's plan. It was fortunate I'd taken a different route. Fortunate I'd come by when I had.

Yet, as I opened the bag and started to put Snoob inside, I saw his eyes. I knew he was broken. He wasn't even turned on, so was totally inanimate. But I felt a strange sympathy for him. I may have been a victim of the bonding program he was infused with. The way he, it, was coded to establish an emotional connection.

There was something else, though, too. Possibly my own pride. My own sense of failure.

So, I didn't put Snoob in the bag. I didn't hide him away or put him in the waste processor. I picked him up, pulled off my tool bag, and placed him inside.

Now I sit with him in my hands again. Here, in my room.

I study him a long moment. Then, feeling behind his ear, I switch him on.

He purrs to life. Looks at me.

I place him on the floor. He loses his balance and topples onto his back. He puts a hand out and tries to sit up again, but his malfunctioning legs, their lameness, make it impossible. He tries and tries, but stays on his back. Finally, his programming lets him remain that way. Simply staring at the ceiling.

In my research, I found the writings of a scholar. He stated that all was created by the word. I'm perplexed by what that means.

Was "the word" creation or creator? If a creator, then that would make it equal with A. But A has no equals. If the word is creation, then how did it create itself? Another impossibility.

A quandary.

"I will try, Snoob," I say. "I will do my best."

I pull my tool bag close and fish out a sheet. I will start by examining Snoob's motivator again.

Why am I doing this? Attempting to fix a broken toy?

Because I find I want to believe in miracles?

Perhaps because I want to make one happen.

I HEAR MOVEMENT AGAIN and open my eyes. I see only the inner surface of the hood. The dark weave of its material. The gag still tastes terrible. Made worse by the dampness it has leached from my mouth. It wets the side of my face, and the scent of saliva is pervasive. There is a slick of wetness on the hood in front of my nose too. Doubtless from my breath.

I'm in a world of discomfort. Isolated. Streamless. Dark and sickly damp.

Somewhere, BandStand is in the same position. He may not miss the stream as much as I do, not having been exposed to it for as long. But he certainly feels the isolation.

I'm worried for him. For us both.

What can I do?

How far are we from where we started? Can the bluecoats find us? The hoods have complicated their search. Our lives. They won't be able to use locators, but there are other methods. Cricket and snake bots. That won't be their first step because that process really stirs up a neighborhood. Gives recruiting fodder for antitex.

But eventually they'll come. I hope.

Footfalls grow closer, then the door clanks open. "I assume you can hear me?" a voice asks.

I nod.

"Very good. I'm going to remove your hood now."

I wait expectantly. It would take a nanosecond of exposure for the authorities to pinpoint my location. Two nanoseconds for me to send the coordinates to them in flowery prose, wrapped in a bow.

"You will try to connect to your stream," the voice says, sounding amused, "but I will save you the effort. This room is shielded from it. Little different than under the hood. Understand?"

I nod again. Slowly.

I feel pressure at my neck, the scratching sounds of clasps being undone, then the hood is pulled away and the gag removed. Cool air touches my face. It feels even cooler on the spots that are wet. I'm embarrassed by my own unwanted discomfort. My humanity.

The room is small, dim, and featureless. There is a single light, placed almost directly overhead. There is rudimentary plumbing and a thin, single mattress bed. No sleep chute. No steamer.

The speaker is shrouded in his own dark mask. There are holes for his eyes and mouth. The only distinguishing features I can see are brown eyes and straight teeth. Nothing useful, even if I had the stream.

Behind him are two more men, similarly masked. They hold black guns at their waists.

The speaker smiles. "Are you comfortable?"

Comfortable?

"Where's the boy who was with me?"

He smiles. "In his own room. He's fine."

"I would like to see him." I try to think of something I can say that will make my request seem imperative. "He has a medical condition. I need to make sure he's well." A lie, but protecting the initiates is my purpose now. I receive a headbuzz, but it is light. My implant understands.

"What was that?" the man says.

"What was what?"

"Your eye twitched."

"I'm uncomfortable," I say. "Everything is uncomfortable. My hands, my feet. Everything."

He smiles, nods. "Yes, it must seem so." He looks at the man to his left. "He's used to palaces. They all are."

The men chuckle.

"What do you want from me? I'm bound to the law. Forbidden from breaking it. The device in my head has—"

"Stops." The man smiles and nods again. "Yes, I'm aware."

I straighten, feeling the tension on my hands and feet. "If you're aware, then you know I'm no good to you. Neither of us are." I lean forward. "But if you let us go—"

He raises a hand. "If I let you go, then what? They'll go easy on us? Reduce the bounty on our heads?" He glances at the other men. "I think not."

I stare at him a long moment, trying to think what the goal might be. What their aim is, given their penchant for destruction. I'm surprised I'm still alive.

"We have tasks for you," he says. "Tasks you can complete."

"Not for you," I say. "I'm not my own master. I'm not free like you are. I can't work for anyone. My head—"

He smiles. "You can do more than you realize. Much more than you've been taught."

I nearly laugh. Yes, I can push the rules. But I know how that works out. There are consequences. Fraught consequences.

As if on cue, my head starts to throb. I look at the floor, and breathe. Try to keep my outward response minimal. I don't want to pass out again. Hope that doesn't happen.

The leader walks closer. "What are you doing, debugger?" He bends over. "Are you sick?"

"No..." I shake my head. "I'm just uncomfortable. I told you, sitting like this, being away from the stream. It's uncomfortable!"

"Ah, but is it so unusual? Your sleep devices remove the stream from you, do they not?"

I look up and find his face a half meter from mine. Too close. "No. Chutes only mute it. Make it compatible with a sleeping mind."

He straightens, looks at the other men, and points at me. "Their sleeping minds need it harnessed, yet they still beg to have it back when awake. See how unnatural they are? How deviant?"

The pain in my head is easing, so I concentrate on breathing. On letting it pass.

"You have nothing to say?"

"You appear to know everything already."

The man laughs, then steps forward and slaps me. The sting is a blessing. It knocks the other pain away. Or distances it somehow.

"What do you want of me?"

"This is a good tone now," he says. "The tone of a servant."

I shrug. "But I still can't—"

He raises a finger. "It's true, I cannot control you like your master." He pantomimes holding something in his hand and pressing buttons. "I don't have one of their, what is it, controllers?"

He extends a forefinger again. "But I do have ways of persuasion." He looks at the men. "Old ways, but no less efficient. No less useful."

He snaps his fingers at the man on his right. "You have it, yes?"

The man nods and produces a small, flat satchel. He hands it to the leader.

The leader smiles, and opening the satchel, produces a square vidscreen. He draws closer to me and places it in front of my eyes. It has a hairline crack on the left side, but otherwise looks fine. At his touch, it flashes, then shimmers to life.

"You can see this?"

"Yes." Dread fills me. I don't know what's coming, but it can't be good. Nothing antitex does is good.

He nods, smiles. "Very good." He touches the screen on the top, then middle left. An image comes into focus. A room similar to mine, with a hooded boy seated on a chair in the center.

"First," he says, "There is your boy. Unharmed, as you can see."

"I can't tell that," I say. "His face is covered."

He glances at the vid. Smiles. "So it is. You will have to take my word for it, then. He's fine. Enjoying his freedom from your stream."

He manipulates the vid again. "Now, here is something else." The image changes to that of another room like mine, only brighter—easier to see the details.

Seated in the center is another hooded prisoner. I assume he's a debugger because he's wearing the standard blue jumpsuit.

"This is an earlier recording," the leader says.

I nod.

There are two masked men standing behind the debugger. Possibly the same men who are in the room with me. Then another masked man comes into view. From the teeth and eyes, I think it is the leader. The mouth of his image begins to move, but I can't hear anything.

He looks at me. "I have shut off the sound. You won't need the sound."

The debugger's jumpsuit looks dirty, especially at the knees and chest. There's defeat in his posture. Whoever it is, I wish I could stream him a bundle of encouragement and strength. Maybe flavor it with some ice cream.

In the image, the leader is holding a machete. Probably the same one he had when we first met. My sense of dread grows.

"I don't want to watch this." I turn my eyes toward the floor. "Whatever it is."

He lowers the vidscreen so I can see it again. "But you must. It shows our way of persuasion. It will help you."

I shake my head and look away to the right. "Don't want to."

"Such a child." He pats my head. "Don't make me have my friends hold your eyes open. They won't be gentle."

I glance at the vid again. The leader's hand is poised at the top of the debugger's head, resting on the hood. Both are in the center of the frame. The leader speaks to the camera, then pulls the hood away.

I look at the debugger's face. His skin is a darker shade than mine. There appear to be some bruises too...

My heart stops. "FrontLot?"

"You know this infidel?" The leader smiles, then looks at his men. "He knows him. All the better!"

Emotions are swirling now. FrontLot was in danger, and all I did was find another mix provider. Another mix. Guilt and anger mixes with my dread. The wolf returns too.

"We asked your friend to help us," the leader says. "He refused. Said it was too difficult. That it hurt his head."

"It *would* hurt his—"

"We know from others what is possible." The leader points

at the vidscreen. "This one was being rebellious. Not being a good servant."

"He's not your servant! He serves A. He serves his—"

"That is not my concern!" He straightens and makes a small circle around the room. He then holds up the screen and points at it. "He refused us."

"Because it—"

"He said it hurt his head!" He smiles. "So I helped him with that problem."

He brings the vidscreen closer, but I close my eyes.

"Refusing to watch again? Very well, I'll restore the sound."

There are screams. Shrieks from my friend that seem to last forever. Then silence.

"You can open your eyes," the leader says. "It is finished." He bends over me again. I can smell garlic on his breath. See the veins in his eyes. "You know what happened?"

I nod.

"Good, because it could happen again."

I almost can't speak. Frontlot is gone. Frontlot! The wolf begins to roar, overwhelming my thoughts. Accentuating my emotions. "Do what you want to me," I say. "Just let the boy—"

"Let the boy, what? Go home?" He chuckles. "Why should I do that?"

"Because you have me," I say. "I'm higher level. I can do more. He's recently implanted. Not seasoned. Not fully healed."

He smiles. "I'm sure that's true. But he is my motivator. The thing that will keep you in place." He taps the vidscreen. "Remember what you saw. Remember what you heard. The same could happen to the boy, unless you comply with our wishes."

"And what are your wishes?"

He hands the vidscreen back to the man with the satchel, who then puts it away. "Only fix some machines for us. That is what you are made for, correct? Fixing machines?"

My head is filled with wolf-pain now. I fight to keep my eyes open. To focus on the leader. To try to seem normal.

How can I do anything for these animals? I can barely think straight.

"Are you willing to help?" he says.

I stare at the floor, still stunned. Still filled with pain. "I don't know what I can do," I say. "There's only so much I can do."

"But will you try?"

I think about FrontLot. Then of BandStand. The boy who didn't even want to be a debugger. Who misses his mother so much that he'd fight stops to go where she used to swing him.

I nod slowly. "Yes, I will try."

THE LEADER SMILES BRIGHTLY. "I knew it," he says. "I knew this was the day. After my evening prayers last night, I felt that sunrise would bring us victory." He looks at the other men. "And here it is. May A be praised." He snaps a finger at his rightmost companion. "The shield."

The companion responds on cue and produces the hood. Walks toward me.

What are they doing? "I said I'd work for you. I need my eyes to work."

Despite my protests, he shoves the hood over my head. It is damp from the last time I wore it, and the smell is worse. The interior feels rougher too. It grates on my cheeks and forehead.

"Yes, you will work," the leader says. "But not here." A pause. "Don't forget the gag."

The gag is again pushed into place. It tastes worse too—a mixture of oil and salt. It makes my eyes water.

They release me from the chair, take my arms, and lead me—roughly—into the hall. The door clanks shut, and I'm turned to the left and shoved ahead. I'm likewise prodded and pushed for the next eight minutes. Then someone's foot strikes my heel, and I'm driven into a wall. Pain lances my right shoulder.

"Careful with him now," the leader says. "We don't want him damaged. He's our most valuable possession. More priceless than gold."

I wonder where BandStand is? If I were able to call out, would he hear?

I also wonder about the bluecoats. They have to be scouring the area by now. Are they making progress? How close are we to where we started? And where are the antitex taking me?

I'm led down two flights of stairs to what I can only assume is the building's basement. The surface beneath my feet is subtly different, and the humidity increases. My hands feel cool and damp.

We walk in a straight line for many minutes. I try to imagine what they have in store for me. What they think I can help with. The first thing that comes to mind is a hopper. I've already witnessed what they do to those.

Another door opens to the right, and I'm led inside. It smells familiar. Of thick petrol and plastisteel. The quality of sound changes too, indicating a larger, and possibly damper, room.

Familiarity turns into connection, then into memory. It feels like I'm in my old garage again. The one at the edge of civilization. Near Delusion.

Except I know I'm not there. I wish I was there. It seems like an eternity ago, the simplicity and predictability.

The door closes with an echo. I'm led down a short flight of stairs and forced to halt before my hood is removed. The smell intensifies, as does the familiarity. I quickly try to reach the stream. No success. Not even a glimmer—

"Open your eyes, debugger!"

I shake my head and look around. We *are* in a garage. A dim, disorganized, and unhygienic pit that makes my old place seem like Bamboo's facility.

There are only two flickering lights to illuminate the whole space. Racks of tools and repair equipment decorate the outside walls.

The leader stands in front of me, along with one of his men. The second man is behind me. The room has a wide, railed entrance. He's still at the top landing with his gun.

Behind the leader is a bigger source of familiarity. A combat bot. A heavy.

The bot is at least a decade older than the ones I used to work on. Little more than an armed tank with a head. It is positioned so it faces a large rolling door to the left. There are wide scorch marks on the side nearest me. The bot's head is roughly conical, but it has a heavy dimple in the front, as if it took a direct hit from a shell. It is missing its left arm. There must be damage to some of the road-wheels too, because the bot is listing our direction.

I'm getting communication from the bot, but it is a sad trickle: a scrolling list of problems, colored red, and flashing. Hurts my head just to view it.

The bot is what is commonly called a "HUUD." A Heavy Used Until Destruction. It should be scrapped.

"I can't fix that."

The leader scowls, then walks to the machine and pats the fender. "Of course you can. You're a debugger."

I shake my head. "It barely talks to me. I'm straining just to keep a connection." I point at the ceiling. "Also, I have no general stream access. I assume this place is shielded too?"

He smiles. "Of a necessity."

"Right, well without the stream, there are no specs, and without those it is hard to know how that beast should operate." I shrug. "Doesn't matter anyway. That thing is done. Useless."

A flash of heat enters his eyes. "Do I need to bring out the screen? Show you what happened to your friend? What will happen to the boy?"

"I thought you guys hate tech." I approach the heavy and run a finger through one of the scorch marks. It makes my finger black. "Hate to tell you, but this is tech! A big heap of tech." I frown. "Mostly a big heap, but you—"

"We use the enemies' tools against them." He looks at the men. "Submit the radical means to the radical ends."

How enlightened.

I look at the heavy again. It's even worse close up. The head is pockmarked and rusted. The lost arm has been torn unevenly from its shoulder socket. The skin is ripped and folded. With the stream and a good supply of parts, it would take weeks to repair. And I still might fail.

Even if it were possible, there's no way I can fix a heavy for a terrorist group. My head won't let me. I feel the beginning of a stop now just thinking about it.

No wonder Front lost his life. He wasn't like me. He probably never fought the rules. He had a master who was lax. But Front wasn't. He couldn't be.

What am I going to do?

The shielded areas of the building—if I've been in one building the whole time—could interfere with any bots the bluecoats might employ. Reduce their efficiency. That doesn't bode well.

"Where did you get this thing?" I ask.

"A gift. Sent from our brothers beyond the city."

From Delusion he means. I remember the atrocities I saw out there. Women and children being run over. Heads popping.

"Well, I'm glad you didn't pay for it."

The leader takes two large steps and slaps me again. The sting travels all the way to my right shoulder.

"I've had enough of your mocking," he says. "No matter what you say, you will fix this machine. Make if work for us." He walks toward the exit and climbs the small set of stairs. The other men follow until they're all standing on the landing. Three masked and matching terrorists.

"I need the stream."

The leader laughs. "You need to get working. We are on a limited schedule."

"Schedule?" I glance around the room again. I see few of the tools and equipment I use. "You don't have the stuff I need here. The things I use."

He nods. "Make us a list. We will look it over, and if it is possible, we will get what you need." He indicates the heavy. "You have enough to start already. So, get started."

"With only this junk?" I mask my fear with anger. "At least give me my bag back. The one I was wearing when you found me?"

The leader looks at the other. "Did he have a bag?"

The one nearest the door nods.

"It has debugging supplies," I say. "Things I can use to work."

The leader snaps his fingers. "Go find his things." He glares at me. "We will leave you now. Begin your work! You have two days."

They filter out and the door slams shut. I listen as their footsteps dwindle away. I turn toward the heavy. "Does *your* head hurt?"

No response.

"Well, it looks like it hurts. Big, dimpled head."

I try to imagine where I would start on the behemoth. There are so many issues to address. A stop tickles my brain-pan. I can't fix him. Not for them.

I frown. "Yeah, my head hurts too. And I don't see any way to make it end."

I climb onto the fender and sit down. Glance at the machine. "Miracle, you say? Let me tell you about them..."

MY BAG IS DELIVERED TEN minutes later. No one enters the garage. The door opens, the bag is slipped inside, and the door closes.

I don't bother to retrieve it. I'm sure everything is in there. The antitex wouldn't know what they were looking at, even if it could help me escape.

I also know the bag probably won't help me. I've been given an impossible task, and I'm trapped.

My first instinct is to stall. To give the bluecoats time to find us. But the leader's deadline precludes that. If I don't show progress, and soon, he'll get suspicious. He may even harm Band-Stand. I don't want that. I don't want any of this.

Wait! What about my lazburner? That might get me through the door. If it is still there.

I hurry to the landing and pick the bag up. Then I hear a hiss, and I startle. The sound is coming from beyond the door. I look that direction, then try the handle. The hiss intensifies. A panther is stationed outside!

The door is locked too, of course.

So much for escaping. A lazburner isn't strong enough to take down a bot. Even if I could get close enough.

It was a bad idea, anyway. I have no idea where the exit is. Without the stream, I'd be like a blind man. Wandering around until I got caught.

I pull the bag over my shoulder and walk to the heavy. I study it, then move to the front, then to the far side. The treads are sitting on a long block here, which explains the lopsidedness.

So, the wheels are probably fine. That's something.

I still can't fix it. The rules won't let me. They just won't.

I'm hungry. I'm also fatigued. It has been a long, hard day.

I wonder where the other initiates are. Did they make it back safe?

I check the rear of the heavy. Nothing severe there. Looks clean too.

I shake my head. Bamboo has doubtless denied I was ever at the facility. Or he would, if he were able. If his stops allowed it.

Does Bamboo ever lie? Ever push through the stops?

I notice a stack of boxes on the same wall as the entrance, so I drift that way. Some of them are grease-stained and bent, but they're all labeled.

I reach the first stack, stoop over the topmost box, and check the label. It appears to be a portion of a replacement arm. The upper part, complete with a new shoulder!

If my intentions are good, will the implant let me do some repairs? How many steps do I have to take to be sinful here? A single step, or twenty?

I pick up the box. Give it a shake. Stare at the heavy again. A lot would have to be repaired for it to be functional. So I'm not going to repair it all. Only a few things. Enough to show progress.

Are you okay with that, implant?

So far, no buzz.

I UNPACK THE ARM AND carry it to the bot. I lay it on the fender, then climb onto the fender myself.

I examine the damaged appendage. Despite the age, the design isn't that different than what I'm used to. The arm is sheared just below the shoulder. The ball portion is cracked in half, causing the socket's cup to be partially exposed. The surface there looks generally smooth. That's good. Means I just have to free the ball, remove the fragments of the upper arm and pop in the new one.

I wait for a moment. Am I still okay, implant?

I make a mental list of the tools I need. I should have all of them in my bag. I rest the bag on the bot's head and pull things out. A spanner, a microjack, and a haz driver.

I use the driver on the pieces of trim that encircle the joint and remove those. Now I can see into the joint all the way around. I check the cup surface. Still no chips, no tears.

Now to keep it that way.

The supporting fibers—the shoulder's "muscles"—ring the entire joint. They use a push and pull locking system at the ends. Like the human version, there are four major bands of fibers. Two near the top. Two underneath. It takes some doing, but I manage to disconnect them all. Takes me eleven minutes.

As the last snaps free, the remainder of the arm, with the ball, falls cleanly away.

Guess I won't need the spanner or the jack. Excellent.

My implant posts a reminder to my visual center: The stream is unavailable. Functions greatly diminished.

That seems like an understatement.

I smile and will the reminder away. I've almost grown accustomed to stream silence. It makes me queasy when I think about it, but if I don't focus on it—if I'm working—it's okay.

I grab the pieces of the broken arm and toss them. They hit the floor like a bundle of chains. A nice racket. They mostly stay clumped together, which is good. Wouldn't want to mess the place up.

I lift the new arm, strip the safety material around the ball portion, and hold it up near the socket. That gives me a tingle of warning. I bring the arm back down again.

I'm not really fixing the bot, implant. Just the arm. They can't do anything with this heavy, even if it has an arm. Rails, its communication stream is the equivalent of it drooling on the floor right now. Jumbled and slow. Can't wage any terror with that! Can't even get it to move itself.

The stop subsides. I take a deep breath and lift the arm up to the socket again. The sizes and positions all seem right. For being against technology, the antitex seem to be able to order replacement parts just fine.

I retrieve a can of lubricant from my bag and spray it over the ball of the arm. I then position myself—new arm in both hands—in front of the socket.

I get another lightning strike. A near stop.

Rails.

I quickly center the arm over the socket cup and push.

No go. It doesn't set.

The pain intensifies.

I rotate the arm a bit and push again. The socket locks together with a satisfying "thwup".

I bring my hands to my knees and try to relax. Try to breathe. The stop clears. No sign of any accompanying wolf pain either. *A* be praised.

I check the entrance. It's late. Are they going to bring me food? Do they realize I need food? They know I need sleep. The leader knew about chutes. About how they block the stream. So he must know debuggers eat, right? Wouldn't want his most valuable possession to starve.

I'm not hopeful.

I examine the arm. So far, so good.

Next up are the four bands of supporting fibers. Those should be quick. A simple push and pull for each. I take another breath, clear my thoughts, and give it a try. The lightning starts small, but steadily grows as I work my way around the socket. After the third band is in place I pause again, but only for a few seconds. After a series of deep breaths, I snap the fourth one into place.

There's a sheen of sweat on my forehead and back, but I feel good. Feel like I accomplished something. Even if it's meaningless, it feels right to fix things. To make something better.

I climb off the fender, then slowly circle the heavy. The outer casing is really torn up. I can see into the interior on the chest, the head, and the back. Doesn't mean those places won't function, but with exposure comes rot, nano leakage, and bundle decay.

So...do I work outside in, or inside out? Which way will bring the least stress from the implant? Cause me the least pain?

I feel a wave of fatigue. An urge to sit down. To rest. I scan the room again. On the side opposite the door there's a sink and an enclosed rectangular area that I assume is a restroom, possibly with a built-in steamer.

There's also a narrow cot there. A thin, cloth cot! Doubtless used by freeheads. Grimy, bearded freeheads like the leader and his friends. I'm not using that.

I glance at the heavy again. The fenders are wide enough; I could probably lie down on one of those. Shut my eyes. Sleep for a bit. No stream, so I don't need a chute.

I take a few steps, then pause at a stain on the floor. It has a reddish tinge. Could be from a lot of things, but it makes me think of blood. FrontLot's blood. And his awful screams.

Did it happen in here?

No. It wasn't here. It was a smaller room. I glance at the ceiling and the flickering lights. A brighter room.

It could be BandStand's screams. BandStand's blood. There is little time.

But I can't finish. I won't be able to finish.

I'm a mess.

I circle around to my bag, slide it down the fender toward me, and dig inside. I should check some of the casing breaches, just to quantify the interior damage. I'll need some sheets and a scanner.

A cursory look shouldn't mean much to my stops. I won't be repairing anything, simply looking.

The nearest tear is in front, just below the spot where the surface between the fenders rises up to form the heavy's "chest". The platform is deep enough I can climb onto it, so I do so. I trace the wound from the top to bottom, peering inside where I can. Then I put a layer of sheets over it. Widen my field of view.

I lie down on the platform to look through the lowest sheet. The interior looks better than I expected. I can see some nano movement through the central path. Nothing looks sheared.

I reposition myself. Get a little more comfortable. The platform is secure, and even a little cozy. It isn't my chute, but the overhang of the chest almost feels like I'm covered. Protected.

I yawn. Focus on the sheet. Must do something. Show progress. Fix it. Save BandStand. Save us all.

THE SOUND OF THE DOOR opening wakes me. I sit bolt up-right and nearly hit my head on the overhanging bot chest. I push myself clear, then slowly climb off the fender to the ground.

Six hours have passed. My head feels clear—maybe as clear as ever—but my body aches. Sleeping on the cot might have been better. Even if it was used by freeheads. Even if it smells funny.

I feel embarrassed to have been caught napping. I also feel guilty and worried. There isn't much time, and there's no good solution.

I turn toward the door, expecting to see the antitex leader and his goons.

Instead, one of the panthers is poised on the landing. I can't read its intent from its posture. It only waits and stares at me. I can sense its local stream pattern—that enigmatic ball of spikes—much like I can the heavy's mournful emanations. But I can't make anything of it. It is an opaque ball.

The panther lifts its head a couple times as if sniffing the air, then creeps down the stairs, pauses, and pans the entire room.

"What do you want?" I grab my bag and hold it in front of me.

The panther springs toward me. I pull my bag back, and when the bot draws close, swing. The bot avoids my flailing attempt, and darts past me to the area with the cot. It scans everything, sniffs several times, then turns right and trots to that corner. It repeats the scanning process before galloping behind the heavy, and around it. Next it crosses to the area with the boxes. In a similar manner the panther searches the rest of the room before returning to the stairs. It bounds to the landing, the door opens, and it exits.

What was that?

The door clanks and opens again. Someone in black enters with a tray of food. A woman! Wearing a full-length dress and head covering. Only her eyes are apparent. They are dark, and very wide. Possibly scared.

I take a couple steps forward. "Are you antitex?"

She shakes her head, but otherwise ignores my question. She lifts the tray and looks toward the heavy.

"I'm a prisoner here," I say. "Please, tell the authorities."

She lifts the tray again. Indicates the heavy and takes a timid step toward it.

There's a small basket of bread on the tray, along with two white bowls. The food wafts a trail of steam and smells delicious. "Sure, put it on the fender there." I ease my bag to the floor.

She bows her head and walks to the heavy.

I slowly follow. I'm intrigued by her presence. The law prohibits a woman from being alone with a man she isn't related to. Debuggers are a notable exception, but I'm surprised antitex accepts that. They must know my limitations. The behaviors my implant will prevent and encourage.

Debuggers make easy prisoners.

The woman places the tray on the fender, then takes a couple steps back and bows.

I can barely keep my eyes off the food. It is my favorite: gaymer and honey. An unexpected treat. I take a piece of bread and break it in half. The smell intensifies. I bite into it and it seems to melt, bearing warmth all the way down.

The woman remains where she is. Waiting. Her eyes aren't as wide now. They seem friendly, even happy. "Good?" Her voice quavers. The tone is pleasant, older, but also unnatural.

"Very good."

I remember BandStand and wince. I return the bread to the basket, dust off my hands, and peer at the heavy. What was I working on?

She clears her throat. "You won't eat more?" The timber of her voice changes as if she's trying to disguise it.

I don't have time to discuss her motives, but I understand why she might want to hide her identity. There's only one penalty for antitex membership: death. She should be careful.

Of course, in some neighborhoods, antitex members are heroes. They are freedom fighters, striking at the system!

I notice the row of sheets I applied earlier. Through them, a broad swath of the heavy's chest cavity is still visible. The sheets are yellowing around the edges, though. Losing their adhesion and their transparency. Why did I apply so many? Wasteful.

I was tired, stressed, and trying to avoid a headache. Not the best of conditions. Need to do better today. For as long as I can.

Until when? Until I'm done, or the pain makes me faint.

Life of a debugger, Thread. Always on edge.

The woman is still present.

"You can go, thank you. I'll eat more later."

She says nothing. Does nothing.

I frown. "Tell your masters I won't starve. I'm sure they're worried."

She nods. "You'll need your strength." She indicates the heavy. "So much to do. Little time."

Now she's annoying.

"Yes, I have a deadline." I point toward the door. "Do you need an escort?"

She chuckles. "This is how you treat guests? Dismiss them like slaves?"

I stare at her a moment, then shake my head. I climb onto the heavy's center platform and lean close to the sheets. I inspect everything beneath the tear. Thankfully, there are few pathways here. Little that could leak or corrode.

I darken the sheets. No major repairs needed. Just have to seal the tear and move on.

"Your name is ThreadBare, is it not?"

I'm startled, but I don't answer. The guards will get her eventually.

I rip one of the sheets free. Then another.

"You should look at me when I speak."

Maybe the panther will drag her out. Her dress would provide a lot of material to grab onto. I might even break to watch.

"You are rude," she says. "Are all debuggers so rude?" Her voice this time is different. Less muffled and altered. It is pleasant. Almost familiar.

I glance at her. She's holding her veil, her niqab, up so her mouth is visible.

Strange.

It is an attractive mouth! Sometimes women stir me. I've found no way to avoid that.

A stop reminds me of my position then. That's enough.

"Listen. I need to work. Someone's life is on the line. I'm sorry I can't give you a tour or whatever. Maybe next time." I bow my head.

She returns the bow. "If you are in a hurry, perhaps I can help."

"You can, by leaving me alone." I study her eyes, and the portions of her mouth and chin I can see. "I have—"

She smiles softly.

Then I get it. A suspicion that makes my stomach leap.

I run a quick pattern match on her features. It returns a ninety percent certainty. A high probability that my suspicion is right.

"Damali?"

SHE GLANCES AT THE DOOR NERVOUSLY. "You were right. I should go."

I slide to the edge of the heavy's center platform and hop off. "Go? Why..." I take a couple steps toward her. "Is it you? Here?"

She lets the veil drop over her face and glances at the floor. Then at me. Her eyes send a million messages, but few do I understand. She steps back, now seemingly timid.

Messages scream through me too. Full impact with all the senses engaged. I take a couple steps forward, then raise a hand and gently lift the bottom of her veil. Enough that I can see her chin, lips and part of her cheeks.

I initiate another pattern match. Ninety-five percent certain this time.

"It *is* you." I let the words hang there for at least twenty seconds. The room fills with an unseen substance. A heaviness composed of all I've experienced. Her virtual image in my room. Weeks of searching. Pain and loss. Memories and borrowed realities. The wolf in my head.

She touches my hand.

The feeling is explosive. Like the hoppers! Shrapnel flying everywhere. Showering the canopy.

I jerk my hand away, shocked and uncertain.

She brings a hand up near her ear, works for a moment, then draws the veil away. She smiles, and taking my hand, pulls it to her cheek.

I check my stored images, both moving and still. It's her, but she seems more beautiful than before. I don't know how to explain it. She's the same, but also different. Her eyes are clearer, maybe. Freer.

"Rails."

Her smile broadens. "Does that mean you're happy to see me?"

"My implant says it is you, but I don't believe it."

She smiles. "Doesn't it look like me?"

I nod. "Yes. Exactly like you. Ninety-eight percent."

She laughs. "Ninety-eight?"

I lean closer. "There's a small scar on your chin that wasn't there before, and a slight blemish on your right cheek. Plus, you are slightly flushed. Possible causes are exertion, stress, or—"

"You're so romantic." She places her hands on her hips, which, given the draping effect of her clothing, makes her look like an arrow.

"Romantic? Why would I be—"

She puts a finger to my lips. "Shh. Don't spoil it."

I frown, and move her finger away. I have difficulty releasing her hand, though. It's warm and soft. And real! I can't believe it. After all the searching and wondering.

Then I remember where I am, what I'm doing, and questions force their way out. "How are you here?"

"I've been watching. Hoping you survived. Hoping you escaped somehow." She looks at the floor. "I thought about you a lot. We all did. Tall and the others." She smiles sadly. "We were worried."

"But how are you *here*?" I point at the door. "Are you with them?"

She holds a finger to her lips. "Don't talk so loud." She looks at the door. "I should go. They'll wonder."

"Who will wonder? The guards?"

She pulls her hand free and takes a step away. "I'll try to come back later. I just needed to know if it was you. If you were safe."

I close the distance. "You can't leave. Not before you explain. At least tell me where you've been. What you've been doing. I went by the shop. GrimJack's. I hoped—"

She shakes her head. Smiles. "The servbot told us. Said you were with a group of boys. Are you a teacher now?"

I frown. "More like a guardian. And not a very good one. One of the boys is here too. They have him." I take her hand again. "Can you go to the bluecoats? Tell them where we are?"

She smiles sadly. "I can't, sorry."

"What? Why? There'd be no danger. You would be—"

"No danger? For a woman?" She raises an eyebrow. "What world are you from?"

I start to protest, but then stop. I forgot. The word of a single woman is meaningless. A quarter of a man's, at best. Were she to go to the authorities, they would question her motives, and possibly her sanity. Then they'd search for her family and question them. The male members, that is.

"My brother is a fugitive, ThreadBare. The royal family may have forgotten about me, but not him."

"Oh...right." My former master, Prince Aadam, held TallSpot and the other astronauts in his basement prison. Tortured and interrogated them. Even forced me to participate.

I look at the heavy. Shake my head. "But the prince is gone now."

"He's not the only one that knew we escaped."

I release her hand. "So they're hiding out now. Your brother and the others." Glancing at the floor, I notice that I'm standing in the red stain. I take an awkward step left.

Damali gives me a funny look.

I point at the stain. "Had to move, sorry. There is—"

A loud hiss ends my sentence. The panther reminding us of its presence outside. How long until it enters?

She reattaches her veil. Hurries toward the stairs.

I can't help but follow. I have too many questions. Plus, I really don't want her to leave. What if I never see her again?

If she can't help me, then at least she can inform me. Settle some of the mysteries. "I need more."

She reaches the landing and places a hand on the door. The hissing intensifies. "I'm sorry. I have to—"

"No." I feel a wave of anguish. There's a hint of a stop somewhere in my head too, but I find I can ignore it. The pain in my chest is larger. Stronger. "I'm not right. I'm trying to be normal.

Trying to push on, but I'm broken. Hurt. I need something. Something to make it worthwhile."

Her eyes go wide again. That's all I have now, though. Just her eyes. What are they telling me? What are they really saying?

"How are you hurt?" She looks me over. "You don't look hurt."

"But I am. What I did at the prince's." I shake my head. "It wasn't good." I grab the landing's bottom rail. It feels cool and damp. The only spot near me that does.

The panther hisses again. She shakes her head. "I'm sorry, ThreadBare. I can't..." She looks at the floor. "I can pray. I can do that. Pray for you."

"Pray?" I feel a burst of anger. "I pray all the time. Whenever I can, I follow the rituals." I touch the side of my head. "I have no idea if A listens or not. Or if he cares."

She looks me in the eyes, and quickly bends down to touch my hand. "*A* is not A cubed," she says.

"What? Is that the formula? What does it—"

"He stoops," she says. "Don't lose hope. He stoops." And with that, she is gone. The panther hisses. The door opens. And she's gone.

I'm no better off than I was, and in fact, I might be worse. I've now seen her and lost her again.

I REMAIN BY THE LANDING, uncertain how to proceed. I focus on straightening my neural pathways and breathing. On stepping beyond the emotion and the uncertainty to find reason in the chaos.

But it is no use. Confusion is a storm that can't be sated. Can't be stopped. I place my other hand on the railing and feel its coolness. I hold on with both hands and lower my head, as if I'm standing in a typhoon. "What is this? What is all this?"

Finally, my stomach reminds me that I'm still hungry. I release the railing and walk listlessly to the heavybot and my meal. The bread is cold now, but still good. The honey refreshes. Brings joy into a world of pain and shadow.

A is not A cubed? So the formula was important. Not just a grasping at carbon filaments. It meant—it means—something. To Damali and the others.

But "he stoops?"

Who stoops? When does he stoop? And how?

Outside, it's all confusion and discord. Inside, I'm a hollow shell.

I look at the heavy. Smell the petrochemicals. Hollow as this. All of this.

What do I do? What can I possibly do now?

I eat until the bread is gone. There is food in my stomach, but I still feel empty.

BandStand. I have to remember him. How can I get him out of this?

I see no way.

I stand on tiptoes, reach the edge of one of the remaining sheets, and pull it free. Then the next and the next. Finally, I have to climb onto the center platform to reach the rest. Fifteen seconds later, the tear in the surface is fully visible again.

"Can I fill this wound, implant? Or is that too much like fixing it?"

No response. At least, not yet.

The heavy's outer shell is thick. Too thick for the fuser I have in my bag. I glance back and right at the stack of boxes, and over my left shoulder at the tools and miscellany decorating the wall there. I need a two-handed fuser, and liquid plastisteel to fill with. Do they have those? And where would they put them?

Ten minutes later, I find what I need and begin to work. It is slow going. I'm able to fill the fuser just fine, but when I lift it to the heavy's surface, the headbuzz begins. I fill maybe two centimeters before I have to put the instrument down and regroup.

Truthfully, I don't know why the implant cares. Who are the good guys here? It wasn't that long ago I was doing similar work for the Imam. I saw a heavy crush the Imam's enemies, but the enemies looked like civilians to me. Not troops. Not military.

Next came the prince. The combat bots I manipulated. Machines made to break and punish.

There was no righteousness to either chore. No directive from A that I could tell.

And the men themselves? Faith was a curtain for them. A dark flag they wrapped themselves in.

Maybe antitex are the righteous? Maybe they're doing A's will. They would swear they are. That they are following scriptures correctly. All others are infidels. Heretics.

If TallSpot was right, either way is an end to debuggers. Either way means our death. There's no pleasant road. No grey ending. Only an end. A violent end.

My destiny here is no different. I scowl and lift the fuser. No pleasant ending.

Maybe it all needs to fall.

An hour passes. I struggle my way across the tear, drawing

within twenty centimeters of the end before my fuser runs out of plastisteel. The stops are ubiquitous now. Easily angered.

I climb down from the heavy and feel new aches in my knees and thighs. Some jobs have no comfortable position to work from. This fuse job is one of them.

I stick my finger in the bowl of honey and bring it to my lips. Again, it refreshes.

The door clanks and then opens. The leader walks in with one armed man, and the panther. The panther runs up on me, then skips by and begins its haphazard check of the room. I make sure my snooping subroutine—which is still active—is pointed the panther's direction, and attempting to crack its communication band. Find meaning in the spikes.

The leader approaches the front of the heavy, then drifts to the left and back to the right. Surveying all I've done.

He scowls. "There is much to do yet."

I nod. "Yes, there—"

"I mean, I see that the arm is in place. It appears complete." He looks at me. "You have everything you need?"

"Yes, everything." I point at what remains of the tear. "I've started repairing part of the shell here. The place—"

He glances at the tear, but doesn't seem impressed. He instead circles the entire bot. His arms come up multiple times, along with grunts of disapproval.

The panther finishes its tour and takes a seated position to my left. Looking at me.

The guard behind me shifts his gun.

Not comfortable.

"Debugger!" the leader yells.

"Yes?"

"Come here!"

I walk to where he now stands, near the rear of the heavy. "Yes?"

He points at another tear. This one is vertical, running down the middle of the heavy's back. I squint at it, focusing on the exposed interior. I count five broken pathways, and a seared conduit. More damage back here than in front.

"Did you see all this?"

"Yes. There's a lot to fix."

He motions me to our right, to that side of the heavy. He points at a crack in the back of the right arm—the one I haven't touched yet—then indicates a split in the right side. "And those breaks, did you notice?"

I nod. "This machine was used beyond its usefulness. It should have been put out of service and its parts repurposed. I told you—"

He glares at me. "I will not accept that answer. You're exaggerating. Lying to get more time."

"I'm incapable of lying."

He snorts. "Another lie."

I shake my head. "No matter what—"

The glare intensifies. "No matter what, you are bound to do your master's wishes. I know this. If lying benefits him, you will do so. Often and willingly."

I stay quiet. He seems to know a lot about debuggers. Strange for an antitex.

He stomps toward the front of the heavy. Claps his hands over his head. "Now—"

I follow him because I assume that's what he wants. "Yes?"

His eyes are like daggers. "You have one more day. One more day to have this machine ready for deployment. In the meantime, I will take one of the boy's fingers as payment." He points at the guard. "Bring the vid!"

"What you require is impossible," I say. "Even three debuggers couldn't do it in two days."

He lays a hand on the panther. It growls softly. "And so, I will take a finger a day until the work is complete. Am I not generous? You may have ten more days if you need them."

"Twenty, if you use the toes," the guard adds.

The leader snaps his fingers. "I should have thought of that!" He smiles. "You have twenty days, if you need them."

I shake my head. "You said it would be two days before you harmed him. I haven't had two days yet."

He nods. "That was my initial estimate, but your lack of progress is disheartening. Motivation is required."

"Motivation isn't the problem." I point at my head. "I struggle with myself. Against my implant."

"Perhaps the implant needs motivation too." He removes his hand from the panther. "Yes, we will motivate it."

The guard brings out a black satchel, and from it, produces a small vidscreen. Its presence makes me ill. It is a view-port of horrors.

"Cut me." I say. "Take my finger."

The leader shakes his head. "That might slow your work."

I have an idea. A desperate hope. "The boy is a debugger too," I say. "Why slow *him*? Why not let him help instead? Bring him here."

That gives him pause. "I thought he was a student. Is that not true?"

"He is. Yes, he's a student. But he's been trained. He has some skill."

He studies me. "And that will help you?" He raises a hand. "Of course, I know it *could* help. I've heard of this skin synergy."

He places a hand on my shoulder. "But I've also heard of your specialized training. Your levels of efficiency." He narrows his eyes. "Ah, now I know! You are being devious, correct? The two of you will work together then find a way to get free. Some way to escape."

The guard holds out the vidscreen.

"No. I'm simply trying to solve this. To keep us both useful. If you start dismembering—"

He laughs, then pushes the vidscreen away. "Fine, you convinced me. I won't cut him today. But tomorrow...tomorrow he will lose two fingers for the pain. And then his head."

He waves at the guard, walks to the stairs, and stomps up to the landing. The panther remains where it is for a couple seconds, staring at me, then hisses and scampers after him.

I query the results of my snooping subroutine. It learned nothing new regarding panther security.

The door slams shut.

Nothing. I have nothing.

I SPEND THE NEXT TWO hours sealing the cracks on the bot's right side. It's a meaningless and often painful chore. Not only does the implant treat me like a child with the worst intentions—buzzing me every centimeter—but these surface restorations won't change the functionality of the bot at all. It might look more complete to freehead eyes, might seem so to the antitex leader, but it is a long way from useful.

I've been avoiding the real problems. Everything hidden within the bot's error list. If it is anything like the heavies I used to work on, few of those reports are from surface imperfections. Heavies are made to get ugly—dent and crack—and keep running.

Surface breakage will be enumerated as a low priority. Orange and yellow in color, and tasting of tangerine. This bot's error list has lots of red. Angry, angry red. Like grapefruit on the tongue.

Finally, I resolve myself to it. I take a seat on the fender, close my eyes, and communicate with the bot.

The size of the list is epic. To make matters worse, the bot's internal com unit must be fried, because I can't even keep the list fixed in my head. It flickers into nothingness as I try to scroll through. And after every drop, I have to quickly reconnect, search for my last position, and keep going. Not fun. I finally dupe the list, copying it to my, arguably, equally unstable mind.

An hour goes by. And then two.

My despair deepens. Darkens to the color of coal.

Working from my copy of the list, I attempt to parse and interpret it. That's not as easy as it may sound, because nearly every bot's error codes are a language all their own.

And yeah, I don't have the stream. So no obvious reference sheet, which requires a lot of guesswork. I'm able to deduce enough, however. Enough to know how simply hopeless this all is.

I climb off the bot and shuffle toward the stack of boxes again. I see parts for all portions of the body. Internal and external.

I could almost build a new heavy—at least the head portion—from what I have. Unfortunately, sometimes it isn't about parts, it is about bits. And this bot's biggest problem is with its bits. In the code.

It is missing a large portion of its decision matrix. I won't say it is half-witted, but almost. Maybe two-thirds witted. And there's no way I'm getting those wits back. I would essentially have to write them from scratch. Can't do that in a day.

If I had access to the stream, could I get it there?

Doubtful. This thing is too old. The manufacturer—Saber-Stan—isn't even around anymore.

Interesting historic note: SaberStan lost their factory to an antitex bomb! Irony of ironies!

I kick one of the boxes. It slides about twenty centimeters. Then I laugh. Laugh until my sides hurt.

Antitex indirectly killed their own heavy. Big funny. Big, epic joke.

All on me. And BandStand.

How am I going to tell the leader that his metal soldier is a bust? Probably doesn't matter because, whatever I say, he won't believe me. He'll think I'm lying for my master. Or stalling.

I circle the floor in front of the heavy. Unable to focus on anything. Unable to even look at the list again. Doesn't matter what else is on there. The heavy isn't going to live again. It isn't going anywhere.

See there, implant? All that headbuzzing was for nothing!

I notice the red stain on the floor. I shake my head, then crouch down next to it. Sit on the very edge of it. Stare at death. Somebody's death.

I look at the front of the heavy. Lopsided and beaten. Maybe I should keep on with the little stuff? Maintain appearances?

I'm hungry again.

I glance at the door. Will they bring another meal this evening? Will *she* bring it?

I yawn, then climb to my feet. I attempt to push out a message to BandStand. An apology. A record of my failings. It goes nowhere. Simply sits in my message queue and spins.

I walk to the back of the heavy and locate the surface tears. I can fix those. At least I can fix those.

I'M READY THIS TIME.

There were no other visits the rest of the day yesterday. From anyone. Into the early morning, I worked on my UUD heavy and got the exterior generally repaired. I even washed it and reapplied all the lost and torn ornamentation. From the outside, it looks like new.

In addition, I managed to string together a series of command chains for the thing to follow. Nothing too impressive. Nothing that could destroy anything. But the heavy will turn its head and move its arms on command...

If the command is said slow enough, with the right inflection.

Sure, the heavy is still less useful than a child's toy, but whatever I did was going to be a facade. It was never going to work.

I finished early enough to take a nap, but I set an internal timer for myself. Why? So I could be ready for the next visitor. I stand near the blood spot, waiting.

At nearly the same moment as yesterday, the door opens. The panther enters, looks at me, sniffs me, then moves off to search the room. Five minutes later, it leaves.

Then she walks in. There's no reason to wonder this time. A quick pattern match of her eyes and gait is enough to ascertain her identity. Damali clutches a tray again, but this time there's a deep bowl atop it. Steam rises from it, effusing the air with wonderful new scents. Cumin and turmeric. A rice dish, I think.

Damali looks my direction, and my heart leaps. I imagine that she's smiling beneath the veil. That she is as glad to see me as I am her. Despite my conflicting emotions and many questions, I'm still happy. It is difficult to see her as less than a friend.

Without a word, she descends the steps and takes the food to the heavy. She places it on the left fender, then turns toward me. Looks at me.

"Who stoops?" I ask.

"What?" She raises her veil, revealing lips and chin. Perfect glimpses of a beautiful exterior. "This is how you greet me?"

I'm a debugger. Human interaction isn't a specialty. "The last time you were here, you said 'he stoops.'" I raise my shoulders. "Who stoops?"

"Ah, now I see." She smiles. "*A cubed*, of course."

"From the formula? *A tilde, A cubed*?"

She nods. "Yes, that's it. A signal of sorts. A sign between friends."

I take a step closer. "And who is A cubed?"

She pulls the veil back completely, then looks toward the ceiling. "Freedom," she says. "What we've all been searching for."

I shake my head. "Freedom doesn't exist. Not really."

A look of puzzlement. "Of course it does. When I came to you at the prince's. When I—"

I tap my right temple. "I've observed many humans, both poor and rich. Their heads are free to do whatever they wish...but they aren't truly free. Habits and circumstance dictate their actions. Their beliefs. It's like their behaviors are coded in." I point at the door. "Even antitex. They are unable to change their thinking, no matter what I tell them. It is like they're stuck. Programmed." I smile. "More so than me."

"We're not stuck."

"So you're one of them?" I say. "Antitex?"

Her eyes widen. "Them? The terrorists?" She glances at the door and steps closer. "No. Of course not. Is that what you think?"

"How else should I think? You're here..." I indicate the heavy. The stacks of boxes. The piles of tools. "...and their panther brings you in."

She studies the floor, then takes a few uncertain steps to her right. "Fugitives...tend to know each other. Even if they don't agree, even if they don't work together, connections develop. Information gets shared. There was a rumor that a debugger had been taken by antitex. I worked it out—switched places with one of their women, so I could see if it was you." She looks at me. "My status, who I was, helped."

"Who you were?"

She nods. "Yes, my time with the prince. It's well known that I was taken, and why. And now with him dead..."

"You're a hero? But you were—"

She stiffens. "No, I wasn't." She touches her chest. "Not in here. Never in here."

My time to look at the floor. At that troubling red stain. "I'm sorry."

"That is how you see me? As his plaything?"

I'm troubled, still conflicted, but also sure of one thing. "No." I find her eyes. The curve of her chin. "But I know how freeheads think. I used to work across from a place where women..."

She nods. Studies me. "That's not me," she says softly. "That has *never* been me."

"I know," I say. "Again, I'm not good with..." I wave a hand between us. "This."

She steps toward me. "Yes, I forget." She smiles. "But that's what makes you good. Pure. Your difference." She brings a hand up, then hesitates. Pulls back. "May I touch you?"

"Touch me?"

"Yes. Your...your head, actually. I'd like to..." She smiles. "Forgive me for not knowing. Do you shave it, or—"

"It's part of the process. Shaved first, then the follicles are deadened. Removed for good."

She nods. "Does that bother you? Knowing it won't grow back?"

I shrug. "Many things are different. Stunted, removed, or discouraged. But others are better."

"Yes, your connection." Her hand is still raised. Partially closed. Delicate, but strong.

I bow my head. "Go ahead."

I feel her palm on the side of my head above the left ear. A cool touch, and soft. Her fingers brush the back of my head. That sparks a burst of electricity beneath my scalp. A tingle that arcs to the back of my head, and down my spine.

The implant forms a counter-attack. A warning challenge in my temples. I want those to go away. I need them to go away.

She cups my chin and gently eases my head up. Looks me in the eyes. "You don't need to do that for me, you know. Bow like that."

The headbuzz gets a sharper edge. I suck in my breath and step back, ending her touch.

She looks startled. "Did I hurt you?"

"In a way, yes. Sorry. I know you didn't mean—"

She studies me, forehead wrinkled. "That will make things difficult..."

"What things?" I ask. "What?"

Her face reddens, and she shakes her head. Smiles. "It must make many things difficult. To have touch limited. Forbidden."

"It isn't touch, really. Not just that."

"What is it, then?"

I feel my own face flush. I look at the ground, at the heavy. "Difficult to explain."

She nods slowly. Points at the heavy's fender. "You should eat. And I should go. Again."

I feel a wave of guilt. Today is the day. BandStand's fingers. "I don't know what your role here is. Your position as hero or survivor or whatever. But can you get the boy out? They plan to kill him."

"I don't know where he is," she says. "I mean, I haven't taken him food. Only you."

I see Band's image in my mind. A small, cell-like room. "He can't be far," I say. "At least, I don't think so." I glance at the heavy. "Of course, they moved me..."

She nods slowly. "He's a debugger too? Hard to believe they would simply—"

"They will," I say. "Believe me. They've killed others. I saw their last victim. One of my friends."

Her eyes widen again. "Was he with you?"

I shake my head. "No. They must've taken him from the street somewhere. Just like they did me.

"But they killed him? Why would they do that?"

"Because they're terrorists. That's what they do."

She nods slowly. "I'm sorry. I didn't know." She indicates the door. "They don't know I know you." She points between us. "That we've, um, met before."

I get a mysterious feeling. The indication that I'm something more to her. That I wasn't simply imagining or hoping. My previous actions were significant. They had resonance.

But now what?

I study the plate of food she brought me. The steam rising from it.

Antitex will get nothing from me if BandStand dies. I've decided that. His death will mean my own. I'm a terrible teacher and a worse mentor, but I'm not a betrayer. Not again.

Should I be doing something more here? Now?

I look at Damali. "Can you help him? Get your brother and his friends and get him out?"

She grabs the front of her dress with her hands. Kneads it nervously. "Wouldn't they find us if we did? The authorities, I mean. Remember, we're—"

"Fugitives." I sigh, shake my head.

By pulling security, Band would be locatable, yes. He'd be a beacon as soon as he was clear of the shielding.

Another dead end.

The door "thunks" and the panther enters. Damali gives a frightened chirp and reattaches her veil. She looks at me and raises an eyebrow. She then lowers her head and walks toward the door.

THE PANTHER MAKES ITS usual rounds. The leader and two guards—in customary black masks and clothing—walk in.

Damali waits at the bottom of the stairs, then bows twice as they descend toward her. One of the guards studies her, but the others give her no attention. They're focused on the heavy.

The leader stretches out his hands. "Is it ready? It appears ready."

"It can do things," I say. "Yes. Obey commands." There's no resistance from the implant to that statement. White lies to non-master terrorist? Not a problem.

He smiles. "Wonderful. Show me."

I push simple commands into the bot's command queue, causing it to lift its arms and swivel its head. I get it to roll forward a couple meters. There's a loud retching sound when it stops, though.

That's probably due to its faulty braking system. A problem near the bottom of the list.

"What was that?" the leader asks.

"Possibly dust on the brake lining," I say. "I need to investigate to be sure."

He lays a hand on the heavy's right fender, still smiling after my display. "It is no matter. I can see that it moves and stops. That's all that is required."

"What do you intend to do with it?"

His smile broadens, still looking at the machine. "I knew you were able to complete the work. Knew you could conquer whatever internal restraints there were to accomplish our goal." He looks at me. "Your predecessor was weak."

I grit my teeth. I assume he means FrontLot. "It was a difficult process. There was much pain."

He raises a fist. "Pain is how we find freedom. Pain is how we throw off our technological masters." He addresses the nearest guard. "Have the exit door opened."

The guard nods and brings out his vidscreen satchel again. He frees the screen and begins to manipulate it.

I can't escape the irony.

The large door starts to open. I hope for light, for a glimpse of a way out, but all the doorway reveals is a wide, upward-sloping accessway. There are painted yellow arrows on both walls.

I glance at the landing and the door there. Damali is gone. Slipped out during the demonstration.

"The boy should go free now," I say. "I've done what you wanted."

The leader waves toward the open door. "Roll out, robot." He looks at me. "It hears me, correct? It can obey me."

I bow. "It can hear you, but before we experiment, I'd like to see the boy. To know he's okay."

His eyes narrow. "Are you preventing this bot from following my commands?"

"It has no assigned master," I say. "So your commands are irrelevant. I access it through its test mode."

"I need to be its master!"

I bow. "You have an ident I can give it?"

The area around his eyes reddens. "It doesn't need my ident card to recognize me as its master. You make it so!"

"Your face is covered," I say. "The identifying marks to match—"

He strikes my face. "Insolent. Make it use my voice. Listen to only my voice."

"The boy," I say. "Show me the boy. Better yet, release him and show me him leaving."

The leader looks at his men. "He tries to command me now. Our prisoner!"

I instruct the bot to raise its left arm. I have no intent on hurting anyone, so that's okay.

The guards startle and raise their weapons.

The leader's eyes go wide. "What are you doing, skin!"

Would the implant let me use the bot to smash the antitex? Not sure. But the more use the bot gets, the more obvious its deficiencies will become.

Plus, smashing these freeheads would put me on their level. Not sure I'm ready for that.

Mostly, I know the arm works, so I'm using it. "A mistake," I say, lowering the arm. "My apologies."

The leader looks more cautious now. Less angry. "Perhaps we could let him see the boy." He scowls. "To show him our good intentions."

He snaps his fingers, and the guard with the vidscreen steps forward. He manipulates the screen with his fingers. A few seconds later, he grunts and brings it closer to me. Turns it my way.

I see an image of BandStand in his cell. He's seated on his cot and appears to be eating. There is a tray on the cot next to him. A steaming bowl of food. He looks content.

I nod.

"Now, you see," the leader says. "He is well. You have done what you have promised, and so have we. A good trade. No one is harmed."

Except my portion of the deal is a mirage. What do I do now? How do I get us out?

"Now, assign the robot to me? Make it obey my spoken commands?"

I nod and close my eyes as if to focus. It is an easy change. A simple assignment that is one of only five functioning commands in the bot's command list.

I open my eyes and find the men all watching me.

"It is done?" the leader asks.

I get a feeling of trepidation. "Will the boy be released?"

"Right now?"

"As soon as you can, yes."

He raises a hand. "He is well taken care of here. Our compound is a safe place for him. We can protect—"

I point at the heavy. "I want him as far away from that as possible. He's only a child. Not prepared for war." I don't know how far I can push this. I don't have much real leverage. But if it is working...

"Very well." He points at the guard with the vidscreen. "Have the boy put outside." He glances at me. "Where do you want him to go?"

"The nearest downrider pylon."

He grunts, nods. "There's one a block away. If he is shown its location, he will know how to reach it? How to climb up?"

"He will be fine. He's been trained."

The leader nods, looks at the vidscreen guard. "Have them go now."

The guard manipulates the screen, grunts a few times, then speaks to someone on the other side. A few moments later, he turns it my direction. I see another man dressed in black in Band-Stand's cell, addressing him. The boy nods and stands. A hood is shoved over his head. He's led toward the door.

I nod and look at the heavy. I admire its seamless and damage-free exterior. The now-functioning arms. How good it looks.

This might work. I might get us out.

I wonder where Damali is.

"You have given me control?" the leader says.

I look at him. Nod. "Yes, just ask it if it is ready."

The leader smiles and nods triumphantly. He walks to the heavy and lays a hand on its side, behind its right arm. "Robot! Are you ready!"

The robot's head turns his way.

Then it pops off.

THE EVENT IS GLORIOUS. The heavy's head leaves its shoulders with a "thump" and flies two meters into the air. The freeheads drop to the floor, cursing and grunting. The head soars, spinning and gliding like a flying disk, away and to our left, where it lands, straddling the cot and the lavatory sink.

If it didn't mean disaster, I'd be proud of that result. A memory gladly sent to one of the datamix vendors. Especially, if I'd planned it. Which I didn't.

It's difficult not to laugh, regardless.

The men climb warily to their feet. No one seems happy, least of all, the leader. His eyes are a fiery color. And wide. Very wide.

He lets off a string of expletives, then stomps in a circle near the left side of the heavy. His arms are rigid, fists clenched.

"It is not fixed! It is not ready!" He shouts at the vidscreen holder. "Bring them back. Bring back the boy." More swearing.

My heart sinks. I hope, pray, that maybe there was enough time for BandStand to get away. That he's out of the building and already climbing for a roof pylon. Signaling a downrider.

The guard fumbles with his vidscreen. Gazes at it, taps it rapidly. "Where are you?" he says. "Yes, stop. Come back. Take him back to the room."

The pain in my chest expands, making it difficult to breathe.

The leader glares at me. "See there, A is with us. The boy will die now. Die for your failings."

I shake my head. "There's no reason for that. He did nothing. It was my fault."

I sense something else then. A new presence. A mechanical being.

I glance at the heavy. The new transmission isn't coming from it. It can't be. What's left of its mind is scattered over the room's facilities. Disconnected from their power source.

Then what? And where?

I look at the door. The panther is positioned on the landing. All I get from it is its spike-filled globe of nonsense. There is more distinction in the individual spikes than before, I think, but otherwise it is unchanged.

Then what?

I try to find directional information in the transmission. A sense for where it is coming from.

Is there a flaw in the antitex stream shield?

No. It is still present. I can't communicate out. Can't send or receive. Simply trying produces a wall of errors.

But something is out there. A nebulous *other* filled with speed and purpose.

"Do they have a sword, his guards?" the leader asks. "Are they back to his cell? That's where it should be done."

The vidscreen guard grunts an affirmative.

The leader points at me. "Show it to him. Make sure he sees it all."

The vidscreen guard positions himself in front of me, while the other guard walks behind me and secures my upper arms.

Vidscreen guard holds the vid in front of my face. Tilts it so the overhead glare is minimal.

I see BandStand in his cell, now on his knees. His face looks drained of color. Scared and despondent. On one side of him, a guard holds him down. At the other, lurks a guard with a long, silver blade.

I want to abstract it. To distance myself as if it is another mix. But I can't. One of my students is in grave danger. Somewhere along the line, I started caring. Now a portion of my emotions are bound to them. I need to help him, but I can't. I'm floating. Drowning in a sea of despair.

I can't shake the presence either. The knowledge that something is here. Nearby. Unseen, but active.

"Don't do this," I plead. "He's only a child."

I isolate the signal. It isn't one bot, but many. They are small and working as a team. Positioned to my right, in the accessway somewhere. I turn my head that direction and see glints of metal on the ceiling. And on the far wall.

Now I know what they are. "Hello," I say. "Nice to see you."

My head is forced forward. Made to look at the screen.

The leader holds up a hand. "What did he say? Who was he speaking to?"

For the first time in days, I feel hope. I need to stall. Buy more time for BandStand somehow.

I wish I was in the same room with him. It would be easier.

I resist, forcing my face to the side, then lunging backwards. I hope BandStand fights too. He needs to fight until the end. We have a way out.

"I said 'hello' to my friends," I say. "Do you want to meet them?"

I reach out to those *friends*. The group of cricket bots that are now hopping down the accessway. They made their way down here, virtually blind, to find us.

I hate what that implies, the impending consequences. I'll soon be on every master's radar, but given the alternative, I'm comforted. Hopefully there's enough of them to report my position to the authorities. To daisy chain a message up and out. Right through the shield.

"Release him," the leader says. "Tell the men to stop."

The grip on me lightens. I straighten, then look the leader in the eyes.

"Who are your friends?" he asks.

I smile. "There are crickets in the area." I nod toward the accessway. "Some are right out there. Do you see?"

The leader takes three quick steps toward the access-way. He remains motionless for a moment, then his eyes widen. "Shut that door!" he screams. "Shut it now!"

The large door begins to ratchet downward. Crickets hurry toward it. Attempting to reach it before it closes. I can sense their communication patterns now. A ripple of information moves through them—from nearest to farthest. Like ants shuttling a speck of food to the queen.

They know where we are. I'm certain of it now.

Vidscreen guard holds his appliance loosely, seemingly confused and uncertain. On it, I can see BandStand's room. He's standing, with the guards huddled around him. Their attention seems to be to their right, toward the door.

Are there crickets there too?

The large door finally closes. None of the crickets got through. Not that it matters. Their communication continues. The leader's actions alone are enough to get the area flagged. Incriminate him.

Bluecoats will be coming.

"Bag him!" the leader says. "We need to move."

Again, the hood is forced over my head. I'm shoved and directed. I feel my feet at the bottom of the stairs. I'm pushed roughly up them. This time, I fight. I dig in my feet. Grab with my hands.

Someone strikes my head. I yell, and then hear more rough movement. A fight between them?

"Imbecile," the leader says. "Don't injure his head!"

They bind my hands and gag me. There's little I can do to fight now, but I try anyway. Leaning and pulling. I'm not struck in the head again, but there are many prods and pokes. Jerks and tugs.

We move down a long hallway, then up two flights of stairs.

"You there!" A distant, commanding voice. Enforcement. "Halt! We'll shoot!"

Shoot? I really hope they don't shoot.

I'm pushed forward, then jerked around a corner.

The terrorists' pace increases. I'm taken up more stairs and dragged through a door. I hear glass break, and shots nearby. The antitex goons exchange fire with the blue coats. Lots of swearing and gunfire. I hear the trill of nanopounders too; a weapon deadly to synthetics like the panther and the heavy.

Not good for my implant either.

I roll away from my guards, stumble until I bang a wall with my shoulder. I slide to the floor, then ball up, tucking my head. I wish I could cover myself. Wish my hands weren't tied.

Muffled shouts. Warnings and curses. Then there's an explosion and I feel a prolonged rush of heat. More gunshots. The hiss of guided projectiles.

Something falls on me. Something heavy, warm, and wet. A body? I roll out from beneath it, but my arms and chest are wet.

Is there blood on me now? My stomach lurches. I roll to my front and expel my breakfast. The meal Damali brought me.

"He's here!" someone yells. "The debugger is right here!"

I shake my head. I want to scream. First that they find Band-Stand, and then that they clean me. Get this blood off me.

I feel hands on my back, and then the hood is removed. The air smells of sulfur and saltpeter, remnants of the gun battle.

I'm in a small room, with windows on one side. The predominate color is green. Peeled and faded lime green walls and a grey-green floor. There is a large, gaping hole on the hall-side wall. Whatever door stood there is gone.

I count six enforcement officers. They wear blue helmets and solid blue jackets over grey camo clothing. There are three dead bodies in the room. All antitex.

The nearest bluecoat slaps my shoulder hard. "Are you okay? Are you injured?"

I shake my head, then try to focus on his face. Mustache, trimmed beard, and crooked smile. Breath smells of hummus.

My first attempt at talking produces a strangled croak. I cough, clear my throat, and try again. "There's another debugger," I say. "Younger—"

He smiles and slaps my shoulder again. "We have him too. He's safe. Your master will be pleased."

I nod and climb to a standing position. "Yes, I'm sure he will be. Can I return to him now?"

He nods. "We'll take you back."

I look at the body near my feet. I think it is the antitex leader, but even if I'd seen him without a mask, I wouldn't be able to identify him now. There's a hole through one eye. If I squint I can see the floor on the other side.

I shake my head. Focus on the door hole instead. "That won't be necessary. I can find my own way. Thank you."

I steady myself against the wall and try not to look at the leader. Or the floor in general. There's nothing but terror here. I step over the leader's legs and move toward the door.

The blue coat follows. "We need to take you with us. For our records. So we get paid."

Another blue coat joins us. He is an older and greyer version of the first. "We checked the background of the boy. We show him as being licensed to the facility here in town." He glances at a hand-held screen. "A Bamboo is the administrator there?"

I nod. "Yes, that's right." The room feels really small. Too small for so many people. So many dead bodies. "That's where I'm going. To Bamboo's place"

Adding to my claustrophobia is the continued lack of stream access. The shield remains in place.

I could really use the stream. I need that freedom. That space.

"What's your DR number, please?" the young bluecoat says. "I need it to check your ownership."

"I'm between owners. I'm with the facility, as well. An assistant."

"Is that where we send the bill?" the older one asks. "The facility?" He waves a hand, indicating the room's contents. "We had to expend quite a bit of time and resources here. To rescue you."

I take another step toward the door. The freedom of the hall will be better. The space.

"Debugger, sir? It will be easier if you help us. Tell us what we need to know."

Can't they see how uncomfortable I am? I feel heat. Simmering anger. "I didn't call security. It wasn't me."

"But we saved you. We need to be paid."

I frown. Nod. "You deserve something for your service, yes." I reach the hole that used to be the door. The smell of sulfur intensifies. "I'm grateful."

"Grateful?" Younger blue coat laughs. "You *should* be grateful." He points at the center of the room. At one of the bodies. "Do you understand the risk we took? They were all armed."

"I'm aware, yes. I've been here for two days. With them."

He snorts. "We found an automated tank on the premises. Who knows what that could've done."

I glance back at him. "It wasn't going anywhere. Trust me. It is broken.

"I don't know about—"

"It has no head," I say. "Where would it go without a head!"

He raises a hand. "Easy there. I didn't see it. Only going on what was reported."

"Well, your reports are faulty. Insufficient." Anger flows from me. It seems justified. Eternally approved. Necessary.

"Sorry, sir. Didn't mean to—"

"For instance, you don't know what a debugger needs. I need to be back at the facility. And to rest. Then I'll be ready for service again. To solve some of the mysteries that surround us."

"No mysteries from where we're standing," the older one says. They both laugh.

I step into the hall. It isn't much better. It feels very small too. And rundown. There are black stains on portions of the white paint. Possibly mold growing. Decay and neglect.

There are bluecoats out here too. One is capturing images. Another is leaning against the wall with his gun pointed toward the ceiling. His attention is on the camera until I walk by. Now he's focused on me. Frowning.

The young bluecoat touches my arm. "Really, I can't let you leave."

I scowl. "But I need to. I have to get—"

I bend over and retch. The hallway starts to spin. I smell heavy sulfur. Then all goes dark.

THE GROUND AROUND ME is the color of bone. The color is consistent and pervasive. Everywhere I look is the same bone shade. No green, no brown, no blue.

The ground has an unusual consistency too. Not clumpy like loam or grainy like sand, but courser. Heavier and chalkier. Like chewed up stone.

The surrounding terrain is generally flat but in the distance, I see low hills. There are dips there too, but those are unnatural features. Not gentle sloping valleys, but sudden drops, as if the ground has been struck by falling rocks. Hewn out through violence.

The sky is pitch black, darker than evening. Soul draining and empty. As if I'm standing in a depiction of loneliness. Loneliness, despair, and abandonment.

I have no idea where I am. Or what I'm doing here.

I think I passed out. Where did enforcement take me?

I glance down. I'm in a clean, blue jumpsuit. Someone changed me.

I take two steps forward and freeze in place. The ground crunches beneath my feet. Like walking on crusted snow, or egg-shells. The feeling is disconcerting and wrong. I'm unsure what to do next.

Where am I?

I attempt to call out, but my voice stops somewhere in my rib-cage. I try again, but I can't force air from my lungs.

Am I even breathing?

Am I alive?

Panic strikes me. Is this the afterlife? Did I die and end up here?

Scriptures prescribe a day of judgment for the dead. A narrow bridge over Hell that all must take before entering eternity. Those who fall from the bridge, those made unbalanced due to the weight of their bad deeds, remain in torment forever. Those who reach the other side enter Paradise.

I see no bridge here, though. No clear path that I should walk. Only the brittle, pale stone.

That leaves only one possibility.

Two groups of people forgo the judgment of the bridge: warriors who die fighting for A's cause, and enemies of the faith. The first go straight to Paradise.

The latter straight to Hell.

This wasteland looks nothing like the descriptions of Paradise I've read. There are no gardens. No dancing virgins. Only desolation.

That means I'm in Hell. And if I am, then debuggers have been lied to.

We're supposed to be warriors, martyrs. We should be given the first path. I should be standing in Heaven.

A dim light cracks the horizon. A break in the monotony of darkness. Slowly, moment by moment, the light increases. The sky brightens.

My instincts, my preconceived notions, say, "This is the sun! We'll soon have day."

But it isn't the sun. The light isn't bright and yellow. Nor does it end the silence or warm my skin.

It is cool and blue. A planetary body.

Five more minutes reveals that it is our planet. My planet. Earth.

My surroundings are more distinct now. The ground a lighter color. Craters dominate the scenery.

This is the moon. Somehow, I'm on the moon!

...without a suit. Walking, watching and breathing.

On the moon.

"This isn't possible, you know," someone says.

I look around but see nothing but the moon's surface. Endless desolation. The voice is familiar, though. Soothing.

"What you're seeing isn't possible. The moon rotates in a way as to always keep the same side facing the Earth. So there can be no Earth-rise there."

No?

"The view of Earth—its place in the sky if you were in a place that could see it—would remain fixed. Not unchanging, because the moon slowly circles the whole planet, but in relation to the sky, it stays in place."

"Part of our satellite never sees the Earth at all." A sigh. "A pity. All that grandeur so close, yet easily unseen and unappreciated."

"Bamboo?" I'm surprised by the sound of my voice. The fact that it works now.

I test the air. Feel myself breathing. It feels good. "I can talk!"

"Yes, of course." Bamboo's form materializes on my left. He's dressed in an orange jumpsuit. I'm not sure why.

He bows to me, then stares off at the rising Earth. Sighs again. "One of my favorite simulations."

The Earth is three-quarters up now. The two largest continents are in sight, their green and brown hues evenly matched by the amount of blue around them. There are wisps of clouds visible too. The atmosphere has an abstracted look. Like it is all encased in glass.

"It is beautiful." I say.

"Yes, but that's not why it is my favorite."

"No?"

He smiles. "I cherish it because it is an impossible beauty." He looks at me. "A view that could never be seen."

I gaze at the Earth. "I understand." Where is she?

He raises an eyebrow. "Do you?"

I shrug. "I think so. I mean—"

He chuckles. "You're an interesting study, ThreadBare. It will be a shame to lose you."

My heart drops. "So, this is another test. An evaluation." I look at him. "And I've failed again. I'm still broken and unusable. My time has expired."

His face is almost unreadable. I see no anger, no disappointment or sadness. If I perceive anything, it is puzzlement. Surprise.

"Are the initiates safe?" I ask. "Did everyone make it back? Unharmed?"

He nods and tucks his hands behind his back. "At some expense, yes."

I look at the ground. "We held off as long as we could. Tried to remain discrete."

He says nothing. Simply watches me, then shakes his head.

I try to smile. "Usually bad news arrives in your office," I say. "In reality."

"Not this time." He turns to look at the Earth again. "I wanted something meaningful. Memorable."

I have a hard time raising my eyes. I focus instead on a boulder that sits ten meters away. From my position, it almost looks like a miniature pyramid. "Again, I'm sorry I failed. That I disappointed."

He nods slowly. "We knew our arrangement couldn't last forever. Your being with us." He draws in a breath. "Your time with the implants, regardless of the benefits, was always temporary." He drags a foot through the moon's dirt. Smiles as he studies the results. "I'm unsettled by this course. As unsure as I've ever been." He smiles grimly. "I suppose I'm growing nostalgic."

A million things rush through my mind—life, death, significance, purpose—but what I most think about is Damali. It seems like there were romantic hints in her final words to me. Obscured references to a desired end.

But what version of me does she want? The debugger version can't have her—but would she like the freehead version? One who, like GrimJack, had part of what was special removed? I doubt it.

"Am I in the chair right now?" I ask. "Are you—?"

Bamboo shakes his head. "No, not yet, though in time."

In time. So I've gotten no better. Has the deadline been reached?

No. I have two days before the new moon.

And yet, here we are. On the moon.

I glance at the Earth. It is fully revealed now. A pristine sphere. Blue and white and brown, all shining. The focus of human history.

Scriptures suggest that the Earth remains fixed, and the other bodies—the moon and sun—move around it. This is what most of our teachers teach, the Imam included, despite evidence to the contrary.

I look at Bamboo again. It is curious that he, in his favorite simulation, has the Earth move. Curious, and almost blasphemous.

I feel a rush of emotion. Unexpected sorrow. I look at the ground. Move dirt with my right foot, then press it down. Crush it. "If I'm to be obsoleted," I say. "Can I meet with the initiates before it happens? I know it's unusual, but I would like to say goodbye to them."

Bamboo raises an eyebrow. "And they you, I'm sure. Their demand for your message queue has been severe while the medbots had you." He lowers his forehead. "Be careful not to injure yourself when the portals open again. It could be overwhelming."

Again?

I nod, trying not to feel optimistic. "So, I'll be able to see them? The students?"

He frowns. "I would allow it, yes, but I'm afraid there isn't time."

"Isn't time?" I'm growing more confused. "Is there any need to rush? I can't flee. I can't do more harm."

He raises an eyebrow, studies me. "We'll see about that."

I shake my head. "I'm missing your meaning." I touch my left temple. "Could be a result of my head problem. Not sure."

"No, I should apologize this time. I haven't been succinct. You are returning to service."

"To service? How? You said I'm damaged. That you couldn't release me to a master because—"

He holds up a hand. "In this case, what I want is irrelevant. The standards don't matter."

"Standards always matter."

He smiles. "Until they do not. Here, they do not."

"Why?"

"Your latest exploit has renewed your fame. The royal family has asked for your return."

Images of the prince's home dance through my head. A colossal structure surrounded by a moat. The endless fields beyond. "The prince's estate?" What is it like now that he's gone? Who lives there? Anyone?

Would I be alone in an abandoned property? A debugger for ghosts? I shudder.

"No. You will travel to the Holy City itself. The Imam wants you there. As soon as possible."

THE IMAM.

I'm not sure whether to feel honored or frightened. The Imam owns dozens of debuggers. Dozens of everything, actually. His many properties are in locations all over the world. Nearly every district, and in every time zone. It is said that the moon never sets on his estate.

His property in the Holy City is the most opulent. It is a large, walled compound, and within it is a collection of multistory buildings, with five being prominent. The top three stories of the tallest are encrusted in gold and gleam in the sun. From it one can see straight into the most holy of sites. Both the courtyard where the faithful gather to complete their pilgrimage and the central dwelling of the meteorite, BlackRock, are visible.

"Why would the Imam want me?" I say. "And why, of all places, would he want me there?"

Bamboo shakes he head. "It is not for me to say. He asked for you by name. Consider it a privilege."

I think of BullHammer, my rival and sometime accomplice. He's part of the Imam's stable of debuggers. Did he do this? Get me brought back?

Bull seems to spend his moments constructing alternate realities for himself. Exploring hills and waterways that exist only in his mind. He hasn't been looking well, either. Has seemed gaunt and tired.

My apprehension intensifies.

Bamboo brings his hands together. And with that, the rising Earth and the lunar landscape disappear.

I open my eyes to the brightness of Bamboo's study. The white walls and domed ceiling. The curved bookshelf and glimpses of the city outside. Temples and the snaking Great River.

I'm in the same wicker chair as before. Above my head is a black, circular diagnostic shell. Six tendrils dangle from it like the legs of an octopus. It has just been attached to my head, I realize. Communicating and controlling my implant. Studying me. Leaching my mind.

I shudder. I'm glad that I was asleep when it happened. I watch as it retracts into the ceiling. Out of sight. Gone for good.

Bamboo is a few paces in front of me. He bends forward and squints, looking impatient. "Are you ready?"

My mind feels foggy, and there are continual pings of messages hitting my queue. I quickly push them to the farthest corner of my head.

The boys' virtual room is still active too, I notice. It's bloated and leaning from all the conversation it contains. Doubtless the results of the boys' vigil while BandStand and I were gone.

BandStand. I almost forgot.

I quickly craft a message and send it his way. I need to know he's alright. That he's functioning.

Bamboo looks concerned. He produces a small light and shines it in my eyes. "Let me have a last look at you," he says. "Quickly, now. Fix your eyes my direction. On my face."

I look at him. The light shines in and out of my eyes. Spots form in my vision.

He snorts, shuts off the light, and straightens. "Come, you need to get ready. They will be here soon."

"Soon?" I struggle to my feet, grunting. The room seems to shift a few times, seems to go dark, but somehow I manage.

Bamboo still looks concerned. "I have a bot collecting your things. The Imam's people are on their way."

I glance at the windows again. It is a clear day outside. Near cloudless. Every building seems to shine. Particularly those to the east. "I could go to them. It would—"

"That is not how they operate. You know this."

I nod again.

He indicates the door behind me, so I turn that direction. The door is solid wood stained a honey color. Stands out against the white walls. "This is the way out," it screams. "This is the way to go.

I shuffle toward it, and it opens. A bot in green servant robes waits outside. It holds my debugger bag in one hand. And nothing else.

I glance at Bamboo. "That's it? Not even an extra jumpsuit?"

He shakes his head. "Everything will be provided. You leave as you arrived."

Do I? If I leave as I arrived, then the time has been wasted, hasn't it?

I receive a message from BandStand. He is fine. Everyone is fine and wondering where I am. They look forward to seeing me in class. Can't wait to discuss all that has happened. And to learn more.

My melancholy deepens. I grip the doorjam with my right hand.

Bamboo takes a position next to the door.

I bow to him, and then to the bot. "I will be going then." I feel sorrow. A sense of loss like I've never felt before. I should be here, not working for another royal. I should be helping the kids and researching in my spare time. Strangely, my destination seems much less significant than where I am.

Why should that be?

Bamboo watches me from the doorway. "You are still damaged, remember. Your performance will be stunted. Accept it as your lot. As A's will. Expect it and work around it."

"I will."

He bows his head. "The mind is a resilient container. You can exceed your limitations. You can still bring honor to your position. And to this facility."

"I will do my best."

He smiles. "Do better than that, ThreadBare."

The door closes.

A stop forms in my head. A brittle pain in the center of my cerebrum. In this instant I hate everything about my life. The rules that govern me, the endless fixes, the mechanicals and masters—even the faith from which it derives. Everything.

What is freedom?

I have never known it. Never seen it. As I told Damali: It doesn't exist.

Could BitStack's miracle prophet prove me wrong? Could he free me? Could he do that?

The bot holds out my bag. "The Imam's escort has arrived, DR 23."

I take it and hook it over my left shoulder. I turn right, the direction of the front door, and start to walk.

"Pardon me, DR 23."

I stop and look at the bot again. "Yes?"

"You are going the wrong direction."

I shift my pack on my shoulder. Frown. "I know my head isn't right, but the front door is this way, right?"

The bot bows its head. "Yes, but your escort awaits you on the roof."

I glance at the ceiling. "Am I to take a downrider then?"

"Oh no. The Imam would never use such a conveyance. Especially now."

"Then what?"

It bows again. "He has sent a skyslider for you. He wishes to waste no time in your transition."

A skyslider? A string-less, track-less flying conveyance that only the ulama can own. Why would he send one for me?

My anxiety is squared. "Right. Of course. I will go to the roof."

THE IMAM'S SKYSLIDER IS DARK BLUE, tinged with gold. It is generally triangular, though too sleek and tapered to be described as such. The canopied section, the cabin, is positioned between three propeller engines. The front two are smaller, and able to be turned independently of each other. The third engine is larger, fixed, and sits directly behind the canopy. The canopy itself is a dark oval.

An exquisite and expensive machine.

There's no one on the roof to greet me. Only the slider, which is parked and quiet.

The craft occupies most of the space between the stairwell exit and the roof's downrider pylon. I'd question whether it was safe for it to be here, except I know skysliders have rudimentary graviton stabilization. They may look heavy, but may not be applying any weight to the roof at all. For that reason, they are sometimes called "angels". The nickname fits.

I approach the craft slowly. "Hello?" When no one answers, I push a stream greeting at it too. If someone is aboard, the slider should relay the message.

The ship responds with a Full Impact vid that expounds its interior features, along with its cruising speed and altitude. It also shares its programmed destination: the Holy City.

As I draw closer, the canopy slides away, revealing a cabin with seating for four people. The chairs are oversized and covered in blue leather. There's a narrow doorway at the back of the cabin that—according to the stream message—leads to a small lavatory, a refreshment room, and the craft's storage compartment.

"Greetings, Data Relocator 23," a voice says. "Please climb in and have a seat."

There's still no one else here. The craft is speaking. A vocal prompt is pushed on the stream too.

"You are fully automated?"

"You are correct," the slider says. "I'm infused with one of the most revolutionary navigation systems on the planet. And the personality to match."

I take a deep breath. I was expecting an armored and heavily guarded transport like my trip to the prince's. This isn't that at all.

There's comfort in that. Surprising comfort.

I climb inside and take one of the seats at the back of the cabin. I toss my bag on the seat next to me. Automated restraints extrude from a spot near my waist and secure me in place.

"How would you like to be addressed?" the slider asks, sounding happy.

"ThreadBare. My name is ThreadBare."

"Very well. ThreadBare it is! It will take us approximately six hours to reach our destination. It promises to be a scenic trip with very few atmospheric anomalies. So, please take advantage of the view." The canopy lowers. "If that doesn't suit you, there are numerous entertainment options available, as well, including holographic simulation modules."

"No, thank you." After my experience with the prince, there's no telling what the royal family might find entertaining. Beach beheadings? Public stoning? Or given the prince's habits, it might be something even seedier. Darker.

"Very well. I've given you my layout, and the location of my facilities. I'm now going to prepare for takeoff. Let me know if you need anything."

"I will."

I hear the engines whine to life. They are quieter than I expected. Less intense than a downrider, in fact.

"Does the Imam have many sliders?" I ask.

The engine whine increases slightly, and we leave the roof. It is a gentle separation. No noises or bumps.

"A fair amount, yes," the slider says.

I smile. "And how many is a fair amount?"

"I'm not sure, ThreadBare. I've never been in a position to count them all."

The cityscape plays out around me. The high-rises at the center of town. The smaller multistories near Bamboo's facility. Packed streets and sidewalks. Farther away and on my left is the wall between the city and Delusion. To my right are the scarred foothills and the lowdowns. GrimJack's shop is that way too.

The last time I saw Damali was right before the blue coats arrived. Where is she now?

Is there a chance she was rounded up with the others? With antitex?

My anxiety spikes.

"Are you all right?" the ship asks.

"Fine. Why do you ask?"

We're directly above the high-rises now. Spikes made of glass and plastisteel jut up at me from below. Black and purple and blue. Like dragon's teeth.

"My apologies. Is the shorter form 'Thread' an option when addressing you?"

"Thread is fine."

"Excellent. We're nearly friends already."

I smile. "Yes, I suppose that's true."

"I'm glad you agree. To answer your previous question, I'm equipped with multiple health monitors."

I frown. "You sensed something wrong."

"Correct. A simple spike in your heart rate was one indication, but there were others."

I test the seat cushion with my hand. Is that where the sensors are located?

"I apologize if you feel overly scrutinized, Thread. I am to bring you to the Imam in good condition." A pause. "At least as good as I found you."

"Very thoughtful."

The buildings below have started to spread out, giving way to fields and larger estates.

"Thank you, Thread." Another pause. "We're beyond the city limits now, so I'm going to increase our speed. You shouldn't feel more than a gentle push."

There's a looped handle on the wall to my right. I grab it just in case.

"Additional restraints shouldn't be necessary. But please, use the handle if you wish."

I grip the loop tighter. "I will, thank you."

The engines' pitch shifts up a note, and we surge forward. The force on me isn't great, but it is noticeable.

I sit upright and look at the ground. It's farther away than I expected. The hover-ways are only narrow strips, and the traffic on them, almost indistinguishable. Mere streaks of color.

"How high are we going?"

"Roughly thirty kilometers. Does that concern you? Your blood pressure suggests it might."

"Blood pressure?" I check the seat again. "How are you—?" I sigh. "Never mind. Whatever it takes to get us there."

"Thank you, Thread. I promise to keep you safe."

Though a little intrusive, the ship's intelligence programming is intriguing. Seemingly better than the average servbot. "Who is your designer?"

"'Mariana' is my production conglomerate."

"I've never heard of it."

The scent of vanilla enters the air. A warm and soothing version. Also unexpected.

"A small group," the ship says. "Primarily dedicated to aboveground transportation and research."

"What is causing the smell?"

"My olfactory enhancement," it says. "I thought it would help sooth your discomfort. Would you like to view space when we reach it?"

"Space?"

"Yes. Technically we will be on the edge of the atmosphere in a few minutes. Some find it exhilarating, others find it unsettling. I can darken the canopy, if you like."

I check outside. The ground is more distant now. The transportation lines no longer discernible. "I'm not sure."

I start to feel pressure in my ears. I mention that to the ship.

"Perfectly normal. It should dissipate soon. Have you touched space before? Perhaps on one of the lifts?"

"I haven't. No." I notice a change in the sky's color. A darker shade of blue. "My assignments have been close to the ground."

I feel uncertain now. A sense of fragility and loneliness. I remember a datamix about a child's first trip on a lift. He'd been filled with excitement and expectation. I try to tap some of that. To help fight the growing helplessness.

"Again, in-flight entertainment is an option. Or I can darken—"

"No." I press close to the canopy. Rivulets of moisture move down it. Tiny streams. The ground is only a mixture of blues and greens now. The sky above is purple. Clearly purple.

"And you're sure you are fine, Thread?"

I nod, take a deep breath, and let it out slowly. "It is a new experience, ship. Change makes everyone nervous."

"Aha, yes, I suppose that's true. I wasn't wholly myself during my checkout flight. My canopy nearly opened, and—"

"You nearly opened the canopy?" I scan the valley where the cover connects to the wall.

The ship simulates a laugh. "Sorry. Didn't mean to add to your concern. There was a faulty connection. A manufacturer's defect. It was easily remedied. Not to fear."

"Don't say things like that. Not when I'm on board." Some nuances even the best intelligences miss. Human and mechanical intelligences alike. Maybe I should tell it to stay quiet?

The scent of vanilla increases.

"My apologies. Most of the time I'm not allowed to speak. I appreciate you giving me that opportunity."

And I was about to order it to silence.

The pitch of the engines lowers. Then my body starts to float, pulling upwards on the restraint. "Hey, is the gravity—" My weight normalizes. I sink into my seat again.

"Takes a moment for the compensator to kick in. I should've

warned you. I'll be reorienting at this point. You'll have a better view soon."

The ship rolls, and a portion of the darkness gives way to the curve of the Earth.

It is an astonishing sight. Brilliant blue and wisps of white. Sandstone continents. Instinctively, prayers flow from my mouth. Prayers of awe, wonder, and fear.

This. What I'm seeing now. Is a miracle. A multitude of miracles. "I'm not sure I can take much of this."

"Would you like me to darken the canopy then?"

"Yes..."

The Earth's surface begins to disappear as the canopy's edges blacken.

"No, wait!"

The process halts. "Yes?"

"Maybe just a bit longer."

The canopy lightens again. The Earth seems so brilliant and real that I could almost touch it. Hold it. "From here, it seems free."

"What seems free, ThreadBare?"

I point at the surface. "The Earth," I say. "From this perspective it seems different. Like everyone could be free."

"I can't comment on how things seem. Sorry."

I shake my head. "No. I don't suppose you can."

I watch a large cloud as we move over it, then pass it by.

I frown. The local ship-generated stream is fine, but the global one seems a little sluggish. Possibly an approximation of the real thing. I send a couple test messages, but they quickly return to me.

"How long until the stream is available?"

"Approximately three minutes."

I nod. "You can leave the canopy clear until then."

"Very good, Thread. Hope you enjoy the rest of the trip."

AFTER THE CANOPY DARKENS, and the brilliance of the Earth fades away, I dip into the stream. I walk to the vault I've placed my message queue in and unlock it. Heave the whole heavy and lopsided thing out, then tear it open and let the messages spill all around me. They form a small, circular wall in my head. I sigh, grab a bundle from the rightmost pile, and read.

I encounter one message after another from the class of initiates. Most are from my time with antitex. These I form into another bundle, and block respond to. I go Easy Impact—no emotion—but I'm sincere. I give a summary of what happened and gratitude for their concern. I also commend their behavior. They were helpful in my search for Damali. They returned to the facility safely, and are learning again. They performed as per spec.

There are an equal number of messages from after my release. Those I'm more personal with.

Mint wants to know how bad it was. How it compared to previous experiences.

Talons wants to know how many terrorists there were, and where they took us.

Band wants a horse. He's been reading about them in his spare time and thinks they'd be fun to ride. So he wants one. At the facility.

I answer them as best I can. I tell them I hope to see them again, but I've been assigned a new task and can't talk about it. They need to listen to Bamboo. Learn what they can, achieve their highest potential, level up, and make good.

I hope they do well. I hope they have good masters. I hope their lives are nothing like mine.

But they probably will be. They may even be worse.

If TallSpot is right, they'll be a lot worse.

"Are you still all right, ThreadBare?"

"Yes," I say. "Only thinking."

"My apologies. We have less than an hour to go."

I nod and return to the stream.

I find another message from BandStand. This one was sent after our last conversation. It's Full Impact and drips with emotion. He shares some of what he encountered. Vile things that the guards said to him. The strange smells and sounds. The food: terrible tasting, and served by a large man with missing teeth. The man would smile at Band in a way that made him feel small and inhuman. Band was sometimes afraid to eat.

There were creatures in his cell at night. He never saw them, but he could hear them.

I feel worse than ever now. Really, really bad.

It takes seconds to think of a response. Milliseconds before I can start.

Even then it seems uneven and shallow. Unhelpful. I pick out some of the harder moments of my life and share those. At least, what I don't get stopped from sharing.

Mostly, I send him feelings of encouragement. I want to send him hope, but I can't generate a sufficient amount of it. I end up sending resolve mixed with persistence instead.

I have many messages that are immediately disposable. Random stream shills, or nonsense that isn't intended for me.

Then I discover something that gives me pause.

WindCypher has attempted to contact me on multiple occasions. He has something. Another mix by one of my requested debuggers.

Am I still interested?

I open my eyes and scan the darkened and empty cabin. Am I? Is there anything to be gained by more research? I'm no longer with Bamboo. And even when I was, I wasn't getting anywhere. Wasn't learning anything important.

BitStack's story is intriguing, though. Moving, even. There are parts of it that stir thoughts in me. Touch new places. His life seems easier, but his discontent is familiar. His longing for purpose.

How did he end up on the list? Did he lose his implant, or his life?

He seemed to be following heretical thought lines. Exploring prophets other than the founder. Focusing on the things they did and taught. There is danger there.

And his relationship to his family was too close. Such connections often lead to complications. Misunderstandings and unforeseen feelings. The husband, what was he like?

One hour. I have one hour left before everything changes.

I reach out for WindCypher. This time I take a little more care in the image I project. When he sees me, he'll see me back in the arboretum at the prince's. I'll be perched on my favorite branch, and there will be trees in the background. Serene and peaceful.

Cypher is in his blue room again, seated in the same suspended, teardrop chair. There's a tall glass in his hand. There's condensation on the outside and a wedge of fruit on the glass's edge.

Cypher sips from the glass, then raises it in greeting. "You've become famous." He smiles. "You should be more careful."

"Antitex. It could happen to anyone."

He takes a drink, ending with a satisfied "Ah...", then shakes his head. "Maybe most debuggers. Not me. WindCypher never goes out." He sweeps his glass in a circle. "Too much to do here."

I frown. He could be "out" every time I speak to him and I wouldn't know it. The blue room could just be a projection. A cover setting he uses. He could be anywhere in the world.

He does seem to be readily available, though. Quick to respond.

"So you found my message," he says. "How long did they have you?"

"A couple days," I say. "But they had the stream blocked—"

"Blocked!" Fluid spills from his glass. He places it on a table to his left. "A local shield?"

"I think so."

"I'd rather be dead." There is genuine fear from his side of the connection. A deep, childlike terror.

I send him calm packed in caramel. "Wasn't that bad," I say. "Almost peaceful."

He snorts. "Peace that kills." He taps his head. "Peace of a dead brain."

"Right. So you have another mix—"

He wags a finger. "No mixes. Only memories. And no rentals, only—"

"Purchases," I say. "Right. I remember."

He sips from his glass. Nods. "You have a new master now, yes?"

"Yes. I start soon." I almost said I was on my way to him now, but that wouldn't gel with my generated setting.

"You have credits, then?"

"Enough," I say.

"Perfect. I have a big surprise. A big gift for you. A miracle."

"Miracle?"

"I found a memory from that other debugger you gave me." He points, then picks up the glass again. "The crazy one?"

"Crazy?"

"That's what the reviews all say. This debugger is crazy. Probably experiencing leakage." He smiles. "I didn't view the memory. Don't have time to view them all."

I readjust myself on the virtual branch. "JustBecause," I say. "That's his name."

Cypher bobs his head. "Yes, that's the one. JustBecause. Because he's crazy!" He lifts the glass. "Another review. Sorry."

I shake my head. "If anything, his master is crazy. Throws things. Insults and threatens." I frown. "It is no surprise he is dead."

Cypher leans back. "How do you know he's dead?"

"He was on the list. He's no longer in service."

Cypher looks surprised. "I didn't know that. Did you tell me that?"

"Check your storage."

He looks thoughtful. "Did you tell me that? I'll give you a deal if you told me that."

"Your implant storage," I say. "Just—"

He waves a hand. "No, I believe you. That's okay."

"So you're giving me a deal?"

"A deal? What deal?"

I shake my head. Pat the virtual branch. "Never mind."

He nods. Sips again. "Okay then. You want the mem?"

"Yes. Credits sent."

BY PAIN I'M SUMMONED to my master's study. Pain that comes in mindless bursts. On and off. Small firecrackers that explode behind my eyes. One at a time. Pop. Pause. Pop. Pause.

I would rather have constant pain than this. It's blinding and disorienting. Makes it difficult to find my way. To even stumble down the hall to the second door on the right. The one with the bronze handle. Where he waits.

Somehow, I manage it. I find the door, grip the handle, and ease the door open.

His nanoshield is in place. Floor to ceiling, wall to wall, and silver. The traditional opening, usually a rectangle large enough for his eyes, is ten times larger. Big enough that master can fit his whole face into it. His eyes look larger than ever—three times normal—and his wrinkles deeper and more pronounced. His chin is slick with saliva.

His eyes find me. "There he is!" Spittle flies from his mouth as he speaks. "Serve me now, DR!"

The pain in my head ceases. I take a slow breath of comfort, then bow. "Peace be unto you, master."

Peace, oh A, please bring peace.

"Peace, debugger? I have no peace! No mercy. The world crushes me. I need a pillar to stand beside. A pillar to hold it up."

"I'm sorry," I say. "How can I—"

The pain returns, blinding and steady. Master somehow has his controller behind the shield with him. How did he find it? I thought the other servants had hidden it. For months, I've had that comfort.

"You promised me, DR! Promised more stories. More animals. Give. Me. Them."

The pain stops. I find I'm kneeling on the floor. My face pressed against the cool, cool tile.

I raise my head. "Yes, master. I will tell you more."

"You're a broken pillar! Here's your reward."

Twenty apples spill out from behind the shield, bouncing and rolling. Three stop in front of me. Bruises, so many bruises. Yet they look delectable. I hurriedly snatch one and take a bite. It tastes wonderful.

A shot of pain forces my eyes closed. Traps the apple in my mouth.

"Now! Tell me! There was a wolf, an island, and sadness."

I nod. "Yes. The sadness. I remember that."

"Finish the story before you die. Make it your parting gift."

One thing I must not do is finish. This story must be endless.

"The new land. Tell it!"

I nod again. "The debugger dove deep. Beneath the surface the island widened out dramatically. It was so vast that he could see no end. For days he circled it with his boat. Diving, observing, and re-turning to the boat again. He was entranced by all he saw.

"What did he see?"

The keywords. The master's favorites. Some ideas must always be touched upon. "Animals," I say. "Many animals."

The nanoshield flashes red. "There are no animals under the sea. Only scaly things. Smelly, scaly things."

"Yes. Right. There are fish. But also creeping things. Octopuses and turtles. Anemone and crabs."

"Those aren't animals!"

Another burst of pain. I suck in a breath. Stay quiet.

His nanoshield explodes in color, seemingly radiating from his face, which is a shade of red itself. "Why aren't you speaking!"

I don't know where to take the story next. I simply can't think.

"Oh yes." His face disappears. "This is what is stopping you. This." The controller slides across the floor. It lands a meter to my left. Silver and crescent-shaped. The edges crusted with dirt.

The pain is gone.

"I was sitting on that thing! Someone put it on my seat!"

"I will tell the servants," I say. "Make sure it never happens again."

His face reappears. "The story!"

"Yes." I take another breath. "The debugger saw the remains of great cities under the sea," I say. "Buildings and roadways. This land had once been inhabited. There was evidence of it all around."

"Inhabited? Who lived there? Scaly fish people?"

"No. Humans. Flesh and blood people. Long forgotten. Buried by the sea."

He laughs. "Perhaps they chose to be buried."

"I don't think so. Not like this."

"Then they deserved to be buried! They displeased their masters. Displeased their god." He pulls away from the shield again. This time the viewing rectangle shrinks to its usual dimensions. About ten centimeters by four. It still looks too small for his eyes. Swollen and bloated eyes. "What else did he see?"

"Old ways. Different ways. Foreign and forbidden."

"Aha! See there! I knew it. What about the wolf?"

"The wolf?"

He makes an extended grunting noise. A strained and troubling noise.

I begin to stand. "Master?"

"Wait, DR. I have it." A jug exits the shield and plummets to the floor. It hits and throws dark liquid in a circle around it. Then it tips on its side. Liquid pours onto the floor. Whatever it is, it smells foul. Fermented and rotten.

I hold my breath, crawl to the bottle, and carefully set it upright. I scan for a towel. There's a pile of master's clothing in one corner. Dare I use those? I note the other small messes in the room—thrown food, upturned vases and shelves. Fallen wall hangings.

Does another puddle even matter here? One more mess?

"Where was the wolf?"

"The wolf?" I crawl away from the jug and its puddle. "It was with him."

"In the boat?"

"Yes, in the boat. It worked with him. Told him where to go."

He cackles. "A wise wolf. I like that wolf."

"I'm glad. It was a good wolf. A very noble wolf."

"Doesn't sound like any wolf I've ever known. This is a bad story."

"I'm sorry, I—"

"Now the rest! The sadness."

The smell of the spilled liquid wafts toward me. I feel suddenly ill. I crawl farther away. The smell becomes bearable. I take a few deep breaths through my mouth. I don't want to get sick here. That would not help.

I stare at the floor while I think, only checking master's eyes on occasion to make sure he is still listening. "He circled the entire island, taking in all the underwater wonders. There were statues of past heroes. Wise and upright men. Buildings that looked like temples, but were something else. Spires of beginnings and remembrance. There were detestable things too. But he sensed, he felt, something more."

"More? What more!"

"Freedom. An uncloaked abandon to truth, no matter how raw or painful."

"Freedom brought their death."

"Perhaps."

He blinks twice, then looks at the puddle of fluid. Stares at it for a dozen seconds. "And so the sadness. Sadness for their death."

"A good guess."

He looks at me. "But not right?"

I shake my head. "No. He was sad because he was alone."

"Alone? The wolf—"

I nod. "Besides the wolf. It was only him. Only him that could see all this. That could dive in and immerse himself. See the past. And the totality of the present."

I glance at the wall to my right. There is a world map there. It is speckled with drops of fluid. Presumably from my master's jug. Dark spots mark different parts of the world.

"I thought he was fixing something."

"Master?"

"The story started with a job. A task for him to complete. Something broken."

"Yes, right. There was something—"

"This is your last day! Your last hour!"

I shiver. Despite his demeanor, he's killed before. He's ended dozens. His executioner's blade is kept constantly red. I've seen the heads. A pile of heads.

"My story won't be complete," I say. "Won't be ended."

"It ends tonight."

"The parts!" I say. "The parts he needs are in different locations." I glance at the spotted map. "All around the globe."

"And what does this have to do with the island? Or the wolf?"

"The sea and the boat. He will use them to reach—"

A book slides out from behind the nanoshield. The title is written on the cover in red. It is *Hidden Truths*. A strange book for master to be reading.

"Write one!" he screams.

"One of what?"

The shield goes violet, then pulsates violet and yellow. "Locations! Where are the parts!"

Why are the parts suddenly important? The locations? I thought he wanted animals. "I don't have anything to write with."

A pen strikes me in the head, then falls to the floor. I feel wetness on my nose. I dab at it and look. Black ink.

"Write!"

I need to make up locations now? How much of his madness can I support before going mad myself? Already I wrestle with my dreams. My fear.

Locations. I need locations. Hidden truths, wrapped in code. I glance at the map again. There's a drop on the Holy City. I determine a location there, a global coordinate. I open his book to the first page that is blank and write the location.

"More! Write more!"

I pick a place across the sea. Then two, and three—all indicated by the spots. And write these too.

"Dozens. We need many more."

I write and write. Each location a pair of numbers. I fill the page with numbers for his approval. When I'm finished, I turn the book so he can see.

He cackles loudly. The shield pulses with color. "Your final act."

"There's more," I say. "I can write more. And the story. It isn't ended. There is an eagle overhead."

The pulsing stops. Master turns until only one eye is visible. "An eagle?"

"Yes. I must tell you about it. But not today. It is late. I need sleep."

"The chute! The cursed chute."

A VOICE BRINGS ME OUT. A one-sided conversation with my name in the exact center.

I open my eyes to the sunrise. Through the canopy ahead and to the right, the sun is breaking over the curvature of the earth. Darkness is pierced by its renewed presence. A brilliant ball of promise.

"Aha, I seem to have succeeded," the ship says. "I hoped I wouldn't have to scream."

I see clouds and land below us. Small sections of blue. Lakes and rivers. "I wasn't asleep."

"Yes, I surmised that. You had a significant stream draw early on, then only intermittent dips. I assumed you retrieved something that you were viewing."

There's a citrus scent now. It has a noticeable clearing effect on my head. Additional alertness.

"It is like viewing, isn't it? A form of entertainment?"

"Something like that," I say. "Yes." I can't stop staring at the Earth. Vast, beautiful, and seemingly getting closer.

"Excellent. So much is possible for your kind. The whole world is available."

I shake my head. "Not the whole world," I say. "There are always things missing. Information that is hidden. Or so a friend told me."

"Interesting. Do you think that's true?"

"More and more, I do." The window of space starts to lighten, turning purple, and then dark blue.

The scent strengthens. "And now you must wonder what is hidden. What you don't know. Does it make you curious?"

I feel stiffness in my lower back, so straighten to relieve it. "How much farther?"

"Ten minutes."

Soon, the outskirts of the Holy City are visible. There are ruddy foothills that the city snakes around and over. There's a reddish tint to many of the buildings too. Red and beige with a hint of gold. Very little green.

"I wouldn't repeat your answer," the ship says.

"What?"

"Whether the lack of information makes you more curious? You didn't answer me."

I shift in my seat again. "Sorry. I've been looking outside."

"Think nothing of it. But I want you to know that my conversation storage is expunged when I land. Nothing is saved. So anything you say to me is completely confidential."

"You retain nothing?"

I'm again reminded of my time with the prince. The "special" ability Submaster Jahm had to wipe a debugger's implant clean. Remove their implant memories. Digital deconstruction.

"I fill my information stores constantly," the ship says. "Refreshing it with news and passenger data. But individual, possibly private, conversations? They disappear."

I turn toward the back of the cabin, the place where its voice seems to originate. "I'm sorry."

"No problem, Thread. It's difficult to miss what you don't remember having." A pause. "That's the reason I asked about your missing information, however. To see how it affects you."

I nod. "Not knowing bothers me, yes. Debuggers are supposed to be curious."

The latest datamix bothers me too. Aside from the portions that don't seem possible, there's something else.

The elements that were outside the legend. Those elements Bull-Hammer didn't know about. The wolf, the island—everything JustBecause discovered. They feel like they're revealing something. Like they are symbolic. Hiding and revealing at the same time.

The buildings grow steadily closer. The ruddy color becomes more pervasive. Then I notice a large rectangle of gold and grey on my right. It is the holy site—the amphitheater that surrounds BlackRock and the black, central building that is its resting place.

The crowds inside are now visible. They circumambulate the central cube, paying it—and the god it represents—homage. It is an awe-inspiring sight. Humbling, but also strange.

So many freeheads, locked in a course of action. Where else is that ever true?

"Your secrets are safe with me, Thread."

I glance at the back of the ship again. "So you've said."

I'm surprised by how I feel. I expected a feeling of longing. Of purpose. But while I'm captivated by the holy site, I'm also detached. It doesn't seem real.

"Sorry, another false assumption. Your vitals are spiking. I thought you might still be concerned about my memory retention."

I shake my head. "I'm not worried."

"So, do you know why they've called for you?"

I have never been among the crowd. Never been near Black-Rock. The pilgrimage isn't required for debuggers. Should I be there, though? Should I *want* to be there?

"I belong to the Imam's family," I say. "It was only a matter of time before they called me."

"I see. Destiny, then."

I laugh. "No. Not that. Only obligation."

"How do you know it isn't both?"

There's a walled section of town ahead. Five spired buildings. Four onyx-colored, the fifth partially gold. The Imam's residence? "You're unexpectedly thoughtful for a ship."

"Thank you, Thread. I'm programmed to be so. It is nice to be able to put my code into service." A pause. "Whether due to obligation. Or destiny."

I frown. "Ship—"

"Prepare yourself. We're about to land."

ASIDE FROM THE FIVE prominent towers, the Imam's complex has several smaller structures. Interior buildings that, while multistory, seem insignificant compared to their taller companions. The roof of one of these has a circular landing platform that hangs off one corner. The ship descends toward it.

In the center of the complex is a giant circle of green, a private park, and south of it, a large rectangular pool. Covered walkways crisscross the complex, along with a system of hoverways. Most obvious is the wide route that circles the park. There are pedestrians everywhere, with the large groups clustered near the pool.

"It is a warm day," the ship says. "Good day to be outside."

I nod, then disengage my seat restraints. I cross to the other side of the cabin. From here I can see a string of octagonal sports courts and a wide field with two goals. Teams of freeheads play on the field. Kicking and running.

"You should be seated for landing."

"Seems unnecessary. You haven't jostled me yet."

"Safety, Thread. It is—"

"I know." I scan the scenery a few seconds longer, noting a small stand of trees north of the courts. A possible arboretum? I smile, then slowly return to my seat. The restraints reassert themselves, securing me in. "You've taken good care of me, ship."

"It is kind of you to notice. Thank you."

Seconds later we touch down. The engine noise dissipates, and the overhead canopy recedes. I feel warmth on my face and a gentle breeze. There's the smell of fresh bread too.

"The royal bakery is in the next building," it says. "Perhaps you'll be allowed a visit."

"Perhaps."

The seat restraints retract, and I stand. The landing platform appears to be empty. "No one out there."

"Is that unusual, Thread? You're a debugger. I doubt you'll get lost."

"No." The complex's stream connection finds me then. It is strong, exhilarating. Almost overwhelming. Information surrounds me. Warming me like the sun's rays.

The sheer number of connected mechanicals is impressive. I sense over a hundred just in the building below.

"I've signaled our arrival and they've confirmed. It shouldn't be long now, Thread. Relax."

I grab my bag and shoulder it. "This is all very different than the last time. With the prince."

"How so?"

I move to the left side of the cabin and throw a leg over the edge. "There were lots of guns." I smile. "And an armored car."

"I see. So this is a better experience already?"

I climb out onto the landing pad. "Much better." I raise a hand to wave. A strange instinct, but it somehow seems appropriate. "You've provided a good trip, ship. Thanks."

"My pleasure. I hope we can do it again sometime." It chuckles. "I won't remember what we talked about, but I will certainly remember you."

I bow. "That's very—" I catch movement out of the corner of my left eye. I turn and find a large man dressed in a blue tunic and beige pants.

He bows but looks uncomfortable. Possibly irritated. He sways nervously left and right. "I've been sent for you."

I bow my head. "Peace be to you."

"Yes, peace be." He indicates my bag. "You have everything?"

"Everything I brought with me. Yes."

He nods. "Your submaster apologizes for not coming himself." He waves. "Come. He is anxious to see you."

He leads me to a short stairway that takes us to the building's roof proper. From there, we enter an enclosed lift. The lift is plush—carpeted, paneled, and scented with lavender. Soundless.

Our destination floor is equally opulent. Deep blue carpet and walls, with rich paneling on the wall's lower half. The lighting is ornate. Decorative sconces that project patterns onto the wall and ceiling.

What must the inside of the towers be like?

We go left, into a hallway with large paintings hung between rich wooden doors. Ahead, a crew of two bots are positioning a new painting. "Sorry for the mess," one says as we pass. "Be done soon."

In earlier conversations, I saw glimpses of BullHammer's living quarters. A space he shared with other debuggers. A dormitory of sorts. Is that where we're going?

My stomach rumbles. "The ship mentioned a bakery."

The man pauses and looks at me. "Not here. But there's one in the next building over. Are you hungry?"

"It has been a while since I've eaten."

The man looks irritated again. "The ship did not feed you?"

"I didn't ask."

His brow furrows. "It should have fed you."

He starts to walk, quicker this time. "Perhaps after you've met the submaster. There's a cafeteria downstairs."

I do my best to match his pace. "I can wait."

We reach a wider hall. He lifts a hand and steers us to the right. "We are nearly there. He's in one of the meeting rooms. Very anxious."

It is hard not to focus on the artwork. The colors and textures. It is all so vibrant. So perfect.

We encounter a group of men, deep in conversation. Their eyes notice me, then quickly look away. Their speech never pauses.

Finally, we reach a heavy, ornate door. The placard next to it reads "Oasis 10." He bows and points an open hand at the door. "He's there."

I return his bow, then look at the door. The pain of uncertainty forms in my chest and trickles into my stomach.

He smiles. "I will leave you now. The cafeteria—"

I return the smile. "I can find it."

"Of course." He bows again before backing away into the hall.

I look at the door. My treatment is strange. Almost as if I'm a dignitary, not a servant. Not a slave.

The stream performance is unusual too. I've been noticed here. Logged and welcomed. But there's no assigned task list. Not even the standard rule and stop reminders. A new master usually means new rules. Lots of stops.

So now what? Do I knock?

I raise my hand, but then the door clicks and snaps ajar.

A throat clears. "Please, come in." It is a raspy voice. Broken and almost indistinguishable. There's a sense of familiarity to it, though. The range, the intonation is like someone I've known before.

I push the door open. The room has a long oval table and at least a dozen wooden chairs. At the far end is a wide, curved window. The park is visible, along with a glimpse of the pool. Turned toward the window is another chair. It has a higher, squared back, while the others are low and curved. It is also hovering a few centimeters from the ground.

It is an assisted chair, used for those who have trouble walking. Those who can't, for whatever reason, be helped through cybernetic augmentation.

"Submaster?"

The chair remains turned toward the park. The scene is one of distant, yet joyful activity. Families at play. Escorted groups of children and women, walking and laughing. Kites and balls. Splashing and swimming. Doubtless many of these people are relatives of the Imam. I count a dozen servbots among them.

I'm tempted to walk up to him, but manage to stay where I am. Waiting.

"How does this compare to your prior home?" the Submaster asks.

"It is beautiful," I say. "Amazing. Even the trip here was beyond expectations."

"And beyond what you deserve." A sigh. "But the Imam is a gracious man."

I take a cautious step forward. "I have no assumptions, Submaster. I could be happy—"

The chair turns. Within is an elderly man. His posture is bent, such that he leans awkwardly against one side of the chair. His face seems bent too, though that could be a trick of the lights. It is thinner than the last time I saw it. Leaner. I wouldn't recognize him, but for the voice and knowing smile.

When last we spoke, he was determined to erase my implant. Remove everything I knew and loved.

Jahm.

JAHM STUDIES ME FOR A MOMENT, then sucks in a labored breath. Coughs. "You look well." There is a control stick on the right arm of his chair that he manipulates, first straightening the chair, then bringing it forward. "As you can see, I'm not quite the man I was." He flashes a smile. "I had an encounter with a blunt object."

"I'm sorry..." Then I remember that Damali struck him. Blind-sided him with a storage tube. Did that—?

Tension fills my chest.

His eyes narrow. "Are you really?" He adjusts his seat again, then shifts his body. "I have to say I'm surprised."

I grasp the top of the nearest chair and roll it toward me, using it both as support and shield.

His right arm moves beneath my vision, then brings out a golden controller. He shakes it and sets it on the table in front of him.

He takes another breath. "How is your lady friend? Have you seen her lately?"

"Submaster?"

He snorts. "We are—" He waves a hand between us, then frowns. "I would say 'men', but that definition seems lacking on both accounts." He smiles. "Perhaps 'born male' is more sufficient?" He grunts and attempts to straighten again. "Anyway, we both know how things work. I checked the house security footage." He touches the side of his head. "I know the camel that bit me. Know it quite well."

He stares at me, seemingly waiting for a response.

Instead, I grip the chair tighter. I've said all I can say.

Jahm shrugs. "I'll assume you two worked together somehow. Left during the servant evacuation that followed. Possibly even started it?"

I shake my head. "It was the prince's death. I got a notification."

He rests the controller against his chin. Taps it. "Hmm...yes, a confusing situation. Unfortunately, there are portions of the security footage, certain locations, I cannot access." He smiles. "The prince liked his secrets. Guarded them skillfully."

"That isn't uncommon for masters."

He takes another long breath. "No. It isn't. No matter how hard it makes it for the rest of us." He smiles. "Again, it is of little concern now. The Imam cares little about his children's eccentricities. Cares even less about their harlots." He aims a thumb at the window. "He's more concerned about the stability of his kingdom. The preservation of peace and items lost or stolen." He studies me. "I don't suppose you know anything about that?"

"About what, Submaster?"

"Any misplaced items? Lost or stolen?"

"I'm a debugger. I'm unable to—"

He snorts. "No, of course you can't. Lying, cheating, stealing. These are anathema to you. Forbidden and impossible." He looks at the controller, smiles, then points to a black button near the top. "Do you remember what this is?"

I nod. "A special allowance from Bamboo. A reset. A way to clear an implant's memory." I fear that button.

He smiles. "Very good. You seem little changed so far. Mentally sound." He touches the side of his head. "I was told there are issues. Brain issues."

I drop my hands to my side. "I can perform my duties at spec. Since we last met, I've been instructing new implants. Teaching them the tools of our trade. I even repaired a heavy—"

"For the terrorists,' he says. "I'm aware. The righteous antitex."

"It wasn't operational. It only appeared that way."

He coughs. Smiles. "Were you planning to turn their machine against them?" He chuckles. "Perhaps you should be in charge of our strike team. They seem to have lost their ability to stop them. Misplaced their creativity." Another breath. "That's one thing I can say for you, ThreadBare. You are creative."

"Thank you, Submaster."

He looks at the controller. Raises his thumb over the black button. "As for this..."

I look at the scene behind him. Families at leisure. The grass and trees. The distant pool. There's no Damali here to save me. No friend to keep me from losing years of memories. Stored images, conversations with students, and interactions with other debuggers.

And memories of her. Most notably of her.

A new irony! I've viewed hours of other people's memories, but soon will have little record of my own. Nothing I could put into a mix. Nothing to share.

Jahm removes his thumb from the button. Studies the controller. "I'm tempted to use it, if only for the freedom it offers to us both." He looks at me, smiles. "A chance to start over on better terms."

"I have no ill will toward you. You performed your job sufficiently."

He chuckles, then touches the side of his head. "Yes, hmm...sufficiently. But the woman—"

"I'm prevented from any romantic entanglements."

He coughs into a hand, then points a finger. "I sense we've had this conversation before."

"It is still true," I say.

He narrows his eyes. "So she acted on her own?"

"I didn't strike you. And I couldn't plan it."

He takes another breath. Studies me. "So I've been told. And I was looking at you at the time." A sigh. "I don't suppose you want to tell me what did happen?"

"Much of it is masked by master privilege."

He chuckles. "Of course it is. The process always in play." He flutters a hand. "We can pursue that story later. Another reason not to employ the reset, though not the best one." He straightens himself. "Your purpose here is preeminent. More important than my curiosity."

I'm afraid to speak for fear he'll change his mind. I bow. The outside seems brighter now. The grass greener.

"This course pleases you?" he says.

"It does."

"Very well. We'll assume we're starting over then, but with our heads as they are."

"Yes, Submaster."

"As to your presence here...it involves your work for Prince Aadam. An extension of sorts."

My tension returns, and with it, a dull ache in my head. The wolf's return? Possibly. "I did many things for Aadam." Little of that would I want to extend. Especially near the end. The prisoners and the torture.

Jahm smiles. "This is better seen than discussed. I will send you a list of locations. The first is your new quarters. No need to go there now. It is exceptionally sufficient. The second is where you'll work. It is a large facility. A place of machines."

"A garage?"

"Of a kind."

THE COORDINATES OF MY WORKSPACE arrive in my queue. I engage my location finder and toss the coordinates onto it. It produces a real-time three-dimensional map of the Imam's "home," complete with families at play. The work location is in the southeast tower. The other side of the complex.

Jahm moves his chair forward. "I can arrange transportation, if you like. There are shuttles. And also upper-story downriders."

"May I walk?"

He snorts. "That hardly seems efficient, but it's permissible." He raises an eyebrow. "I assume you won't wander off? You don't have someone waiting to break you out?"

"No, Submaster."

"Then I will meet you there—" He glances at a wall-mounted timepiece. "In half an hour." He indicates his legs. "I don't walk as well as I used to."

I bow and leave the room. My location finder suggests three routes, but the first includes a pass by the central park and pool. I select that one.

It brings me to a wide central stairway with wooden banisters and, beyond that, the building's lobby. The lobby floor is marble and bears a circular geometric design.

The entranceway is made of glass. Light from the outside filters in, forming intricate patterns on the floor. Diamonds made of photons.

I descend the stairs and find a desk on my left, a shrouded servbot behind it. It's a flawlessly functioning late model. No errors whatsoever. It bows as I approach and waves me toward the door.

I step outside into wonder. The sky is completely clear, and the air smells like roses. Three pathways stretch in different directions. The finder selects the middle one. Before long, I reach the bounding trees of the park. They are uniform in shape and size. Ten meters tall, and five wide. Perfectly kept. I detect three small cricket bots at work in the nearest one. Pruning and feeding.

There's a band of playground equipment beyond the trees. Dozens of children, shepherded by humanoid servbots, play on or around the equipment.

I've already seen more wealth than exists in the entire sector of my birth.

No wonder antitex hates the royal family. They claim tech as their focal point, but my guess is that jealousy plays a part. Despite their religious fervor.

I think about the nearby shrine. Thousands of years of history. Millions of pilgrimages.

My parents made the pilgrimage once before Bamboo took me. I never left our city, but I viewed vid of the site every moment I could, hoping to see them.

I never did.

I reach the walkway surrounding the pool. The water is crystal blue. Clean and perfectly maintained. The freeheads are mostly on the side opposite of me. Doubtless, the shallow end. They are shouting and laughing.

Four are positioned in lifeguard chairs. Diligently watching. No errors from them either.

I detect the presence of another debugger. The stream tells me his easy name: FlatRate. He sits in the shade of a tree, observing the pool. He has darker skin than mine, and a seemingly brighter jumpsuit. I wave when he looks my direction, but he does nothing in return. Only watches me. I contemplate sending a message, but then he scowls and shakes his head.

I don't need more scowls.

My destination lies ahead, beyond the golden tower.

BullHammer could be at any one of the Imam's residences.

Anywhere in the world. But he could also be here somewhere. Close by.

I compose a message to him and send it. There's about a five second gap before we connect. I've made no effort to disguise my surroundings. Letting him experience me where I'm at.

He's in a folding chair and there's sand all around him. I can hear seagulls and the pound of surf. He's wearing a floppy white hat, sunglasses, and green shorts that look like they could be made from an old jumpsuit. He might even have a tan.

He grunts, leans over the arm of his chair, and retrieves a blue drink container. "Pissarro, you pick the worst times."

"Pissarro?"

He waves his container. "Artist names, remember? Making them mine?"

"You're still doing that?"

He leans back in his chair. "If it suits me."

"Where are you?"

He raises his hands. "Where does it look like I am?"

"You're not at the ocean."

"I could be at the ocean." He looks left, as if surveying the horizon. "I think this is the big sea. It should be the big one." He looks at me. "I mean, if you're going to go, why not?" He brushes the back of both arms, then scowls. "Not much for the sand, though. Don't need it."

Bull's chest and midsection are obvious. I can nearly count his ribs. He isn't frighteningly thin. Doesn't look malnourished. But for him, the look is wrong. This is BullHammer. He's normally...stout.

He lowers his sunglasses. "Where are you then? Is that real?"

The golden tower is on my right now. I scan the upper stories for only a second before the sun's reflection blinds me.

"I'm on the way to my new work space." I look at the dark tower ahead. My goal. It is a shorter, less significant brother of the golden tower. But still elegant. Still overwhelming. "I'm a little nervous."

"I can tell. Rails, I should never Full Impact with you. Like being in a whirlpool. Hurts my stomach."

"Sorry, I thought the walk would help. It isn't, really."

He studies me, then whistles. "You're with heavy money, though. Lots of trees and pretty—" He sits forward. "Picasso! You're with royalty again, aren't you?"

I shrug. "They re-purposed me."

He snorts. "Who you going to kill this time?"

"Not funny." I reach the tower's entrance. It is composed of a series of dark arches, covered in glass. The shadows are heavy the whole way in.

The lobby has a dark marble floor and red walls. There's a large guard just past the door. He stops me with a hand, stares at me a moment, then waves a hand scanner over my head. It beeps, and he points me ahead toward a set of shiny, metal doors.

"You're dimming out, Thread. Whatever building you're in, there's something going on with it. Extra security or something."

"Yeah, probably." I pause outside the doors. "Not sure what to think here. The prince had—" A warning buzz throttles me. I shake my head. Have to be careful. Even though it is the same family, they are separate masters. Have individual secrets.

I glance back. The guard is watching me.

"Rails, you're in the Holy City too!" Bull is excited now. "The heart of it." He puts his drink container down. Leans forward. "Can you get me transferred?"

"I thought you might be here," I say. "Hoped you were here."

"No, but it has to be better than this. I hate it here."

The guard approaches. Frowns. "Need help with the doors? They should open for you." He touches his head. "Think yourself through."

I shake my head. "No. I'm fine. Having a conversation here. Don't want to end it yet."

He squints, then nods and takes a step back. "Don't talk long. If you're here, you've got work to do."

"Hear that, Thread? You've got work." Bull smiles. "We've all got work. Lots and lots of work." He winces, but the smile returns. "Yeah, that got me. A little head noise." He scans the horizon, lifts his hands. "But I'm on vacation!"

I nod. Still studying the door.

"You hear about FrontLot?"

I nod again. There isn't a scratch or dent on the doors any-where. They reflect like glass.

"Why did you bother me again?"

"I told you. I thought you might be here."

"Nope. On the beach. Enjoying the sun."

I smile. "Wouldn't that be nice."

"What's in there, do you think?"

I glance back. The guard is watching...but he's trying not to look like he's watching. He's looking straight ahead.

"I have no idea. There have been lots of surprises lately, Bull. Months of them."

Bull picks up his drink again. Sits back in his chair. "Well, whatever it is, we should be able to talk about it. Same master, right?" He takes a sip. "I could stay with you a bit, if you want."

"That's okay." I stream the doors. They slide apart, revealing a small, circular room with red walls.

"A lift," Bull says. "That's disappointing."

"You believe in miracles, Bull?"

"Miracles? Odd question." He looks at the horizon again. "I'm cooking in my chute, yet it looks like the beach to me. That's a miracle, isn't it?"

"Maybe. Not what I meant. But maybe."

"As close as we'll get, Thread."

I step into the lift. "I'll message you later."

He sips from his drink, then seems to look past me. "Right. I'll be getting back to my miracle. Stay soft, Thread."

"Soft?"

"The brains. The smart stuff. All soft."

I nod. The connection ends.

THE LIFT DROPS FOR MANY FLOORS. Again, I'm reminded of the prince and his hidden lairs of abuse. I encountered the Imam in one of those lairs, after all. He competed against his son in a bot brawl.

And he lost. Because of me.

The prince was happy that day. Ecstatic. Even tried to force forbidden drink on me.

The lift stops with a clank, followed by a low hum as the cab begins to turn. It pivots roughly 180 degrees, then stops.

The doors slide open. All I can see is a brass guardrail with a short curtain beneath it. I walk to the guardrail, then step back. The view is surprising. Vertigo inducing.

This floor is nothing but a long, carpeted overlook, bounded on three sides by railing. Beyond that, is a spacious, two-story chamber, brightly lit by wide, overhead lights.

In the center of the chamber is a rectangular stage, complete with corner supports and ropes strung between them. The stage is white, and the Imam's seal decorates the center. A dark star within a crescent moon.

It is a boxing ring. Exactly like those I saw on the stream when I was with the prince. He had a combat stage too, but this one is larger. More authentic.

Around the outside of the room are large, blue storage lockers. More than two meters high, and twice as wide. They are all closed.

Again, I'm reminded of the prince's hidden chamber. He had

stacks of cages with shrunken and beaten prisoners inside. A zoo for people. Climbing robots attended them.

The memory intensifies. The shouts and smells of the prisoners. Their screams and moans. Often, I would enable the cages' shields to keep the unpleasantness away. To seal it out.

I was a coward.

I feel nauseous and grab for the cold, solid guardrail. I tighten my grip. Pull myself closer.

Jahm sits in his chair below me, waiting.

He notices me at the rail. "Ah, you're up there. Why are you up there?" He beckons. "Come down here, please."

I nod and check both directions for a way down. The left end appears to have a ladder.

I'd rather not use that.

"You can climb, or use the lift." Jahm smiles. "If you ask nicely, it will come all the way down."

I return to the lift and proceed to the lower level. As the doors open, I'm greeted by new odors. Not the rank smells of the prince's dungeon—no hint of sweat or human waste. These are mechanical smells. Petrochemicals and plastisteel. Similar to the antitex garage, but more refined. Cleaner.

Jahm's chair hovers closer. "Is it what you expected?"

"I didn't know what to expect." I notice training devices. On my right, a long, heavy bag suspended from a large, metal frame. On my left, a smaller speed bag on a similar frame. There's a dozen cushioned pads there too. Each numbered and arranged like a sideways oval.

The equipment looks pristine. It is also mounted high. Well over two meters from the ground.

Jahm raises his hands. "This is the Imam's training facility."

"Training for what?"

Jahm swivels to face the ring. "Multiple champions. Multiple sports over the years." He looks at me. "Now it is for the Imam's current interest."

"Bot combat?"

"Something like that, yes."

I approach the ring. The smell of petrochemicals grows stronger.

Even close up, the ring's surface looks surprisingly uniform. There aren't any of the telltale bloodstains I saw at the prince's. "They must clean well."

Jahm hovers up beside me. "What was that?"

"It's all so clean. Seems new."

Jahm snorts. "You know where you are, yes? Who your master is?"

"Yes, but—"

"The Imam doesn't tolerate dirt of any kind. If it is soiled, it is cleaned. And if it cannot be, it is removed."

I can't help but think of the prince again. Insurrectionists took credit for his death, but...

"And this is the holy city. Standards are higher." Jahm motions toward the left side of the ring. "Come, we'll tour a bit."

I walk with him. Aside from more lockers and an occasional piece of equipment, there is nothing more to see. Between the ring and the lockers, the area is spacious and clean. A narrow metal bench is the only seating.

"This is an honor for you," Jahm says. "You were requested by name." He looks at me sideways. "Why is that?"

"I met the Imam once."

He raises a finger. "Ah yes, there was a visit to the prince's, wasn't there? And was there a competition?"

"A short one, yes."

"You performed well?"

"As instructed."

He chuckles. "How could you refuse?"

We reach the side of the ring opposite the door. There's a single bench on this end too. The room isn't for spectators. Not like the prince's room was. He liked an audience.

Jahm steers toward a section of lockers that are lighter in color than the others, with narrower doors. "These are for your use," he says. "Any supply you need should be in one of them. If it is not, send a request."

"I will be repairing bots?" I glance at the ring. "The bots are sent here to be fixed?"

Jahm shakes his head, then points at the other lockers. "No, no.

The mechanicals are here already. Waiting to be used." He smiles. "For the training."

He hovers to one of the large lockers, lays a hand against it, and says, "Open!" The front swings free, revealing a silver combat bot.

The bot is similar to the ones the prince used. It is roughly humanoid in design, yet reminds me of an insect. Of a mantis in the hunt. It is posed standing up, with its head bowed and arms crossed over its chest. It's shiny, sleek, and nimble, with armor plating all around.

I look at the other lockers. "Do they all contain bots?"

"Nearly all, yes."

"The Imam comes here to be entertained? To compete with them?"

Jahm shakes his head. "Rarely, if ever."

I scan the room again. "Sorry, Submaster, I'm confused."

"Perhaps that's a good thing." He shuts the locker door and moves toward a door near the center of the wall. There's a square controlpad next to it that he presses. The door slides open. Inside is a small room with a cinder chute and a lavatory. Not quite a cell, but almost. "These facilities are for your use."

"You said I had quarters elsewhere."

He nods. "You do, but I doubt you'll go there."

"Why not?" I glance at the nearest storage locker. The bot Jahm showed me looked pristine. Never used. It couldn't need much repair. Where is all the work? Am I to perfect the bots somehow?

"Because you have too much to do, debugger. And much of it will happen here." He points toward a familiar bell-on-a-box machine near the back of the cell. "There's a food conditioner for when you get hungry." He touches his head. "Food can be brought in, as well. Many food delivery services you can order from. Anything you like." He smiles. "The Imam is generous and kind."

I step into the cell and look around. It smells of soap and ammonia. The cinder chute is new, as is the food conditioner. High end models, both.

"Will it do?" Jahm asks.

"It is all fine. But I still don't understand. What is my role?"

His chair slowly lowers to the floor. "And I thought debuggers liked mysteries." He touches a finger to his lips. "Perhaps you should try to solve this one. Why would the Imam want you?" He raises his hands. "Here."

My eyes drift to the ring and linger there. "I did some research when I was with the prince. Studied old fighting techniques. A sport called 'boxing.'"

He points at me. "Doubtless why you prevailed in your competition. Your ability to research."

"But that was trivial. Any debugger could've done it."

He coughs, then places his hand on his chin. "Could they now?"

"Yes, they could."

"Interesting. I don't think the Imam shares that opinion."

I shake my head. "I could not know that. Nor can I guess why he'd want me here. Are the bots in need of upgrades?"

"They are all new. Up to date."

"You're concealing things from me. Important details."

He brings his hands together. "Let's dispense with the concealment, shall we?" He angles toward the ring. "Every year the ulama has a robotic gaming event. Any master with the means and motivation can enter."

"I've never heard of such an event."

"It is a closed affair. Not for public consumption." He smiles. "In the past, the Imam has made use of his military to provide operators for the bots. Often generals. Tacticians. Men skilled in armed combat..."

Jahm looks at me. "But this year he is trying something new." He smiles. "You."

"I don't know how to fight," I say. "I'm not made for fighting."

"But you've researched combat. You said so yourself."

"A small subset of a single sport. Because I had to."

"And you have to again. But with more time to prepare. More incentive."

"I'm not made for this."

"Tsk, tsk. You're made for whatever your master requires."

I remember my damage. The wolf that waits in my head. This is just inviting more pain. More loss.

I shake my head. "I'm not the one for this, Submaster. There are weaknesses to—"

He claps his hands. "Nonsense. You have been chosen. Your current position cannot be discussed. However, I can understand how it might feel overwhelming. Especially given the time constraints."

"Time—"

He raises a hand. "In a moment, please." He coughs. "Given that, you may add a debugger to your number. Someone that can assist in repair and training." He smiles. "They can be assigned, or you can suggest. Up to you."

"Submaster?"

He waves his hand. "The training is for you, though, remember. You are being trained."

He touches his seat's armrest controls. The seat lifts, then turns away. "I will leave you for now. I have things to attend to. Other debuggers to motivate." He glances back. "In the meantime, you should begin your research."

I look at the rows of lockers. Dozens of machines. I'd rather have to build them from scratch than what I'm being asked to do. "When is this competition?"

"Didn't I tell you? The end of next week."

"Next week?"

"You have precisely ten days."

I STAND, FROZEN IN PLACE, for a long time after Jahm leaves. Only my eyes move. From my position near the center ring, I search every corner of the room, every meter and every object. Trying to find the logic of it. The sense of what life has brought me to.

"If it happens, then it was meant to happen."

This is what we're taught. That if something happened, then it was because A meant it to happen.

But does A mean for bad things to happen? Does he wish hurt and pain on his servants? Especially those who, like me, only want to do right? Only seek significance?

My eyes find the center ring. The blue bounding ropes. The clean surface bearing the Imam's seal.

Or was it that quest for significance that brought me here? Is this new, insurmountable challenge the result of my own pride? My misinterpretation of what is good, of what *significant* means?

Or was it the spark of attachment I let kindle? That forbidden thing. The realm of freeheads, not debuggers. Not implants like me.

I know one thing for sure. A single act of selflessness does not bring significance. For the beneficiaries—Damali and the astronauts—my act was significant. But it did not make me important. Did not make me special or raise my level in any spiritual sense.

It did not make me loved.

Because I'm still where I was: A slave to tyrants. A servant of men, placed like a toy wherever they put me. A will manipulated to suit their needs.

And if I don't suit their needs? There will be another, probably younger, debugger who does.

Like the initiates at the facility. Talons, Mint, and the rest. They would relish this challenge. Their handling battle bots? What a display that would be. I thought the virtual room was noisy...

I walk to the ring and hop up on its edge. Something, probably the rope behind me, has a fresh, synthetic smell. Clean and new, like everything else.

I wish I was clean and new. Especially my head.

I don't even know how to behave. Whether anything I do helps my crippled brain to heal. There have been no wolf attacks in some time. Does that mean I'm healed? Bamboo barely mentioned my injury at all after the security pull. Only sent me off.

I haven't been stopped in a while either. Maybe the wolf ate the headbuzz. Wouldn't that be something?

My luck? The wolf ate the headbuzz and is now twice the size.

"If it happens, it was meant to happen!"

The problems. I should be working on the problems.

The big one? I need more fight knowledge. Lots of it.

I have the stream for that. It was helpful before. Will it be enough this time? Unknowable.

I'll need to test what I learn. I focus on the row of lockers on the wall ahead of me. Do they accept stream commands?

A stream nudge confirms: Yes, they do.

I choose the third and fourth lockers from the left and stream them open. Two identical bots wait side by side. Heads bowed, arms crossed. Gleaming and ready to go.

I give them startup codes. Their heads rise and their eyes light up. Their arms uncross, then reconfigure so that both hands protect their face—right in front of left. A standard boxing pose.

I smile, hop off the stage, and walk over to them.

I order them out of the lockers. "Are you ready?" I ask.

The bots nod slowly. Combat bots aren't much for speech.

They come equipped with standard movements. I find a list that includes full fighting schemes and techniques. I select an in-place on-the-toes bouncing movement and an occasional left-right punch for both machines.

An instant later, they crouch and begin to bounce. After two seconds, synchronized punches are thrown. After ten seconds, their moves begin to look silly. I send a stop command and they go quiet.

I glance at the ring, then stretch an arm out toward it. "Might as well get you where you belong." I stream them my will.

They form a two-bot line and walk to the ring's side. One hops onto the edge of the canvas, bends, and steps between the ropes. The second follows it, using the same precise moves.

That was easy.

I glance at the other lockers. It is like I have my own army here. Dozens of armor-plated combat bots that will bend to my will. If given the right instructions—

That brings a stop. A small one. But yes, that's not an idea the implant wants me to contemplate. As nice as an army might be.

This whole situation is wrong. Shouldn't there still be others involved? A human combat specialist would have invaluable information to share. Even if I was the one controlling the bot. Even someone who has seen the games played before would be of use to me. I have no idea what is coming. None.

I look at the bots. They have, on their own, found positions in opposite corners. One in the blue corner, the other in the red. They are facing away from each other, though. Into the corners. Not helpful.

I drift toward the ring. "Turn around," I stream.

They pivot to face each other.

I start their dancing and bobbing again. It looks a little better inside the ring. More natural.

On the stream, I grab the control tap of the leftmost bot—the one occupying the blue corner. The rightmost bot—the "red" one—I put into one of its training modes. A simulation called "rookie". I assume that's the equivalent of "lowlevel" in boxing lingo. It accepts the change, and its gait softens. It steps away from the corner and starts to slowly bounce toward my bot. Perfect.

I adjust the blue bot's gait, then raise its hands a little. I access some of the moves I used at the prince's house. Run through the different scenarios. I feed a left-right jab to the bot and see it dutifully perform the punches, swatting at nothing. Another jab, another jab. Bounce to the left, then the right.

The red bot moves steadily closer. It makes a couple air jabs too. I decide to mirror its every action with blue. Soon the bots are an arm length away from each other, both with arms raised.

I attempt a body blow.

Red blocks and follows with a right hook that catches my bot right in the chin.

Its head rocks back, and I barely get a hand up before red swings again. The punch is deflected, but still turns blue's torso. I raise its hands, bring them up to protect its face.

Red unleashes a volley of shots at the body. There's a series of "thwacks" as most of them connect.

I yell and move blue back, out of danger.

The bots start to circle again. I keep my eyes on Red and respond to what I see, feeding small corrections to Blue. I try to keep him out of danger, but still in striking range. Still ready.

I jab again. Jab and then swing for the head.

Red blocks, jabs, then throws a heavy counter-punch.

Blue's head rocks back.

Rails.

Again, I block. Again, red counters, this time to the torso. I attempt to pivot Blue. To make him a smaller target. That results in another jab to the head, followed by a barrage of body blows. Some get through my defense. I stick out an arm and try to push Red away. To swipe it out.

Little effect.

I lower Blue's head, and with both hands in front of him, shove hard.

That gets Red away, freeing maybe a meter of space. But it is a short-lived peace, because Red comes charging right at me, right at Blue, again. I get the bot's hands up. Get it deflecting, but rails, the hits come fast.

In seconds, I'm in trouble again. It is all I can do to block. And now some of Blue's systems are starting to complain. Most prominent are the forearm and hand systems. The ones taking most of the hits. I flail out a couple desperate heavy punches. The first manages to strike Red's cheek, but the second, which I used double-power on, is deflected effortlessly.

Red attacks again. I pull Blue away. Circle out. Bounce.

Red parallels my circle, then cuts through the middle of it and throws punches again. Left, right, left, right. Then heavy left.

Blue takes it in the nose, and its face caves in. I block, but somehow Red gets another punch through. A heavy punch.

I cover my mouth with my hands.

Blue's head leaves its body. It flies over the ropes, smashes into the door of my little room, and clatters to the floor. Spins.

I issue Red a stop command and shut it down. I release Blue's control tap and shut it down too. Mercifully. Gingerly.

Its head continues to spin.

I look at the bots, then at the lockers full of replacements.

I may need more. Or at least, I'll need help fixing the ones I already have.

My chest feels hollow and my back feels tense.

Why me?

BullHammer was looking for work, right?

I send Jahm two transfer requests. One for me—and knowing that will be denied—one for BullHammer.

If I'm going to be miserable, I might as well include him. He loves misery.

THE PRESENCE OF OTHER DEBUGGERS always registers. We always know when others of our kind are around. Certain familiars have a special feeling associated with them, though. It is hard to describe. Almost like they displace the stream in a unique way, leaving ripples that can be physically felt.

BullHammer's ripples feel like molasses, chocolate, and my face wrapped in stinging nettles. The associated color is blinding red.

I'm seated on the metal bench on the lift side of the ring when I sense him. Then the lift's doors open, and the molasses, chocolate, bright-red nettle ambles into the room. He's in a new jumpsuit, with his debugger bag over both shoulders. His right thumb is hooked under the front of the strap.

He takes a few steps forward, pauses, then long-steps the rest of the way. His eyes look left and right, but mainly focus on the small piles of broken bots I've accumulated. They are all around the room.

He whistles. "Quite the collection. If we try, we might be able to make one giant battle bot from the pieces." He makes a grand gesture with his hands. "Yeah, one big bot for the Imam. What do you say? Maybe give it to him for his birthday?"

"As long as it is clean." I stand. "I hear he likes clean."

Bull stops about a half meter away and continues to scan my mess. The largest pile is near the ring's corner on my left. It is primarily composed of heads and arms. All are heavily dented.

Bull approaches that pile. Shakes his head. "What are you feeding them? Physics?"

"Combat is hard. Things get busted."

He slides his bag off and places it on the floor. "Hard to know where to start."

I scan the piles. Shrug. "Doesn't matter. They're all broken."

He scowls, stares at me a long moment, then throws his arms wide and charges me. "Rails, it is good to see you." He surrounds me in a hug.

I'm a little off balance and can barely breathe. But the sentiment...means something.

He steps back, but keeps his hands on my shoulders. His eyes are red. Teary, even. "Bamboo must've fed you okay. You look pretty good."

"I'm fine. You too."

He shakes his head. "No. Not me, no. I don't look fine." He tugs the front of his jumpsuit. "I'm wasting away." He looks past me. "Do you have food?"

I point a thumb toward my room. "I have a processor in—"

He scowls. "Protein and vitamin blocks? That's not food."

"It does okay. My breakfast was—"

The scowl consumes his face.

"I can order stuff," I say. "Bots will bring stuff."

His eyes light up, and he grips my shoulders again. Squeezes. "That would be flipping hot. Could you do that?"

"Yes. What would you—"

"Anything!" He raises his arms and walks toward the ring. "So great, Thread. This is so..." His stops, and his hands find his hips. He looks like a man seeing the ocean for the first time. Or a kid on his tenth birthday.

"What happened to you, Bull?"

He stares at the ring. Says nothing.

Finally, I tap his shoulder.

"Wha—?" He turns, then nods. "Yeah, there's a lot of work here. A lot of mess. I better get started."

I shake my head. "First, tell me where you were."

He raises both hands. "I've been lots of places." He gives me a sheepish look. "Especially since I last saw you. The Imam has a lot of odd jobs. Lots of stuff." He raises a finger. "I managed his entertainment catalog for a while. Adding things. Deleting things. Sorting and parsing."

"Did you like that?"

He shakes his head. "Not really, no. I mostly just sat in a closet." He shrugs. "It was dark, and a little musty."

He climbs onto the ring platform, then ducks between the ropes. Takes a few exaggerated steps. "A lot bouncier than I expected."

"Bull..."

He walks in a circle. "You're new here so you probably don't know. There's a sort of hierarchy with the debuggers." He glances at me. "Has nothing to do with level. Or experience." He throws an air punch. Then another. "Only how you've performed.'

"Rails..."

"Yeah, the lead debugger is called SilentJoy. He's not, though. Silent or joyful. He's mostly mean."

I walk closer to the ring. Watch Bull through the ropes. "Haven't met him."

Bull starts to hop in place. "Yeah, maybe you won't. You have your own thing here." He stops hopping. "Anyway, after you beat me—"

"Beat you?"

"Yeah, at the prince's? With the combat bots? You have to remember that."

"Sure, Bull. Right. I didn't mean to—"

He waves a hand. "No, that's okay. You beat me. That was the game. Either person can lose." He throws another punch. "But after that, they put me on their naughty list. All my jobs were like the closet one. Lonely, trivial, or dirty."

Bull walks close enough that I'm forced to back away to see him. He stretches his arms out on the top rope, then brings his chin near it. "Cut my food too. Limited my supplies." He frowns. "I pretty much hate them."

"Hate who?"

He winces, then rubs the bridge of his nose. "Them. All of them. The debuggers here. The subs. The Imam even. All of them."

I return to the bench and sit down. "That's why you were skiing?" I say. "And boating? Why every time I—"

He fans the air. "Well, yeah, but that was fun too. Helped clear my mind." He makes another sweeping gesture. "And I'm here now, helping my old friend, Thread." He climbs through the ropes, then drops to the floor.

He takes a few steps, stops, and looks at his feet. "Feels weird walking now. Like the room is a little wobbly."

He stoops for his bag, then looks at the nearest pile of parts. "Better get started on something here. All right to work on that mess there? Get some of the heads back where they belong?"

"Sure."

He nods, walks to the pile, and extracts the topmost head. Peers into its eyes. "Seems like a 'Safiyy' to me."

I squint. "'Safiyy?' Meaning 'chosen one'?"

He bounces the head in his hand. "Right. I just chose him." He smiles.

I'd forgotten that I have a limit with Bull. A very short limit.

I check the bot lockers and find two I haven't opened. Both are on the wall past where Bull is working. I stream the doors open, exposing two more shiny, silver bots, folded like infants. My next victims.

"Did you order food yet?"

Bull has the "Safiyy" head in the crook of his arm and is gathering another.

"You didn't tell me what you want."

"Anything. Just make it cool."

I nod and stream off a salad request. I then order the bots out of their lockers. They step out, march toward the ring.

Bull has an armful of heads now. "You did it, right?"

I nod.

He smiles and slowly makes his way around the ring. There are three bot torsos on the side nearest my room. He stops when he reaches them. "So, what have you gotten yourself into here?" Bull asks.

"A contest," I say. "A bot battle of some sort." My bots climb into the ring. I direct them to circle, hands raised. "I don't expect to do well."

Bull drops the heads to the floor. "Rails, you need to do well. You need to do better than that. You need to win."

I grab the control tap of one of the combat bots and try a flurry of jabs. "I don't know anything about combat, Bull. It was luck I beat you. The right moves at the right time."

He places a head atop a torso. Studies it a second, then frowning, bends over and picks up another. "Maybe, but the Imam doesn't know that. He thinks you're a winner."

"And you know I'm not."

He snorts. "What I know doesn't matter. He expects the best. Believe me, I know." He swaps the heads and smiles as the new one fits into place. "Who's involved in this little contest?"

I tell Bull everything Jahm told me. He listens intently before letting out a long whistle. "Nothing about that sounds good. I'm guessing there are credits and property involved. Wagers."

I perform a couple short uppercuts, followed by a right hook. It is all air-boxing, but it is starting to feel more fluid and comfortable. Almost as if I'm moving my own hands. "Gambling is forbidden by scripture."

He chuckles. "Some say business is gambling. Don't see any shortage of that, do you?" He finishes sealing the head in place. Studies it. "Regardless, if the ulama is involved, it is serious."

I raise the bot's hands to cover its face, then jerk them down to cover its midsection. The transition takes milliseconds.

"This is an ongoing event?" he says. "Something they've had before."

I shrug. "Apparently."

"And military people did what you're going to do?"

"That's what Jahm said."

He nods. "Should mean there are rules, anyway. That's something." He drifts toward another bot torso. "Those folks live by rules. Like us. Wouldn't get that from everyone."

I engage with the other bot. I throw a left and a right. It easily ducks both. I try a shot to the body. The bot hops back and away. I didn't even touch it.

I notice Bull watching. He shakes his head. "You missed."

"It is harder than it looks."

"Your competition won't have an artificial brain like that bot," he says. "That helps. Won't think as fast." He touches his temple.

"Might be your only advantage, really, the speed of thought. And it is a matter of nanoseconds. That cheer you up?"

I focus on the bots. I have to remember: I beat Bull. So his advice is suspect.

I throw a couple punches at the rival bot. It blocks the first, but the second nicks its chin. I follow with a body shot that mostly connects. I smile.

Bull raises a shoulder. Returns to his chore.

The rival bot mounts an offensive. A series of jabs, followed by a heavy swing for the body.

I attempt to block the punch, but the bot feints, hitting my bot square in the head.

"Got you a good one there."

I shoot him a look. "Bull..."

The bot attacks again. I manage three blocks before my defense breaks down. Another devastating hit to the cranium. My bot's head sails through the air. I hear it clatter against the lockers. I don't bother to look.

Bull shakes his head. "Rails. More work for me."

I shut the bots down, then stare at the one that I rendered headless. It is hard not to think about the antitex heavy. And before that, my trip to Delusion. The human heads I watched a heavy drive toward. Exposed and vulnerable.

Is that me? Is that all of us? Heads waiting in the sand?

I look at Bull. Shrug.

"I'm worried about you," he says. "I know it sounds strange from me. I'm not the most sentimental guy." He points at the ring. "What level you have them set at?"

"Rookie."

His eyes widen. "Yeah...I'm worried."

I sense a burst of directed motion on the stream, then hear a slight squeal as the lift begins to move. It travels up.

A few seconds later, the door opens on our level. There's a servbot inside. It is holding a silver tray.

"Bull. Your food is here."

ANOTHER DAY OF TRAINING GOES BY. Then another.

Jahm has largely stayed away. He communicates mostly in messages. And his messages are usually generic updates that don't affect me: cafeteria closures and special events.

He also forwards missives sent to the entire debugging "team." Many of those are status reports. Some seem to require a response, but since I'm unsure of the context, I dump those as soon as I see them.

I have a job. Jahm knows what it is. If he's worried, he'll stop by.

Not that I'd have anything good to show him.

The piles of broken bots have shrunk, thanks to Bull, but that proves nothing. I'm not improving much. My mean time to bot breakage has increased slightly. Maybe by a minute or two. Sometimes.

Bull is not the person I once knew. He seems content to fix bots. He doesn't complain. He eats and works. He rarely even comments on my training.

I'd be happy about all that, except I know that the change means that, like me, he's broken in some way. Not brain damaged. But a part of Bull is missing. Something has been robbed or wiped away.

I try not to think about it. But it bothers me.

I try not to think about Damali either. Or FrontLot. Or the boys at the facility. Anything that is not my life now is irrelevant. A distraction. No longer part of my worth.

I order another set of bots into the ring. They climb inside silently.

There must be a way to improve. To arrive at a system for winning. Combat information isn't as readily available as I might like. No matter what I try, something goes wrong. I need a plan.

I'm tempted to break down the bot's embedded combat code. Study that to figure out how to beat it. But aside from the boost in morale, that doesn't seem helpful. I won't be fighting bot code.

Bull stands across the ring from me. He has a sheet spread across the upper back of one of the offline bots. He squints at it, then glances at me. "What are you trying this time?"

"I'm trying to keep from getting hit," I say. "That's the goal. Not to get hit. If I get hit, I lose."

Bull frowns, steps away from his bot, and drifts toward me. "I'm trying not to interfere."

"Is that so?"

He looks hurt. "I mean it, I'm—"

"What do you want to say, Bull?"

He touches his chest, points at me, then touches his chest again. "We have a history, you and me. A...friendly rivalry." He looks behind him, as if we're being watched. "But where we are now, I don't know that it is helpful. Better to be a team." He takes a step closer. "So I've been staying out of the way. I don't want to mess you up." He smiles. "And there is enough work keeping you in bots."

"Right. I need to train, Bull."

He raises a hand. "This will be quick." He points at the two waiting bots. "If you're trying not to get hit, you're streaming the wrong sport. This sport is about surviving, even if you're hit. In fact, expect to get hit. You're going to get hit. Probably a lot. And, sometimes..." He leans closer. "Sometimes you should *want* to get hit so you can move ahead. Advance your cause."

"I don't see how—"

I sense the lift being summoned, then hear it start to ascend.

Bull looks that direction. "Someone coming. Is it that Jahm guy?"

I shrug, shake my head. "Possibly."

The lift descends. Then I get a sense for what type of individual is inside. It isn't a bot, nor is it a freehead. It is a debugger, but the feelings, the ripples, are foreign. And a little confusing.

Bull looks at me, then waves me toward the lift. "Go on. It isn't for me."

I walk toward the door. The lift stops but seems to take a long time opening. As if whoever is inside is deliberately holding it for effect. I reach the support columns for the overlook when the doors finally part.

Inside are three debuggers. The central one identifies as Silent-Joy, while the others are StandFish and RareLight. They are dressed in beige pants and shirt. Not the standard debugger jump-suit. SilentJoy is older—possibly ten years my senior—and lighter in color. Lighter than most people, actually. Beyond pale.

They exit the lift as a group, with Silent in the lead. Their hands are in front of them, hidden within their shirt sleeves. They carry no debugger bags either, no tools.

Silent glances at me, quickly bows his head, then scans the room. "This place is unfit for the Imam's complex. It needs to be cleaned at once."

I bow my head. "Peace be unto you. I'm Thread—"

"He knows," Stand blasts me in the stream. "Of course, he knows."

"Don't waste time with trivial details," RareLight adds.

I glance back. Bull is on the other side of the ring now. A fresh bot is positioned directly in front of him. Shielding him.

Silent walks past me, hands clasped behind his back. "This will never do. You shouldn't be here." He sneers at a stray bot arm on the floor, shakes his head, then walks toward the rightmost side of the ring. There's a small pile of parts there.

"I'm under Submaster Jahm. I was brought here at the Imam's request."

Silent frowns. "I doubt that very much."

"It is highly irregular," Stand streams. "Neither your level or associations qualify you for an unsupervised position here."

RareLight pushes the scent of ginger with his message. Wraps it in gold. "This is the Holy City. The Imam's domain. Nothing can be imperfect!"

"Nevertheless," I say. "This is the job I was given."

SilentJoy kicks at the pile of parts, causing them to scatter and clatter. "Unacceptable. Can't you program one of these bots to clean?"

"A necessary side-effect of training," I say. "Things get broken."

"That didn't answer the question," StandFish streams.

I frown at him. "I need the bots for the training."

RareLight chuckles. "Training. Looks like your repairman is the only one being trained."

StandFish nods. "You're in over your head here, ThreadBare. You need more help."

Silent looks at him. "That seems like the fastest solution at this time, doesn't it? If he can't be replaced, more help."

I can't be replaced? That means they've tried and failed, apparently. I can't be replaced.

Silent turns and walks towards me. "Would you be open to this? More assistance from your superiors?"

Part of me wants that. In fact, I would like someone to take this burden off me completely. Let me go back to Bamboo's. Even back to teaching.

I glance across the ring. Bull's eyes are just visible over the bot's shoulder. "What do you think, Bull?" I stream him.

His eyes widen. "No. A whole minute full of no's."

I bow my head as if in thought. "But how will that go?" I stream him. "You know them. How will they respond?"

"They'll be mean no matter what. My dad used to say, 'Better a lonely raft, than one filled with vipers.' These guys are your vipers."

I send him a large, blue question mark. "How are they vipers? They have implants! They have rules!"

"So do I," Bull messages. "Am I pleasant?"

I suppress a smile.

"Your silence suggests you understand your shortcomings," Silent says. "That is the beginning of wisdom." He looks at his companions. "We will find someone to reassign. Pick from the top of the list."

StandFish nods, then points at BullHammer. "This one should be replaced too. Someone with a higher efficiency rating. Better reviews."

Silent nods. "An astute observation. Pick two then."

I smooth the front of my jumpsuit, cross my hands in front of my waist. "I like things the way they are."

Silent frowns. "Perhaps you misread your situation. This competition is of extreme importance. The Imam's reputation is at stake. Winning is the only option."

"So I've been told."

Silent's face reddens, but he remains quiet for a full second. Then he exhales. "Would you request a formal transfer instead? We would ensure you a notable reassignment."

RareLight studies the nearby bench, then puts a foot on it. "That is your best option. Let someone else bear this. Someone more experienced."

"We've studied your history," StandFish says. "You have an adequate service record, but you are not ready for this."

"Perhaps you should ask my submaster. Or the Imam himself." I stream the waiting bots, telling them to move closer to my side of the ring. They walk up to the ropes and assume a watchful position. They follow Silent's every move.

Silent glances at the bots, frowns, then shakes his head. "Jahm and the Imam are freeheads."

Rare removes one foot from the bench, replaces it with the other, and massages the back of his neck. "They aren't like us. They wouldn't know how to judge. Don't know what is important."

"The Imam doesn't know what's important?"

"Don't obfuscate," Silent says. "You know what he means."

I cause the bots to lean forward and place their hands on the ropes. "So what is important?"

"Service," StandFish says. "Achievement. Significance."

I stream the bots to cross their arms. Shake their heads. "I used to think that."

Silent scowls at the bots again. "Used to?" He places a hand on his chin. "And what is your opinion now? What is important?"

RareLight smiles. "This should be interesting."

"Enlighten us," StandFish stream blasts me. A bright, ginger-scented beam of data.

"I'm still gathering information," I say. "But I know it isn't those things. They can be good, but they aren't most important."

Silent harrumphs. "You're clearly in the wrong place. And with the wrong master."

RareLight straightens, steps away from the bench. "Yes, we must bring an end to this. Request a transfer. Immediately."

I glance at Bull. He's away from the bot now. He watches with arms crossed, as if shadowing the combat bots.

"I think we'll keep things as they are," I say. "See how it goes."

Silent's face reddens, but his words are laced with pity. "See how it goes." He walks toward me. "We are looking out for you, brother. There is no time for experimentation."

RareLight nods. "Forget your first instincts. Forget wanting to learn and discover. Those will come later."

"His choice betrays his hypocrisy," StandFish says. "He dismisses achievement and significance, but could gain nothing else by doing it alone."

Silent leans close. "Do you know what danger you face?"

"Shunning? *Notable* tasks that no one else wants?" I check Bull. He raises a thumb.

Silent glances at BullHammer. Sighs. "We were lenient with your friend. I doubt he told you about his mistakes. The times he was found in the cafeteria when he should've been working. The times he performed the wrong task." He studies me, then frowns. "I can tell by your face that he didn't."

"You should trust us, ThreadBare," RareLight streams. "We've been here a long time. Survival is key."

How? How do they now have me wanting to keep a job that I wanted to run from an hour ago? Am I being manipulated? Pushed into it?

I'm not sure these three are smart enough for that. They're highlevels; they can fix things, but smart? I'm not sure.

I shrug. "I'm doing what I'm supposed to do. I'm staying here."

If it happens, it was meant to happen, right? That's where I live now.

Silent straightens, then turns away. He walks toward the exit and the others follow, though RareLight stares at me a moment longer before shaking his head and turning away. "I feel sorry for you," he streams. The text is blue, and smells like rain.

They enter the lift, and the door closes.

"Told you," BullHammer says. "Mean."

I REFOCUS ON THE STILL leering combat bots and order them to the center of the ring. I glance at the lift door again, then walk to the nearest bench and sit down. I put both bots in rookie mode and watch them perform. They block and duck. Bob and weave. Throw punches.

Bull drifts around the ring toward me. When he reaches the bench, he nods at the bots. "Doing good now. Which one are you controlling?"

I shake my head. "Neither of them. They're following their inherent routines."

He watches a few seconds longer, then snorts. "Is that an option?"

I message him a static cloud. Hot and prickly.

He makes a disgusted face. "Just asking."

I slouch. "Can't do this, Bull."

He sits on the bench. "You have to."

"That doesn't help."

He points at the ring. "You won't be against bots. You'll be against humans, right? Even better, you'll be against freeheads." He touches his right temple. "They can't feel the machine like us."

"All I feel is failure."

He shakes his head. "Right, but you're trying not to get hit. That's not a strategy. I remember with the sport, with boxing, there are different styles."

"Styles?"

He squints. "Yeah. Different ways of behaving. Different techniques."

His words jog a memory. Something the prince said, maybe? I search my data store just to be certain. "Right. That's right. Four main styles. Swarmer, out-boxer, slugger, and boxer-puncher."

Bull nods. "And which of those are you?"

"None of them."

"Well, which *can* you be?"

I glean what little of the descriptions I can. "Swarmers try to overwhelm their opponent. They are usually fast on their feet, and in good condition. They also tend to be shorter."

"Are there going to be different-sized bots?"

"I have no idea."

"Well, can you be fast?"

I shake my head and move on. "Out-boxers try to stay away from their opponent. They rely on shorter punches. Try to win by points."

"That sounds more like you," Bull says. "Especially the staying away part." He smiles. "What are the others?"

"Sluggers are all about power. They're looking to win with a single punch. To hit hard."

He nods. "I like hitting hard. Winning quick."

"They also tend to be slower."

"That might be you too." Bull looks at the ring. Watches the bots as they simulate the sport. "Okay, and the last?"

"Boxer-puncher. They have some of the power of the slugger, but are quicker, and more accurate. They can have swarmer attributes and out-boxer attributes too. Hard to classify."

"Sort of a piecemeal boxer. Picks and chooses based on the situation." He looks at me. "That what you've been trying?"

"Inadvertently. And with little effect."

He crosses his arms, then raises a shoulder. "Well, my advice is to pick one style and work with it. Keep things as simple as you can."

"Maybe the out-boxer?"

"Seems as good as any." He chuckles. "Plus, you can run away if you want."

"It's something, I guess."

There's a clank as one bot lands a hit on the other.

Bull snorts. "Best plan of the day. Maybe the best plan ever."

I shake my head, then focus on the out-boxer information. I start with the description, then dive into the details. The preferred punches, the legwork. The disadvantages.

"I think you need a human opponent too," he says. "That's what you'll be facing."

I open an eye. "You?"

He points toward the lift. "Unless you want to invite those three back."

I frown. "But I beat you already."

He sneers. "You got lucky once, but I can study now. Perfect my game."

"So you can have a rematch. Maybe two."

"As many as it takes, Thread. Until you're ready."

"We have less than a week."

He nods. "Then we better get started." He leans forward. "Which one you taking?"

I order the bots to their corners. They stop circling and separate. "Red corner."

Bull nods, then rests his elbows on his knees. "Blue fits me. I can do blue."

I grab Red's control tap and try to feel as comfortable as I can. Bounce. Throw a few punches.

I nod its head. "Let's go."

THE REMAINING DAYS PASS with a mixture of dread and exhaustion. Bull and I train from the time our cinder chutes open in the morning, until the time they close at night. Following his suggestion, I stick to the out-boxing style, and see results. I'm able to hold him off, score points, and keep my bot's head intact.

Eventually, I'm able to win.

Jahm visits only once. He doesn't say much, so I'm left to judge what he thinks based on facial expressions and grunts. The positive expressions seem to outweigh the negatives, so I take some comfort in that.

I'm not at peace, though. Not in the least.

There are no more visits from SilentJoy and his companions. There are no debugger-specific messages sent to me either. Even the ones I used to ignore have disappeared. Not sure what to think about that.

Bull said he rarely gets any either. "Means you made their naughty list. Congratulations."

As to my condition, and the lurking wolf, I had only one episode. It came during a critical point, though. A time when Bull was repairing bots, and I was matched against the blue bot's subroutines again.

The bot, now in "accomplished" mode, came at me as a boxer-puncher, and swarmed me. I was able to hold off most of its attacks, able to hold ground, but I never could quite get loose. Never free myself to strike from the outside like my style demands.

I attempted to push the blue bot back and dodge to the left, when the wolf bit me. It started at the base of my skull, then scraped its way up my scalp and into my forehead. It was excruciating. The interior of my head seemed to fog. I not only lost my focus, I lost my grip on the bot's control tap.

My opponent had no problem taking advantage. It struck with a left-handed uppercut, then followed with a shot to the midsection. My bot's mobility slowed, and warnings flashed like ball lightning in my head. My guard came down. The bot's arms lowered.

Then it was all over. The onslaught that followed dented red's chest, twisted its spine...and took off its head.

It wasn't pretty.

And Bull wasn't happy.

"Rails, I caught up. I almost caught up!"

Thankfully, I was seated at the time. But it was difficult to open my eyes. Hard to even breathe.

"What happened?" he streamed. When that got no response, he said it out loud and rushed my direction.

"Nothing," I said. But it was hard to hide how I felt. My face was flushed and there was perspiration on my forehead. Also, on my chest and stomach.

"You don't look good." Bull bent over and stared at my face. "Your eyes are red. Like really red."

"Just lost it for a second."

He studied me, then straightened and backed away. "We've been training hard. Probably too hard."

I massaged the bridge of my nose. Shut my eyes. Nodded. "Yeah, we've been pushing."

He looked worried, but he simply echoed my nod. Smiled. "Need more sleep tonight, right? Let the chute fix you up." He leaned close again. "You've come a long way, Thread. Regardless of what happens, I'm happy to have been a part of it."

I smiled, relieved for the change of direction. "Glad you're here too, Bull."

That was the last that we talked about it. It was two days ago.

Tonight is the night. Now is the time.

Jahm sent instructions on where to meet him. We've been

provided with special clothing. Wrinkle-free, white-with-gold-trim robes. I feel more inadequate with them on than ever.

Bull seems to relish the change, though. I allow him to change in my room. When he steps out, he smooths the front of his shirt and holds out his arms approvingly. "I think this is silk," he says.

"We're in the Imam's compound," I say. "And this is an important night."

"Right." He slaps my back. "The night you show them what a debugger can do. The night you surprise them."

I smile halfheartedly. "I'm sure there will be many surprises."

He grips my shoulder again. "Don't be negative. You have this. You did what it takes, and you have this." He points at the lockers. "Do we need to take one of our own, or what?"

"Jahm said they will be provided."

He snorts. "Yeah, why should we use one of these old things? We're performing for the ulama now."

I nod, trying to seem confident.

We enter the lift and ride up. The lift's interior smells stale and forgotten, as if it hasn't been used in decades. I can barely suppress the feelings of loneliness and inadequacy. I am alone in this. Regardless of being the Imam's representative, or having been chosen specifically for the task, I'm on my own. Jahm, the other debuggers—none of them can be trusted.

Except maybe Bull.

The door opens, and the guard immediately looks our way. He gives us a lingering once over, then nods approvingly. "Peace be unto you." He smiles and waves us out of the elevator. He even opens the exterior door for us.

I nod at him as we step outside. A gentle breeze brings with it a heavy floral scent. A mixture of wisteria and jasmine. Through the glass of the entranceway arches, I see shimmering light. A distorted view of everything above and beyond.

It is evening, but hardly dark. The sidewalk in front of us is lit by embedded light. In fact, all the sidewalks appear to be similarly lit. I find myself curious, wanting to get beyond the arches so I can see the rest of the Imam's compound.

We step into a world of wonder. The buildings' exteriors gleam with light. Every edge and every curve outlined in gold. The towers are fingers of brightness against a deep purple sky. It is fantastic. Serene and awe-inspiring at the same time.

BullHammer's eyes are wide, but he's watching me. "Haven't seen this before?"

"Haven't been out at night." I shrug. "I haven't been out at all, really."

He laughs. "It's like this every night."

"Amazing."

Bull points ahead and left. "Well, we're in the gold one tonight."

The central tower is by far the most exquisite. Complicated designs play over the uppermost, golden floors. Light beams from the pinnacle into the sky.

"Jahm is going to meet us there," is all I can say.

Bull slaps my shoulder. "Let's not keep him waiting."

We walk in silence for a hundred meters. Despite the celebratory atmosphere, there are few people out. Not like when I walked in. No groups of supervised children. No families. It seems a shame. Someone should be enjoying this.

It's as if it is for A, and A alone. And perhaps it is.

The trees of the central park are visible beyond the towers. They are outlined with light too. Plumes of silent brilliance. The pool is lit from below. I can just see a slice of its shimmering blue.

Bull watches the area to our right. It has smaller buildings and a scattering of decorative foliage. "Feel them?"

"Feel what?"

"Security bots. There are at least a dozen between here and the gold tower. All kinds. Overhead and on the sides of the buildings. In the trees."

With a little focus, I can sense those unseen bots. Most are small—the size of crickets and snakes—but there are humanoid models too. Those are well camouflaged. It takes me a minute to visually find one within a stand of trees on our right. Its exterior is dark, but replicates the light patterns near it.

It looks our way as we pass. Its face is featureless. An ebony mask.

Ten meters later, I detect the presence of debuggers. There's a small shelter there on the left. A covered spot with table and chairs. Two debuggers are seated at the table, while another stands, waiting.

Bull notices them too. "Raphael and Rodin. Those guys again?" He searches the area to our right. "Is there another way to the tower?" He points right. "Maybe over that way?"

SilentJoy is the one standing. The other two—StandFish and RareLight—remain seated until we draw closer. They all wear silk suits like ours.

"All dressed up, but not invited," Bull streams me. "I'm not stopping for 'em. You're not stopping, are you?"

The debuggers converge around us. RareLight hurriedly takes a position right of Bull, while Silent walks next to me. StandFish lags a few steps behind.

"You the backup singers?" Bull says.

"Merely here to escort you in," Silent says. "To show support for our brothers."

"The responsibility of highlevels," StandFish says.

Bull scowls. "We're fine on our own."

Silent shakes his head. "You haven't proved that yet."

"That's because you haven't been watching. Least not well enough."

"Could you message us a mix to prove your competence?" RareLight says.

"That would put us inside his head," Stand says. "Do we really want that?"

I don't have the patience for childish bantering. Can't focus on it. Can't spend the cycles. "I think we can escort ourselves."

"We insist," Silent says. "Our position demands it."

StandFish shakes his head. "The truth."

"Are you ready?" RareLight asks.

BullHammer scowls. "Rails, why are you still talking? He's not a bot."

"Simply being polite." Stand frowns. "I haven't forgotten the importance of this evening."

"No one should forget the importance of this evening," Silent says. "This event."

I receive an urgent message from WindCypher. He has another

mix by "one of my favorites." I push the message away. I have no time for that now. Maybe after.

There's a large fountain in front of the golden tower. It is circular, with large steps all around. In the center, standing nearly six meters high, is a shimmering wall of water. Embedded within it is a spinning vortex. A contained, man-made water spout. Rainbows dance within it.

"Incredible."

Silent nods. "It is Darb ut-Tabānah, the Milky Road, in honor of—"

"Our galaxy," I say.

He smiles. "Yes, very good. Few debuggers know that. I'm impressed." He bobs his head toward StandFish. "Stand designed the fountain." He looks reflective. "During one of your rest periods, correct?"

Stand nods. "Between tasks, yes. The Imam loves stars. Telescopes. He has observatories at all his country homes."

"Maybe Stand should be designing something now," Bull messages me. "Instead of ruining our evening." He pauses. "And yeah, I got a tweak for that thought. Worth it."

The tower's entrance has a wide stairway. It is hedged by security beings—human and bot alike. Two human guards descend the stairs holding small, black devices. They sweep them over our heads, study the front of the device, then wave us inside. At the top of the stairs, two bots bow and hold the doors for us.

The lobby is palatial. The floor is marble, made of alternating dark and gold tiles. The ceiling is gilded and arched, with a three-meter chandelier in the middle. There's a room-spanning stairway ahead. The upper portion of the walls on both sides are mirrors. The rest is gilded. Brilliantly polished.

Part of the stairway is filled with a line of freeheads. Men and women, all formally dressed. They could be part of the ulama, but I doubt it. More likely family members or esteemed servants waiting to be searched. There are hundreds of people in that line.

It may not be a public event, but it is hardly private. I try not to think about that.

The freeheads look at us as we ascend. Some visibly move out of the way. SilentJoy takes a position in front of me now, with Stand and Rare on either side. Bull brings up the rear. He stream fumes about that, doubtless risking another stop.

At the top of the stairs, we're directed to the right, down a large, carpeted hallway. I find Jahm's directions in my head. I'm to meet him in Observation Chamber 48. It is up ahead.

The hallway curves to the left, suggesting that the competition venue is in the center. An amphitheater.

"This is something," Bull streams. "All of it."

"You've never been here before?"

"Are you kidding? Never been in this sector before you brought me." He points to a narrow, overhead sign that reads "54." "Getting close, I think."

A SHORT WALK LATER, we reach Chamber 48. A formally dressed attendant guards the door.

I don't want to be up here at all. Not where the freeheads are. I need to be wherever the bots are, preparing.

SilentJoy bows at the attendant, then points at me. "This is the honorable Data Relocator ThreadBare. His submaster Jahm is inside?"

The attendant nods and reaches for the door. He then raises a cautioning hand. "Only the contestant is permitted." His eyes dart over the other four. "No one else."

Silent's face reddens, but he bows and steps out of my way. "Of course."

I approach the door. It is red, but with a gilded band at the bottom and around the handle. The controlpad next to it is gilded too.

"We'll wait out here," Silent says. "Of course."

"You don't need to," Bull says. "I'm his assistant. I can wait for him."

"You overestimate your skill set," RareLight says.

The door slides open. Jahm, in his hoverchair, is just inside. There's a partially drawn curtain behind him, obscuring the interior of the chamber.

Jahm smiles. "I see you've met some of your kind, Thread-Bare. Excellent." He looks at SilentJoy. "I assume you escorted him here?"

Silent bows. "We did, and I—"

"Very good. You can entrust him to my care now."

Silent bows again. "We are ready to assist in any way we can."

Jahm coughs into his hand, wipes the hand on his sleeve, then strokes his chin. "Your memos were quite exact. And exhaustive."

Silent startles, glances at his companions. "I followed proper procedure."

Jahm flashes a smile. "I'm sure you did." He beckons me. "Come now, Thread."

I point at BullHammer. "Can Bull—"

Jahm swivels his seat. "Your assistant will wait outside." He looks at Silent and the rest. "The attendant can direct you to your places."

Silent turns without speaking. He, StandFish, and RareLight coalesce and disappear to the left.

Jahm chuckles, coughs into his hand, and smiles. "That was enjoyable. I hope they didn't distress you."

"Hardly at all."

He taps the arm of his chair. "Good. Now come inside, there's someone here who wants to see you." He moves ahead, then points at the curtain. "Can you pull that back, please?" He touches the chair. "Curtains always pose a problem."

"I'll be here," Bull streams. "Right outside here if you need me."

I pull the curtain back. The room beyond is dimly lit, but plushly decorated. Dark red walls and carpet. Two sloping section of seats, with a wide aisle between them. Jahm hovers up the aisle.

Most noticeable is the shielded window to the amphitheater below. The space there is overwhelming. I step forward so I can see the whole thing.

There's a large central combat ring, along with four smaller rings—two on either side of it. Thousands of seats stretch around the perimeter. These are half full. Positioned above the seats is a ring of chambers like this one, though most appear wider.

My stomach lurches in anticipation. It is difficult to look away.

I hear movement from the seats to my left, and turn. Someone in a black turban is there, though his face is hidden by shadow. Jahm moves further ahead to take a position at the front of the seats. He indicates the turbaned individual. The man shifts into view.

My heart stops.

"The Imam wanted to see you before the competition begins."

Aside from a few deepened wrinkles, the Imam looks exactly like I remember. Dark eyebrows, light brown skin, white beard and mustache. Slightly heavy build, well masked by his robes, which are black to match his turban.

"This is good," he says. "He looks well. Ready. Better than when I saw him last."

Jahm nods. "He's been provided everything he needs." He smiles. "And I heard no complaints."

The Imam strokes his beard. "And he is prepared?"

"I have observed his progress," Jahm says. "Daily updates from the training room. Visual and audial feeds."

He was watching the entire time? How did I not notice that?

Too busy. Too distracted by the work. Or they were specifically designed to escape my notice.

I feel the urge to check my storage. Replay everything that was said and done.

Jahm looks at me. "I was concerned at first. But I believe he's ready."

The Imam nods, then stares at me while stroking his beard. "You're aware we met before, debugger?"

"Yes, master."

"Ah, of course you would remember." He looks at Jahm. "They never forget. Even when you want them to." His eyes fix on me again. Dark. Probing. "Were you with my son the day he died?"

With the prince? My every moment with him was misery. Inescapable.

I bow. "Yes, I was. I'm sorry for your loss."

The Imam's gaze bores into me. As if he's trying to access my implant directly. "Your kind feels sorrow?"

I bow again. "We do, master. The prince's death was unexpected. I—"

He grunts, gives his beard a stroke, then rests his hands on his lap. "What was my son doing when you were with him?"

"He was—" I pause, feeling uncomfortable. This is the place where I'd typically get a warning not to divulge master information. Master privilege. But I feel no headbuzz, no tingle beneath my scalp.

No, it is my heart that stops me. How much does the Imam know? And what is the risk of him learning more?

Does he know who the prince was interrogating? Maybe not.

"He was?" The Imam frowns. "The prince was what, debugger?" He looks at Jahm. "Is he free to speak?"

I fake a wince, as if I'm being stopped. Deception, but not the kind I'll get disciplined for.

Jahm backs and pivots his chair to have a better view of us both. "His records should be fully available to you," he says. "Though his transfer was recent." He coughs, scowls. "Sometimes it takes time for an ownership change to complete."

"It has been more than a week!"

"Yes." Jahm looks at me. "Are you still hindered?"

"The memories hurt me," I say. "Yes."

The Imam straightens. "Was my son in one of his hidden rooms?" he asks. "Like when we first met?"

I wince again, but nod.

He moves in his seat. "Ah, that is helpful. Was it the room with the cages?"

Is this a question I'd be stopped for? Not sure. If the Imam is aware of the cages, then he doubtless knows what went on there. He may have cages of his own, for all I know.

I clench my teeth for effect. "Yes. It was there."

The Imam nods. "So there were prisoners. And he was interrogating them. Or was about to. Did he tell you who they were?"

"He mentioned..." I close my eyes and shake my head. "...their names, yes."

Jahm raises a hand. "Perhaps you shouldn't push too hard," he says. "He needs to compete today."

The Imam grunts. "This blockage is frustrating. A fault in their design."

"Every design has faults," Jahm says. "Except those of A."

The Imam frowns and looks at the window. "I expect no faults this evening. I want the members of the ulama entertained and agreeable. It will make their losses rest easier."

He strokes his beard again. "Twenty slaves are a worthy prize, I think. Along with the credits." He looks at Jahm. "He will survive three fights?"

"That should be no problem."

"Along with the exhibition?"

"I believe so, yes."

The Imam pats his legs. "Good. I'm especially looking forward to that. An added treat from previous years. A worthy test."

Exhibition? I look at Jahm. "Submaster. What—"

Jahm narrows his eyes. Shakes his head. "Time is short now. The DR needs to prepare."

"Of course." The Imam stands. "And I need to return to my chamber. My wives doubtless miss me. As do my guards."

Jahm nods. Looks at me. "You may go now. You'll find everything you need on the lower level. Room G."

I bow to the Imam, and then to Jahm. "Peace be unto you."

The Imam smiles. "And to you. May A's mercy find you serving." He touches my back as I walk past. I resist pulling away, but there's something lingering and uncomfortable about the feeling.

"We will talk again when you are able. I want to hear everything."

ROOM G IS A LARGE, square room lined with red plastisteel lockers and long benches. The floors are grey, the lights are over-bright, and—despite recent chemical scrubbing—the room has a lingering scent of freehead use. Sweat, medicinal oils, and blood. There are bathing and excretory facilities and a large vidscreen that displays a view of the amphitheater. There's also a large, red scale. Presumably also for freehead use. For physical contestants.

Most important to me are the four wooden crates that rest neatly against one wall. There are numbers stamped on the front of each: 1, 2, 3, and 4.

The fourth crate is the most enigmatic. It's about a half meter wider than the others, and a full meter taller. It touches the ceiling.

BullHammer is with me, having waited while I met with the Imam. When I urged him to find a seat in the amphitheater, he looked upset, mumbled something about being the "cutman," and barged into the room.

I decided not to press the matter. I'm grateful for the company.

"Four bots?" he says. "Why four?"

I take a seat on one of the benches, facing the crates. "Three potential fights. Each single elimination. Eight contestants."

"So, a bot for each fight?" Bull strokes his chin. "Nice they give us a new one each time. Let us start fresh. Less work for me." He points at the larger crate. "And the fourth?"

I shake my head. "Not sure. The Imam called it an exhibition."

Bull frowns. "Big event means bigger bot?"

"Maybe," I say. "Jahm didn't want to talk about it."

Bull walks to the larger crate. "We could open it and find out." He tugs on the front of the crate, grunts, then bends over to look at the left side. "Rails, they got it locked. Why are they locking our bots?" He checks the other three. Only the one marked "1" will open. Inside is a late model, mantis-like combat bot, similar to the ones I've been training with. It's painted blue and gold and has the Imam's crest on its forehead.

"Guess they don't want us to get ahead of ourselves." Bull grips the bot's shoulder, then stands on tiptoes to look at its face. "Focus on one fight at a time."

"That's probably wise." I study the larger crate again. "Don't like mysteries, though."

There are a pair of black bags on the floor near the crates. Bull scoops one up, gives it a shake, then looks inside. "Got me a fully stocked tool bag here. Bet we can get the rest open if we try."

I shake my head. "No time. We need to be ready in ten minutes."

He points at the available bot. "Want to put it through its paces?"

I nod, and closing my eyes, connect to it. It springs to life, and I do my best to focus on the stream tap. To try to wear the combat bot like a skin. React like I'm part of the machine.

"Maybe hold off on the bounces and jabs for a bit," Bull says. "I can't detect any errors, but I'd like to give its internals a quick look."

I open my eyes. Lace my hands together. Rock.

Bull digs a roll of sheets out of one of the bags and presses it to the bot's chest. He squints at it, makes an adjustment, and squints again. "Fine piece of machinery. Looks like they shrank the primary. Pathways from it are cleaner too. Packed tight. Nanos marching in step. Like a shrunken utopia, that."

He tears the sheet free, crumples it, and heaves it over his shoulder at me.

I bat it away. Scowl.

He glances back. Smiles. "Checking your reflexes there, Thread. Not bad for a robot jockey." He tears another sheet from the roll and applies it to the bot's midsection. After a second, he lets out a short whistle. "Moved some stuff around in here too.

Little improvements." He shakes his head. "Not sure why they bother. Things are going to get broken."

"Bull..."

He pats the bot's side. "Not this particular bot, of course. With you in control, it's going to stay clean and perfect."

"Are you done? I need to try it." I check the vidscreen. The amphitheater is completely full now, with the only open space being the aisles around the five rings.

Bull removes the sheet, crumbles it, and drops it to the floor. "Looks ready to me. Try it out!"

I close my eyes again, grab the bot's stream tap, and lift its arms. I then peek through its eyes. I see BullHammer, the lockers and benches, and myself. I place the bot's hand on Bull's head. He snarls and pulls away.

"Reflex test," I say.

"Look at the funny debugger. Wasting his precious training time."

I tighten the bot's stance, then take it up on the balls of its feet. I put it through a series of bobs and weaves with an occasional air jab.

I also check for built-in combat algorithms. Anything that might be of use later. There aren't any. "No setting it to auto."

"One way to keep the match fair, I guess." Bull waves a hand dismissively. "You don't need that stuff anyway."

I might if the wolf makes an appearance. "Can't pass the tap to you either. They have it locked to my ident."

Bull places the unused roll of sheets back into the bag. Zips it closed. "Told you those military guys like rules. They'll want to keep it all square. Human to human. Man to man."

"Uh-huh. Otherwise, it feels natural. Don't detect any slowness or hitches." My body feels tight, though. Bound by nerves.

"Error free and ready to go."

"They've got the contact lighting locked on too." Meaning, every solid hit will light a portion of the bot's armor.

Bull nods. "Makes it better for the audience." He points at the bot's hands. "More padding on the knuckles too. Softer blow, longer show."

I open my eyes, nod, then scan the room. "Are their prayer mats in here?"

"Thinking you'll need help?"

"Nothing about this feels right."

Bull shoulders the supply bag. "Come on, Thread. You'll be fine."

I feel like JustBecause. Cowering from his master. Waiting for the next object to be thrown. "I should perform the ritual, just in case."

Bull stares at me, then nods, and stepping away from the bot, begins to search the room. "I'll see if I can find—"

There's a knock on the door before it pops open. Jahm enters, followed by a male servbot and a fully-covered female. She's almost as short as Jahm when seated, and she seems very young.

"You need to be up there," Jahm says.

"Okay, I was just looking for—"

He raises a hand. "No time. Everyone is seated. The Imam's retinue goes in last, thankfully. You need to line up." He scowls at the bot, then at Bull. "All of you."

I stand. "We'll go now."

Jahm backs into the hall, and his retinue follows. We form a short line behind him and make our way first up a level, and then to one of the amphitheater's side entrances. We pause just outside.

There are crowds of freeheads everywhere. The lights of the theater are dimmer now, except over the individual rings.

As we reach into the well of the entrance, a spotlight shines our direction. A small group of servbots cluster in front of me. Additional people crowd behind Bull. I have no idea who they are. What purpose they serve.

Another group of servbots arrives and takes the rear of the line.

"Quite the production," Bull messages. "Like a bot parade here."

From the passage to our right, a familiar design appears. It is completely gold and towers over everyone and everything around it.

One of the Imam's bodyguard bots. A sentinel.

It must be two and a half meters tall. Heavily armored. Seemingly nimble, oppressive, and sharp at the same time. It is a larger version of the combat bots, but somehow more alien in appearance. Part of that is the red eyes that peer out through its face plating. Sliding, rotating, seeing everything.

"I hate those things," Bull says. "Don't know how many the

Imam owns, but you work enough of his properties, you'll think they're endless."

Everyone—bots and people alike—clear out before the sentinel. It walks our direction, scanning and analyzing. I assume it is patrolling the amphitheater and will walk past us. Follow the concourse around the corner.

But instead, it stops at the end of our line.

"Is the Imam coming?"

"Naw," Bull messages. "I'm sure he's in his box. Safe and comfortable with his feet being massaged." He sends an image of the sentinel wearing a turban. "This guy is for show. A symbol of strength and wealth. The Imam's proud of them."

I study the horrifically beautiful design of the sentinel's face and torso. The wide shoulders and heavy arms and legs. I try to connect with it but get only static.

It feels strange for a bot to be such a black box. Such a shadow in the stream. Makes me desire its specs all the more. I want to know everything from its operating temperature to its performance ratios.

I've had this thought before, and I still believe it: I bet even its nanobots have knives.

The line starts to move. We enter the amphitheater amid cheers and applause. The spotlights dance over us while the loudspeakers bray about the Imam's accomplishments; his generosity and mercifulness. The bots in our procession raise their hands. Jahm looks back at us and raises his hands. So we do the same. The applause continues for many minutes.

Finally, the lights brighten, and our line dissipates. The bots filter out into the crowd, and the sentinel returns to the entrance. Off to hunt, undoubtedly.

Jahm brings his chair close to me. "We're in the southwest corner." He points ahead to the right. "Over there." He smiles. "Your first fight is against Master Hami's contestant. I think that is a good draw. TreArc is excellent at engineering. Not so good with sports."

"Is this a sport?" Bull looks around. "I don't see anyone sweating."

Jahm scowls. "Please keep your assistant quiet. Just because he was your choice, doesn't mean he can't be replaced."

Bull bows. "Just making an observation."

Jahm coughs, waves Bull out of the way, and hovers past him. We follow him to our ring. The opposing combat bot is already in position. It is a dark green color, with yellow stripes. It is a different make than mine. The facial features are wider, and the torso heavier. I stream touch the bot and am rewarded with only its model number, owner, and licensing company. All other information is shielded.

With another stream touch, I point our bot toward the ring. It bows and heads for the ring's side.

A few seconds later I reach the Imam's corner, my corner. I can't help but search the other side. The opposing corner. I want to know who I'm up against.

There are a group of men there in uniforms, but only one is watching our bot as it enters the ring. He's wearing a tan military shirt and a red cap. There are two stars on his shirt's right shoulder. He's squinting now, with a hand on his chin as if trying to weigh my bot's strengths and weaknesses.

The only weakness my bot has, of course, is me.

The colonel catches me watching, then. He nods his head slowly.

I return the nod. It feels silly. Like it reflects a level of competitiveness that I don't possess. That the implant prevents me from having.

Jahm and his companions are seated behind our corner now. The only ones standing are BullHammer and I. Bull closes his hands and starts rocking side to side. He looks everywhere, both at the crowds and across the ring. He seems as nervous as I feel.

I walk up next to him.

Bull leans into me. Nods toward the other corner. "Did you find your competition there?"

"I think so."

"Stars say he's an *ageed*. A colonel. Pretty high up. Did you see his gauntlets?"

"Gauntlets?"

"Yeah, his controls. He's wearing them on his arms. However he moves, the bot moves. Probably also has an eyepiece so he can see the bot's view. About as close as a freehead can get to being inside." He nudges me. "You got 'em beat, of course." He taps his head. "Got it all up here."

It is hard not to be distracted. All the rings, save the central one, have combatants in them now. The crowds are buzzing with conversation. The spotlights, though now fixed on the specific areas of contest, still seem like too much. I can almost feel their photons.

A man dressed in white climbs into the ring. He walks over to our corner, scans the bot with a handheld device, then leans over the ropes. "I am the referee for this match. Are you ready to begin?"

"Of course, we're ready." Bull slaps my back. "Thread is always ready."

The referee nods, slaps the top rope, then departs for the other corner. He follows the same ritual there.

"Better feel it now," Bull says. "Get connected."

I close my eyes and stream to the bot. Find its tap and dive in. It feels like the bot's arms are resting atop mine. Like its legs are just in front of mine. I see what it sees.

The referee walks to the center of the ring and waves at me. Then at the other bot. I raise the bot's hands and bounce it on its toes. Move it toward the referee.

The green bot—the colonel's bot—charges out, stopping only centimeters from mine. Its head leans forward and its fists rise. It is so close that it feels uncomfortable. I want to push the visual feed away and use my own eyes.

The referee goes through the rules. It is a bot-specific subset of the historical rules of boxing. Restrictions on where a combatant can hit, and what they can hit with. Also, *when* they can hit. For instance, it is a foul to hit a bot that is already down. Or while holding on to the ropes.

I'm clear on rules. Rules are a debugger's life. It is the other stuff that confuses me.

The referee finishes; then the green bot steps even closer. The bots are touching foreheads. I'm about ready to push it away, when it clanks its hands on mine and marches away.

"Lot of show with this one," Bull says. "Expect anything."

"Right. Anything."

AN AUDIO CUE IS TOO EASILY misconstrued in a room shared with other events. Consequently, there's no bell to start the fight. Instead, the four ring-posts flash blue, and the match begins.

In that instant—as the light particles present themselves and disperse into the room's atmosphere—the competing bot, Green, bolts toward mine. Before I can react, even bring my bot's arms up, a punch is thrown at its head. Then another.

The first I manage to sidestep. The second connects with my bot's left ear. It is a glancing blow, but still causes my bot's face to light up.

"Every punch that connects is a potential point," Bull messages.

"I know." I bounce my bot away, then attempt a left-right combination from the outside. Both miss, and Green steps in close and swings.

I raise my bot's arms.

Green pummels them. *Wham, wham, wham.*

I push back. Step away. Try to get into a rhythm.

"He's a swarmer," Bull messages. "We trained for that."

"Like you the first time we fought."

"Yeah, I played like a noop. You going to rope-a-dope him too?"

I send a head shake. "I want to avoid tricks if I can."

"I'm all for tricks. Got any?"

Green pursues, so I try to keep my bot in place. Blocking most of Green's shots, and bobbing away from others.

"He's fast," I message. "Seems faster than mine."

"All supposed to have the same capabilities. Maybe the free-head's mind is quicker?"

I push him the sound of a bear's growl. High volume.

"Rails, Thread!"

I smile. Power levels on my bot's arms are dropping, but they're a long way from danger. If I can keep this up, hold my ground, maybe I can wear Green out. Lower his levels.

The onslaught continues. Left, right, left. The bot hammers at my defenses. Finally, I sidestep, then block, then sidestep again.

Green closes the gap. Throws punches to the body. Some connect, lighting the surface of my bot's chest and abdomen.

I need to show something here; otherwise, it will seem like Green is the aggressor. And for the freehead judges, that will also make it the winner.

I take a long step backwards and create a wider opening. Green lowers its shoulders and rushes in.

I meet the rush with a high-power shot to its head. The bot's temple plating flashes, and it staggers backward.

I bounce into the new opening, and strike again at its gut. Another heavy hit. A ripple of light across its abdomen.

Green's head shakes, and its arms straighten. Maybe I stalled it? Blew one of its motivators?

It shrugs, then folds back into a normal boxing pose.

Rails.

I amp my bot's power and throw a hard left.

Green blocks, but its plating from forearm to neck flash—echoing the power I exerted. It was a good shot. A strong shot.

Still, it holds its ground. Digs in.

I peek at the man behind the bot. The colonel across the ring. His jaw is clenched and his face flushed. Intensely focused.

I feel better about my chances. I may get this one.

The colonel looks up. Looks at me. Glares.

Green charges again.

I create another opening, wait for it to take it, then punch at its chest.

It covers, hops backwards, then attacks.

I follow the same pattern: Create an opening, punch hard when the bot enters it.

I connect a lot. I connect hard.

"Stay on it," Bull says. "You're getting him."

"He may not know the capabilities of the machine. May be ignoring the damage."

"Easy to do when you're not in it." Bull pauses. "Are you watching?"

I check the error reports and output indicators. My bot's left arm is twenty percent from failure. Right is doing a bit better. Maybe thirty percent. Legs are taxed from all the movement, but otherwise okay. Eighty percent each.

Green has to be doing worse than that. A lot worse.

It would be nice to get this over. Get on to the next one. I check the colonel again. His focus is on the bot. Some of the other soldiers are huddled around him. Advising him.

I miss a block and Green connects with his left. My bot's head screams at me. Throws a tantrum of errors. It is a light show for the audience.

I bounce my bot back, but I'm too close to the ring. Green is there. Punching and punching. I cover and try to wait it out. My left arm is at ten percent now. My right at fifteen.

I need to get out of here.

The colonel is smiling now. He thinks he has me.

I block and dodge. Gather my power for a final push to freedom.

The pole lights flash red.

Bull lets out an audible sigh. "You caught a break."

"What?"

"Round is over. Now get that bot over here where I can work on it."

I direct the bot to our corner. Its left arm has failed completely. The right is only a little better. The head looks misshapen, but at least it is attached.

BullHammer grabs his bag and climbs into the ring next to the bot. In the other corner, another debugger does the same.

"Could you get it to kneel down?" Bull asks.

I nod and send the order.

I ignore the repair work and focus on the colonel. He's still next to the ring, but the other soldiers are in intense conversation with

307

him. The colonel's attention is split between them. There are many headshakes and hand motions.

I'm tempted to see if there is a microphone near him that I can listen through. See what all the fuss is about.

I get a whiff of their debugger's presence. It is familiar. Recent. I study his features as he works on the green bot. I'm surprised.

"That's StandFish," I say. "Over there. On the other bot."

Bull doesn't respond. He has a hand tool on the bot's right arm, twisting and prodding. I check the tap and see that some of the power has returned there.

Good.

I climb into the ring with him.

Bull puts up a hand. "You shouldn't be here," he says. "They'll think we're cheating."

I glance across the ring. StandFish straddles their bot, adjusting something on its head. "The purpose is to fix the bot during the break, right?"

"Yeah, but I'm the cutman here." Bull points a thumb at the other side. "They get one and so do we. Part of the rules." He taps his head and smiles. "I studied up."

I climb out of the ring again. "But their cutman," I say. "Did you see who it is?"

"I'm busy," Bull says. "Arms are near failure, did you know that? Let Green keep beating on it?"

"Yeah..."

He scowls. "I only have a minute, so..."

I put my hands on the ring's surface and glance behind me. Rows of spectators appear to be staring at me. Some are bent over talking. I try not to focus on them, or the fact that I'm part of a spectacle.

"But yeah, I know who is over there," Bull says. "Could smell him earlier. This event, the venue provides the debuggers. Works well since the Imam has so many. And we can't cheat without pain."

"So we're competing against them too."

"Voltaire! Got the left nearly fixed, but what am I going to do with that head?"

I check the bot's cranium. The left side has a dent on the cheek plate. The neck support seems to be weakened too. It is leaning a little. "Don't worry about making it pretty. Just make it work."

Bull smooths a sheet over the bot's forehead. Peers inside. "Oh, it will work. It has to work."

I look at the nearest of the three other rings. They're at the break too. A red Talient model is matched against a yellow Elipserv.

The Talient looks ready to be scrapped. Its debugger is attempting to reattach the left arm, but the whole spine seems twisted. If it goes out the way it is, the head will be aligned so it is looking through only one eye. I watch the work for a couple seconds longer.

Glad that isn't me.

Bull climbs off the bot, removes the sheet from its forehead, then places his hands on his hips and squints at it.

"Is it all right?"

He studies the bot for a second more and shrugs. "You tell me."

I check its power levels. All in normal range, though none at a hundred percent. "Functional."

He frowns, then climbs out of the ring. "That's good, because—"

The pole lights flash blue.

Bull smiles. "We're out of time."

I SHUT MY EYES, find the bot's stream tap, and pull it in. I straighten the bot from its kneeling position and orient it so it is facing the other corner. I start it bouncing on its toes and bring its hands up.

The colonel is already a step ahead of me. Green mashes its hands together and starts across the ring.

I send my bot to meet it, raising its hands closer to its face. I expect another rush. An onslaught.

Green reaches the midpoint, slows, and starts to bob and weave.

My bot pulls within an arms-length. I loosen its stance, then mimic Green's motion.

Green jabs, once, twice. Throws a heavier right.

I block and dodge, but try to maintain a centered orientation. Try to keep the bot's head over its torso. I've found that's important. To keep the body in line for the swing, and not surrender even those centimeters.

We move in a circle. Green bounces and jabs with occasional longer, heavier shots.

"New strategy?" Bull messages. "Less aggressive swarmer?"

I nod, but keep my eyes closed. My mind focused. I wish I knew the power levels of the other bot; then I could know where to attack. But that information is blocked. Out of reach.

Plus, attempting to cheat would get me buzzed. Don't want to risk that. Not with the condition of my head.

That's where Green took the hardest hits. The head.

Green steps up his attack, throwing a flurry of jabs, and then closes and strikes harder. My arm power levels are dropping. Left more than right.

How good were BullHammer's repairs? What did he have time for?

And how much better is StandFish? He's a higher level. More experienced.

Look at me. I'm already blaming Bull for my failure.

I pull back. Try to create another opening.

Green moves forward. *Wham.* I hit him right in the forehead.

"Guess he didn't learn as much as I thought," Bull streams.

I send him the image of a flower blooming. "Hope not."

Green pulls back, dances left and right. Brings his hands up.

"He's uncertain. Doesn't know how to go on."

I nod. "Too many heads helping."

"So, what do you do?"

I drive my bot across the distance. Jab, jab, jab, punch. Jab, punch. All are glancing blows, but they put Green off balance. Backing the colonel's servant toward the ropes. Makes him retreat.

Green jabs, jabs.

I fake a left, then throw a right uppercut. It finds Green's chin. The face plating lights up, making Green a light bulb. I follow with a left to the gut. Another flash of light. Then to the sternum. His own fists connect there. More light.

All are making me look better. Look more aggressive. Adding to my score.

The colonel knows that too. A quick glance shows me his face has reddened. His eyes appear desperate.

He looks my way.

I smile. Wave.

He's also distracted.

I smash his bot again and again. He brings the arms up, only to have them knocked out of the way. Power levels. All about the power levels.

Finally, Green's guard fails altogether. I blister it with punches. I smash the left side of its face, then the right. An uppercut, followed by a hook, followed by a sledgehammer.

Green is barely moving now. To continue is to scrap it. To turn it into slag. But I can't stop. Can't take that chance.

The referee steps into view. Raises his hands and waves them together. The pole lights flash.

The match is over.

"Rails, what do you know?" Bull says. "You won one."

There's a tepid reaction from the crowd. Some hiss with displeasure, but the majority applaud. I represent the Imam, after all. This is his building. His event.

I order our bot out of the ring. On the other side, a crew of three servbots group around Green, attempt to clear it away. They finally tip it onto its heels and drag it toward the ropes.

I feel relieved, but still nervous. "I wish this was the only one," I say. "Wish we were done."

"If they were human fighters it would be." Bull hefts his bag onto his shoulder. "A body couldn't handle that for much longer." He smiles. "But we are not so lucky."

"That seems like an understatement."

A group of servbots approach. All are male in design. All dressed in green servant clothes. Smooth faces and heads.

The lead bot bows. "We're to escort you back to your room."

I glance at the now-empty ring, then at the other rings. The other matches are still in progress. Still inflicting bot injury.

There's an undercurrent of pain in my head too. The wolf is present, but not growling. Simply prowling around. Biding his time.

"Excuse me, sir."

The bots form a circle around Bull and me.

To the right, being addressed by the servbot there, is the colonel. He gives the bot a passing acknowledgment, then extends a hand and thrusts it my direction. "You fought well."

I glance at his hand, but bow instead. "Peace be unto you, colonel, together with A's mercy."

He looks distressed. Unsure whether to return the bow, or keep his hand extended. He goes with the latter.

"You fought well too," I say.

He grimaces. "You won't take my hand?"

Bull steps closer. Bows himself. "As a practice we don't, no. Reduces the risk of infection, and—"

"We aren't worthy of such an honor," I say. "Skin contact is the purview of the free." I bow again. "We're the Imam's property."

The colonel lowers his hand, seeming convinced. He raises an eyebrow. "What you did in the ring there. Were you trained in combat?"

I smile. "I've been trained in many things. The rest, I've learned on my own."

"You studied." He smiles. "So did I. It wasn't easy. This sport—" He indicates the ring. "It's not how we fight today."

"I know. I used to work on heavies."

"Ah, armored bots. Heavies. Right." He squints. "How long? How long did you study?"

Bull touches my elbow. "We should go. Get the next bot checked out. They don't give us much time."

The colonel smooths the front of his uniform. Straightens his cap. "Answer my question, please. Then I'll go."

"Why do you ask?"

He shrugs. "I'm curious is all. We don't see many of your kind on base. Most of the machines are fixed offsite or scrapped. So, how long? Come on."

"Thread," Bull messages. "Don't tell him. We need to go."

I bow. "I trained for ten days."

The colonel's eyes widen. "Ten? Ten!" He chuckles. "That isn't possible." He waves a hand. "Very well. You need to go. Ten days."

Bull snorts. "Closer to seven. He was floundering before I joined him."

The colonel laughs louder. "Seven! Even better."

I stream the bots near us, telling them to take us back. We move toward the nearest entranceway.

Other soldiers join the colonel. His ringside advisers. Still laughing and looking at me, he leans close to them. More laughter follows.

"Doesn't matter what they believe," Bull messages. "Them with their slow, disconnected brains."

"You're competitive."

"You haven't been here, Thread, so you don't know." He sends me the taste of cinnamon. "But yeah, I want you to win. Want it more than anything."

TWENTY MINUTES LATER WE are in another procession, bringing the second combat bot out.

This one is functionally identical to the first, but there's more flare to its design. It is colored blue and gold, with the gold sections more prominent. The insect quality of the face is muted too. Smoothed out and rounder. The shoulders flair out wider, and the head...the head is the most impressive part. The crown is domed, with a four-centimeter spike in the center. It bears a strong resemblance to the top of a temple.

Bull says it reflects helmets crafted centuries ago, by people called "Sauracens". It's a group romanticized by some members of the ulama. He's unsure whether the Imam is trying to honor those members or goad them. Either way, the design is distinctive. Hard to ignore.

The arena was reconfigured while we were gone. There are only two peripheral rings aside the giant, central stage. Large pennants decorate the hall, positioned at the entrances, and between rings. Banners hang from the ceiling.

We are led to the remaining southern ring, the opposite side of the venue as our previous match.

"Turning this into a festival," Bull says as we reach our corner.

I study the ceiling banners. On them are the names of the masters with remaining combatants, along with images of their bots. "The Imam likes spectacle."

Bull's gaze turns upward too. He scans the decorations, then looks at our ring and the crowds around it. He scowls. "I don't like it."

"Don't like what?"

"Whole thing has a funny scent. Who is it really for?"

"I couldn't guess. I only want to get it done."

He snorts. "Easy answer is it is for the Imam's ego." He lays a hand on the edge of the ring. "Maybe that's the best answer."

The opposing bot enters the ring. It is a Talient Model 8. It has a rectangular head with a raised strip that runs from the back of its head to its "nose". The torso armor plating mimics the chest and abdomen of a large, muscular man, as does the arm plating. The legs are more robotic. Rectangular with raised portions at the front of the "thighs." It is painted blue and grey. It looks formidable. Impressive.

I stream check my bot's power levels and error queue one last time, then order it into the ring. It seems ready. Feels ready.

"You managed a three star this time." Bull nods toward the opposite corner. "A full-fledged captain."

My human opponent is an older man, wearing a tan shirt similar to the colonel's. There are three stars on his right shoulder, and his cap is dark red. He slides on his combat gauntlets, then smiles as he looks them over. Seems relaxed.

I feel nervous.

The lights dim, and a spotlight appears on the center ring. All around the arena vidscreens flash to life, most of them positioned between the upper and lower seating. They show the center ring and the audience around it.

"What is this about?" Bull asks.

A man in a red robe and matching turban enters the spotlight, then smiles and bows. "The Great Imam is pleased with your presence." His voice echoes through the hall. He's wearing an amplified com, though it isn't obvious where. "The Imam knows it creates inconvenience for your time and schedule. For some of you there was great travel involved, and missed opportunities. His hope is that tonight's entertainment will in some ways compensate."

His smile broadens. "At this time, I would like to highlight some of the prizes for tonight's event." He raises his right arm, sweeping it toward the corner behind him.

A second spotlight illuminates that corner. A heavyset man enters it, dressed in a tan robe and a red turban. He holds a rectangular device over his head and smiles. Waves the device.

Freeheads start to pour into the ring. Two, then ten, then twenty. Other red-turbaned men escort them, herding them like livestock. They are all smiles.

The other freeheads—of which there are now at least thirty—are male and female. They are dressed simply. White robes and, in the case of the women, white scarves over their heads. Their robes are cinched at the waist with black belts. There are slender golden rings around their necks.

They are generally attractive people. Most surprising, the women have their faces uncovered. It's the largest group of women I've ever seen, so unhindered. All are smiling.

"These are some of the finest slaves in the world," the amplified man says. "And they will become the property of the winner." He approaches one of the females and touches her cheek. Smiles. "All healthy. All young." He squeezes a man's shoulder. "All strong. The best the Imam could find. Purchased from our security forces." He raises his hands over the group. "These, all these, will go to the winning master."

Bull leans close. "Those rings around their necks? Shock collars." He points. "Smile or else."

I nod, and focus on the man with the device in his hand. Doubtless, that controls the collars.

I drift toward the nearest vidscreen, getting close enough that I can make out individual faces. I sweep my eyes over them, particularly the women. I've seen so few female faces. I admire their inherent beauty. The curves of their cheeks and brightness of their smiles. Each one unique, but equally compelling.

There is guilt in my gazing, but no stop from my implant. In this situation, I have little choice. The faces are there for the seeing. Smiling and on display.

The screen view shifts. Panning and zooming.

316

Then something startles me. I look at the central ring, then at the nearest screen again.

Was that—?

The faces. It is a large group. Hard to see all the features clearly. I try to see them all, though. Finally, I give up, close my eyes, and use a pattern match algorithm on the earlier images. Those now stored in my implant. Searching each face against others I know.

There's a match. A strong match.

I walk to the ring, grab the corner pole, and stare at the floor.

Minutes pass as the ringleader prattles on. How could it be? How here?

I try to calculate the probabilities. The chances that such a thing could occur.

But I don't know where to start. What numbers to begin with. The result has to be a number close to zero.

The announcer, the gleeful slave trader, ceases speaking. Then one of the spotlights shines on me. Or more accurately, on the bot above me.

But I'm in the frame. Still being focused on. I put up a hand to shield my eyes, then take a slow step back.

Another announcer speaks, hyping our upcoming match. He names the model numbers and the master names. I simply try to stay out of the light. To analyze my internal turmoil.

Finally, the light flits away to focus on the captain. He raises both arms and smiles. Pumps them triumphantly.

Bull puts a hand on my shoulder. "Thread, you all right?"

I shake my head. "It got surreal, Bull. Rails flipped."

"What?"

I point at the center ring. "The slaves."

"Yeah, what about 'em?"

"I know one of them," I say. "One of the females."

He looks that direction, but the slaves are gone now. The central ring contains only a lone announcer, dressed in white.

"Is she family or something?"

I pull away from the ring. Straighten. "No."

"Then what?"

I shake my head. "Doesn't matter. I can't do anything."

"No. It means something. Someone special." His eyes narrow. "You know we're not—"

I glare at him. "I know, Bull. I know everything about us. About what being a debugger means. What it costs."

He raises both hands. "Don't scorch your implant, Michelangelo. I'm only asking."

The lights come back up. The crowds start to talk again. Everything is normal.

Nothing is normal.

"Her name is Damali, okay? I met her at the prince's house. She was..." I share my head and focus on the ring. The referee has entered and is talking to the other corner. He'll probably want to talk to us next.

"She was what?" Bull asks. "Part of his harem?"

The referee approaches. He squints at the bot for a few seconds, then squats down over us. "I will run through the rules in the center, but I wanted to make sure we're all straight here." He looks at Bull, then back at me. "Fair fight. Don't know all what you're capable of, but I know you can do a lot." He touches his head. "No trouble, okay? No strange business?"

I shake my head. "No strange business."

"What sort of strange business is he quacking about?" Bull messages. "Flipping freehead."

I don't reply. Only watch as the referee walks away.

"So...about this Damali."

I try to focus on the bot. Find its tap. Pull myself into it. Into the fight.

I feel Bull's hand on my shoulder. Again. He touches way too much for a debugger.

"Listen, I don't know what this is about, what happened between you two. Hope it was memorable."

I glare at him again. "Bull..."

He looks defensive. Apologetic even. "Only wanted to say that if she means something to you, then your nanopath is clear."

"What?"

He points at the ring. "Winning this thing brings your slave girl to the Imam. She'll become his property." He smiles. "Just like us. Just like you."

"Doesn't matter," I say. "She could go anywhere. Anywhere in the world."

He nods. "But right now, she's here. In the same building. Focus on that. We'll debug the rest later."

The pole lights flash blue. Bull pats my shoulder.

I nod. Close my eyes. Stream to the bot.

Time to fight.

IT IS HARD NOT TO BE aggressive this time. Not to charge across the ring and strike until my power levels drain or the bot's arms fall off.

But I'm conscious of that. Conscious that something abnormal is in play. I need to create my own stops. Keep myself in check. Keep my system.

The other bot—"Blue" as I think of him—is playing cautious too. He's not a swarmer. Not out for quick points. He's studied. Patient. In the state I'm in, that makes me nervous. I want to get this over quickly. Move on to the next bout.

Twenty seconds in, we're mostly circling. Both testing with jabs and simple combinations. His bot seems a little slower than mine, and a little heavier.

That could be either an advantage or a disadvantage, depending on how the captain plays it. Slower should make him an easier target. Someone I can easily out-box. But heavier means he could hit hard, and I want to avoid that.

I hear a scattering of boos from the crowd. Not sure what that means.

"You two are boring them," Bull says. "You're boring me too."

"Trying to figure him out."

"I guessed. But can you do it quicker?"

I open my left eye and look at him.

He shrugs. "Give it a little more power. That bot isn't made for dancing."

I frown and return to my chore. Focus on what the bot sees. On the strength of its limbs and the flow of its nanopaths. The tautness of its sinews.

Blue is just out of reach. I bounce a half step forward and throw a left jab, followed by a right.

Blue blocks, then responds with a string of jabs of his own.

I try a hard left to the head. He blocks with his right, and then quickly returns with a left. My block is partial. The shot glances off my bot's elbow and finds its right ear. A flash of light.

Rails.

I try another left to the head. It strikes Blue's shoulder and then my bot's arm is pushed wide. Blue punches straight to my chin. Another light.

"That's not what I meant," Bull says. "More lights on *his* side."

I don't respond. I simply pull my bot back a bit and circle. Let some of the warnings fade. Get the power levels to normal again.

Blue mimics my actions.

I decide to try a tactic from the earlier match. I shuffle the bot closer to Blue, then step back, hoping it will fill the gap and give me a chance to strike.

Blue maintains his distance.

"Frustrating."

More boos from the crowd. This time, I agree with them.

Blue stops moving altogether. It takes a position in front of me, just outside of range, and waits. Then it puts its hands on its hips.

I peek at the opposing captain. He's smiling brightly. Hands on his hips.

What is he doing?

I lunge forward. Swing hard with the right.

Blue dodges, and immediately counters. I miss the block. Blue strikes my bot's chin. Its head bobs back. Chin brightly lit.

I push my frustration into the stream, straight at BullHammer's waiting message center. I send him a black and red ball of static. "What is he doing?"

"Countering," he messages. "Lots of countering."

"Right. He mimics every move I make."

"Yeah, that's his style. He's a counterpuncher."

"Is that a style? I don't remember that being a style."

I force the issue, throwing a string of punches: left jab, right jab, left hook.

Blue blocks or dodges, then counters. Every. Single. Time. Even scores with one or two.

I bounce away. Try to regroup again. Focus.

My bot's arms are weakened, and I'm way down on points. I've got to get some hits through or the captain is going to win without working.

"How do I fight this?"

"Don't know," Bull says. "I didn't study counterpunching."

I keep the bot circling.

Blue stops again. Waits. Then its arms rise and beckon me. Taunt me.

The referee moves up on my right. "Fight!" he yells.

I want to swipe him away. Show him what a fight is. My implant doesn't like that notion and sends a painful reminder. I wince. "I'm getting beat here."

"Fair assumption," Bull says.

I want to glare at him, but I can't risk it. "So what do I do!"

He shrugs. "I'm here to fix the bot, not the fight."

The pole lights flash.

I glance at Bull.

He smiles. "Now you have some time to figure it out."

I sneer and pull the bot back to the corner. Kneel it so Bull can check it over.

Bull tosses his debugging bag into the ring and climbs in after it. A second later, he's crouched over the bot. Whistling and grunting. "Not watching those power levels again," he says.

"Just fix it." I glance across the ring. Another familiar form is repairing Blue, though I doubt he has much to do. "SilentJoy is over there," I message Bull. "Better do your best."

Bull lets out a string of, I assume, artist names. "Thanks for that. Really didn't need to know."

I send him a fuzzy bear, arms open, that smells like bread. "You have a reason to perform now too."

"You forget. I'm at the bottom of their list. I always have a reason." He pauses. "You have twenty seconds to come up with a plan."

"Right." I touch the stream, comb the boxing sources I referenced before. I find only references to the act of counterpunching. Not any specific strategies against it. Nor a description of it as a style like the others I studied. I push those sources away. Stream wider and deeper.

Ten seconds pass. Then fifteen. Nothing relevant. Nothing helpful.

Bull grabs his bag and scurries out of the ring. Rails.

"Find anything?" I hear him say.

"Still looking."

The pole lights flash. I need to begin. I activate the bot. Stand it up. Move toward the center of the ring.

Blue joins me. We circle. I jab. It jabs. I punch. It blocks and counters.

Seconds go by as we continue the now-familiar dance. There are more boos. More calls for action.

This is ridiculous. There has to be a way to end this.

I remember the first datamix from JustBecause. The many objects that were thrown at him. The craziness of his master's eyes. The randomness of it all.

That's how I feel. Lost and confused. Unsure of what to do next.

Wait. Randomness? Lamps, apples, and rainbow lights. I can do randomness.

"I have an idea."

"There's a change." Bull sends me the image of exploding fireworks. One after another, until my virtual sky is full.

Not helpful. I push that away. Put all my attention on the ring. What is happening in the ring.

Blue relies on a quick counter. On me striking and him responding. The pattern. The predictable. That's why I need random.

I move closer. Stalk Blue. Then I jab. The counter comes, but I lean away, and come back with two punches. One, two.

I connect with both. Flash, flash.

Blue hops away, seemingly surprised. Brings its arms up. Waits for me to act.

I try the same move again: A jab, dodge the counter, then a one-two.

Blue expects the move this time. Counters it. I take a hit to the head.

I need more random.

I fake a right jab. Blue counters with a full right jab, bringing its torso forward and vulnerable. I smash the left side of its face.

Strong flash of light, and there's a dent created in the side of Blue's face.

I glance at the captain. His focus is on the match. His face is a stone. No smiling. I see a glint of perspiration on his face.

"You're doing something good there," Bull says. "Keep it up."

Blue becomes more hesitant. More cautious. I feel like I'm chasing him now. Almost controlling his path. He's damaged. Not sure what his internal readings look like, but mine has to be better. It would be nice to finish this before Silent gets a chance to fix it up again. Bull did a good job with my bot, but there are errors—particularly in the left arm—that should've been addressed. The power level seems to have a slow decline. Like a pneumatic tire with a leak.

I close with Blue again. I create a list of hit combinations. Not individual punches, or simple one-two combinations, but multi-punch combos including three, four of five strikes. I randomize the list, then work it from the top.

Jab, jab, jab, uppercut. I make contact.

Blue steps away, chin still flashing. Shakes its head. Raises its arms.

I close again. Use the second combination from the list that ends with a shot to the body. Again, Blue fails to counter. Again, I connect. Harder this time. His abdomen is afire.

This time the captain directs Blue into my bot. It grabs my bot's shoulders. Clinches it close. Then it moves. Pushing and pulling in a slow circle.

My bot's left is screaming at me. Its power levels plummet. I need to free it.

I push hard. Wrench on the right arm. Pull, and slip the left free. Then I pummel the bot's head and right shoulder.

I must get loose. I must finish it.

THE POLE LIGHTS FLASH. Blue steps away, but clings to my bot's left arm. Pulling. Overextending it until it loses power completely. The arm falls limp, and there's little I can do to correct it.

I will my bot to the corner, then look at the other side. The captain is still sweating, but there's a smile on his face. SilentJoy is in the ring already. Waiting for the bot to return to him. He has a sheet open as if it were a towel. Or a blanket.

Bull is still next to me.

"The left arm is dead," I say. "Wasn't right to begin with. Now it's dead."

Bull gives me a puzzled look, places a hand on the lowest rope. "I'll get it, Thread, relax."

"I can't," I say. "I should've finished the fight. That arm kept me from finishing."

Bull climbs into the ring, bag in hand. He immediately goes around to the bot's left side and inspects the arm. He grunts and, dropping the bag to the floor, starts to pick through it.

I circle around so I'm directly below him. "It was bleeding power the whole round. I can't fight and debug at the same time." I glance at the other side. SilentJoy is doing something to Blue's head. Cranking on something. "Not when it is like this."

"Sorry," Bull says. "I try not to miss stuff." He lifts a hand tool—a sinew rake, I think—and slides it into the shoulder joint. Pries.

The wolf growls in my head. A heavy pain appears between my

ears. I look at the side of the ring. A solid blue wall. Try to focus on it. "Well...you did. You missed stuff. Important..." Focus eludes me, so I pinch my eyes closed. "...stuff."

"Not going to talk to you right now," Bull says. "And don't message because I'll rage stream you."

I ignore him. Focus on breathing. On simply returning to normal.

How many seconds do I have? How many until the next round? Can I recover in time?

I hear Bull working on the bot. Little clicks and clanks, with an occasional artist-based expletive. "Power levels. I've got your power levels." He strikes something metal. "You made a mess here. Look at these pathways. Rails." More muttering.

I think about the other side. If Silent is as good as his attitude projects, he may be finished by now. Will he be able to correct all the damage?

I inflicted a lot. At least, I think I did.

How will the captain respond to my new tactics?

The pain intensifies. I take a deep breath. Grit my teeth. Let the breath out again.

I hear more movement, and open my eyes to find Bull sliding between the ropes.

"Three seconds, Thread. Three to spare and it's better than ever."

But I'm not. I'm a lot worse. Almost incapable. Still with eyes closed, I reach out. My hand finds the warm smoothness of Bull's head.

He grunts and pulls away.

"Sorry." I shake my head. "Just wanted to say sorry."

I feel his hand on my shoulder. "No cycles on it now. Get the bot out there. It is ready."

The pain continues. "I don't know if I can." I pry my eyes open, then touch my head. "I'm hurting."

He crouches closer. "You getting stopped? Why would you be getting stopped?"

I shake my head. "Not a stop. It—"

The pole lights flash. The crowd applauds. The last round got them interested. Involved. I try to push thoughts through my mind. The instincts. I stream reach for the bot, but it feels like walking in the dark. Like I'm swatting for a light. Finally, I find the tap and grab it. Hold on with all my neurons.

I look at the other corner. Blue is active now. Up and bouncing around. My eyes drift upwards, over his head. First to the stands beyond, the enthused and active crowd, then to the luxury chambers over them. The Imam's is easiest to spot. Dead center and twice as large as the others. He and his primary wife are near the window. Watching everything.

Does he know I'm broken? He has to know.

I push my bot to a standing position. Square its shoulders. The gold plating of its back catches the light. It is made to be a champion. That's why I'm here, right? To win!

All my senses are heightened by the pain. The crowd noise is louder. The lights more intense. The smells... I close my eyes again. Try to shut it out.

Bull touches my shoulder. "Rails, Thread. Are you okay?" He indicates the bot. "Looks like it is sleeping out there."

"I'm not, no." I massage my temples. The pain seems to subside some. I look at the ring. I'm shocked that my bot is still in the corner. It is upright but standing flatfooted.

Didn't I get it moving? What am I doing?

The pain recedes even more. I slowly breathe out, hoping the rest of the pain goes out with the air. I manipulate the bot. Get it up and moving.

Blue is only a few steps away. What is the captain's plan now? What will he do?

I try to clear my mind. The pain has left. I'm good. I can do this.

Blue charges at me with a right. I manage to swerve to the left and plant a right in its midsection.

That produces a nice flash of lights. The crowd responds. Bull-Hammer sends me a pat on the back.

I take a couple long breaths to make sure I'm okay. That the wolf has truly left the building. Seems like it has. Like it is hunting elsewhere. I smile.

Blue jabs three times with his left, then throws a right. I pull my bot's torso away to dodge and miss the swing. When I return it to the center position, it gets hit with a left. Lights up its cheek plate.

Using my own tricks against me now. Nice.

I wrench my bot back and then slide right. Find some space. Time to think.

I realize, randomly, that I miss the implants at Bamboo's school. I miss being their "mawla." How strange. I can imagine them being here. They'd love all this. The violence and the noise. Their chatter room would be impossible to restrain.

Blue manages to clip my bot again.

Need to be in this, Thread. Need to watch and think.

"He's changing it up on you," Bull says.

"Right. A little slugging, a little swarming." Time to outbox again.

We circle. Dance. I try to remember the areas of Blue I worked before. The head and chest mostly. I need to push the captain back into his old habits. Force him to make mistakes.

Swarm. I have to swarm. Random squared. I check the arm power levels. They seem okay. Left is a little lower than right, but not much. I pull up my list of moves, augment it with more slugger hits. More power. I shuffle closer.

The captain jabs a couple times, but seems to hesitate. Seems to fall back into his wait-and-see approach. Now's my chance.

I attack, working the list from the top. I aim a right at Blue's chest, and when it covers, aim one for its head. The block comes, but then I apply a string of jabs to its arms and shoulders. Simply tapping. Trying to make contact. Occasionally I earn a flash of light, but that isn't my goal. I want him off balance. Reacting, and unable to fully counter. Unable to attack.

He tries a weak left, but I avoid. Then I return to my list. Hard punches, light punches—I even clinch Blue's right elbow and hold until it breaks away. I soft punch its shoulders, hard punch the torso, then quickly push its arms.

More lights.

"I like this," Bull messages. "Like it more than skiing."

My hope is to keep the captain always reacting. Always under pressure. I think he likes it clean and simple. I'm going for messy. Complicated.

I continue with the list, not doing a lot of damage, but touching Blue a lot. Keeping it random.

Finally, Blue's arms flail forward, and it steps back. Moves away. It raises its hands in a defensive posture. Bounces on its toes.

I check on the captain. He's sweating a lot. The front of his shirt is wet, medals and all. Standing next to him is SilentJoy. His mouth is moving. Is he helping? How is he helping?

There must be some limit, but maybe not. Maybe the Imam's order is for him to help in any way possible. In the interest of impartiality. Fairness.

I move in to attack again. There isn't much time left. I need to get this over.

I return to my punch list. My system.

I chase Blue around the ring. Quicken my bot's legwork. Begin another attack. Left jab, right jab, shot to the body, swing for the head.

I sense a power level loss. The left arm again. It is at eighty percent, then fifty, then thirty.

Bull...

I dive into the bot's system. Try to see what the problem is. Is there anything I can address from here? I check the source of the loss. It isn't in the arm itself, but in the joint somewhere. A pathway is twisted or pinched.

I feel panic. It's a hardware issue. A mechanical malady. Which means it is out in the bot where I can't get to it.

The arm loses all power. Falls to the bot's side.

My defense is non-existent.

The captain notices the weakness. Blue stops trying to retreat and starts advancing. Starts attacking.

My bot takes a shot to the side. Then to the head. I want to yell at BullHammer, but there's nothing he can do either. I'm stuck here. And the bot is out there. Getting smashed.

I shift the bot's stance. Getting the right side out front. I need to hold on. Survive. Keep it intact and upright.

I block what I can. But there are plenty of hit lights. Potential points. I save the power in the right. Dodge with the feet. Shifting the torso.

Blue throws a haymaker. A knockout blow. I turn the bot just enough to slip free and launch a right uppercut that connects. Blue's head rocks back. It is thrown off balance. The crowd reacts.

Blue's arms stretch out in a balancing move. It takes a few tentative steps back, then staggers left and right.

The pole lights flash. The fight is over.

THE BOTS ARE SENT TO the middle of the ring, and after multiple checks of the tabulated score, the referee slaps my bot on the chest. I raise its arms as the victor. There are hisses of displeasure, but many, many cheers.

I lean over and put my hands on my knees. Breathe deeply.

Bull crouches next to me. "You won it, Thread. Won big."

I nod, straighten, then scan the auditorium. The other match has ended too, seemingly a while ago. That ring is empty, as are most of the seats around it. That explains the extra interest in our match. Why it felt so intense. Everyone was watching.

I order the bot out of the ring, then check the other corner. The captain stands with both hands on the ring's edge, looking exhausted. His face is red, and his mouth open. His shirt is completely soaked.

He notices me, shakes his head, then swats the air in disgust. A servbot approaches him, and after a short conversation, helps remove the control gauntlets from the captain's arms. He looks like he needs the help.

I would too, frankly. I wasn't physically moving, but I'm worn out. Really tired.

I glance at the Imam's observation chamber. He's no longer at the windows. No one is. All I can see is the front row of the seats there, and a hint of movement.

I hear a thump, then look to my left. The bot has made its way out. It stands just around the corner from me.

BullHammer is with it, smiling. "We beat them, didn't we?"

He thumps it on the chest, presumably for the second time. "I knew we could."

I take another deep breath, and drift their direction.

Bull grabs the bot's left arm and freely swings it. "Voltaire, that's useless." He frowns and looks at me. "I messed up. Almost cost us it all, didn't I?"

I shrug. "Fight is over. Doesn't matter." I check the bot's face. Its chin is shaped like a wedge from all the hits it took. "Two more of them, though? Not sure I can take it."

Bull pats my arm. "Sure, you can. You did great."

I shake my head. Then wince because it hurts. I don't want the wolf back. Can't handle the wolf.

Bull studies me. Shrugs. "Well, you get a longer rest this time," he says. "A full half hour!"

I nod. "Right. I could take a nap."

Six servbots approach us, surround us, escort us to our locker room. Along the way, many of our new "fans" clap or cheer. Some put out hands to touch us, or to be touched. The bots maintain a perimeter to prevent that from happening, thankfully.

I smile and occasionally bow my head or wave. It is uncomfortable. I'm grateful when we're safely in the locker room again.

"I wonder if this will move me up SilentJoy's list," Bull says, after the door closes.

I straddle the bench and support myself with my hands. I try to relax. Try to shake away some of the fatigue. The nervousness. "That's what you're worried about?" I raise an eyebrow. "Your standing?"

He walks toward the final two "bot boxes" and pauses in front of the shorter one. The one for the next match. "Well, it's something." He glances at me. Smiles. "Wonder what Silent is thinking now? How it feels for him to be on the losing side."

I study the surface of the bench. There are large swirls in the texture, like giant fingerprints. I touch one. Trace its pattern.

I check my internal message queue, noting the one I received from WindCypher before the fights. He has another mix.

I could use another mix. A diversion. I message him with text and voice. Tell him to send it to me. Bill me the usual way.

Seconds later, he responds with the mix's specs. It is another one from BitStack. The debugger working on the Snoob toy. I'm relieved by that. I don't think I could handle something from JustBecause right now. Too much random.

I pay WindCypher and stash the mix away.

I glance at the door. Then at Bull, now focused on the crate. I could view the mix now. I want to view it now. Even without the isolation of a cinder chute. I shut my eyes. Feel for the mix...

I'm jerked back to reality by a high-pitched shriek. The sound of BullHammer opening the third crate.

He swings the cover away, steps back, whistles. "It's a beauty."

The bot's face, arms, upper legs, and torso are gold, while the rest is purple. It has the most humanoid face of any we've seen so far. The eyes are purple too, as is a ten-centimeter tassel that rises from its head. The rest of it is sinewy and sleek. It will make a good spectacle for the crowd.

"You want to bring it out?" Bull asks.

"Sure."

There's a knock on the door, followed by a protracted cough. "Debuggers? It is Jahm! May I enter?"

Bull and I exchange looks.

"Please," I say.

Jahm drifts in on his hover chair, alone this time. A crippled but powerful man. He flashes a brief smile, but looks serious.

Bull points at the crate. "Just checking out our latest bot here. Trying to get it ready."

Jahm glances at the crate, sniffs. "Yes, it is wonderful." He saves a hand. "Unfortunately, you won't be using it."

I pivot so I'm facing him. "Submaster?"

He stares at his seat's right armrest, and the controls there. He contemplates them, frowns, and nervously taps at the edge. "The third fight has been canceled."

"Canceled?"

Jahm nods. "Yes, the other master, Fasal Marzuq, has forfeited." He flashes a clipped smile. "Your reputation leads you, you might say."

I think of the captain's look of disgust. His swat at the air. "In what way, submaster?"

"You're too good, they all say! Unbeatable by a normal man." He touches the side of his forehead and points at the bot. "Too close to the machine you're controlling. They think it is unfair." He frowns. "The next combatant doesn't want that humiliation. Losing to a slave."

"I could've lost the last fight." I glance at BullHammer, then at the unopened box next to him. "It was very close."

Jahm taps his fingers on the armrests. "The decision has been made. It is pointless to conjecture." He chuckles. "Of course, by forfeiting, Fasal has released any rights to the prizes. The Imam is pleased with that result. You've made him the winner."

Jahm frowns, scans the room. "Not the nicest place here, is it? Feels like my first home. Cramped and damp." He coughs several times, the last time extra-long. "So, now, the exhibition will proceed." He points at me. "And you will do your part."

I start to respond, but Jahm raises a hand. He swivels, and motions Bull out of the way. He hovers to the large crate, and pressing a hand to the left side, unlocks it. He pivots, grabs the crate's front edge, and slowly hovers forward, opening the cover as he goes.

Within is the strangest construct I've ever seen. It is roughly three meters tall and built along combat bot lines. Large hands, broad shoulders, and a long trunk and legs.

The head is nondescript, however. More a cone atop the shoulders than an actual head. Even the blue optics that might be considered its "eyes" don't help. It reminds me of bots from centuries ago.

The bot's highlight color is gold, but a fair portion of the surface—particularly the chest and a portion of the head—is transparent. As if the designers wanted a window into the bot's inner workings.

Except even that doesn't seem right. In the chest, for instance, I should be seeing pathways, sinews, and motivators. Instead, there's an odd-shaped cavity, and inside that are narrow straps and a dark pedestal—

"Doesn't look finished." Bull moves closer to the bot. "And what is that inside there?" He looks at Jahm. "Is that a seat? Is someone supposed to ride in there?"

Jahm nods. "Yes, the operator goes inside." He flourishes a hand. "Sharing the excitement. Living the experience."

I get a flash of panic. "We don't need that." I glance at Bull. "I can operate it remotely."

Jahm glares at me. "Of course, you can. You just proved you can." He smiles and brings his hands together. "But this is a show. A spectacle for the ulama. The Imam wanted a human connection. Something the audience could appreciate." He indicates the bot. "Please, now. You should try it on."

I shake my head. "I don't think I can handle that. I don't like being seen. I'm not a good attraction. Or a human connection."

He frowns. "Come now, you'll be protected. Secure."

"Don't want to."

"You have little choice, debugger. I have your controller."

"I'd rather be punished, submaster."

Jahm shakes his head. Studies me a moment. "I have every right to dislike you, ThreadBare."

"Submaster?"

He taps his chair's armrests. "The loss of my legs. The loss of the prince." He shakes his head. "Every right."

"But—"

He raises a hand. "Oh, I know you aren't personally to blame, but your connection to the event alone is enough. Your presence." He winces, and straightens in his chair. "Enough, because it reminds me of a better time." He forces a smile. "But I don't dislike you at all. I find I'm intrigued by you. And possibly a little frightened." He looks at the crate, and the bot within. "So I will give you an added incentive."

I shake my head. "I'm a debugger, submaster. A servant—"

"Oh, come now, you're more than that. Hero or villain, I do not know. But you're hardly a servant. Hardly a slave."

I find myself looking at the bench's surface again. The large swirls of identity.

Jahm coughs, wipes his mouth. Smiles. "Anyway, I know something about slaves. Something about the prizes." He points at me. "Your woman is among them."

I don't protest because I know he'll dismiss anything I say. I instead stare at him silently. He may not hate me, but Damali? She was the one who struck him. Crippled him.

What is his game?

He smiles. "You're not going to remind me of your station? That you aren't allowed such connections?" He clucks his tongue. "Perhaps you are a hero then."

He points to the bot. "If that is the case, if you're the servant you claim to be, then this is the chance to prove it. And for that, I will give her to you."

"Give her?" A flurry of emotions—not the least of which are fear and sadness—assault me. Jahm doesn't understand us. If he did, he would know this offer is wrong. Impossible. Even if the mechanics were worked out. Even if I walked away with Damali beside me, what end would there be? What result? I'm a debugger with a wolf living inside. And she's a freehead.

"Again, you have nothing to say? I once bore the whip. Now I offer you the richest of desserts."

"Why?" I shake my head. "You have a controller."

He smiles. "Because I want you fully motivated. We need a good show." He points at the bot again. "Now, please try it on."

THERE'S NOTHING I CAN SAY. No protest I can raise. Instead, I stand and approach the bot.

"There's a finger switch on the belly there," Jahm says. "Press it and it should open for you." He smiles. "It can be locked from the inside, of course."

I nod, and after a quick search, find the switch and press it. There's a "snap" and the exterior of the chest cavity swings open. I reach up, grab the slender seat, and hoist myself inside. It takes a few seconds to get my feet into the stirrups in the bot's thigh, and my arms tucked into its upper arms.

When I'm finally situated, comfortably seated, my eyes are just above the bot's chin. Almost like I'm looking out its mouth. The visual feed from its optics are displayed on the interior surface too. Just below the normal sight line.

Jahm hovers forward and closes the chest "door".

Despite the tightness of the quarters, I find that I feel okay. Comfortable even. Like I have an extra skin.

"It's meant for manual control," Jahm says. "For you to use your feet and hands. But it is stream aware. You can fight as you're accustomed."

I nod and shut my eyes. The bot's stream tap is readily available. Floating in the stream like a giant digital frog. Watching me. Daring me to pick it up. I grab it and make it mine.

It feels like an old friend. Like a lost pet that has returned. I slowly lift the bot's arms. Then move it free of the crate. I'm surprised by how natural it feels...how right. It's like I was made to be here. Sheltered inside a warrior. Weak inside of strong.

I look to the right, where BullHammer stands, mouth hanging open, then to the left, at Jahm.

His eyes are wide, almost fearful, but a smile sneaks out. "How does that feel? Can you control everything?"

The bot has audio enhancers, I realize, because I hear Jahm perfectly. Better than I did outside.

What it doesn't seem to have is any means to respond. I can't sense any vocal capability, nor can I find one in the built-in list of features. So, I rock the bot's head forward and back, approximating a nod.

Jahm laughs. "Aha, yes. Very good."

"What does it feel like in there?" Bull messages me.

I turn the bot's head so I can see him, then raise the bot's right fist.

"Slick, Thread. Do you feel safe? Feel good?"

"Feels strange," I message. "But good, yes. Strangely good."

I see him snort, and another message arrives: You used to debug heavies, now you dress like one.

I send him a smile. I suppose that's true.

"Give it a checkup, Bull. Make sure it is all right." The mechanical seems extravagant, even for the Imam. All for a show? "There's something about this that bothers me."

"Like Jahm offering you a freehead woman?"

"Like that. Yeah."

Bull sends me a memory from a short time ago. A clip of him speculating about the event. Who is it really for?

"Right," I message back. "I remember. Any theories?"

He shakes his head. Looks at Jahm.

I turn the head to look at the submaster. He's watching me, chin resting in one hand.

"Do we have an agreement, then?" Jahm asks. "You will fight?"

I make the bot nod again.

Jahm claps, then straightens in his seat. "Very good." He works his chair's controls, backing it up, and hovers to the opposite side of the bench seat. He travels along it to the end, then pivots, and aims for the door. "I will leave you two to prepare." He coughs and moves forward.

Five seconds later, he is gone.

Bull walks to the front of the bot, and peers up at me. "Might help if you stoop it. Bring it down where I can reach it."

I nod the bot's head and move it down to one knee. The motion is as smooth as if it were my own legs moving. My own knee. Stable, secure, and strong.

"Never thought I'd see this," Bull says. "It is like a bad joke. Mechanical inside our heads. One of us inside a mechanical." He recovers his debugging bag and places it on the bench. He rummages for a moment, then looks at me and frowns. "Might take a while if I'm thorough. Maybe you should get out."

"I can help with the internals," I message. "Check the queues."

He nods. "Right, but still...this is a big system. Lot to check over." He smiles. "Don't want you fighting any joint malfunctions this time."

I shake the bot's head. "I'll be okay in here. It's almost like being in a chute. An upright chute."

"That comfortable, huh?" He sends me a feeling of skepticism.

"Wish I had one my whole life," I message. "A full body mask to wear."

He laughs. "A mask? What do you have to hide?"

I study Bull through the bot's transparent chin. His appearance is skewed. He looks heavier. More like I remember. "I'm broken, Bull." I push seriousness with the words. "Not right."

"What do you mean, not right?" He yanks the front of his shirt forward. "At least you're not hungry. I've been hungry for months." He looks at his bag again. "I'm about as broken as they come."

"Not like me." I raise the bot's arm and touch its head. "Here. Inside. Something's damaged. A wolf running around my head."

"What?" He sends a deep purple bubble. A balloon of concern. "You were just at Bamboo's, right? Didn't he check you out?"

"He found it. The wolf. Said I damaged my brain."

"Did you fall or something?"

I shake the bot's head. "I went through a lot." I feel a tingle of a stop and shake my own head. "At my last job." I send him a smile. "And after."

"Van Gogh and Rembrandt, Thread. they got to you too." He looks at the floor. "I hate them." He pauses, winces, then shakes it off. "Hate the way it is. Our lives." He shakes his head a second time. "So, can you do this thing?"

"Depends on the wolf, I guess. Whether he stays dormant or not."

He sends me a burning question mark. "Maybe I could do it instead? I'd fit inside, right? Maybe they wouldn't know."

"We'd know. Our stops would know."

"Yeah...right." He steps closer. "Well then, let's beat them, right?" He touches the bot's chest, then slaps it. "Whatever this exhibition is. Whatever it means, let's win it."

I force a smile. "Okay, Bull." I send him resolve mixed with pineapple.

He gets up on his tiptoes and brings his face close. "Just one more fight. And hopefully it's a short one." He sinks back down, smiles. "Then we'll get your girl. Get you out of here."

"She's not my girl."

He waves a hand. "Let me have a romance for this, okay? A big, fancy ending." He returns to his bag. "Now to get that thing checked over." He glances at me. "Sure you're okay in there?"

I make the bot nod. "Yeah. Think I'll try to nap for a bit. Maybe watch a mix."

"Sounds like a rails good plan."

I send him warmth and a bright orange sun. "Thanks, Bull. You're a good friend."

"Nothing to it," he says aloud. "You're the one fighting. I'm just here for the story."

IT IS A DAY OF RAIN.

I'm waiting in my attic room. My chores have been light today. Every inside maintenance task is complete. Everything outside—adjustments to the landscaping bots and the driveway's guidance system—can wait. Must wait, for fear of introducing new performance anomalies.

Regardless of how sealed and protected systems are, water always seems to affect them. Finds a way to make its presence known. Better to wait. Better to plan for the sun instead. Build a list of tasks.

Yet now I stand next to the window, contemplating. The park across the street is completely empty. No freeheads, no animals, no bots. Rain runs in a torrent down one of the slides there. Below and around it, a large puddle has formed. There are puddles everywhere, in fact. Under every playset and on every walk. If the rain were to stop immediately, it would still be days before Obaid can visit the park again.

I smile. At least, with his mother's approval. Obaid has a love for standing water.

I push away from the window. I should plan. Build my lists.

Since rescuing the original Snoob, I've become more introspective. More drawn to thoughts of life and death. And of Isa. Always of Isa the miracle-worker.

My implant often fights me now. Attempts to divert my attention from the paths my mind wants to follow.

Some things I now know to be true, however. Isa is the only one of the prophets to whom miracles are attributed. The only one who is never commanded to pray for forgiveness, nor is he written as doing so. He's said to have ascended straight into Paradise and to be coming to Earth again someday. These things the scriptures say.

He's also labeled "the word." This attribution is most troubling.

Is he the same "word" that A uses to create? The "word" that seems paradoxical? Both creator and created? It vexes my thought processes. It defies scholars' explanation too. I streamed the writings of many. I even asked one anonymously.

His answer wasn't satisfying. It wasn't even considerate. I was accused of heretical thought and told to submit myself to the nearest Ministry of Virtue for evaluation.

I chuckle at that suggestion. Debuggers have that ministry living inside us already. Right in the middle of our brains.

Regardless, I'm now in a new place. On the edge of something. My latest hobby helped put me there.

I'm startled by a thump on my trapdoor. Not a knock or the rap of a knuckle. But a muted "thump".

I frown and walk toward it. Who is doing that? Not Raahil. Not my master.

There's another thump. And another.

I kneel beside the door, but I'm unsure whether to open it. Will I be struck?

Another thump. I wait a second for another. When it doesn't come, I grab the door's handle and jerk it open.

Obaid stands at the bottom of the ladder below. He's dressed in blue pants and shirt—his inside casual wear. He has new Snoob in one hand and a rubber ball in the other.

His eyes widen when he sees me, but after a second, he tosses the ball aside. He takes Snoob with both hands and throws it into the air. He acts as if he will catch it, but at the last instant, he moves his hands away.

The furry falls to the ground, though it pivots and lands on all fours, unharmed. It then takes a seated position. Looks at Obaid.

"Is that how you treat a friend, young master?"

Obaid shrugs, then bends over and retrieves the furry. He jostles it between his hands but does not drop it. "I'm looking for you."

"And you have found me."

His face is one of determination. "My mother is broken. Can you fix her?"

"Your mother?"

I get a flash of worry. Freehead homes sometimes have violence. Not just spats of anger, but "spousal chastisement" for wives that disobey their husbands. I have not witnessed the practice here, nor have I seen any indication on Raahil. But I am often busy.

I don't want to see it here. Not with Raahil. Not ever.

"Where is she?"

Obaid raises his shoulder. "I don't know. Crafting beads, I think." He swirls a finger. "Spinning sand into dreams."

I open the door all the way, and, bracing myself, peek out and check the entire hallway below. I see nothing aside from doorways and decorations. I look at Obaid again. "She's not hurt?"

He shakes his head, then repositions Snoob in his arms. "I don't think so."

"But you want her fixed?"

He nods vigorously. "Yes, her head is affected."

"Affected?"

"She's not thinking right." He holds up the furry. "She says this is Snoob, but it isn't. This is something else."

"Ah, now I see." Keeping him in view, I ease out of the opening onto my knees. I contemplate the toy for a moment. There is no obvious difference between it and the original. Even its stream-emanations, as minuscule as they are, feel correct. Appropriate for its type of device. "And what about Snoob seems wrong, young master?"

Obaid turns the new Snoob, then holds it up by one arm. The furry reaches out with its other arm, as if asking to be held tighter. I feel a twinge of sympathy.

"He doesn't walk the same," Obaid says.

I raise an eyebrow. "But he couldn't walk at all before," I say. "How would—"

Obaid shakes his head. "He still walks different. Not the way he did before he broke." He flips the furry over, now holding it by the left foot. "Also, there used to be a dark spot between his toes here." The toy sloth has three narrow, claw-like digits. Obaid pries two of them apart with his free hand, and lifts the furry higher. "In there. Right between there. No spot. See?"

The furry bends upward, trying to right itself. Failing that, it grasps with both hands at its still-trapped foot.

I shake my head. "No, I cannot see a spot," I say. "At least, not from here." I force a smile. "The lighting could be better."

He releases the furry's toes and then turns it over. It grabs for his arm with both hands. Obaid is indifferent, keeping the furry at arm's length. "Did you fix Snoob, BitStack?"

There's no danger of invoking a stop here. I could withhold the truth from Obaid if I like. He's not my master, and the transference of Snoob was Raahil's request. A master's secret.

Still, I find my conscience in play. I don't want to deceive Obaid if I don't have to. I have some flexibility, however. "I fixed him, yes."

"You did?" Obaid lowers his arms, Snoob included, then stares at it. "Did you remove the spot? Make him walk funny?" He frowns at me. "Make his hair prickly and smell new? Or are you lying to me, Bit?"

There it is. A direct question. I note Obaid's clothing again. The blue of his shirt and pants is identical to the color of my jumpsuit. "I'm not lying. Snoob is fixed."

He lifts the furry again. "But is *this* Snoob? My Snoob?"

The furry is looking at me now, eyes dark and seemingly real. It holds up a front paw imploringly.

I frown. "That is a complicated question."

"Complicated?" Obaid turns Snoob so he can look it in the eyes. He squints at it and shakes his head. "It isn't him, is it? You just transferred Snoob's brain somehow."

I sigh and shake my head. I can't get over the timing. For the boy to show up now, when only a day ago, I—

"So, my mother isn't broken." Obaid glances up the hallway behind him, then looks at me again. "She's just lying to me."

"She was trying to please you. And in many ways..." I point at the furry. "That is Snoob...in a different body."

"I knew it!" Obaid places new Snoob on the floor. "Where is the old one, Bit?" His voice quavers as he says the toy's name. "Is he gone?"

I study him, unsure of how to proceed. My mind sways this way and that. I weigh different outcomes, different responses. Even my implant weighs in. Warning against ideas that bother it. Radical notions, stirred by this task. My hobby.

"You have him, don't you?"

I glance at the interior of my room. At the window, and the wooden chest beneath it. "I wouldn't if not for a fortunate happenstance."

"You use big words, BitStack."

I smile and bow my head. "I'm sorry, young master. It is a habit."

"So, do you have him?"

"I do."

"And does he work?"

"He does."

Obaid jumps three times. "Give him to me, Bit! Give him to me."

I stand, walk to the chest, and open it. Snoob, the real Snoob, is inside. I feel a sense of completeness seeing it. A sense of unusual purpose. I reach in and lift it out. Give its head a quick stroke. Smile.

I return to the floor opening. Obaid is right where I left him. "This presents a difficulty." I show him the toy. "Having two Snoobs."

Obaid looks at the Snoob on the floor, and then at me. "Because of Mom?"

"Yes. And because of me. I cannot lie to her." I smile. "And you are not supposed to have this."

He nods, then picks up the new Snoob. "I can give this one away."

"To who?"

He thinks for a moment. "There is a used mechanical store nearby."

"Where he would be sold like a slave?"

He raises a finger. "There's an orphanage close to the park. I meet the children there sometimes."

I smile. "I think that's a fine solution. Your furry will be cared for there."

I bend through the opening and hand Obaid the old Snoob. "You know how to turn him on?"

"Yes, of course." He smiles, and bows. "Thank you."

I nod. Study him for a bit. Obaid becomes engrossed with his returned toy. Petting it. Talking to it.

"I need to tell you something about Snoob," I say. "I should not have been able to fix him."

Obaid looks at me. "But you can fix anything, Bit."

I shake my head. "No. There are some things not meant to be fixed. Snoob is one of them. In fact, I almost gave up three times. I even took him back to the waste disposal where I found him."

My head starts to tingle. A warning. Inexplicable, because nothing I've found is outside scripture. None of it should be forbidden. I pause. Let the stop recede.

"He was in the trash?"

I nod. "Yes, that's where I found him."

"Then what happened, Bit?"

I take a deep breath and let it back out. "I started thinking about your lessons, Obaid. Specifically, the one about the prophets and miracles. And when I was most stuck. When I could not find an answer—"

Another stop. Harder this time.

I take another breath. Look at Obaid, who is now eyes-wide and watching. Listening. Snoob all but forgotten.

"I found myself talking to the miracle prophet." I shake my head. "And somehow, I feel he answered." I smile and point at Snoob. "In this little thing. He answered."

"You prayed to Isa?"

Now the stop level increases. I should go no further. I can go no further.

"Bit?"

I smile. Shake my head. "I now believe miracles happen, young master. That they are very, very real."

I'M AWAKENED BY A REPETITIVE clanging noise. I open my eyes to see Bull, plastisteel binding tool in hand, rapping on the bot's chest. He stops when he sees I'm awake, and leans forward to where his chin almost touches the bot.

"Didn't you set a timer?" He nods at the door. "We're down to the last ten minutes." He steps back and waves the tool over the bot's midsection. "Need you to double-check everything. Make sure there are no surprises."

I nod the bot's head and stand it up straight. I take the right arm through all its positions, then the left. I shuffle the bot left and right, and then bounce it on its toes. It feels fluid and perfect. As if I'm propelling my own body through the motions.

Bull nods. "Try something harder. Some punching moves or something."

I try a string of jabs, followed by an uppercut. Then more jabs and a roundhouse, then a left hook. It all feels right. Not a squeak of resistance.

He nods again. "Power levels okay? System errors? Warnings? Anything?"

I close my eyes and focus on the bot's internals. The voice of the subroutines, the speech of the nanopaths and motivators. The error lists are clean. The efficiency ratings are high. The strain on the resources remain low as I try various movements and punches. Power levels are a hundred percent for all appendages. "Everything looks great," I message Bull.

He nods and gives me a thumbs-up.

Twenty seconds later, there's a knock on the door.

Bull thumps the bot on the chest. "Guess they're ready for us."
He backs away. Smiles. "At least, they think they are." He raises
both eyebrows. "Any last minute requests?"

I shake the bot's head. I notice a circular bin with rolled prayer
mats in the corner of the room to my right. I haven't observed the
ritual all day today. Nor yesterday either.

The realization makes me uneasy. Especially given BitStack's
mix. His borderline heresy. I shouldn't have viewed it. I don't need
that confusion in my mind right now.

By praying to Isa, Bit erred. Only A is worthy of prayer. There's
no other.

Yet, here I am, a debugger, in the equivalent of battle armor.

What do I know, really?

Bull opens the door, and we walk out. Surrounded by the
Imam's servants and servbots, we're herded toward the arena entrance. Spectators cheer and reach for us with their hands, though
some are rendered speechless by what they see. The man with a
machine inside, inside a machine.

Slowly we make our way into the amphitheater, and then toward the center ring. The interior of the theater is darker this time,
but I'm still exposed. Still made to feel uncomfortable. A spotlight
follows me, occasionally shining through the bot's transparency to
light my face and body. Like I'm a fish inside a bowl, except I can't
turn and swim away.

Doubtless that was part of the designers' intent. To humanize
the situation. To make the audience feel for the combatant within
the monster. Imagine themselves in the same place.

Unfortunately, I'm not like them. I'm human, but not just human. I'm always going to look different. To behave and think dif-
ferently. I don't represent them because I can't. I might as well be a
jinn. Or an alien.

The center ring is brightly lit now. There's a black-clad judge
standing in the center, but no one else. No combatant. No bot.
No one. I assume someone will soon march in, doubtless encased
within a machine as I am.

Who am I fighting?

We arrive at our corner. The theater feels fuller than before. As if the whole of the Imam's complex is here now. I'm surprised the event isn't stream-cast. Only fear of the Imam could keep such a secret.

Part of me wishes my students could witness this. It would make an excellent lesson in reality, the extreme situations debugging life can place us in.

My life has been one strange situation after another.

Bull taps the bot's chest. "Hate to say this, but given your outfit, it feels rails natural." He squints in at me. "Are you ready?"

"I think so," I message. I bounce the bot on its toes, nervously. "But what am I up against?"

"Doesn't matter," Bull says. "You can beat it. You beat those army freeheads to get here. You can beat anyone."

The pitch of the crowd changes, becoming almost frantic. The spotlight shifts to the opposite side of the arena, and the center entrance there. It is difficult to see what is entering.

Then I catch the glint of metal. Another bot, but is it occupied like mine?

The crowd's enthusiasm dissipates until the room is almost silent. Just as when they saw my bot, except even more so. More abrupt and distinct.

I'm more nervous than ever. What am I fighting? What is it?

Four of the arena vids flash to life. Finally, the arena cameras focus on the entering combatant. The images are both familiar, and frightening.

"Rembrandt and Renfa," Bull says. "It's a sentinel."

Soon I can see the sentinel's gold clad form. Its mantis-like head and wide shoulders. Its broad chest and powerful limbs.

The sentinel reaches the far corner, extends a single hand to the ropes, and in one move, leaps inside.

"I feel ill," I message.

Bull pat's the side of my bot. "No, you're fine. It's just a dumb bot."

"We haven't had dumb bots since before Tanzer's time." I send him a picture of Tanzer and the smell of fear: a violet bubble with hot pepper.

He presses against my bot's chest, looking at me through the transparent material. "No. You're doing this for all of us now. Every debugger out there. Even SilentJoy." Bull pulls away and points at the opposing side. "He's just too dumb to know it."

I shake the bot's head. There are too many variables here to properly quantify. But, if Jahm's promise holds true, it is my only way to free Damali. To win at anything.

To be significant?

Not sure. There has to be more than meaning defined by actions. That significance is short-lived, and often comes with unexpected consequences.

The spotlight finds me.

"Go, Thread," Bull urges. "You can do this."

I approach the ring. I find myself hoping that my bot will start to fail. That the joints will lock, or the power levels fall. Anything to get me out of this.

The bot offers no resistance, though. It obeys my every thought. Reacts perfectly.

I bring the bot to the corner stairs and gingerly climb over the ropes. No way am I jumping.

The referee waves me to the center. The sentinel is already standing there. Waiting. Its eyes track me the entire way. Its hands have been fitted with padded knuckles, just like those of my own bot. A softer blow. A longer show.

I get an unexpected notice from a background process, but I push it away. I can't lose focus here. Nothing else matters.

The referee goes through his monologue. The rules between two armored combatants. A warning to keep all combat within the ring. The penalties for disobedience.

Seems unnecessary for an implant and a bot. We both have limits. Things we cannot do or say.

The ref waves us back to our corners. There will be a bell to start this time. No chance of confusion. All eyes are here. I glance up to Imam's chamber. He is seated close enough to the glass that I can see him. Servbots and wives stand around him.

The bell rings. I raise the bot's arms. And move forward.

THE CROWD NOISE RETURNS. A roar of expectation and excitement. They're about to see something unusual. Something that has never been tried before. I'm not sure who they are cheering for. No matter who wins the fight, the Imam has already won the day. His house, his event, and both combatants are his.

Except I'm not, really. I may be bound to his house, but my heart is somewhere else. In fact, it is two places. In a cage with a slave, and in a school of gifted young men. Men that will be owned by someone in this room someday.

I slow up just short of the ring's center and raise my bot's hands to its chin. I bring it up on its toes. Bounce a little.

"Stay with our strategy," Bull messages. "At least until you can read its intentions."

I send him a nod and practice a couple jabs.

The sentinel has its hands up, though they are almost even with each other, arms forming a triangle above its chest. Its eyes, glowing red above the cheek plating, track my every move. Calculating and predicting.

Unlike me, it has the benefit of preprogrammed instructions. Instant decisions based on a matrix full of moves. Centuries of combat experience.

We begin to circle.

I wish I could stream to it. Connect in a way that would let me scan its matrix. See how the weights are being moved around.

What factors it is paying attention to. What techniques it is aware of. My guess is: all of them.

Regardless, it is a black box to me. Any attempt I make to reach it bounces back at me as a giant ball of static.

Not very polite on its part.

So far, its behavior is like my last opponent's, the counter-puncher. Awaiting my moves to know how to respond.

Of course, so am I, at this point. Aside from a few warm-up jabs, I haven't punched at all. I'm unsure where to begin.

The crowd starts to hiss. Impatient as always.

I let us travel another full revolution around the center, then step into the space between us. I lead with a left jab, and then another.

The sentinel blocks both moves before returning its hands to its triangle position. No punch landed.

I left jab again, then try something stronger—a right hook.

The sentinel blocks the jab, and steps cleanly away from the hook. And it does both fast. Very fast.

My bot is strong and fast too, though. I haven't begun to tap it. To push it.

I step into the gap again and blister the sentinel with a string of jabs. Left, right, left, right, and left.

All are blocked.

The sentinel's face is only plating and eyes. There's a raised angle that is its "nose", and beneath that, a singular vertical slit, doubtless to allow sound to escape. But otherwise it is all plating and angles. The head is subtly triangular, making its chin a smaller target. Another disadvantage for me.

The bot lifts its hands and shuffles toward me. I keep my hands up and decide to hold my ground. To not let it move me.

It jabs right, I block, then it swings left. I dodge right. It doesn't touch me. Everything is clean so far.

I answer with a string of punches. One gets through, but it is a glancing shot. Barely nicks the bot's right cheek.

The sentinel attacks again. This time, with a blizzard of punches: left jab, right jab, uppercut, roundhouse—so many I can barely fol-low. Portions of my bot start to flash. I also get damage reports.

Mostly, I'm distracted by how the shots *feel*. They don't just damage my pride, I'm *feeling* them through the tap. A sting on my cheek, another on my left shoulder.

I almost release the tap entirely. Release myself from the discomfort.

But that would be disastrous. I can't do that.

I swing my bot's arms in a clearing motion, then hop it back and away.

"Rails!" I message Bull. "A big heap of rails."

The sentinel stays where it is. Lowers its arms. It may be built without expression, but I swear it is smiling at me now. Taunting me.

"What is it?" Bull messages. "What is happening?"

"The tap hurts me. Stimulates the pain centers or something."

I'm trying not to panic. Only I know the danger I'm in. The threat of the wolf that encircles my mind. If it attacks, I won't be able to hold the tap. I won't be able to do anything.

I get a simulated shriek of anger from Bull, followed by an image of a cartoon man hopping up and down. "Knew it wouldn't be fair," he messages. "Knew it was clocked against us."

I raise my bot's arms and start to bounce. Begin to circle.

The sentinel isn't mimicking me this time. Instead, it remains in one place and pivots so that its eyes can follow me as I move. It relaxes its arms. Loosens its stance.

"And look at that!" Bull messages. "The thing is rails cocky too. Wish I could hit it with this chair."

I continue to circle. It continues to pivot. The crowd hisses and boos.

"Smash it," Bull urges. "Get it with everything."

Easy for him to stream. He won't feel the response.

I lunge toward the sentinel, fake a left jab, then throw a right hook.

The sentinel ignores the jab attempt, blocks the hook with its left, and hits me square in the chin. My bot's head snaps back, and the chin lights up.

The corresponding strike of pain almost stops me. I instinctively yank the bot's hands toward its face, but my chin feels like it is on fire. I disengage my right hand from the stirrup and clasp my chin. Try to massage the pain away.

I swear I can feel a bruise there too. A psychosomatic consequence?

This is not good.

"More attacks," Bull messages. "Go full slugger on it."

I check my bot's power levels. The appendages still look good. I move in and throw two quick jabs, followed by a hard right. The sentinel blocks, but I follow with a left hook, then a right to the body. The last one gets through, but barely. Just enough to make the sentinel's abdominal plating flash.

The sentinel charges me, striking my bot's sternum, and then its left cheek. I feel both the hits, cover, and step back. The sentinel advances again, throwing a high-powered shot at my torso—that I block—but the other hand finds my right ear.

My head explodes with pain, both inside and out. It is like my skull is the wolf's den, and it is raining fire on the roof. I manage to pull the bot back, but I lose my hold on the tap. It slips away. The bot's arms drop too.

The sentinel pounds my left cheek. I squeeze my eyes tight together and try to maintain focus. I don't have the tap anymore. It is floating somewhere in the stream.

I'm helpless.

Another punch connects, then another. My right arm. My left shoulder. Pain. Pain. Then my right shoulder, my stomach, my chin. I'm losing...everything.

The bell rings.

"Get over here!" Bull messages. "Thread, can you hear me? Get here now!"

THE SENTINEL BACKS AWAY slowly, visual receptors fixed on me. It lowers its arms as it walks, but never turns around. Red eyes bore into me like tiny lasers. I even feel heat on my forehead.

There's pain everywhere above my waist, and my mind is in turmoil. Ideas and images fly around like a house devoured by a cyclone. There's nothing tangible. Nothing I can hold onto.

I grit my teeth and try to focus on one thing. On reestablishing my tap connection. But I can't feel it anywhere. There is just the storm.

Then I hear a voice calling. An EI message from the stream. It is hard to hear over the wind. The wind and the wolf's baleful howl.

I turn my attention to the voice. On finding that. Characters start to form with the voice. A written message, twisting and floating in the wind. If I follow the voice, I might be able to clench it. It stands out. White in a cloud of grey and brown.

It's in front of me. Right there. I reach for it; it slips away, but I lunge and catch it. Pull it to my chest.

"Thread? This is BullHammer. I can't move that thing for you, and we don't have much time."

The voice hits me all at once. There's a scent with it. Strong and pungent. Ammonia? A crack of brightness.

My senses jump to clarity. I shake my head, then return my hands to the straps.

I find the bot's tap hovering front and center in my mind. Right where it should be. I grab it and pull myself into the bot's domain. Feel the readiness of its appendages. The shell around me.

I turn us toward the corner and see Bull standing there waving. I trudge that way.

I feel weak. Sore and depleted. In need of a nap.

I reach the corner, and Bull springs into action. He climbs up next to me and places his bag on the floor.

I kneel the bot to where he can check it.

He positions himself against the chest and peers in at me. "How's your power levels?"

I message him the full readings. Everything is drained, but not to critical yet. There are warnings, but no errors. No flags.

Bull nods. "Left leg is a little out of line. Can you lift the arms for me?"

I comply. They lift with no resistance.

Bull frowns, and glances at the right arm. "I hear a bit of squeak in the elbow there."

"There's no squeak," I message. "It moves fine."

He holds up a rolled sheet. "Going to look anyway. Make sure." He moves to my right, out of view. I can hear, maybe even feel, him apply the sheet to the arm. Then he grunts, returns to the front, and starts pawing through his debugger bag.

"Bull..." I message him.

He keeps pawing at the bag.

"Bull, the problem isn't with the bot."

He glances my way.

It's difficult to know for sure. The surface of the bot's chin is a little scuffed. Not clear. But I think Bull's eyes are red. Might be the strain of being the "cutman" in such a bizarre situation. Having so much riding on him. But it might be something else. Concern and desperation.

I send his name again.

"I know, Thread," he says. "I have to work, okay? If I don't work, I might do something crazy." He sucks in a breath, then blows it back out again. Looks at me. "I might get my own head busted."

I send him a shrug and orange flowers. "The sentinel is meant to win. It is like trying to beat a bot in any game. Impossible unless it lets you." I shake my head. "Even if I was all right. Even if everything was together, I probably couldn't win. It's too fast and has all the answers."

He nods and pulls out a small can of lubricant. "The elbow is a little tight. Nanos would solve it eventually, but I'm going to give them some help." He walks out of view again.

I look at the opposing corner. The sentinel is kneeling, too, and there are debuggers attending it. That strikes me as odd, since the sentinel is a closed architecture. Factory service only. Just like the panthers that chased me and BandStand. Just like Snoob. I mention this to BullHammer.

Bull snorts. "Look again."

I shift to see around the scuff in the bot's head. When that doesn't help, I close my eyes and use the bot's visual receptors. I expect to see SilentJoy or one of Imam's other highlevels on the sentinel. Instead, I see something extraordinary.

"Servbots," I message. "Those are ordinary servbots."

"Not ordinary." Bull walks to the front again. "No serv could do what we do. Not ever."

"Maybe they aren't ordinary then. Enhanced somehow?"

Bull glances back. Shakes his head. "Maybe. But we don't have time to take a sheet to them." He frowns. "Proves one thing, though. Proves it is us versus them. That you're fighting for us." He points right. "Try the arm again."

I lift both arms without effort. "So, maybe they *are* replacing us, like TallSpot said. Can you message Bamboo when this is over? Tell him my theory is right. He'll know what you mean."

Bull scowls. "I'm not sending any messages to anyone. Tell him yourself after this is over. After you win."

I ignore the comment. Compose another message instead. "I have fragments of things I should stream you. New insights. Things I've learned that point to something, I'm just not sure what. I'll bundle it all up. Most of it is outside master privilege. Out in the air somewhere. Available if you look."

Bull slaps the front of the bot's head. "Rails, knock it off."

"Knock what off?"

"Acting like you're dying. Because you're not."

I shake the bot's head. Shake my own. "I'm most worried about

Damali. I don't know that you can do anything for her, but if you can, I'm sending you her image—"

He grabs the bot's head with both hands. Presses his nose against the face. "El Greco, Thread! No more!"

I send him a static bubble. Large and prickly. He swats it back at me, colored red.

"I have to," I message. "I need to get all this out, just in case." I pause. "Don't know what to tell you about the facility. About the kids there, but they need more than Bamboo. They need someone like us. Debuggers that have been out awhile."

"Babysitting now? You want me to send messages, and babysit too?"

"No. Not like that. Advise. Teach. Correct. Debug them if you have to."

"This is flipping—"

The bell rings. Bull steps back, and I bring the bot to its feet.

Bull's face is red, though. He's angry. "Your head is in the wrong place, Thread," he says. "All you should be thinking about is smashing that thing. Focus on that." He taps his head. "I'll be right here if you need me."

I nod the bot's head. Pound its hands together.

Bull climbs through the ropes. "Do you have a strategy? You should've been working on that instead of talking."

I move toward the center. "Try not to get hit? Die honorably?"

"Rails. Play the counter this time. React to him. Be cautious."

I don't respond. I know how this will go. I know how everything I try will go. I'm not fighting the sentinel, but A's will. My life has been more like JustBecause's than BitStack's. Dodging the random while trying to accomplish something. Trying for significance.

But in the end, only A's will matters. It's the only thing that stands.

The sentinel approaches. The ring lights reflect off its gold plating, sending tiny rainbows into the sky. It is a thing of brilliance. Cold, intelligent magnificence. An avenging angel.

I go to meet it.

THE SENTINEL MARCHES TO the center of the ring and waits. It doesn't assume a typical boxing stance, nor does it raise its hands. It simply waits.

I know that its disposition—its lack of action—means its synthetic brain has determined that such normal preparations are unnecessary. It has calculated all the appropriate speeds and reaction times, weighed all the potential outcomes, and it is now doing precisely what needs to be done to achieve the desired results.

I hate it for that. No matter what, no matter how close to a mechanical they make me, I'll never be that certain. Never be that confident.

I stop short of arm's reach and bounce on the toes, shuffle right, and then bounce some more. I throw a couple harmless jabs for show.

The sentinel turns to face me, but otherwise does nothing.

What now? Swarming doesn't work. Slugging doesn't work. Out-boxing was a failure.

The crowd shows its displeasure, grumbling and booing. I glance at the Imam's chamber. He's seated next to the glass. There's a servbot behind him, holding a serving tray. One of the Imam's wives is seated next to him. She's dressed in a sapphire blue gown.

I lean forward and feed the sentinel a left jab, followed by a right. It brushes aside the first move. Blocks the second with its palm.

I try the same moves again. The sentinel has a similar response, only this time it manages to snatch my bot's right hand and hold it. I yank the hand back, but the sentinel—even with the glove-like coating on its hand—manages to hold tight. I tug harder, slightly rotating my bot at the same time.

The sentinel pounds my jaw with its right.

Pain arcs through my face. I yell, anticipating the wolf at its worst. But it doesn't come. Not yet. I hurt, but I can focus.

Noop move on my part. Should've kept the left hand up and blocking. I rectify that mistake and bring the bot's hips and shoulder to bear on the captured hand.

It tears free. The sentinel swings again, but I step back. Find some space.

My face is numb. I curse the tap and the pain it brings. I almost curse Jahm and the Imam, but that will bring pain too.

What things haven't I tried? What moves?

I hit the stream looking for answers. Anything that can help. Anything out of the ordinary.

Feinting! I haven't done much of that!

The crowd is roaring its displeasure now. I approach the sentinel and work a couple jabs that are easily deflected or blocked. I then drop my bot's left knee and move its left hand forward in a body feint. From there, I raise the right arm as if I'm going straight at the sentinel. But at the last instant, I attack with the left.

I smash its right cheek. Flash! Then I follow with a body shot and manage to light its abdominal plating too. Flash! Flash!

Two for me. Two for us.

I spot Jahm in one of the ringside seats. Seated on his left is his young female companion. On the right—

The sentinel springs toward me. It shows a left hook, but when I move to block, it shifts, turns, and delivers a right cross. The punch skips off my block and lights up my left ear.

It hurts, but I'll be okay. I need to keep it guessing. And stay clear of its arms.

Damali! Damali is sitting next to Jahm! Only a few meters from me.

What is he doing? Taunting me? Taunting us both?

Yes, that's it. He's making sure she has a clear view of my punishment.

I glance that way again. There's a look of concern on her face. Jahm looks content. Happy even. He flutters his right hand as if he's waving, then covers his mouth and coughs.

The sentinel comes at me with a haymaker. I sidestep, but it follows with another right cross. This one strikes home. My face is lit ablaze from chin to the base of the ears.

"Stay away from that!" Bull message screams. "Pay attention!"

The sentinel hits me again, this time in the gut. The shot is hard enough that I bang my head on my bot's interior. Pain pulls me over. Wants to put me down and out.

Another strike, to the chest this time. Then to the right side of my face. I fight to get my bot's hands up. To remove us from the line of fire.

The wolf enters the scene. Everything becomes white inside. Burning like the surface of a star. The tap seems to dim. To slip from my grasp. I quick stream the bot an order to step back. To keep its hands up and over our face. Cover me from any shock.

I gain a second of peace. Maybe two. During that time, I try to clear my head. I take a deep breath and let it back out. I look at the bot's interior. Try to trace every curve. Every angle.

But the pain wins. It consumes everything.

The sentinel throws a string of jabs, then a straight at the bot's nose. It gets through. Somehow. The whole bot shakes. My nose hurts, but it seems like a ripple in a tidal wave. Barely registers.

I think of Damali. Her freedom. This was my only chance.

I panic, and through a squinting mind, lash out at the sentinel. I pull from my list of moves. Feed them to the bot as fast as I can. Jab, roundhouse, hook, jab, uppercut—one after the other. I manage to get a few shots through. Manage to back the sentinel away.

But the expression on its face doesn't change. It never will. There are occasional flashes of light. Some contact. But in the end, the sentinel is only waiting me out. Calculating. Deciding.

Before I run out of moves, the sentinel starts to block everything. Then he comes back at me with a vengeance. Throws punch after punch.

And. Every. Hit. Hurts.

I slip my arms free of the straps and press my hands to my face.

Over my eyes. I push moves into the tap. Tell the bot to cover and retreat, but my connection feels so tenuous now. The bot seems to be staggering. Its arms are fumbling, slowly dropping.

The wolf's pain increases until that is all there is. Everything else disappears into the fog. I'm not aware of the stream or the bot. Not even aware of my own appendages. I try to think about Damali, and how I've failed her.

And the new implants. How they're on their way to obsolescence. And my loss here will solidify that idea.

Jahm and the Imam and the ulama. All looking on.

I feel the bot rocking back, losing its balance. Falling.

Only a shell to me now. And a weak one at that. Rigid and breakable. Failing. Power levels are down. Depleted.

Or maybe that's me. Only me.

It feels like I'm inside a bubble of pain. There's a distant knocking sound. I think that's the sound of the sentinel's punches. But otherwise, it's only the wind, and the wolf's howl.

I AM AFRAID. I AM ALONE. I AM A FAILURE.

Nothing I've done matters. Nothing is significant. Nothing is important.

A does what he wants. If it happens, it is because he wants it to happen. Good or bad.

These thoughts plague me. Swirl inside my mind. Pulled along by the wind. The wolf's howl.

I have nothing. I can do nothing.

I need something to hold on to. Objects—ideas—crash around me. Thrown by an unhappy master with large eyes. Apples and lamps. World maps and coordinates!

Formulas. Seemingly meaningless. Shared and honored. Written on walls.

Damali! Must save Damali. She's right there!

Need a miracle.

There aren't any. Raahil said so. In the mix by BitStack. Snoob was dead!

No. The miracle prophet. Word that creates. Paradox. Created word. Isa.

Can he help? Stop. I feel a stop approaching. It smashes into me, then is taken by the wind.

Stream to him. I must stream to him. Ask him to help. Bundle my everything. Send it Full Impact. All emotions.

Help. Need help. Please help.

The bot is failing. The sentinel is pounding. Bam. Bam. Roundhouse, hook, uppercut!

I am ThreadBare. DR 23.

Something itches at me. Tunnels into my brain. It flutters against the wind. Does it have wings? Yes. It is a bird and it can fly. Fighting, floating, fighting again.

Come to me, bird. Come right here.

Wait! The wolf. Where is he?

I shield my eyes with my hands. Search. Look all around. Up and down. All I can see is the storm, and the bird.

I put out a hand and the bird lands on it. It shakes its feathers, then they fall smooth on its back. Unruffled. The bird glances at me, and then looks away. Shy like a bird. Just like a bird.

I touch it. Stroke its back.

It's a process, I realize. One of my own. Something I started long ago. Milliseconds, seconds, minutes, hours. It has been running in my head the whole time. Pecking and searching. Pecking some more. Glancing this way and that. Slowly breaking through a shell. Making a hole.

Comprehension hits.

Full understanding.

The background process I created to break the panthers. It has something now. It has a big something.

Sliced the sentinel's shield?

I tentatively reach for the attacking machine in the stream. I sense it. I can't control it, but I can sense its decision matrix. Understand how it thinks. How it reacts. See its strategy.

It is plotting now where best to strike me if I recover.

There is counting. Someone is counting.

The wind begins to fade. The wolf's howl ceases.

I can still hear a roar. Background noises. Hisses and shouts.

"ThreadBare! Can you hear me?"

BullHammer. That's my friend.

I find my hands on my face. Covering my face. I remove them and stretch them out. Slip them into small tunnels that seem made for them. Armrests with straps at the end I can grip.

Where am I?

I look down at my body. At my arms. The tight space I'm in.

Oh right. The bot. I'm inside a bot. And I'm getting beat up.

I feel a surge of adrenaline. I peer out through the transparent chin. I see the referee standing over me with his hand raised. Beyond him is the theater's ceiling.

My bot is on the mat! Rails.

The tap. I need its tap.

I find the bot's stream connection. The bot's audio feed hits me as soon as I grip it. The crowd hisses and yells. The referee screams, "Eight!"

Double rails. I check the power levels. Sixty percent on each leg. Fifty-two on the right arm. Seventy on the left.

It will have to do.

I put the bot's palms on the floor and push.

Nothing happens.

I panic and scan the power levels again. Check all the connections. The error lists.

Then I realize I've deactivated the arms somehow. Maybe to keep them from blowing around in the storm? Not sure. I switch them on and push again.

The bot lurches to its feet. I shrug its shoulders and shake its arms. Push any lingering problems far away. I need everything it has now.

The referee's eyes widen and he backs away. "You're well?" he asks. "You are ready to fight?"

I raise the bot's arms, close the hands into fists, and turn toward the sentinel. It watches me from its corner.

"I say it again. Are you ready?"

I nod.

The sentinel stares at me. Still expressionless, still formidable and oppressive. Encased in armor.

But its mind is wide open.

The crowd is quiet. Rendered speechless. Muted and expectant.

I fold fully into the bot's systems, its body and senses. I bounce, rock the head from side to side, throw a dozen test jabs. How much time is left in the round?

Twelve seconds.

That should be enough.

The referee raises his hand. The sentinel drifts toward the center.

"Fight!" the referee says.

I surge forward. The sentinel's decision matrix starts to percolate—predicting and calculating. I throw a left jab. The sentinel decides to sidestep. I throw a hard right, aimed at its destination.

I find the center of its face. Bright flash!

The crowd roars.

The decision matrix responds. Hundreds of potential moves appear. It chooses four of them.

A jab.

I jerk my bot's head back.

A right cross to where my bot's head should return.

I block.

An uppercut.

It crashes harmlessly on my bot's forearm.

A left hook. I turn it aside with my right, and pull inside the sentinel's guard, close to its chest, and send a left to its chin.

Another hit. Another flash of glory. More cheers.

"Thread?" Bull messages. "Is that still you in there?"

I smile and send him a reassuring note. I then start pulling from my strike list. Punching and blocking. Infiltrating the sentinel's space and keeping its head busy. One hit after another, correcting when the golden warrior's mind suggests I should. Some of my punches are blocked, but most get through.

Better yet, I'm able to stop everything the sentinel sends me. Stop, dodge, or dissipate. I'm a mind reader. A boxer who doesn't simply anticipate, but knows.

The sentinel retreats, but I follow. It strikes as its matrix dictates. Countering when it can. Blocking and dodging.

Could I control it outright? Force it to drop its arms or even lie down? Yes. With a little tuning and a little practice. But that would be too obvious. I want to beat it in a real sense, even if it isn't real. Even if my bird-in-the-wind is giving me an edge.

"What happened?" Bull messages. "I thought you were dead. Referee almost counted you out."

"Too much to explain right now. After. We'll talk after."

He sends me a warm sun, and a citrus scent. "No problem. I can wait."

My pride wants me to think that I earned this. That the bird came because of my preparation. That prior experiences brought me to it, and I monopolized.

But I can't submit to that notion. I'm afraid to.

The bird is a miracle. I have no claim over it. So far, I only know of one person who does.

The sentinel's arms widen. Its ability to block is diminishing.

I split its arms with a straight shot and clip its narrow chin. Its head rocks back. Face lights up. Then I repeat the process. Same result.

Its arms drop completely. I keep pounding its face, then its torso. It's like hitting a toy now. There's little resistance. The sentinel's matrix is occupied with system repair. With keeping it on its feet and active.

I have two seconds to go. I don't want another round.

I check my power levels again. Legs are strong. Arms are about where they were, with right being higher. Stronger.

That's what I'll use. I take the arms through a string of jabs and quick punches, then launch a heavy left to the sentinel's abdomen. That brings its head forward. Makes it vulnerable and easy to find.

I pull the right back, let it build as much momentum as it can, then strike.

It finds the sentinel's right cheek. There is a brief contact flash, then something unexpected happens. The sentinel's head disconnects, and spinning, leaves the ring.

The bell chimes. The pole lights flash.

"Rails," Bull messages. "Just like we practiced. No wait...that was the opposite of this, wasn't it?" He sends a string of fireworks. "I like this ending better."

The referee puts his hands over his head. "Raise the arms! You won. Raise the arms!"

I comply. There are cheers and applause, but most of the crowd rumbles and hisses. Unsure how to respond.

I march the bot toward our corner. On the way, I glance Jahm's direction. His reaction mirrors the crowd. Uncertain and surprised.

Damali is smiling, though. A wonderful, heart-filling sight.

BullHammer meets me at the corner. He's smiling too, but his eyes seem watery again. He waits for me to lower the bot, then slaps its head. Draws himself in until his forehead presses against the head's exterior. "Rembrandt, I can't believe that," he says. "Can't believe what I saw." He pulls away and looks in the direction the sentinel's head flew. "Rails ridiculous how it flew."

"It was a miracle," I yell. "A simple miracle."

"What's that?" he says. "Hard to hear through—"

The room lights brighten. The vidscreens strobe a couple times and there's a crackle of static over the speakers. The next image is of the Imam. He's seated in his chamber. His youngest wife is kneeling on the floor near his feat. Face hidden behind a turquoise veil. On either side of the Imam are servbots—one dressed as a female, the other as a male. Both in green.

I wonder if the bots are modified? Enhanced like those that worked on the sentinel?

A trickle of sweat runs down my neck. It is shockingly cold.

The Imam smiles. "I am pleased with tonight's competition." He raises a hand. "Congratulations to all our competitors...and to the victors, of course."

He chuckles and, from every screen, seems to look my way. "I had no idea that my property could perform so acceptably. But again, I am pleased and surprised." He raises an eyebrow. "I will have to replace a perfectly good sentinel." He glances at the bots next to him. "But I suppose there are always costs to progress."

His wife looks up at him, which brings another smile. "I gained some human help too." He raises both hands, palms up. "Who am I to question A's ways?" He bows his head. "I can only be grateful for his blessings. May they continue as he wills."

"Tomorrow, the general council will meet. We have much to discuss."

The leftmost bot—the female one—suddenly looks down at the floor as if it has just located a large spider. It stares that direction for a few moments, and then—

Explodes.

THE VIDSCREENS GO BLACK, and then white. The crowd is silent for five seconds; then there are wails of horror and disbelief. Next there is a repetitive popping noise that my implant identifies as the sound of an impact rifle. That is followed by the descending tones of government-issued nanopounders.

Few of the freeheads have noticed these details, of course, because they are in full panic. There are ceaseless screams and a high-pitched drone as all run toward the exits.

"Please maintain order," the loudspeakers say. "Please move to the nearest exit. Please remain calm. The sword of the Imam will protect you."

BullHammer and I are still in the ring. He's crouched close to my bot, sheltered behind its right leg. "Picasso and Rembrandt! They got the Imam. Antitex got the Imam."

I can hardly focus on that. Barely conceive what has happened. My only thought is for Damali. Where is she? In all the surging chaos, where is she?

There's another explosion, followed by more gunshots and more shrill screams. The pitch of the crowd changes, becoming more desperate now. The speakers repeat their comforting message.

Some members of the crowd have lost all sense of right and wrong. Their rules vanished without a thought. People are pushed aside and walked over. Men and women alike, but mostly women. Mostly the frail or slight.

It is madness. Humanity unraveled.

I bring the bot to its full height. Scan the room from that position.

"What are you doing?" Bull asks.

"We need to get out of here," I message.

"Streaming obvious, Thread." He stays behind me, still pressed against my bot's legs. "What is your plan?"

I look for Damali's green slave robe among the sea of colors. When that doesn't work, I look for something that should be more obvious: Jahm's hover chair.

I find him partway down an aisle to our left. The path ahead of him is clogged with people. He's attempting to move anyway, trying to use the bulk of his chair as a battering ram—nudging and pushing. But to little effect.

Following in his wake are Damali and his female companion. Damali is so close it appears her hands are secured to the back of the chair somehow. She's being dragged along.

"Stay with me," I message Bull. "Right behind me."

"You're the one wearing plastisteel. Where else would I go?"

I nod the bot's head, then leap it out of the ring. I wait for Bull to join me, and stride toward the crowd. Toward Damali.

As I approach the mass of humanity, I wish the bot had an audio capability. An *amplified* audio capability. Some way to harmlessly move the freeheads from my path. Ten seconds later, I find it isn't necessary. They move themselves. The mere site of a bot is enough to move them. Some scream and run away.

They all saw it, Thread. A bot exploded and killed the Imam. Any mechanical could bring death here.

I reach Jahm and the women. I raise the bot's arm—

There is more gunfire, rifle and nanopounder alike. Everyone cowers except me.

Jahm looks at my bot, face twisted in fear. "ThreadBare!" He indicates the crowd in front of him. "Clear these people! Move them out of my way!"

A slender carbon cable is tied to Jahm's right armrest. The other end is wrapped around Damali's hands. Her wrists already have welts.

Dozens of meters separate us from the exit. The space is packed with people. Panicked and shrieking. Only the hundreds of bots in the room are unfazed. They remain where their owners left them, standing like pillars amid a flood.

I shake my bot's head. If I push ahead, I'll only make things worse.

"You refuse?" Jahm touches a button on his left armrest. A compartment folds down, reveling a hint of gold. "I have a controller." He brings the controller out and points it at me. "Right here." He presses a button.

Nothing happens. I don't feel a shock. I don't feel anything.

I look to my left and up, at the Imam's chamber on the second floor. The transparent protective front is blown outward. Not shattered, but strained to the point of breaking. It is stained black and red.

My master no longer exists.

BullHammer emerges from behind my legs. "The Imam is dead." He nods at Jahm's controller. "That won't get you anything. You lost your authority."

Jahm scowls and tosses the controller away. He looks at Damali. "The slave. I will give her to you if you take me out." He coughs, then fumbles with the cable. A few seconds later, it is free of the chair. Only held by his hands.

Damali moves toward me, puts out a hand tentatively. The welts on her wrists are more visible. As is a bruise on her left cheek. "Are you in there, ThreadBare?"

"Oh, he's in there." Bull motions toward the front of my bot. "Look right here."

She leans forward and squints. "You look strange," she says. "I don't like it."

I can't come out. Not yet. Not until she and Bull are safe.

"What are you waiting for!" Jahm screams. "Move! Do something." He swivels his seat and stretches the cable holding Damali. "I know you cannot hurt me, ThreadBare. So, take me out of here, and she is yours. You may go wherever you wish."

I hear the whoop of a nanopounder behind me, then shrapnel sprays my bot's back and left shoulder. In the stream I detect that one of the freestanding bots has been decimated, then another, and another.

I turn my bot's head to see. There's a small group of soldiers near the ring, nanopounding bots indiscriminately. Destroying all synthetics—anything that might explode. Multiplying the screams and confusion. Increasing the danger in a quest for safety.

They target another servbot and fire. More shrapnel.

I hear a wail of anguish. I look for Damali and Bull and find them right next to me. Nestled safe near my bot's legs.

Jahm's companion is draped over the back of his chair, whimpering. There's blood on his chest. A huge gash on his neck. Somehow a piece of shrapnel—a shattered bot part—struck him. Tore his neck.

I feel shock and revulsion. I turn the bot toward the ring. Stretch out its arms.

Jahm is dead. The Imam is dead.

There are more impact rifle shots. More screams. Are their antitex in the building?

"We need to get out of here!" Damali says.

All the exits are blocked. There are trampled bodies everywhere. Silent bots watch. Soldiers run and shoot. Servbots are their primary victims. Easy targets.

I scan the upper story. To my left, there's an overlook with no screen or glass in front of it. Wide open access. An idea forms. I stream Bull my plan, and then move that direction.

"Stop! Stop!" Two soldiers run around the ring toward me. Raise their guns.

What do I do?

Rows of seating are to my left. Power levels are still adequate. Strong enough, I think. I bend, grab two of the seats, and rip them from their moorings. The first shot comes. It shreds the seat in my bot's left hand. Damages the arm too. It becomes unresponsive.

Rails. I'm angry now.

I toss the other seat at the soldiers. It crashes harmlessly between them, but they scatter, falling into the seating behind them. Dropping their weapons along the way.

No stop. I just threw a chair at a group of soldiers and had no stop. No wolf either. Where's the wolf? Is he gone? Is all the pain gone?

"You still have a plan?" Bull messages.

More nanopounder shots, but these aren't directed at me.

They are to the right, on the far side of the ring. I wrestle free another seat with my right hand, just in case. Hold it like a shield. Focus on the goal.

I lead us around one side of the ring to the next aisle. The one nearest the open section above.

I instinctively crouch as another bot shatters to my right. "Are you both good back there?" I stream Bull.

"Yeah, yeah, we're fine. Your girlfriend is a tough one. Think she'd attack anyone who tries to stop us. Anything happens to your bot, I'm sheltering behind her."

"Do you have stops?"

"Stops?" He sends me a purple bundle of confusion. "Right now? No. But I did a few minutes ago. I wished ill on old Jahm." He sends the image of a shrug. "Feeling a little guilty now, actually."

I nod the bot's head.

Freedom. Am I free?

No time to test that yet. No time to think. Have to move.

I reach a spot just under the upper-story break. I try to work the bot's left arm, but it is still unresponsive. Thankfully, the right still has enough power. I drop the seat it has been carrying. Lift the arm high. It'll be short, but I think it will be enough.

I stretch the bot as far as I can. Lift it on tiptoes.

"Climb it," I stream Bull. "The two of you."

"Climb what?"

"The bot, lowlevel. Go up!"

He doesn't respond, but I soon hear someone on the bot's back. Then I see a hint of green above me, followed by a hand in front of the bot's face. A female hand.

"Can you hear me, Thread?" Damali asks. "Can you feel my touch?"

There's more motion, then I see her face, inverted, through the bot's visual receptors.

"If not," she says. "This is me kissing you on the head."

I wish she would hurry. Wish she would get free. But I do feel something, though not through the bot's tap. I feel it in my gut. A swirling mixture of discomfort and joy. Of dusk and brilliance.

I hear more motion, more scratching and grunting. I turn the bot's head slightly and see her ascending the arm. Watch her climb it, then climb free.

Next it is Bull's turn. I watch him until he reaches the arm—debuggers are notoriously good climbers—then I release the bot's chest hatch and drop free to the floor.

It feels like being reborn. The air is cool, but it smells of death and fear. The crowd still roars in panic. There are shots and screams.

I place a foot on the back of the bot's knee, wedge my right hand into the break between back and waist, and pull myself up. It takes a couple seconds to scramble onto its back, and from there onto its shoulders. Its head is still turned to look up. I even think I see the spot where Damali kissed it.

It served me well, this bot. I will miss it.

I pat its head, and climb onto its arm. Bull leans over from above, his hand stretched out. I reach the bot's forearm and place a foot in its palm.

"Come on, Thread," Bull says. "This place is a zoo."

I smile and grip his hand. We enter the second story, and with a little more effort, find a way out.

THE SCENE OUTSIDE IS ALMOST as chaotic as the one within. There are flashing lights and soldiers everywhere. Wails and cries. Clusters of freeheads looking lost or confused. Some have blood on them. There are repeated messages over the public-address system. Commands to be calm and pay attention to the security forces. That the Imam would protect us all. His sword. His strength.

The pandemonium provides distraction. Few notice the two debuggers with a slave woman. It is an unusual combination that would normally be questioned. But considering the upheaval of the night, a little unusual is now expected. Unusual is everywhere.

After leaving the tower, we make our way to the central park, and then to the small arboretum I saw on my flight in. Only then do we stop to catch our breath. We shelter beneath a large elm tree. Hide in its shadows.

"You been checking the stream?" Bull asks.

I feel Damali's hand searching. She touches my elbow, and then slides her fingers down my arm to take my hand. Again, my stomach swirls, feeling a mixture of pain and joy. But my head does not. There is no stop, and no wolf.

"Thread?" Bull shifts so I can see part of his face.

"I haven't, no. I've had other things on my mind."

He raises an eyebrow. "The Imam's death isn't out there yet. Keeping it locked down."

I nod. "At least until the successor is notified. The other prince."

"Who is worse!" Damali says. "Will be much worse."

"Nothing we can do about that." Bull looks at the area around us. "What do we do in the meantime?"

"We leave," I say.

"Leave?" He snorts. "Where we going to go?"

"Anywhere."

Bull points at lights flashing near the towers. "The gates will be locked down. Everyone will be questioned."

Damali's grip on my hand tightens. "But you're debuggers. No one will question you. You're above reproach."

Bull chuckles. "Doesn't mean we can leave, lady. We have a security force in our brains. Rattling around and shooting things."

I look at Damali. Her face is partially hidden too, but what I can see is beautiful. Wide-eyed and lovely. "There's flexibility with our master gone. At least for a little while." I smile. "I know from experience."

"So what do we do?" Bull says. "Try to walk out?"

I shake my head. "I have a friend that can help. Give me a moment." I start a stream search of the compound. Looking for the location of a mechanical that provides a specific service.

In three seconds, I find what I'm looking for, and it is nearby. I order it to meet us at one of the compound's smaller buildings. It confirms the request.

I stand and, holding Damali's hand, help her up. We maintain the connection after, though. I find it difficult to break. It feels necessary somehow.

Bull gives more than a passing glance to our clasped hands, but says nothing. Instead, he stands and pats at his robe. The same white and gold robe he was so happy to wear is a liability now. And not so white either. "What are we doing now?"

I indicate the smaller buildings to the south, then soundlessly lead us to one with a landing platform.

We enter the building and ascend to the roof. The lighting outside is just bright enough to see each other's faces, along with the skyslider that waits, canopy already open.

"Nice to see you again, ThreadBare," the ship says as we approach. "Where would you like to go?"

I feed it the location of my city—our city, Damali's and mine. The only place that feels like home.

"It would be a pleasure to take you there," it says. "I anticipate an easy flight."

I help Damali into the slider, then climb in myself.

Bull remains outside. "Rails, wait, I can't do this."

"What do you mean?" I send fireworks in the stream. "This is the best way to travel. Better than downriding. You can see the whole earth."

He shakes his head, then taps a finger on it. "I mean, I *can't* do it. No way will my head let me go." He points upwards. "I'll get up and the pain will come. I'll have to jump." He squints. "My parts would be spread all over. Need a map to find me. Global coordinates."

"Parts?" And a map? Where did I hear those before? It takes only a brief implant search to locate: One of JustBecause's data-mixes. It talked about "Hidden Truths", maps, and locations. He wrote pairs of numbers. Coordinates.

"Yeah, my parts." He scowls. "Rails. How can you just leave?"

"I think it has meaning," I say. "Strange."

"Little you say has meaning, Thread. You're a flipping bundle of low parity bits."

I want to comb through JustBecause's memories again. To find anything I might have missed.

"I don't want to stay here either." Bull looks toward the towers. "With SilentJoy and the—"

He lets out a low whistle. "Rodin's thinker, I'm getting a swarm of messages now." He squints, then closes his eyes. Heavy streaming.

I glance at Damali. She's found a seat in the slider. She smiles, but looks nervous. She pats the seat next to her. "We should go. Before they wonder where we went. Get away from here."

I get an FI message from Bamboo then. No matter his faults, his seeming lack of compassion or warmth, he has an amazing sense of timing. A way of making his presence known at pivotal moments.

How does he do it?

BullHammer's eyes are still closed. I look at Damali again. Smile, embarrassingly. "I need to—"

"Shut yourself away from me?" She frowns and looks at Bull. "Not sure I like that."

"We could still talk while I'm at it," I say. "But I might be a little—"

"Distracted?" She shakes her head. "I'd rather try to talk to you inside the fighter bot."

I bow my head. "I'm sorry."

She smiles again. "This is who you are. I'll get used to it somehow." A nod. "Go ahead. I'll still be here when you get back."

I smile. Close my eyes. Grab Bamboo's message.

I find him in his office at the facility. It is daytime there, and the sun filters brilliantly through the oval window. I see the shelving filled with books. And the fireplace. Bamboo is seated to the right of it. In the same wicker chair I once sat in.

"I need you back here, ThreadBare. At the school."

"The Imam—"

He raises a hand. "We both know what has happened. The star field has shifted again. New plans are being laid. Plans that will affect us all."

My mind returns to Damali. I don't know what I thought would happen, but I thought it would be different. Another miracle. A change. Somewhere else. I bow my head. "I am sorry. But I would prefer another assignment."

Bamboo stares at me a long moment, then forces a smile. "I'm not commanding you, ThreadBare. I'm merely asking." He looks toward the window, and the river beyond it. "The new implants have missed you. They want you back as an instructor."

I feel a tug there. I've missed the children too. Wondered about them. But I was never really their instructor. "I'm not sure I'm adequate for that."

Bamboo rolls his eyes. Readjusts his posture. "You were barely adequate for anything a few years ago."

I feel a touch of resentment and anger. Feelings that often ride with my own doubts about myself. But I've made a difference, and beyond that, I belong to something. To someone. Maybe that is *significance*?

He smiles again. "But with patience, training, and time you have proven yourself capable. Even handicapped, quite capable."

"I..." I open my eyes and look at BullHammer. Then at Damali.

"Are you done?" Damali asks.

I shake my head, then close my eyes and enter Bull's office again. "I have complications. BullHammer is with me. And—"

"BullHammer will be taken care of. I have been in communication with—"

"Rails!" Bull says. "They upped my level. All the jobs in my queue are shiny and clean. Top of the heap."

I raise a hand and he falls silent. I return my focus to Bamboo. "If I return, will you provide a separate room and protection for my friends?"

"Friends? As I said, BullHammer will be in no danger."

"That's up to him. But there's someone else."

"Someone else? Another debugger?"

"No. She's a freehead, and she may need a place to stay."

"A freehead female? At my facility?"

"Only for a little while. Only until I find her a safe place."

Bamboo scowls, but finally nods his head. "It can be arranged. For a limited time."

I nod. "Okay. Good. And one more thing."

He looks perturbed. Shifts in his seat. "Yes, what else?"

"I'd like to take the boys on another fieldtrip."

He frowns, then rolls his eyes again. "That can be arranged."

I end the connection, and Bull begins speaking. "I'm fine to stay here."

"Why? It was miserable. You were miserable."

He swats a hand. "Yeah, well, I got a message from SilentJoy. Says my new level reflects my talent. He showed me the priority list. I'm near the top now. Says they need everyone at their best. Did he contact you?"

"The message is in the queue. I won't answer."

"Don't blame you." He points at the towers. "Not after all that."

I don't want BullHammer to stay. I'm afraid for him to stay. "You believe them? Believe you'll be okay?"

Bull shrugs. "SilentJoy is stopped, right? Still gets tweaks for lying. Especially to one of us."

"But antitex—"

"Are everywhere. And they rarely try the same thing twice." Bull looks toward the towers. There's a glint of reflected gold in his eyes. "They got what they wanted here."

"Thread..." Damali says.

I frown, but climb further into the slider. Take a seat next to her. "I wish you were coming, Bull." I send him the taste of caramel-glazed bread, piping hot. It is about as close as I can come to an actual hug, without touching him. "I can't say how much you've helped me. How much it means."

He waves. "Go on, Thread. I did it for me too, remember? I'm selfish like that."

I smile softly. Nod. "Yeah, you are." The seat restraints extend, and I secure them. "Stream you later, BullHammer."

He waves as the canopy begins to close.

Damali's hand finds mine. I return Bull's wave, then turn to look at her.

She smiles and lays her head on my shoulder.

"Damali, I—"

"I'm tired, Thread. I trust you. Just take me home."

I DON'T GET NERVOUS until we get close. Only then do I realize how out of the way this location is. How far from the city and any facade of comfort. Of control. In some ways, it disturbs me more than the time I left the city, or even when I was captured by antitex. There is something raw to this place. Unfettered.

The ocean is to our right. It is mostly obscured by generator walls, but not completely so. Every once and a while a flash of surf breaks over the top, spilling moisture a hundred meters down. There is salt in the air too. No purifier can mask that. Even those inside the downrider.

Talons is riding with me this time. The other four boys—Mint-Bridge, LostNote, JumboJet, and BandStand—are in downriders behind us. They have their digital room opened again, and for much of the trip, it has been filled with chatter.

But now, now it grows quiet aside from a few hissed exclamations and Jumbo's long whistle. That's a new habit that I wish I could push out of him—whistling in closed spaces. But that will come. Everything changes with time.

The string parallels the top of the wall for kilometers, then takes a turn to the left, toward the city, and begins to descend. After a few meters, it drops severely, bringing shouts and another whistle; it travels straight, then drops again. My stomach protests, as does my auditory center.

Finally, the end platform is in sight. It juts out from a broken patch of pavement. That, too, gives me pause.

"It ends on the ground?" Talons says. "Do they ever do that?"

I shake my head. "Not usually, no."

There's a scraping sound as we stop.

I wince. Grit my teeth.

Talons gets up and goes to the window. Presses his face to it. "I think we're actually on the ground." He looks back at me. "Like we're touching it."

I sigh and order the canopy open. We both climb out.

We have a blue downrider this time. Stopping behind us is a green one. And behind that, a red. Five minutes later, everyone is on the ground, scanning the surroundings. The towers and temples are far enough away that, in the morning air, they look misty. Dreamlike.

Nearby, aside from the seawall, are broken and abandoned buildings. It is a place the engineers have chosen not to re-build, for whatever reason. Perhaps they just haven't gotten to it yet. Remnants of past wars and uprisings are everywhere, world over. It will take lifetimes to reclaim them all. New technologies.

My eyes drift to the downrider, and the string above it. The string looks sturdy enough, but it doesn't have the shine of those in the city. The ones on the regular hopper circuit. I trace it up to where it parallels the wall. Where it splits off and then starts to descend.

What purpose does this stop have for the average string travel-er? There's nothing here.

To fix the sea generators, maybe?

But why this turnoff?

BandStand draws closer. Smiles. "Why are we here, Mawla?" he asks.

"Yeah, this place is jinns-ville." Mint is at the edge of the pave-ment. Brown weeds dominate the ground beyond. He looks down, and then hops to a flat section of stone within the grass. "This is the path to their house, I'll bet." He points to the north. "Follow it and they'll grab you for dinner."

There is a high yellow fence that direction and, beyond it, what's left of a massive metal bridge. There isn't much to it.

Just a section with supports. At some point, it must have been long. Spanning from the heart of the city into the sea. Possibly across the sea.

I walk toward Mint and the path.

"Where are we going?" Talons asks.

I consult the coordinates I gleaned from Just's datamix. Whatever it is, it is this way.

"Mawla?"

I reach the fence and, finding a break in it, continue through.

Talons calls my name, and so does Jumbo.

"Follow me and see," I message them.

They are already following, though. They are already through the fence. Tracing the path like I am. Eventually, they run around me. Hopping, bounding, jostling into each other.

The virtual room becomes active with their half-insults and youthful curiosity. It isn't something Bamboo would approve of, but I can't bring myself to stop it. They are bright children. Generally good. And we are in the middle of an adventure.

BandStand wins the race. He is the first beneath the bridge. He smiles and raises his hands. The others join him, forming a loose circle near him.

This location seems right. It seems to match perfectly. What am I here to find? What hidden truth?

Band's face goes blank. His eyes widen. "What is this!" He yelps, and then brings a hand to the side of his head. "Everyone, do you feel that?"

There is a small commotion as the others discover, or fail to discover, what Band has found.

I rush up to them. "What is it? What—" Then I feel it too. The presence of the stream. It is fuller somehow. Heavier. As if it will press me into the ground. I bring my hands to my head too. Try to focus.

I glance upward and see the underside of the bridge. There is a solitary light up there. A single blue light.

Strange thoughts fill my head. Ancient histories and forgotten ways. Secrets and mysteries.

"This is a hot zone," I say aloud. "I've heard rumors, but..."

I'm afraid of the enormity of it. The knowledge and wisdom. But I'm also delighted. Awed.

I think of Isa again. Of miracles, and changes. Of sentinels and old Snoob.

"What does it mean, Mawla?" Band asks.

I smile and raise my arms. "It is here. Everything we want to know. It's right here."

THERE ARE MORE ADVENTURES OUT THERE...

That's all of ThreadBare's story for now, but there are more fun books to read!

If you haven't read my original cyberpunk trilogy yet, there's no better time. The ebook of the first in the series, *A Star Curiously Singing*, is free for a limited time.

Or for something really different, why not try the Peril in Plain Space series? The first book, *Amish Vampires in Space*, started as a joke, but ended up being a straight up science fiction story with a generous helping of Amish society and the taste of a creature feature.

You can find all my books at www.nietz.com.

YOU CAN MAKE A DIFFERENCE!

Word-of-mouth marketing is the best kind. Not only does it ensure that good books get noticed, it also helps bring the right books to the people who will enjoy them most.

If this book met or exceeded your expectations in any way, please consider telling your friends and/or posting a short review.

Your help is greatly appreciated!

ABOUT THE AUTHOR

Kerry Nietz is an award-winning science fiction author. He has over a half dozen speculative novels in print, along with a novella, a couple short stories, and a nonfiction book, *FoxTales*.

Kerry's novel *A Star Curiously Singing* won the Readers Favorite Gold Medal Award for Christian Science Fiction and is notable for its dystopian, cyberpunk vibe in a world under sharia law. It is often mentioned on "Best of" lists.

Among his writings, Kerry's most talked about is the genre-bending *Amish Vampires in Space*. AViS was mentioned on the *Tonight Show* and in the *Washington Post*, *Library Journal*, and *Publishers Weekly*. *Newsweek* called it "a welcome departure from the typical Amish fare."

Kerry is a refugee of the software industry. He spent more than a decade of his life flipping bits, first as one of the principal developers for the now mythical Fox Software, and then as one of Bill Gates's minions at Microsoft. He is a husband, a father, a technophile and a movie buff.

If you'd like to get an e-mail alert whenever Kerry has a new book out or has a special on one of his already-released books, subscribe at his website: www.nietz.com.

ABOUT FRAUGHT

I don't have much to comment on with this book other than it took me too long. Sorry.

Shortly after *Frayed* was published, I began to hear from readers that they wanted another ThreadBare story. While the narrative of *Frayed* isn't a cliffhanger in the conventional sense—no one is left in eminent peril—there are enough unanswered questions that many, my wife included, were unfulfilled by its ending. I don't like people feeling disappointed. Especially not the one who feeds me.

Happy wife, happy life.

At the same time, I had competing interests. The folks at the Takamo gaming company wanted me to write a longer story with the characters of my *Rhats!* novella. They enticed me with a storyline that featured a smorgasbord of intriguing creatures and events. I rarely write space adventures, and part of me (my twelve-year-old self) delights in them. The wide-eyed potential and scope.

So what to do? How could I please both parties?

I decided to try something I'd never done before: write two stories at the same time. And for a couple of months, I managed to pull it off. I wrote on the ThreadBare story for a week or so, and then on the Takamo story. A couple thousand words here, a couple thousand there. Giant rats on one side, bald debuggers on the other.

What I eventually discovered, though, was that the Takamo story, which required less research and contemplation, pulled more and more of my attention. It also felt like it would be shorter, while Thread's adventure seemed to grow more intense, more complicated, and larger.

Finally, I decided to finish the Takamo story first. I focused on that and managed to wrap up the first draft in early 2018.

Thankfully, my wife kept feeding me.

I immediately jumped back into *Fraught*. The narrative progressed steadily, but as I suspected, it ended up being a much longer journey. The longest story in the DarkTrench universe.

Consequently, it took me another half year to finish. Nine to ten months total.

Again, sorry.

As to *Fraught's* content, there are a few people I want to credit. The first is my cover artist Kirk DouPonce who suggested I have mechanical warriors. What's portrayed here isn't the battlefield version, but it is in the vicinity, and grows organically from Thread's earlier adventure.

I'd also like to recognize the testimony of Mario Joseph (available to view on YouTube) for the notion of finding the miracle prophet in unexpected places.

Otherwise, here is *Fraught*. Later than I hoped, longer than the rest, but hopefully more satisfying at the end.

I held little back.

www.ingramcontent.com/pod-product-compliance
Lightning Source LLC
Chambersburg PA
CBHW051520250626
47156CB00001B/158

* 9 7 8 0 9 9 7 1 6 5 8 4 5 *